THE
PROMISE
OF
REST

REYNOLDS PRICE

THE
PROMISE
OF
REST

SCRIBNER PAPERBACK FICTION

PUBLISHED BY SIMON & SCHUSTER

SCRIBNER PAPERBACK FICTION
Simon & Schuster Inc.
Rockefeller Center
1230 Avenue of the Americas
New York, NY 10020

First Scribner Paperback Fiction edition 1996

Excerpt from "Little Gidding" in Four Quartets, copyright 1943
by T. S. Eliot and renewed 1971 by Esme Valerie Eliot,
reprinted by permission of Harcourt Brace & Company.

Excerpt from "One Art" from The Collected Poems 1927–1979
by Elizabeth Bishop. Copyright © 1979, 1983 by Alice Helen Methfessel.
Reprinted by permission of Farrar, Straus & Giroux, Inc.

Manufactured in the United States of America
1 3 5 7 9 10 8 6 4 2

The Library of Congress had cataloged the Scribner edition as follows:
Price, Reynolds, 1933–
The promise of rest / Reynolds Price.
p. cm. — (A Great circle)
"This book concludes the trilogy by R. Price which began with The surface of Earth
(1975), and continued with The source of light (1982) — CIP info.
I. Title. II. Series: Price, Reynolds, 1933– Great Circle.
PS3566.R54P76 1995
813'.54—dc20   94-48086
CIP

ISBN 0-684-80149-3
0-684-82510-4 (Pbk)

FOR

MICHAEL HOWARD RAYMOND JORDAN

FOR

FORTY YEARS

We die with the dying:
See, they depart, and we go with them.
We are born with the dead:
See, they return, and bring us with them.

T. S. ELIOT, *"Little Gidding"*

O N E

BOUND HOME

APRIL 1993

For thirty-odd years, this white narrow room at the top of a granite building in the midst of Duke University had been one place where Hutchins Mayfield never felt less than alive and useful by the day and the hour. For that long stretch he'd met his seminar students here, and this year's group was gathered for its first meeting of the week. There were fourteen of them, eight men and six women, aged nineteen to twenty-two; and by a pleasant accident, each had a winning face, though two of the men were still in the grip of post-adolescent narcolepsy—frequent short fade-outs.

This noon they all sat, with Hutch at the head, round a long oak table by a wall of windows that opened on dogwoods in early spring riot; and though today was the class's last hour for dealing with Milton's early poems before moving on to Marvell and Herbert, even more students were dazed by the rising heat and the fragrance borne through every window.

In the hope of rousing them for a last twenty minutes, Hutch raised his voice slightly and asked who knew the Latin root of the word *sincere*.

A dozen dead sets of eyes shied from him.

He gave his routine fixed class grin, which meant *I can wait you out till Doom.*

Then the most skittish student of all raised her pale hand and fixed her eyes on Hutch—immense and perfectly focused eyes, bluer than glacial lakes. When Hutch had urged her, months ago, to talk more in class, she'd told him that every time she spoke she was racked by dreams the following night. And still, volunteering, she was ready to bolt at the first sign of pressure from Hutch or the class.

Hutch flinched in the grip of her eyes but called her name. "Karen?"

She said "*Without wax,* from the Latin *sine cere.*"

"Right and what does that mean?"

She hadn't quite mustered the breath and daring for a full explanation; but with one long breath, she managed to say "When a careless Roman sculptor botched his marble, he'd fill the blunder with smooth white wax. A sincere statue was one without wax." Once that was out, Karen blushed a dangerous color of red; and her right hand came up to cover her mouth.

Hutch recalled that Karen was the only member of the class who'd studied Latin, three years in high school—an all but vanished yet near-vital skill. He thanked her, then said "The thoroughly dumb but central question that's troubled critics of Milton's 'Lycidas' was stated most famously by pompous Dr. Samuel Johnson late in the eighteenth century. He of course objected mightily, if pointlessly, to the shepherd trappings of a pastoral poem—what would he say about cowboy films today? He even claimed—and I think I can very nearly quote him—that 'He who thus grieves will excite no sympathy; he who thus praises will confer no honor.' I think he's as wrong as a critic can be, which is saying a lot; and I think I can prove it."

Hutch paused to see if their faces could bear what he had in mind; and since the hour was nearly over, most of their eyes had opened wider and were at least faking consciousness again. So he said "I'd like to read the whole poem aloud—again, not because I love my own voice but because any poem is as dead on the page as the notes of a song unless you hear its music performed by a reasonably practiced competent musician. It'll take ten minutes; please wake up and listen." He grinned again.

The narcolepts shook themselves like drowned Labradors. They were oddly both redheads.

One woman with record-long bangs clamped her eyes shut.

Hutch said "Remember now—the most skillful technician in English poetry who lived after Milton was Tennyson, two centuries later. Tennyson was no pushover when it came to praising other poets—very few poets are—but he claimed more than once that 'Lycidas' is the highest touchstone of poetic appreciation in the English language: a touchstone

being a device for gauging the gold content of metal. Presumably Tennyson meant that any other English poem, rubbed against 'Lycidas,' will
show its gold or base alloy."

Though Hutch had long since memorized the poem, all 193 lines,
he looked to his book and started with Milton's prefatory note.

> "In this monody the author bewails a learned friend unfortu-
> nately drowned in his passage from Chester on the Irish seas,
> 1637."

Then he braced himself for the steeplechase run-through that had never
failed to move him deeply.

> "Yet once more, O ye laurels, and once more
> Ye myrtles brown, with ivy never sere,
> I come to pluck your berries harsh and crude,
> And with forced fingers rude,
> Shatter your leaves before the mellowing year."

From there on, along the crowded unpredictable way to its visionary
end—with Lycidas rescued and welcomed in Heaven by a glee club of
saints and Christ himself, giving nectar shampoos—Hutch stressed what
always felt to him like the heart of the poem, its authentic cry. It sounded
most clearly in the lines where Milton either feigned or—surely—poured
out genuine grief for the loss of his college friend, Edward King, drowned
in a shipwreck at age twenty-five, converted in the poem to an ancient
shepherd named Lycidas and longed for in this piercing extravagant cry
with its keening vowels.

> "Thee shepherd, thee the woods, and desert caves,
> With wild thyme and the gadding vine o'ergrown,
> And all their echoes mourn.
> The willows, and the hazel copses green,
> Shall now no more be seen,
> Fanning their joyous leaves to thy soft lays.
> As killing as the canker to the rose,
> Or taint-worm to the weanling herds that graze,
> Or frost to flowers, that their gay wardrobe wear,

When first the white thorn blows;
Such, Lycidas, thy loss to shepherd's ear."

Ten minutes later at the poem's hushed end—*"Tomorrow to fresh woods, and pastures new"*—Hutch was even more shaken than he'd meant to be. Strangely he hadn't quite foreseen a public collusion between Milton's subject and his own ongoing family tragedy. But at least he hadn't wept; so he sat for five seconds, looking out the window past the creamy white and cruciform blossoms toward the huge water oaks with their new leaves.

Then he faced the class again and repeated from memory the central lines—"Thee shepherd, thee the woods, and desert caves. . . ." When he thought they'd sunk as deep as they could into these young television-devastated brains, he said "Estimate the wax content of those few lines."

Even Karen looked flummoxed again and turned aside.

Hutch tried another way. "—The sincerity quotient. Does Milton truly miss the sight of young Edward King, King's actual presence before the poet's eyes; if not, what's he doing in so many carefully laid-down words?" When they all stayed blank as whitewashed walls, Hutch laughed. "Anybody, for ten extra points. Take a flying risk for once in your life." (Through the years, except for the glorious and troubling late 1960s, most of his students had proved far more conservative than corporate lawyers.)

Finally Kim said "He's showing off"—the class beauty queen, lacquered and painted and grade-obsessed.

Whitney said "Milton's almost thirty years old, right? Then I figure he's stretching—he's using King's death as a chinning bar to test his own strengths. *Can I write this thing?* he seems to be saying, right through to the end." Since Whit was one of the midday nappers, his contributions were always surprising in their sane precision.

Still fire-truck red, Karen finally said "I think Milton's discovering, as the ink leaves his pen, how terribly his friend drowned and vanished—they never even found the friend's corpse apparently. I think it sounds like Milton truly longs for him back."

Hutch said "Does it *sound* like longing, or does he really long?"

Karen winced and withdrew.

Whitney said "What's the difference? Nobody can gauge that, now anyway."

Hutch said "Why not?"

"It's too far behind us, nearly four hundred years. The words have all changed; we can't hear their meaning." Whit lowered his near-white lashes like scrims down over green eyes.

Alisoun said "Then let's all go home." She was six foot one, and any threat to unfold her long bones to their full height was always welcome.

Hutch asked her to explain.

"If four hundred years in the life of a language as widespread as English add up to nothing but failed communication, then I don't see any point in encouraging the human race to live another year. Let's just quit and vacate." She was genuinely at the point of anger.

The other women looked officially startled; their mothering genes had felt the assault.

Erik turned his face, that was always stern, a notch or two sterner and set it on Alisoun. "Get serious. *I* anyhow understand every syllable—not one of them's moved an inch in three centuries—and I'm no genius of a reader, as you well know. Milton is literally desolate here, right here on this page, all this time later. The fact that he's also phenomenal at words and rhyme and music doesn't disqualify him for sincere grief. If that's been the problem about the poem since old Dr. Johnson, then it looks like critics are short on reasons to fan their gums."

Hutch said *"Touché.* They mostly are."

But to general surprise, Karen recovered gall enough to say "I have to disagree. Milton's mainly bragging, the way Kim said. The poem's primarily about himself—'Watch my lovely dust. Recommend me to God. Buy all my books.' "

Hutch smiled but raised a monitory finger. "Milton didn't publish a book of poems for eight whole years after 'Lycidas.' "

So tremulous Karen took another long breath, faced Hutch unblinking and thrust toward the subject that no other student had found imaginable. "Mr. Mayfield, have you written poems about your son?"

Startling as it was to have the question come from Karen, Hutch realized he'd waited months for someone to ask it. *Now the demon's out and smashing round the room.* In Karen's halting, plainly sympathetic voice, the question sounded answerable at least. Her boldness surely had to mean that the news of his son was widespread now and accepted as mentionable. Yet when Hutch looked round to all the faces—some class was breaking up early outside; the hall was a din through the shut glass door—all but Karen were blank as slate again. So Hutch offered the minimum he thought they could use. "My grown son is sick with AIDS in New York. Till today no known AIDS patient has won. And no, Karen, I haven't written a word, on that subject anyhow. I doubt I ever can."

Karen had the grace not to push on and make a connection with Milton, though she thought *Anybody in genuine grief couldn't sit and write an intricate poem, not one we'd keep on reading for centuries.*

But Hutch could read the drift in her eyes. "Don't for an instant make the tempting mistake of thinking that I share Milton's powers— nobody else in European poetry, not since Homer anyhow, can make that claim."

Kim said "Not Virgil, Dante or Shakespeare?"

Hutch shook his head No and suddenly felt a surge of pleasure—a strange boiling from deep in his chest of pleased excitement to plant his feet down and crown John Milton supreme in all the great questions of life. He said "Milton knows more than anyone else, in the western hemi- sphere in any case, in verse anyhow; and he's nine-tenths right on almost every question. Shakespeare is all a zillion bright guesses, bright or pitch- dark—not one single answer. Dante knows just one big urgent thing."

Whitney said "Which is?"

Hutch said " 'No rest but in your will'—the *your* means God of course."

Kim scowled, the regulation atheist.

And Karen's eyes plainly showed that she felt Hutch had short- changed the subject she raised—his son's present illness.

So he faced her directly and tried to give more. "Even Milton will have found that not every loss, however picturesque, and not every joy, however rhythmic, will submit itself as poetry fodder—as food for new poems."

Karen accepted that but wanted still more. "Can you think of a sadness or a genuine pleasure that wouldn't submit when you yourself tried to write it out?"

Hutch knew at once. "In fact, I can—oh many times over. But one in particular strikes me today. I'll be dealing with it again—in my life, not my work—in another few hours. Soon as I leave you today, I'll be driving up to my family's homeplace in the rolling country north of here, up near Virginia, for what should be a mildly pleasant occasion. We'll be celebrating the 101st birthday of a cousin of mine, named Grainger Walters. I've known the event was coming for a long time and have tried more than once to write a poem that would say what that man's meant to me since the day I was born—a kind of older brother when my mother died, a surrogate father when my father died young, even a species of bighearted alien from some kind of Paradise, guarding and guiding me fairly successfully for six long decades. But a poem won't come, or hasn't come yet."

Whitney said "Do you understand why?"

"Not fully, no I don't. But I'm fairly sure the problem's buried somewhere in the fact that I'm all white—pure Anglo-Saxon and Celtic genes, to the best of my knowledge—and Grainger Walters is part black, the grandson of one of my Aryan great-grandfathers on up in Virginia, in Reconstruction days."

Whitney suddenly strummed an imaginary banjo and sang to the tune of "Way Down Upon the Swanee River,

> "Hankey-pankey on the old plantation,
> Far, far away."

Alisoun said "It's already been written."

Hutch was puzzled.

"By Mary Chestnut in her famous diary; by Faulkner, in every paragraph—by Robert Penn Warren too, a whole slew more. Won't that be the main reason you're stymied? The job's been *done*."

Since Hutch was a poet, not a novelist, the fact had never quite dawned that harshly. He instantly suspected *She's at least a third right*. But he said "Wouldn't the fact that every one of you is white, that a black student at this university—or any other—very seldom takes courses in literature, mean that you're wrong? Far from being done to death, the subject of race in America—race in its deepest historical and moment-by-moment contemporary ramifications—has barely reached the level of audibility in our literature, much less the level of sane portrayal. A world of explaining remains to be done."

Alisoun's answer was long-since ready. "I've noticed how scarce blacks are in this department, yes; but the reason for that has got to be, they *know* you'll tell them nothing but lies—our solemn white poems and stories about human one-ness, all our feeble alibis for common greed and meanness and worse: torture, murder. Every black student here, and I know quite a few—I've made it my little white-girl project for the past three years—has got those lies bred into their *bones*. They don't need to read Old Master's effusions. What have we got to tell them, we Western white folks, in poems and plays?"

Her immaculate pale green cotton sweater and short string of pearls had misinformed Hutch; he was shocked by her force. *I'll think about that on the road today.* For the present he could only say what he trusted. With all the self-trust of a lifelong teacher, his mind chose to seize the wheel of the talk and turn it his way. "What conceivable subject—any subject comprehensible to humans at least, of whatever color—hasn't been done to death? The fact that Milton wrote 'Lycidas' has hardly prevented the writing of later great poems about dead youth."

Alisoun said "Name two."

Hutch said "Take three, off the top of my head—Tennyson's 'In Memoriam,' Arnold's 'Thyrsis,' Robert Lowell's 'Quaker Graveyard in Nantucket.' "

Erik said "But isn't the theme of early death a whole lot more universal and available than the historical accident of Anglo and Afro-American miscegenation for three hundred years in a highly particular steamy place called the old Confederacy?"

Hutch waited, then had to say "Thanks for the question; I need to think it over. I will admit I don't think William Faulkner is a genius compared to, say, Tolstoy or Dostoevsky. Faulkner knew a small hot patch of ground he invented; it lacked huge chunks of the actual world—real women, for example: just half the human race unaccounted for. And responsible fathers, which many men are. Mothers who can love and not smother their young. Faulkner *was* the best student of wild and tame animals I've yet found in fiction; but as for his using up any large subject you'd meet in the real world, except maybe whiskey—you recall Hemingway always called him 'Old Bourbon Mellifluous,' a well-aimed spear from one who'd consumed his own share of gin—well, all Faulkner exhausted was runaway English; country show-off prose.

"And no other writer, since Faulkner drank himself out of sane action by the age of fifty, has really dived deep into that huge maelstrom called miscegenation on Southern ground—the feeding of white on black, black on white—though the problem has gone much further toward both solution and utter insolubility than Marse Will Faulkner ever dreamed possible."

Hutch looked up to Alisoun, who'd waited him out, and smiled broadly at her. "I'll prophesy for you what I'm likely to feel, if I think your question through for years—I very much doubt that any reality that's widely experienced by human beings is ever worn out, not so long as the right he or she takes it up in flaming-new language."

More than half the class now realized that the teacher had left himself open for a body blow. *Are you the right man, and where're your deathless flaming-new words?* But every watch showed the hour was ending.

So Hutch said "I promise you more of an answer; but for now, one final word from the foreman here—words as freshly minted and potently thrusting as the words of 'Lycidas' all but never come out of a human mind for any reason less than enormous feeling, a nearly stifling pressure to *speak*. My money anyhow is on John Milton's being mightily moved by his young friend's drowning—by the chance that such a random disaster could fall on himself—and by the near-sure existence of a just afterlife. But believe what you will, if the poem will support you. I'll see you on Wednesday. Read Andrew Marvell."

Only Kim slid her chair back to rise.

Late as it was, the others seemed held in place, unsatisfied.

Hutch actually asked himself *Are they facing their own eventual deaths?*

And they held still another long moment—even Kim balked, unsatisfied but gripped.

To free them, Hutch said the only thing that came. It was anyhow truthful. "This poem—'Lycidas'—means more to me than all but a few of the humans I've known, more than most anything I've ever owned or tried to keep. Except of course for my lost son—he's lost to me; *how* I can't bear to tell you. If the world hadn't turned up creatures like Milton— or Keats or Handel—every century or so, I doubt I could live through the thought of my young son dying in pain, too far from me, refusing any help and even his mother's." He knew it sounded a little mad, maybe more than a little.

But none of their eyes betrayed fear or laughter; and even when they'd filed silently past him toward their crowded unthinkable lives—Whit's hand touched his shoulder as he went—the rising in Hutch's chest boiled on. *What in God's name has got me happy?*

2

THE rising continued as Hutch stopped by his office to check the mail. He'd no sooner sat, though, before someone knocked—a tall man behind the opaque glass. A little annoyed, Hutch called "Come in." The dark-haired, dark-bearded man was familiar on sight anyhow—Hutch had noticed him on the stairs and in the hallways for maybe two years. He was almost certainly a graduate student; but he held in place on the threshold, not speaking.

Hutch stood. "I'm Hutchins Mayfield. May I help you?"

Entirely serious, the man said "I very much doubt you can."

Then check out immediately. But all Hutch said was "We may never know if you don't fill me in." He motioned to the single red-leather chair that stood by his desk, for student callers.

Then the man launched a sudden spectacular smile, stepped in, shut the door and took the red chair. When Hutch was seated, the man held out a hand. "I'm Hart Salter, sir, a doctoral candidate. I've watched you for years."

"I've noticed you around, yes, but didn't see you watching me. You're bound to be bored."

Again Hart took it seriously. "Not bored exactly. Not fascinated either.

I guess I've always tried to guess how poems get into your head from space."

Hutch had taught one genuine lunatic student a few years back. *Is this a fresh psycho?* He thought he'd try first to lighten the tone. With both hands far above his head, he indicated the shape of a drainpipe running from thin air through the top of his skull. "There's a long invisible pipeline, see, from the spring of the muses directly into my cerebral cortex."

Hart said "I've got no doubt about *that*."

"Good. I only wish it were true."

Hart said "You fooled me. I've read all your poems; you're a real self-starter."

"Warm thanks, Mr. Salter. I'm a cold engine now, a minor dud." Then dreading what was almost surely the answer, Hutch asked the question that seemed required. "You write poems yourself?" The thought of a manuscript thrust at him here felt as real as a knife.

"Not a line of poetry, not since high school. No, I guess you're wondering why I'm here."

"I had begun to wonder. I'm due out of here in the next ten minutes—"

Hart sprang up at once. "I don't want to hold you."

"No, sit by all means and tell me your errand."

So Hart folded his endless legs again and sat. "I'm in deep water, sir. It's in my marriage. I figured a poet might help me swim out."

For the past three decades, student strangers had occasionally dropped in with personal problems for the resident poet. One excruciating twenty minutes had followed when a young man with hideous face burns had walked in to show Hutch the poems he'd written about his fate—a gasoline bomb that had left him a monster. *But has any lovelorn certified adult ever asked for love-help? Almost surely not.* Hutch said "My record on love is dismal, Mr. Salter. I'm alone as a dead tree."

"Call me Hart, please—Hart." He smiled his winning smile again. "This is idiotic of me, I know; but since I've committed this ludicrous folly, let me ask one question."

Hutch held up a finger and laughed. "One question then, entirely free of charge."

"How do you ever convince a woman that you actually love her?"

Hutch had noticed Hart's wedding band. "You're presently married?"

"Yes sir, for three years, fully sworn at the altar with God and man watching—"

"God and *humankind*, Hart. Maybe you need a crash course in—what?—'gender-sensitive language'?"

"Sir, if I get any more sensitive, my blood will ooze out of these fingernails." Hart showed ten long thick fingernails, well tended. "The problem is, my wife can't believe me. I'm loyal as any Seeing Eye dog, I do well over half the chores (she works full-time in the Botany greenhouse), my body has never once cheated on her, I say the word *love* to her on the quarter-hour whenever we're together, but she says she literally cannot believe me. This morning she said she felt as abandoned as the world's last swallow."

Hutch smiled. "Assuming she meant the last *bird*, I like her image."

"Oh she can crucify you, by the minute, with images."

Hutch said "Try writing her short letters maybe, that she can keep and reread at will. Try your first adult poem."

"I guessed you'd say that."

"What else could I say?—you called on a poet."

Hart flushed as fiercely as Karen, last hour. But he leaned back, thrust a broad hand into his jeans and brought out a single folded index card. "I wrote the poem, just now in the local men's room. May I read it to you?—I think it's a haiku."

"By all means then—no epic recitations though."

Hart opened the card, spread it on his right knee but never looked down as he said

> "In all this thicket of straight white trees,
> A single burning bush, concealing you."

Hutch said "Well, it may be a little too bold to be a haiku; but it's striking all right. Will she mind the touch of eros?"

"No, that's one thing that's never been a problem."

Hutch said "Oh bountifully lucky pair!" Then he pointed to his phone. "Call your wife right now; read the poem to her, more than once. *I'd* be glad to hear it from any mate of mine." He was suddenly eager for

Hart to succeed, so eager he threw off his usual caution about recognizing real poetry, however modest. "I've got to leave, Hart. I'm overdue for my own family business. But use my phone for as long as you like; just shut the door as you leave—it locks itself."

Hart half rose. "I couldn't."

"You can. You already have, with your poem. Now read it to— who? You never said her name."

"Stacy. Stacy Burnham—she's kept her old name."

Hutch was on his feet now. "If you think it's appropriate, you can say *I* believe you."

Hart said "I may need to deep-six that." But then he could smile. He rose too, shook Hutch's hand again, then sat and carefully placed the phone call.

Only when he'd heard Hart's voice say "Stacy?" did Hutch shut the door behind him and go.

3

Two hours later, for whatever reason, Hutch was still nearly happy. The feeling that had sprung up at noon, in class, had only strengthened with the start of his trip. And against strong odds, it had lasted till now when he was in sight of his destination. At first he'd thought the change was caused by the day itself—an early April afternoon, new leaves overhead, the deeps of the woods splodged with redbud and dogwood, the air desert-clear. The landscape twenty miles northeast of Durham had begun a slow change through another forty miles into what was still the land of Hutch's childhood, the only nature he'd loved on Earth, though he'd stood in various stages of awe in the presence of sights from the Jericho wilderness north to Lapland, west to Beijing and south to Rio.

In calm defiance of rusting billboards, trailer parks and all other man-made waste and ruin, the country Hutch drove through briskly was caught in its nearly invisible rolling—a broad-backed brown and green undulation beneath dense evergreens and a wide pitched sky as royal-blue as the eyes of a watchful year-old boy or the banner at a high chivalric tilt in dark-age France. To Hutch it seemed, as it always had since his own father told him, the actual skin of a slumberous creature the size of a quarter of east Carolina and southside Virginia—a creature that might yet prove benign if it ever roused and faced the living.

And as always, again Hutch pushed on silently across the broad hide, hoping at least to pass unseen in his odd elation. Or was his pleasure a simple prediction of the evening ahead, a birthday supper for his ancient cousin? Hutch slowed a little for the final curve, glanced to the rear-view mirror above him and grinned at his face.

After all these years it still surprised him to see how, this far along in life, he'd come to look like Rob his father who'd died a younger man than Hutch was today. Not that Rob was an unlikable model—the same braced brow and jaw, the brown unflinching eyes, the still dark hair with its broad swag of white. So Hutch actually spoke to himself, "You're bearing up better than you ought to be." It was true but the words hardly touched his pleasure as he entered the drive and stopped past the main house, by the vast oak—his father's old homeplace, which Hutch had rented to friends years ago.

He sat still a moment and tested again this strange new feeling. Despite the bitter sadness and loss he knew was bound toward him—him and his family—Hutch felt like a lucky man on a hill. And he guessed it was not some temporary boost, ignited by the weather or a quick jet of natural endorphins in his blood. He'd had long stretches of joy all his life and he trusted pleasure. It had lasted for two hours alone on the road, and it somehow promised to last a good while. For an instant, it even crossed his mind that his sexual force might come back again. Except for occasional bouts with his own hand, sexual will had all but left him months ago when he learned for sure that his son was desperately ill at a distance. Yet he knew all feeling, all longing for love, must hide now—for weeks or months—till he buried his only child, his son who was dying in upper Manhattan, refusing phone calls or visits from home.

Hutch reached for his cousin's birthday gift and climbed out into pure good-smelling sun. He shut his eyes and let the light warm his face and neck. Then he looked around him. No other car or truck, no other human in sight or hearing—Strawson and Emily must be in town. But Hutch had known this house and its setting all his life. He'd spent the best part of his boyhood here; it knew him well enough to let him arrive with no boisterous welcome. Only the fat old Labrador bitch on the porch turned to check; and once she knew him, she spared herself barking. Hutch called to her "Maud, it's the Friendly Slasher—go back to sleep."

Maud ignored the news and resumed her watch on the empty road.

So Hutch walked on toward the squat white guest-house beyond the stable. The clapboard was freshly painted, the roof was sporting new bright green shingles, and every window was shut and shaded against the light. Once Hutch was there though, the door stood open. Even the rusty screen was propped wide.

A single day-moth made a lunge to enter, then fell back as if a broad hand had struck it.

Hutch paused at the foot of the three rock steps and spoke at a low pitch. "Anybody breathing?" A keen-eared child, or a bat, might have heard him. He was testing his cousin's ears and brain.

The voice that answered was lean and light, a note or two higher than in the old days but firm and unbroken with no growl or husk. "One mean old soul in here; that's it—enter at your own risk."

Hutch said "I'm hunting a birthday boy named Grainger Walters. You seen him today?"

The voice stayed put but spoke even stronger. "He's not your boy but I've seen him every time I looked in the mirror for one-damn-hundred-and-one years today."

"You're not in there with some young girl?"

"Haven't seen a girl in thirty, forty years. You coming in or not?— I can't stand up." But there were sounds of a creaking chair, a tall body unfolding itself and then steps toward the door. A man was slowly there in the doorway behind the screen—long powerful hands, skin the color of the starched khaki pants and shirt, brown eyes that had turned almost a pale sky-blue.

At first that seemed to Hutch the one sign of unusual age—the eyes and the skin that lightened with every year as if time were canceling the first fact about this palpable body: its mingled blood. Hutch hadn't seen the old man in nearly four months. If there'd been a real change, it was maybe the eyebrows. The last of the snow-white eyebrows were gone, and the head was as hairless as any bronze bust. Then Hutch realized that the skull itself seemed larger and grander, grown to accommodate the huge filmy eyes. Otherwise the old man stood straight as ever since Hutch had known him—a little shrunk in the chest and thighs but bolt upright and balanced steadily. "Happy birthday, Cousin Grainger—and a hundred more."

Grainger Walters had given up smiling long since, except at unpredictable moments for unannounced reasons; but he showed the remains of his strong teeth now, and he tipped his bare head. "Fall down here in the dirt on your knees, and pray I die after supper tonight."

Hutch said "Whoa here."

"Whoa nothing—I'm tired. Haven't slept since Christmas."

"Why?" Hutch had asked without thinking.

"If you don't know my reason, fool—if you been sleeping good yourself—then leave that package here on my stoop and head on out." Grainger turned and vanished back to his chair.

At first Hutch edged his way to the door and laid the gift where he'd been told to leave it. A powerful urge to *run* shot through him. If anyone living knew Hutch Mayfield from sole to crown, it was this old soul who'd say what he meant if he felt the need or the merest whim. Hutch waited the urge out; then climbed the steps and entered, shutting the screen door behind him. It took a whole minute before his eyes had opened to the indoor darkness, and while he waited he said "You'll ruin your eyes in this dark."

Grainger said *"Trying* to. What do I need to see?"

"You might like to see how well I'm doing. I've trimmed off eight pounds since last Christmas; everybody thinks I'm ten years younger."

"Not me" Grainger said. "You're sixty-three years old and look it— sit down."

Hutch said "My birthday's not for six weeks. Don't rush me please." But he sat in the rocker across from the automatic chair he'd bought as a gift the previous spring when Grainger turned a hundred. You pressed a button; it gradually rose and stood you up with no exertion. When Hutch's eyes could finally see, he looked around the space for changes.

Nothing obvious, just the same strict order Grainger had laid down all his life, wherever he lived. This main room had its two good chairs and a long pine table against the wall with dozens of pictures framed above it—various kin whom he and Hutch shared, caught in photographs ranging from the 1850s to now.

The center of the cluster was a single oval tinted picture of Grainger's wife Gracie, long gone and dead. The other face that caught at Hutch was his own child Wade at about age ten, in a fork of the oak tree not fifty yards from this dim room. Beside it was a tall dark picture of Rob, his own dead father and Grainger's great friend. No one had ever looked finer than Rob, not the way he was here, in summer whites for high-school commencement more than seventy years past—a smiler as charged with electric attraction as the magnetic poles. All the others were distant kin and friends, a few stiff generals from the First World War (and oddly the Kaiser with his comical mustache) plus three or four modern Democratic politicians and Jacqueline Kennedy, a stalled gazelle of inestimable worth.

Otherwise there was only a big oil stove, a television and the neat narrow bed. It all looked as new and nearly unused as when Hutch had paid for Grainger and two boys to build the place thirty some years back. The kitchen and bathroom doors were shut.

When Hutch didn't speak but went on looking, Grainger said "You planning to sell me out? It's worth every penny you paid me to build it—two thousand, three hundred, twenty-two dollars and eighty-six cents. I got the receipts." He actually pressed his chair button to rise.

"Sit still please—sit as long as you want. Every piece of this is yours and has always been."

"Emily don't think so."

It riled Hutch instantly. "Emily's dead wrong."

Grainger pointed through the wall toward the main house. "She's all the time saying how much it cost them to keep me warm."

It was then Hutch realized the oil stove was burning, though the front door was open. He put his palm out toward the heat. "You know this blast furnace here is roaring?"

Grainger said "I do."

"Shall I shut the door?"

"Shall not. Mind your business." But he may have smiled again. "I'm drying my clothes."

Hutch looked—had Grainger started fouling his pants? Then he noticed another khaki dress shirt, neatly hung on a wire hanger from the window ledge near the stove, and a pair of white socks. "You put out a wash? I pay Emily money to wash your clothes."

Grainger said "She don't get them dry enough—make my bones ache."

"I warned her about that here last Christmas."

"Remind her again; her memory's failing."

Hutch said "She's a whole lot younger than me."

"You failing too." Grainger suddenly focused on Hutch's face and gave it a thorough search. He'd watched it make every change it had made, through six decades.

"Me failing?" Hutch grinned. "I'm in fairly good shape; taught school today." He flexed both arms in their blue sleeves.

Grainger shook his head firmly No. "You're worse than you ever been in your life; you'll be worse soon."

At first Hutch thought it was old-man meanness or hard-edged teasing. But then he wondered what Grainger knew. Hutch had never mentioned his grown son's illness; Emily and Straw knew little about it, if anything; surely Ann hadn't blabbed. Hutch said "You know something I don't know?"

Grainger froze up slowly through the next long minute. He sat in place perfectly still; then again his eyes found Hutch's face as if they'd dug up the bones of a hand with scraps of skin. His old eyes were brimming.

So Hutch said "Wade? You heard from Wade?"

Grainger nodded but offered no more.

"When?"

"Just now. First thing this morning, still dark outdoors." Grainger pointed to the telephone screwed to the wall by the head of his bed.

"Wade called you today?"

"Wade calls me every birthday I've had since he could talk."

"He told you he's sick?"

Grainger said "I could hear it."

"You ask how he was?"

"He told me himself."

Hutch suddenly felt cut loose from a chain and flinging through space. "He tell you it's this terrible AIDS?"

"What?"

"This plague that's speeding all over the world, that kills you by wiping out your whole immune system so you're helpless to every germ and virus—"

Grainger said "I watch the TV. I'm not on the moon yet."

Hutch could grin briefly. "But Wade told you himself, today?"

"You don't know how your one child's doing?"

That hurt more than Hutch's own deep self-blame. He said "Wade hasn't talked to me in three months."

"Try calling him up. They invented the phone when I was a boy."

Hutch said "He won't answer me, hangs up soon as he hears my voice."

Again Grainger waited to estimate if Hutch could take the fresh news. He finally said "Then you don't know he's blind."

"Oh my Jesus—" For an instant Hutch felt he'd pitch flat forward on the bare oak floor.

Grainger just nodded.

Then another man's voice called from well out of sight somewhere in the yard. "Mr. Walters, you seen that out-of-work poet we used to know?"

Hutch knew it had to be Straw, Strawson Stuart—the friend to whom he'd rented the place for nearly thirty years. Nobody but Strawson called Grainger *Mr. Walters.*

Grainger looked to Hutch and waved his hand slightly at the door. "Go show him it's you. Tell him I ain't dead."

Hutch was still too dazed to obey. So he and Grainger waited, silent, as footsteps came toward them.

Though Hutch had seen Straw on campus at Duke for a basketball game a month ago, there was always a welcome jolt in running across him in person and seeing how little his excellent face and body had changed in the forty years since he was Hutch's student in prep school in Virginia—Hutch's first real job and his first strong taste of what seemed love at its full hot tilt. And here, for all of Grainger's news about Wade,

Hutch stood up smiling to shake Straw's hand—an enormous hand that always engulfed you a second longer than you intended and, above it, the nearly black eyes that would have looked natural in the face of a hurtling Mongol rider.

They were set, a little slant, in a head as strong and encouraging to see as any antique head of a grown man—the Dying Gaul or Augustus Caesar in the prime of power, a face you'd follow through narrow straits. Hutch had lasted well enough too, but he always had to remind himself that Straw was only seven years younger—fifty-six years old and tanned by bourbon like a well-cured hide yet untouched at the core by the years he'd breasted.

Straw let go of Hutch's hand and turned to Grainger. "How long's he been here?"

Grainger said "Time don't mean nothing to me. You ask him." He hooked an enormous thumb toward Hutch.

Hutch went to his chair; but since there was no seat for Straw but the floor or Grainger's bed, he stood and faced Straw. "I've still got some of my faculties intact—I can estimate I got here twenty minutes ago. You charging parking time in the drive?" Hutch was only half joking; something was wrong here. Was Straw on the verge of one of his drunks (they'd grown increasingly rare in recent years but could still throw him badly for weeks at a time), or had Grainger let Straw know about Wade?

Straw said "Oh no, I'm just guarding Mr. Walters. He promised he'd rest all afternoon so we wouldn't wear him out tonight."

Hutch looked to Grainger and could see no sign of impatience or fatigue. But he also reminded himself he could see no adequate sign that this live body had lasted one year more than a century.

Grainger lifted a hand for quiet. "Old Mrs. Joe Kennedy—Miss Rose Fitzgerald, you know, the President's mother? She just turned a hundred and three, going strong up yonder on the Cape Cod beach. Nobody tells *her* when to sleep or wake."

Straw was suddenly as peaceful as the boy he'd been when Hutch first knew him, before the first drunk. He said to Grainger "Well, Hutchins and I aren't President yet and you're no rose. Emily's up at the house now cooking the party. It's the size of a circus and headed your way. So

Hutch and I plan to find beds and lie down to rest up for it. Let's stretch you out for a little nap too." Straw went to the old man and took his elbow to help him rise.

Grainger shook Straw off and pressed his stand button.

Hutch went to the other side to help Straw guide the frail bones to bed.

But once the chair had stood him upright, Grainger held in place to loosen his collar—the pearly button; he never wore a tie. Then on his own he moved to the bed with no sign of age but a kind of dream slowness like fleeing in a nightmare with no hope of rescue.

First Grainger sat on the edge of the bed, then laid his head back and drew up his legs. Only then did he ask for help. "Strawson, take my shoes off."

Straw untied the clean black brogans and slipped them off. Beneath them the feet were in high thick cotton socks, spotlessly white.

Grainger said "Hutchins, help smooth out my pants."

Hutch arranged the khaki pants along and around the legs they covered—smoothing wrinkles, straightening creases.

The old man's eyes were shut by then, the eyeballs big as pullet eggs through the thin tan lids. He hooked his thumbs in the waist of his pants. "Now both of you cover my feet. I'm cold."

Straw looked to Hutch; both silently grinned and together unfolded the green summer blanket and laid it over the legs, to the knees.

They were shutting the door when Grainger said "Too mean to die."

As Hutch glanced back, he met the opalescent eyes, open on him again.

Grainger told Hutch "I'm talking about nothing but me. Nobody you know."

Hutch said "I've known you every day of my life." It was literally true and he had clear memories from as early as two and three years old of this same soul here.

But the old eyes shut again. "That's what you think. Live on in the dark." Grainger gave a rough grumble and waved the boys off—two tall men in late midlife, whose ages combined exceeded his by a mere eighteen years. Before they'd both got down his front steps, he was gone in sleep, entirely serene.

4

OUTSIDE Hutch turned toward the main house. A nap might not be a bad idea, or an hour alone in deep country quiet.

Straw, though, had turned left toward the pine woods. From a hundred yards' distance, the trees were so dense they looked more like a bulwark than trees, some old fortification abandoned but guarding still its forgotten cause. When Hutch didn't follow, Straw looked back. "We need a short walk."

Hutch fell in five yards behind him. They didn't make a sound between them till they were deep enough in the pines for all other signs of human life to be screened out so thickly that civilization seemed denied. Hutch thought he and Straw might have been air-dropped on an island owned by nothing but evergreens, a brown bird or two and the dark gray owl they startled awake (it flew ahead like a spirit guide in an Indian tale).

He and Straw were in sight of a small clearing with a single white-barked sycamore before Hutch knew he was being led down the same dry path they'd taken thirty-seven years ago after they'd buried Rob, Hutch's father, and Straw had flunked out of Washington and Lee in his first semester and moved here with Grainger while Hutch went back to England to finish his graduate study. Hutch even spoke out now. "You picking this same old trail on purpose?"

Straw never turned. "What trail?"

"The one we took in '56 when I flew back from Rome for Rob's funeral."

Straw said "Sure, since you noticed, I *did*. Walk on a short way."

The leafy ground began a slow decline toward the valley, and step by step Hutch could barely believe the near-silent show of early spring fullness. There were spry red cardinals every few yards. At his feet there were frequent blooms of a shape and color he'd never seen, and overhead there were glimpses of a sky so blue it seemed to be working to match the pleasure he'd felt today on the road. But what kept slamming against Hutch's eyes was not this masterful calm unfolding—a natural life indifferent to him and all his kind, proceeding along its immortal rails—but the new raw idea of his son's face, blind with all its other punishments, if Grainger was right. And what Hutch asked himself every step was *What am I doing on a sightseeing hike five hundred miles from my only child, who needs me whether he'll say so or not?*

After the better part of a mile, Straw pushed on faster ahead, then stopped with his back toward Hutch and waited stock-still.

Hutch came on and stopped in reach of Straw. Only then did he realize they'd come to a place he'd never seen, not in the childhood years he'd roamed these woods alone or with Rob or Grainger. Fifty yards downhill from where he and Straw stood, a wide creek ran in banks so even and clean that the whole scene looked manmade and tended.

The bed of the creek was deep and apparently clear of rocks; but hundreds of rocks in every shade of brown and white paved the banks and made a thick border, far as Hutch could see, to left and right. In broad clumps, scattered among the boulders, were flowers a foot high—a bright egg-yellow. *Late wild jonquils maybe?*

The scene was admirable but a little funny. It had the look of an accidental stretch of city park, spliced in here and lost. Hutch looked to Straw to check for signals. Was he meant to laugh at the incongruities or praise whoever had curbed raw nature into this tame stretch?

Straw's eyes brimmed tears, though none had yet fallen.

Hutch said "It's handsome. Who do we thank?"

"Grainger."

"Grainger gets down here to tend all this?"

Straw hadn't faced Hutch, but he knuckled at his eyes and sat on the dry ground. "Grainger spent most of his spare time, twenty-odd years ago, making this place right. He'd sometimes be down here in the near-dark, hauling rocks till I'd come down and make him quit."

"What was he planning?"

Straw said "He never told me and I never asked. You know me—I leave people to their own designs."

"But somebody's keeping it up, I can see—not Emily surely?"

Straw said "Emily doesn't know it's here. Hell, Em doesn't know we live in the country, not for all the looking around she's done. Never walks an inch beyond the garden. No, I keep this place up, after every big storm—pull on my hipboots and gouge it out again. I put in a hundred new bulbs last winter; every one of them lived. I take pictures of it for Grainger to see—he hasn't been down here for, oh, eighteen years."

Hutch had also sat and by now the sight looked more appropriate. The water even sounded pure and free-flowing from some intentionally guarded source way uphill from here. "Why do you think he did it, back here where nobody much would see?"

Straw finally faced Hutch; his eyes had a trace of their old ferocity— eyes you might see as your last sight before violent death. But his voice was low and steady on. "Mr. Walters told me, flat-out plain, the day he finished. He'd asked me, weeks before, to leave him be—just let him work down here alone. But finally late one fall afternoon, he quietly found me when Em was in town. He led me to this spot, sat me down and said 'It's all I can leave you, Strawson.' I begged his pardon; I didn't understand. So he tried again. He laughed a long time—he'd almost quit laughing, even back then—and he said 'Your *inheritance*. My deathbed gift. Keep it clean in my memory.' I thanked him and then said 'You killing yourself some evening soon?'

"He picked that over in his mind and laughed again. 'It hasn't come to me that directly, no. Very few black people kill themselves—you noticed that?—not with razors or guns, not fast anyhow. No, I'm just thinking I'm past eighty years old. The Bible doesn't promise but three score and ten; and very few of my family, black or pink, lived nearly that long.' So I told him I was sure we'd celebrate his hundredth together. He said he partly hoped I was right. Then he never mentioned the place again—never came back down here, not to my knowledge; never asks me one word about it, even when I show him the pictures I take."

Hutch owned all the land they'd crossed to get here; he owned this valley. Years back he'd tried to give it to Straw when Straw's daughter was born, an only child. But Straw had said he didn't want to "lay up treasure"; instead, let him keep on supervising the Negro tenant who worked the tobacco and running the place on straight half-shares (Straw had money from his own dead mother). So Hutch thanked Straw for tending Grainger's peculiar improvement.

And Straw agreed as solemnly as if they'd concluded a treaty exchanging some isthmus or bridge.

Hutch couldn't help smiling. "Hell, we may have the core of a gold mine on our hands—buy the rest of the county, clear-cut all the trees, build a cinderblock music hall for tacky stars from Las Vegas and Nashville, run a paved road back here, build parking lots, lure in busloads of senior citizens; and I'll sell tickets when I retire. That'll be any day."

For a moment, as he generally did, Straw took the idea seriously. Then his mouth seemed to fill with bile; he turned aside to spit. When he spoke to Hutch's eyes, it came straight as a tracer. "I can *see* what you've turned into, friend. You can thank your Jesus that Wade is blind; he won't have to watch."

Hutch actually thought *Nothing anyone's said till now in my life was harder than that.* In another ten seconds it still felt true. Hutch still hadn't smelt any liquor on Straw; he couldn't recall an offensive word he'd said to Straw in two decades (it had been twenty years since he'd criticized Emily for her Puritan-mother primness and jealousy). Had some postponed toll for years of self-loathing come down on Straw and poisoned him bad enough to flush hate from him—not only hate but unearned nonsense, however well phrased? *What does he see I've turned into?*

Hutch thought through that before he registered Straw's main news. *Straw knows about Wade. So Grainger's told him.* Hutch had known since Christmas that Wade still phoned Grainger every few weeks, but he'd had no inkling that Grainger knew about the plague and its symptoms. And he'd never asked Grainger to keep anything he knew about Wade from Straw and Emily. Hutch himself, though, had kept it from Straw and everyone else except his own ex-wife—Wade's mother Ann. Ann had been on her own for more than a year since leaving Hutch when she passed sixty-one.

Straw said "You don't deserve that from me." He knocked a fist on Hutch's shin.

Hutch waited, thanked him but then said "What have I turned into?"

Straw looked him over thoroughly again, shook his head in honest bafflement and said "Can we talk about Wade instead? We might help him."

"What don't you know?"

Straw said "How long have you known Wade's sick?"

"Since late last summer, eight or nine months."

"Did Wade tell you outright or call his mother first?"

Hutch thought *Might have known Straw would go for the quick.* He almost laughed. "Wade came for a visit two winters ago. I hadn't quite guessed what Ann had in mind, and I doubt Wade knew before he arrived, but Ann had her own plans cooking by then. She was already hunting modest quarters to start her 'lunge at self-reliance'—honest to God, she was calling it that. So sometime during that three-day visit, she brought young Wade in on her thrilling secret, and he helped her find the place she's rented out toward Hillsborough on Pleasant Green Road.

"Sometime on that same visit, Wade told her his trouble—by then he'd only had minor infections—and asked if he could count on coming home when he got bad. According to Ann, Wade asked if she could stand to move back in with me long enough to see him through to his own end, if the end-time came and he needed help? You know how Wade had shied off visits this far south in recent years, how he'd barely see us when we went to New York and then nowhere but in public restaurants or dark theaters—he and his super-Afro friend."

Straw said "Wyatt Bondurant?"

"None other, the scourge of pink Caucasians. Anyhow, back to my sad story—Ann's squatty little self-reliant house can barely hold her and her big designs on self-improvement, much less a man at least as sick as anybody left on Earth. But Ann told Wade she'd give all she had; she couldn't speak for me—he must ask me himself. For whatever reasons, though, Wade left without asking me; and Ann didn't mention one word of his trouble till after she'd been on her own for long months.

"Then she called me one evening and asked to come by on the pretext of bringing me some jackass gadget she'd bought for my kitchen. In fifteen minutes she backed up that great truckload of sadness and poured it on me. Till then I'd got fairly used to the idea that Wade's friend Wyatt had turned him against us. But hearing that my son couldn't trust me with the news of his death—and hearing it from Ann in the midst of this skit she's waltzing through—well, it put an even harder freeze on our dealings, Wade's and mine." If Hutch had more to tell, it failed him.

Straw said "So Wade is at the point of death in New York City, alone as any street-corner psycho, because you and Ann are peeved with each other?"

"That's likely to be a small piece of it, yes. It may be part of why he won't take my phone calls."

"Forget the damned phone, Hutch. *Walk* to New York, if that's what it takes."

"I've thought this through a billion times—Wade's still a grown man, Straw. I don't have the right."

Straw said "Pardon me but I fail to comprehend how any quibble about your rights can be strong enough to keep a man, kind as you've been in your best days, from a son in a pit as low as this?"

Hutch was too full to speak.

Straw said "Set me straight on a few things here—Wade is not a junkie, right?"

"Don't cheapen this."

"Don't worry; I'm not. I'm exercising my rights as I see fit. You may have forgot but I remember, clear as this minute, standing by Wade when he was an infant at the christening font and swearing to be his faithful godfather."

Hutch shut his eyes and agreed. He could see it plain as Straw.

"Last time I looked, Wade wasn't a needle-drug addict. He's sure-God not hemophiliac."

Hutch said "No, Wade would barely take aspirin till this came on him."

Straw's voice was like a voice that has reached the last conclusion available to humans, that exhausted and mild—"What other brands of adult catch this plague?" When Hutch stood silent, Straw stated his finding. "So Wade is queer." It was far from a question.

Hutch faced him; their eyes were no more than three feet apart.

Straw could watch you for hours on end and not blink once; he was steady-eyed here.

Hutch said "That's an admirably educated guess."

"It's the truth, mean as barbed wire; it's been the truth since before Wade finished grade school surely."

Hutch said "I doubt it was early as that; recall he loved more than one fine girl." He paused, then mutely agreed to Straw's finding. *All right, we've both known it always.* But he and Straw had never so much as broached it between them, not till today.

"Is there some kind of freeze-dried Baptist hypocrite hid down in your soul and holding you back from Wade Mayfield at the edge of his grave?"

Hutch said "Not to my knowledge, no. I was never a Baptist, as you'd remember if you honored our past. If any one of your friends has loved pleasure, it's surely been me—taking *and* giving." Hutch paused and met Straw's unbroken stare. "I'd have thought you remembered. God knows, I seldom forgot our times."

Straw watched Hutch again for a long quiet minute. Except for handshakes, no parts of their bodies had touched in nearly four decades. And for Straw that had never seemed a real deprivation, despite their pleasure. Now though, this close to Hutch's body, Straw saw again how well made his friend was, how nearly his face had refused to age and how his eyes had only strengthened in both directions—Hutch drank in the world and sent it back out; something in his eyes always said *Come. There's a better place here, an actual dream.*

Straw asked himself now why he'd stopped answering. He broke his gaze and looked down to Grainger's all-but-maniacal water park below them. Then a memory he'd lost came back. "You remember Wade nearly drowned, right there." Straw pointed to the central pool of the cleaned stretch.

Hutch said "Lord, no." They'd kept it from him. "When was it? Who saved him?"

Straw thought Grainger's name and recalled the event. But all that past suddenly seemed meaningless against the pressing weight of now. He faced Hutch and said the unavoidable thing. "Let me drive you to New York tonight. We can bring Wade back. He'll listen to me." Straw suddenly drew back and flung a small white flint, an arrowhead he'd found underfoot. It missed every tree between them and the valley and thunked down in the midst of the creek.

Shocked as he was, Hutch at least turned the idea over. *Wade tonight? Would he so much as answer the door, much less join them?* At first Hutch could only think to ask "Where would he stay? I'm teaching straight through till the end of the month."

"There's Duke Hospital, for an obvious start. There's his mother in her house, ready to serve. Emily wouldn't object to Wade being here; I'll take him on gladly."

Hutch said "He won't move."

Straw waited through half a long minute. Then he said "Christ, do you love your son or not?"

"Friend, I honest to God don't know," but by then Hutch's own eyes had watered, and the sound of the words was criminal nonsense. The total weight of the postponed fact that Wade Mayfield was dying blind five hundred miles north, the only thing Hutch had expected to last of all he'd had a part in making except a few poems, the only human he'd loved with no real reservation since his own father died—that whole weight caved in on him here. All over his body under the clothes, his actual skin begged to be held and touched. Hutch had waited too long, much more than a year, since any welcome hand had touched him. Now though, he couldn't ask or reach out for touch. So he stood, looked down to the creek a last time, then turned and headed back toward his car— the main house, the car, the road, wherever.

Straw called out "Answer yourself soon, boy. You've got to know"— know whether Hutch truly loved Wade or not. It didn't feel like a cruel question to Straw.

Hutch failed to answer though, failed to look back. And soon he was almost out of sight before Straw fell in behind him and followed. Straw made no effort to overtake Hutch; and when they were out of the woods into daylight, Straw paused at Grainger's to check on his nap while Hutch walked straight to the main house, the upstairs room that was always his on overnight visits.

5

An hour later Straw had already gone on to Grainger's with most of the meal, so Hutch and Emily came down the high back steps with only a tray of the last hot dishes and a box with the gifts. In the short walk Emily said, out of the blue, "Hutch, we're heartbroken for all your family."

If she'd flung off her darkish old-maid clothes and thrown herself on him, Hutch could hardly have felt a stranger surprise. In thirty years Emily had said very little to him that an unbiased witness might have

called warm or generous. And it took Hutch a few yards of silent walking
before he could say "Em, it's awful. Thank you."

"Whatever we can do, whatever on Earth—"

*Have she and Straw huddled on some plan to bring Wade here and
see him through to whatever end? Have they told it to Wade and has he
agreed?* It was hardly the worst thing that might happen next, but the
thought of shouldering what was his duty onto others here—even onto
Strawson who truly was Wade's godfather and had loved him—was painful
for Hutch and scraped on his sense of failing to tend the single person
alive who had full claim on his care. He shocked himself by saying
"Strawson just mentioned us going to see Wade—him and me, soon."

Emily's small white face burned a kind of fervor that Hutch hadn't
seen since the early days when she'd tear into him and fight for her share
of Straw's time and notice. "Strawson very much wants to go with you,
I know."

"Since when, Emily?"

She paused to answer carefully. "I think it was two nights ago, maybe
three—Strawson came back up to the house from Grainger's and said the
old fellow had made him call Wade."

"Straw talked to Wade a few days ago?"

"I thought Strawson told you—"

They were in earshot of Grainger's door; it was open again. Hutch
quietly said "Straw's barely told me he's alive, not for some years." He
thought it would please her.

But again she surprised him. "You're the only person, alive or dead,
that I've never heard Strawson low-rate or laugh at or slash to ribbons."

"He's known a lot of people."

"In the Biblical sense." Still Em's face was showing a life it had
seldom showed, a fined-down purpose that could drill through rock. "I
well know people have lined Strawson's road; but I've told you the truth,
Hutch, the bare-knuckle truth. I thought you were in the business of
truth—teaching school, writing poems."

By then they'd arrived at Grainger's front steps, and Emily had
climbed the first one before Hutch touched her elbow to stop her. When
she turned, he said "I needed reminding." His eyes were not cutting.

And she understood that. She also knew it was as near to thanks as she'd get from Hutch Mayfield. She shut her eyes, ducked her chin, then raised her voice and called "Mr. Grainger, we're all here with you."

Hutch wondered since when she'd called Grainger *Mister.*

Inside Grainger said "Stop where you are."

Straw's voice laughed. "Easy, Mr. Walters. We know them both. They're bringing provisions. Just let them unload."

Inside, when the screen door shut behind them, Hutch saw that Grainger had changed his clothes—a starched white shirt and gray wash pants with sharp creases, the small gold eagle-pin he'd found and polished not long ago (some relic of his infantry service in France in 1918). *Can he dress himself; does Strawson help him?* Again Hutch felt accused of failure—this old man was literally his nearest live cousin, of whatever color. Grainger had been as strong a prop to Hutch's childhood as anyone, alive or dead—as watchful, honest and guard-dog loyal. *I should come on up here, soon as class ends, and stay till he dies.*

But the clear fact was, Straw and Emily had been far closer to the old man than Hutch for decades. They'd lived with him daily throughout their marriage; they'd worked beside him as long as he could work; and they'd brought him up to the main house and nursed him through double pneumonia just last winter, not to speak of a hundred daily attentions. Hutch moved toward Grainger, gathered the long bird-bones of his shoulders into an embrace and said "I owe most of my life to you."

Grainger whispered slowly at Hutch's ear. "Colored men bearing down on you tonight, big knives in their fist. Haul out of here now." It was said in urgent indelible conviction.

Hutch stepped back but said "I think we've got a little time. Let's eat Em's supper."

If that assurance meant anything to Grainger, he gave no sign. His eyes were still urging Hutch toward the door.

By then Straw and Emily had slid the table out from the wall, set the extra chairs that Straw had brought and spread the food. There was a good-sized roasted turkey breast with dressing, baked yams in their skins, macaroni and cheese, home-canned green beans, fresh biscuits, corn chowchow, a pitcher of milk and a bottle of good California red wine. Straw guided Grainger to his place at the head, assigned the right-hand chair to Hutch, the left chair to Emily and the foot to himself.

Then Hutch said "Old cousin, you bless it."

Grainger looked as distant as the outskirts of Cairo, not confused but gone.

Straw said "Mr. Walters has pretty much quit on the Lord Above. You bless it, Hutch."

Hutch had likewise been far less than observant since he gave up on all known Christian institutions during the boiling acid and blood of racial integration in the South, when the churches behaved at least as abominably as the Klan (a good deal more so; the churches knew better). But after a short pause now, he said "Thanks for the three of you and this much food. Thanks above everything for Grainger Walters' life that has given us such long care and that goes on among us. Watch everyone we love who's not here with us." Only at the end did Hutch realize he'd addressed his blessing more to Strawson than God.

But eventually Emily said an "Amen," then began to serve Grainger's plate a heaping plenty. If she knew what she was doing, then his appetite was healthy.

And once he had the food before him, Grainger set in at once to salt it heavily and slice the turkey into minute cubes. Then he ate it, not stopping, the way they'd all seen him eat for years. He'd neatly consume a particular item till it was exhausted—the beans, the bread—then move to another, around his plate clockwise. With each new item he'd fix his eyes on one of the three white table partners. He showed no detectable smile or frown to any of them. Maybe he couldn't see them at all but watched some memory from his long supply; but he never spoke, even when he turned to his tall glass of wine and downed it slowly in an unbroken swallow.

The others ate Emily's likable cooking in normal ways and traded the all but meaningless remarks of longstanding friends; but though the three of them kept mild faces, their separate minds were circling tightly.

Straw thought of nothing but Wade—alone, he guessed, in a city where no strong man should live, much less a godson with the worst disease since white men sold smallpox-ridden blankets to American Indians and wiped out whole tribes, no trace left, not even their language. Straw's own child—a textbook editor now in Georgia, pleasant to see and as cold as a bottle—was as far from his mind as the strangers of Asia.

Emily thought *Someway I'll wind up with Wade on my hands. My hands are full. How in God's name can I hold on to more?* None of that was just mean-minded; with all her fears, she'd kept a decent heart alive in her.

Hutch thought almost entirely of Grainger. Whatever secret personal things this old man had been throughout his own life, he sat here tonight for Hutch as a relic of more than a century of his own family's unfillable hunger—its adamant aim to survive and print its demands on a line of faces called Mayfield, Drewry, Kendal, Gatlin and whatever part-black Walters kin lived on from Hutch's white great-grandfather who'd wasted no chance to pass his traits down whatever human route would give him hot entrance.

Only for a moment did Hutch let himself think that—with Grainger barren of any offspring and Hutch's own son racing toward death now with no more leavings than the memory of pleasure in a few young men as barren as Wade—then one long line of bold contenders from one patch of ground was fading and sinking to Earth at last.

And though all the others assumed that Grainger was either asleep, upright in his chair, or had wandered into some thicket of memory, it was simply a fact that none of them except Grainger Walters—in their thoughts here now—had moved on into fresh knowledge and hope. Since a year ago when television brought him the ghetto riots from Los Angeles—whole days and nights of fire and pillage by young black men— Grainger's mind had frequently called up memories he'd heard in childhood from his slave-born great-great-grandmother Veenie.

Veenie had been born around 1820 in southeast Virginia and was halfway grown when a preacher named Turner led his short revolt of a few black men that managed to kill some fifty white people in the summer of 1831. Veenie had even told Grainger she'd stood not twenty yards from the scaffold and watched Turner hanged in the county seat when she'd been sent to town for one spool of thread. And somewhere in his trunk in this room, Grainger still had the buckeye—the dry horse chestnut— that Veenie had found near Nat's swinging corpse as she left the sight that morning and walked to the master's kitchen where she worked every day from sunrise to bedtime. That much pain and iron endurance had come and gone in the live presence of a woman Grainger had loved and leaned on, not fifty miles from where he sat tonight with three white people he'd worked to serve, one of whom was his cousin. Yet Veenie's cold blood, thick as a dragon's, crept through him tonight.

So the mixture of those two ominous thoughts—the California riots and old Veenie's memories—had preyed on Grainger ever since; and lately he'd spent long hours each day, and many whole nights, in the vivid certainty that wholesale righteous dreadful slaughter waited for every soul he'd cared about, live and dead (he specifically thought that the dead, white and black, would also rise at the Judgment with their strength renewed and turn on one another with pitchforks, butchering axes and hand-forged knives). And none of it worried him all that much since, in his mind, Grainger likewise knew he had enough Negro blood in his veins (he was more than half black) to be permitted to save two souls when the gore streamed at last. He'd long since chosen the two he'd rescue—his dead wife Gracie, who'd abandoned him many years ago, and one young white man that sometimes (now in Grainger's shifting mind) wore the face of Rob Mayfield, then Hutch's own face and sometimes Straw's, then Wade's face the way it had looked in childhood: clear as a clean plate with two keen eyes, not bone-thin and blind, which it must be now.

The other thing that wove through Grainger's mind as he sat at the head of this bountiful table was a line of numbers he tried to recall—1–1–2–2–something–5–8–9–9. He barely knew it was Wade's phone number his mind was hunting; but he finally thought it was urgent to ask for somebody's help, whoever these people here might be—he was no longer sure. So he reached for the fork on his empty plate and rapped the plate hard.

Straw said "You don't plan to eat more tonight, Mr. Walters? We'll be up till day."

Grainger ignored him but looked to Emily and said "Tell me what this number means." This time he could only say "1–1–something," then "9–9–9."

Emily went blank.

Even Straw was stumped.

Hutch quietly said "He's working on Wade's telephone number." Then he said the whole number clearly toward Grainger. "Wade's telephone number in New York City is 212–732–5899. You want to call Wade?"

Emily gently said "No—"

Strawson said "Let Mr. Walters say. It's his damned party; he's got his own plans."

But Grainger's eyes had shut down firmly. He might very well have been dead upright.

And Hutch took the possibility seriously. He reached out, turned Grainger's wrist and held two fingers against the skin that was dry as any adder's. It was chill to the touch, and at first Hutch could find no pulse or motion. But he lightened his pressure till, finally, there seemed to be the wide-spaced thud of ongoing life. He moved his fingers to Grainger's neck, the hollow below the back of his jaw. There Hutch could sense an actual beat, still faint and slow.

Emily whispered "The wine was too much for him, this late."

Straw said "He fades off like this a lot." When Hutch had taken his own hand back, Straw said "Mr. Walters, we've got this cake to eat."

Emily said "He can have cake anytime. Let's put him to bed."

Straw said "He's fine, just playing possum."

Hutch said "First possum to live past a hundred. Let's lay him down."

But though he spoke gently, Straw insisted on his own rights. "I want to remember this night; get the cake." He'd drunk more than half the bottle of wine, though he showed no sign of more than his daily heat and focus.

Through the screen Hutch saw that the night was almost on them, and the air had turned cooler than he'd expected. He'd already seen Straw's camera by the door; so he said "Take a picture if you want to now, but I doubt we'll need reminders of this."

Grainger said "I don't show up on film no more." Then he actually laughed, the first time in three years. His eyes stayed shut another long moment; then Grainger looked to Emily. "Em, let's light us a bonfire and eat it."

At first nobody quite understood; then Emily realized he meant the cake. "I just put one candle on your cake, Mr. Grainger. Last year you started over on your age."

Straw laughed. "Last year we nearly had our own firestorm."

Emily stood and went to the kitchen counter, lit the one green candle and brought the cake forward—the caramel cake that Grainger had asked for, rich as any oil billionaire and made by a half-cracked widow down the road. Emily waited for Hutch or Strawson to sing; but though they faced her, they both stayed quiet.

So Grainger said "Everybody's too old to sing but me" and croaked his way through a curious version of the first line of "Happy Birthday." Then he went mute again to eat the sizable slice Emily gave him. And when Straw stood to bring on the presents, Grainger only said "I don't need a thing cash money can buy" and held out his long raised palm to Straw.

Straw set the three boxes back by the door. "You'll enjoy them tomorrow." The contents were socks and a pair of red suspenders and, from Hutch, a framed photograph of his mother—Hutch's own mother Rachel, whom Grainger had known and helped years back. Till now she'd been absent from Grainger's wall of pictures; her death, in childbed, had pained him too hard.

To that point Straw had seemed cold sober, his alert best self. But when Grainger balked him from giving the gifts, Straw's face had gone slack. Then every cell around his eyes and mouth had crouched.

Hutch thought *He's about to say something else mean.*

But what Straw did was stand up soberly and go to Grainger's bed. He sat on the near edge, took up the phone and punched in eleven digits slowly.

If Grainger understood, he sat very still and thought *I was right. Here comes what I dread.*

Emily guessed at once what Straw was attempting.

Strangely it didn't dawn on Hutch. He was watching Grainger again, that lordly face, taking the sight of it back to his own first memories.

When they'd put the phone out here a few years ago, they'd hooked it up with a twenty-foot cord so Grainger could call for help from any-where. Now Straw walked with the white receiver toward the table; and a moment after he stood by the old man, the number answered. Straw quietly said "Wade, did I wake you up?" Then, with waits, Straw said "We're all down here for this big event" and "I'm glad to hear it" and "Tell it to Grainger." Straw put the receiver against Grainger's left ear.

Grainger's hand didn't come up to hold it, but he seemed to listen for half a minute. What he finally said was "You can't see me." Wade must have answered something like "No, not on the phone" since Grainger said "Here now in this room. You're looking right at me but I'm all gone." If Wade was still there, he either said nothing or launched a monologue—Grainger said nothing else.

So Straw took the receiver back.

But Grainger's hand came up and seized it. He said to Wade "Just do this for me." Then he leaned to hold out the phone to Hutch, to give him this chance.

It didn't startle Hutch or rile him. It was plainly as much a piece of this day as the ancient life that was still beside him in Grainger's body, a part of the course that Hutch had always understood to be laid down before him, a step or two ahead of his feet. He said "Evening, Son."

"Evening sir." Wade sounded younger, by maybe ten years, than the last time they'd talked.

"I've missed your voice."

Skittish as Wade's mind had got in recent days, he'd thought of such a moment for months. A great run of stored scalding words waited in him. But he held himself back enough to say only "I've missed a lot more than your voice, believe me."

Grainger was still in his chair, watching Hutch. His eyes hadn't blinked in maybe two minutes.

Emily and Straw were in the kitchen, scraping plates.

That near to Grainger—and all Grainger signified of their shared family's reckless waste—Hutch was suddenly free to say to his child "When can I see you?" It felt like the first words ever between them.

And Wade's voice was still young and hard as a child's. "I can't see you."

Hutch thought he referred to the blindness Grainger and Straw had mentioned. "I've heard about that. I'll help all I can."

But Wade had intended a bigger refusal—he couldn't imagine the sight of his father, after what had passed between them in recent years. He said "I've got all the help I can use."

"That much relieves me. But I'd still value the chance to see you. I finish classes in three more weeks."

Wade seemed to be gone—the wait was that long. Then a voice that was almost certainly his, though younger still, said "What if I told you to come here right now—by dawn at the latest?"

Hutch said "I'd start driving."

"Tomorrow?"

"Tonight."

Wade took a real wait. "How long could you stay?"

"Long as you need me, Son."

"You just said you had three more weeks of class."

"I'll get a stand-in; that's my least concern. You say what you want."

Wade drew a long breath but couldn't speak.

"Some friend's there with you tonight, I trust?"

Another pained wait, then finally Wade said "I'm by myself."

"For how long?"

"Another few minutes, maybe an hour."

"Wyatt's still with you, right?" Wyatt had been Wade's companion for nine years; he'd quickly become the main obstruction, and then an all but impassable wall between Hutch and Wade.

Wade said "Not Wyatt."

"He's left?"

"He's dead." On its own, Wade's voice made a high rough cry like a wail on the TV news from Palestine.

Hutch thought *Thank God* but he said "Oh no. I thought he wasn't sick at all."

"Wyatt shot himself, downstairs, out on the street—February 18th."

At first Hutch could only think *Has Ann known this and not told me?* But he knew not to ask it. *Keep pushing on.* So he said it again another way. "Wade, you're not all alone there, are you—not in the night?"

"My neighbor checks in twice a day and runs errands for me. A man from the AIDS center comes every morning. I haven't seen a doctor in weeks, haven't needed to—thank Christ for that."

"But you're blind, they say."

"Did Grainger tell you? I asked him not to."

Hutch said "He's here beside me right this minute. We've eaten his birthday cake, and it's past his bedtime by hours." Hutch could see that Grainger's eyes had shut and his head had drifted down onto his chest.

In the kitchen Straw and Emily were quiet, clearly waiting on Hutch to end the call.

Hutch was so overloaded with feelings, he could hardly think. "Son, we need to let Grainger lie down. Can I call you back in half an hour?"

"No, professor. I need to get quiet."

"Then I'll be there tomorrow."

"No. Leave me *alone*, Hutch." Wade had called Hutch *Father* all his life till today.

Hutch heard the change and thought it was hopeful. He said "I'll call you back in a little. If you don't want to talk, don't answer the phone."

But Wade was gone—had he heard the last words?

Hutch called his name again once, then rose and replaced the phone.

By the time Hutch turned back toward Grainger's chair, Straw was leaning to the old man's ear. "Sleepy time down South."

Grainger didn't respond; his head stayed limp on his chest, no sound.

For whatever cause, Hutch felt again the rush of strong pleasure— was it pleasure or a strain of panic, he wondered?—and he thought *Let him go*. It was Grainger he meant—let him go on now to death and eventual rest, at the end of this night when the old man had flung what might be a bridge between father and son, both frozen in silence till this full night.

Straw already had Grainger out on the bed. Hutch watched him unbutton the collar button, the cuffs of the starched shirt; then as Straw moved lightly to loosen the belt, Hutch untied the high-topped shoes and shucked them, then laid the blanket back on the old man, foot to chin (Grainger often spent whole nights in his day clothes).

Grainger said to the air in general "I told you they're coming with sickles, cutting a road, but nobody heard me." He was gone then, asleep, not ready to die; or death was not yet ready to take him—no one else ever had or would.

When Hutch followed Straw down the steps, he walked a little behind in hopes of a quiet few minutes to print on his mind that last sight of Grainger. He might well see him tomorrow morning before he left—he might be leaving tonight if Wade said "Come on" again—but Hutch understood that, once he'd spread that blanket up three minutes ago, he'd made his final try at thanking a man: an openhanded unsparing kinsman, whom he'd never see matched in this world again.

The mold was as long gone as whatever mold made the architect of the Great Wall of China, the goldsmith who beat out the pure death mask for Tutankhamen's withered face; as gone as the captain of the last clandestine slave ship that worked the south Atlantic in the girlhood of Grainger's great-great-grandmother and who still plowed on through the old man's mind, though powerless to appall him now.

At the foot of the steps to the main house kitchen, Straw turned and saw Hutch lingering in the dark yard. Straw spoke out clearly. "Take the air you need. I'll be inside. Call for me if you need me. I'll ride to Mars if you need me that far."

Hutch bowed his head and waved and stayed by the big oak, seated against it, looking back through his blind son's life to the days when they'd run around this same tree—Wade in the years before he was twelve, Hutch in his thirties, both flung by love like hawks by a storm.

6

It was past nine o'clock and fully dark before Hutch entered the main house and climbed to his bedroom on the second floor. It was the space he'd occupied when he lived with his father Rob in the country—usefully lonely adolescent years with a man more likable than most, though one who was apt to cause frequent pain, and with Grainger beside them much of the time. Straw and Emily, for thirty-odd years, had used Rob's old bedroom downstairs. It was directly under Hutch's; but though Hutch had left his door open now, he heard no sound except the normal creaks of a dry house older than Grainger.

Hutch had cleared his thoughts fairly well in the yard. He thought he understood that his forced encounter on the phone with Wade was the cause of the clairvoyant pleasure he'd felt through the day—not pleasure in a son's far-off agony but in contact restored—and Hutch had planned his next sure move. He wanted to sit here a few more minutes in a room that had sheltered much of his life, then to go back down and phone Wade again as he'd promised.

He'd repeat his offer to drive north tonight; he could be at Wade's West Side apartment by early morning and do what was called for. If Wade would agree to accept his help and come home, Hutch could simply lock the New York apartment, get Wade to the car by hook or crook and leave the chores of packing and shutting down a life till some decisive choice had been made, by death most likely. Life with a dying son in Durham would need its own plans. Hutch had a shaky confidence that somehow a path would open before him once he had the boy home.

A boy—right—thirty-two years old who had strong warnings of the danger he risked but who walked, open-eyed, into this destruction. The first need would be some reliable help, a companion or nurse. Surely Durham, a town with three huge hospitals, could offer qualified practical nurses to tide them through the last weeks of school. Then Hutch could take over full-time till the end. He'd already set his mind on the hope that Wade could die at home, the comfortable house where he'd grown up.

What will Ann try to do? Once Hutch had helped Ann move into her new life, he and she had hardly communicated except for business matters (and then mostly by letter); and—strangely, though they used the same grocery store and shared many friends—they hadn't met face-to-face in nearly ten months. Their mutual friends were not talebearers. Ann's new job kept her off Duke campus. And Hutch had gradually managed to fill, with friends and work, what had seemed like a sucking wound when Ann spent her first night in three decades outside their marriage—outside the idea of their marriage at least; they'd of course been briefly parted by business trips. The thought of Ann tonight, with Wade's phone voice still strong in Hutch's ear, felt as distant and cool as a handsome old house seen from a fast car, trailing off in the dusk of a rearview mirror. *It's me Wade has asked for, if anybody.*

Hutch looked up, intending to head downstairs toward the nearest phone; and there stood Strawson, silent on the doorsill, both hands raised like a cornered thief. He'd changed into a dark blue polo shirt and black cotton trousers. Oddly Hutch thought *Pallbearer's clothes.*

Straw said "Don't shoot."

Hutch said "Why would I?"

"I've stood here watching you a whole long minute. I know all your thoughts."

Hutch shook his head No. "We've lived apart much too long, old friend. I'm in deep hiding." It was only halfway meant as a joke. Like everyone, Hutch overestimated his own complexity.

Straw said "You want to go get Wade tonight. You want to have all his death for yourself—you and him in a room till it's over."

"Tell me what's wrong with that."

"You well know, Hutchins."

"I wouldn't have asked you if I really knew."

Straw said "There's somebody still alive called Ann Mayfield, born Ann Gatlin—used to be your wife; gave birth to your child. Wade loves her too."

"You don't understand that Wade ordered both of us out of his life, long years ago; or so his friend Wyatt said by phone and fax and every other known means but letter bombs. Once you got Wade on the phone just now though, it was me he asked for—not his mother."

Straw said "You truly sure Wade was in his right mind?" It was not meant cruelly. Straw had read that dementia was often a late result of this plague.

"I'm going downstairs right now to call him back."

Straw said "Can I go with you?"

"Downstairs?—it's your house, friend."

"No, it's yours; I'm just the loyal tenant. I mean can I ride with you to New York?—you'll need some help."

Hutch said "No I won't."

"Hutchins, the last thing Wade Mayfield needs is a doting father dragging his pitiful body downstairs through a big apartment building and trying to navigate the eastern seaboard single-handed."

Hutch said "Look, I don't even know that I'm going. When you called Wade at Grainger's, the first thing he told me was 'Come tonight.' The longer we talked, the more he circled; then Grainger conked out. So I told Wade I'd try him one more time before bed. If he doesn't want to answer, he won't. He hasn't in months."

"Christ, Hutch, of course he'll want to answer you."

It came out of Straw with the old singeing force that had brought them together, almost as a matter of logical course, weeks after they'd met in a prep school classroom.

And it moved Hutch nearly as much as in those days—few men past sixty get bearable tributes from a trustworthy source. "Thank you, Strawson, but Wade may be exhausted."

"Wade's still got ears." Straw glanced at his watch. "It's past ten now; go call him. I'll wait here."

As Hutch pushed past him, Straw entered the room and—once he heard footsteps going down—he silently stood in the midst of the rag rug, nothing to lean on, nothing to brace him. His arms extended a little from his sides, and he tried to ask for whatever mercy was possible this late in his life, a life that he knew was littered with failure and was not done yet with small but calculated meanness. Whatever hopes or demands for payment went through Straw's mind, his body stayed perfectly still in place, though the last time he'd worshiped anything but a naked body was in his lost childhood.

Straw stood in place the best part of two minutes till at last an enormous blunt shaft of pain forced downward through him, shaking him brutally. A mute bystander might have thought this excellent man with perfect eyes was dying where he stood, bludgeoned somehow by an unseen hand. Straw, though, took it to be the only answer he'd get, the only answer he'd had in years of terse claims on God or fate; and he knew he must take the answer straight to Hutch.

7

WHEN Straw got to the dim long kitchen, Hutch was still at the counter by the hung-up phone. It looked like a baited iron bear trap in reach of his hand. Hutch seemed alarmingly older than he had a quarter hour ago—gray and slumped. He didn't look up but at least he didn't ask Straw to leave.

Straw said "I know the number if you lost it."

"I got the number."

"Somebody else answer?"

"No, it was Wade—pretty certainly Wade. He sounded really stunned but he asked me if I'd ever lived through a dream where I couldn't find the walls or the floor, however high I flew or dived. I told him No; he waited and said 'A man I know is there this minute. Right this red minute.' Then he dropped his phone or left it off the hook—I've tried twice more and just get a busy."

Straw came a step closer and said "I'm driving you up there then."

Stunned as he was, Hutch could think of no reason to wait. "When?"

"I can leave this minute."

Hutch slowly looked around this room where he'd spent so much good time as a boy. *Any rescue here?* In fact, though the room still had its old long proportions, its old self was smothered under long years of Emily's apple-green paint, framed spurious coats of arms, stitched mottoes and furiously cheerful refrigerator decals. Apparently no rescue at all. So Hutch said "Lead the way." Then he risked facing Straw—he dreaded a collapse if he met those wholly demanding eyes. But here they were milder; and Hutch felt a little steadier, on a new pair of legs. "Many thanks, old friend."

Straw would have liked to leave it at that and hit the road, but he had to deliver the hurtful message he'd got upstairs. "First, you need to call Ann Mayfield."

At once Hutch agreed and touched the phone, but then he said "Why?"

Straw prodded him onward. "Just say I told you to do it, tonight."

"What else do I tell her?"

"You're a grown man, Hutchins. You take it from there." When Hutch made no move to pick up the phone, Straw said "What do you really want to say?"

Hutch knew right off. "I want to tell her I'm bringing our son back home to die, the home she left long months ago. Wade spent the first two-thirds of his life in a house she's abandoned; she can stay gone now."

Straw grinned. "You used to be a Christian gent."

"About ninety years back."

"Wait—ask Ann to help you. Just two or three words."

"I don't want to see Ann. Not in this life."

"She's got rights in this," Straw said. "Look at me."

Hutch actually looked at Strawson's eyes and recalled a fact that was easily forgot—Straw was the fairest referee he'd known, however crazy.

Straw told him "This is no child-custody case. A grown man's dying like shit in the road."

Hutch took up the phone and surprised himself by knowing Ann's number (he'd called no more than twice in the past year).

In twenty seconds Ann's firm voice said "Yes." Even here, its smoky resonance was sufficient warning of her steel-trap mind and her heart that had never yet trusted anyone's love for two steady hours.

Hutch said "Don't tell rank strangers 'Yes' in the night, alone as you are."

Ann was silent but she stayed on the line.

Hutch could taste her confusion and anger, so he tried to talk straight. "Ann, I don't know when you saw Wade or talked to him last, but I've had no recent news till tonight. The quick truth is, he sounds really awful; so I'm driving up there tonight to get him. I thought you should know."

"Are you at home?" Ann's voice wasn't choked but odd and uncertain.

Hutch heard her word *home* and wondered if he'd waked her. Was she drinking? Surely not. No company with her surely. Anyhow he said "I'll bring Wade back to one of my homes—I'm at Straw and Emily's; Straw's riding up with me."

Ann said "Let me speak to Strawson please."

Hutch knew she lost no love on Straw, but he held the phone toward him.

Straw refused. "Tell her No. This is your and her business entirely."

Hutch agreed, then told her "You and I'll settle this."

Ann thought she'd glimpsed the trace of a chink in the wall Hutch was already building against her. "Settle what? What's this we'll settle?"

"Wade Mayfield's death."

Ann was adamant. "You don't know he's dying."

Hutch said "This thing kills everything it touches."

"It may have looked like that till now; but Hutch, there are people who've been infected for years, some for more than a decade—I just read about them in *Time* magazine. They're somehow hanging on, doing their jobs. Don't kill Wade yet. Don't scare him to death—you know how contagious anxiety is." When Hutch kept silent, she thought *This won't sound maternal, whatever I feel*; but she went on and lightened her voice to say "I finally talked to Wade night before last; he seemed clear-headed and said not to worry." Then for the first time in many weeks, Ann lost grip on her own smothered feelings. Still she thought she managed to muffle the groan that broke from her, helpless.

Hutch heard it though. "We'll know a lot more when Wade's back home. I'll very likely need you." He hadn't foreseen he'd say that much; and for a bad instant, he thought of denying it.

But Ann said "You know I'll help, day and night."

There was only one thing left for now. Hutch lowered his voice. "You know Wyatt's dead."

"Yes, his sister wrote me."

"Wyatt had a grown sister?"

Ann said "Very grown; she writes a fine letter."

"And you didn't feel compelled to tell me our son was alone?"

Ann paused a long while. "No, Hutch, I didn't. Wade asked me not to."

"Asked you tonight?"

"In the letter—Wyatt's sister's letter."

Hutch felt a surge of revulsion that, though he'd never touched Ann in anger, might have ended in violence if they'd shared the same room. He waited it out, then could only say "I guess this means Wade is ours again." Before the words were out of his mouth, Hutch heard their strangeness. He'd always half concealed from himself his conviction that Wyatt Bondurant had shanghaied Wade Mayfield from his home and borne him off to the glaring impasse where they'd all stood wordless till tonight. Hutch had never quite said as much, even to Ann.

But Ann echoed his sudden discovery of an old sense of ownership in Wade. "Ours?—I guess."

"You say you talked with him two nights ago?"

Ann realized she'd stretched the truth. "It was probably more like a week ago. We talked fairly normally for maybe five minutes; then he hung up on me; and when I've phoned him since, nobody answers." Whatever desertion Ann had doled out to Hutch, her voice here sounded bruised with regret.

Hutch said "All right. I'm leaving for New York."

"Will you let me know exactly what happens?"

"I'll call you from there—you working tomorrow?"

Ann said "All day. I'll tell them to put your call straight through."

Hutch said "Till then."

But Ann held on and gentled her strength. "I'll go anywhere or do anything that you or Wade need."

That was one more piece of news to Hutch, so new that it almost angered him again and he almost laughed. *She won't take simple requests from God, much less her legal mate.* But the sight of Emily standing in the kitchen door made Hutch say at least "Thank you" to Ann.

When he'd hung up, Emily said "Sandwiches and coffee won't take me a minute. Strawson, find the quart thermos; then you won't need to stop." No mention of how she'd heard or guessed that Straw was in on this belated lunge.

Hutch didn't know how long Emily had stood here or what she'd heard, but she had it all right—no word to slow him or to stop Straw's going—so he thanked her too.

She went to the counter and began to slice turkey.

Then there in the midst of Rob's old kitchen—a kitchen that had served nearly two hundred years of kin and slaves, returning freedmen and the rickety children of wormy white tenants—the wall that had held grief back inside Hutch broke and fell. He gave a single cry like an animal watching its own leg torn from the socket.

Straw acknowledged the sound. "That may be all any of us can do. Let's go anyhow."

Hutch agreed and sat with Straw at the table while Emily packed food; and though Hutch tried to think of old Grainger to steady his mind, he thought *What if Grainger dies in the night?* and was briefly troubled till again, in the silence as his mind turned to Wade, a slim flow of pleasure began in his chest.

8

IT had been twenty years since Hutch had actually driven to New York, longer still since he and Straw had been alone together in a car for more than ten minutes; but exhaustion swamped him in the deep night in Delaware, and Hutch had to ask Straw to take the wheel. For half an hour Hutch stayed awake, feeling a duty to keep Straw company (though they barely spoke); but as they crossed the New Jersey line, Hutch settled his head against the side window. In five seconds he was deep asleep; and after three miles—once Straw had looked toward him and silently granted his greater need for rest—this dream came to Hutch, an astonishing gift.

The moment it started, his watchful mind recognized it as fact— mere history, an accurate memory of an evening forty-four years back, the day he'd first made love to Ann. They'd met in their freshman year of college, both new students in a bonehead composition class; and though they were each as virgin as snow, they'd seriously liked each other on sight—their looks, the keen young air around them—and after a month of smaller meetings, Hutch had quietly worked toward a way they could meet entirely while the fall warmth lasted. Meet and go past the little they'd learned apart, in separate high schools with high school loves about as adventurous as day-old calves.

He'd borrowed his friend Jack Hagen's car—illegal for a freshman— and driven Ann out one Wednesday near sundown to a place he'd already scouted in the woods. They'd parked on the road, walked inward (not even holding hands) to a site as thunderous as any Hutch knew of between Carolina and the caves of Virginia—a range of granite bluffs that climbed some hundred feet above a small river with its own serene rapids. They'd drunk the bottle of cider Hutch brought, tart but unfermented, with a box of cheese crackers; and then he'd actually fallen asleep to the sound of the water, darkening below them—no sleep at all the previous night, a zoology exam. The nap was wildly unexpected and no part of his plan; he was still too green not to be overcome.

And he'd have slept hours if Ann hadn't waked him a half hour later by stroking his eyes. When Hutch looked up, she was curved above him— her face some twenty inches away. In a few more seconds of bearing that awful distance between them, it seemed a literal prohibition against life itself. Ann was that good to see, that good to smell close. He didn't reach out though; she didn't reach down (her stroking hand was back in her lap).

So Hutch did the next thing he knew to do—it boiled straight up from some old but never-used chamber of his brain, some legacy maybe from his bold grasping father. Very slowly, moving like a man in dense water, he stripped his clothes from neck to toe and stood bare beside Ann Gatlin, still seated. Hutch couldn't see it but his face, chest, arms, his groin and sex were shedding around him, like clean strong light, the only half conscious splendor of his frame, his flawless skin and the promise of his power.

Ann studied it all, grave-eyed as a girl on a Greek tombstone; then she also rose and—a whole yard from him—she followed suit with no trace of shame: a slow but determined unveiling of gifts even grander than any Hutch owned or had dared to want. The hair of her sex alone seemed both the safest thicket for hiding and rest and likewise a masterly crown of thorns, some medieval jeweler's handiwork to set on an ivory Christ in glory, back in victory from death and famished.

When Hutch reached toward her, to close the gap, they found they knew—from longing and dreams—each move to make next, each move in order, each more stunning than its previous neighbor: Paradise. In the dream, as it had in actual life, no sight had ever given Hutch more; no human being had known like Ann (that first best evening) his every hope and how to win them in smiling silence, passing them on with open hands.

And in the car, four decades onward, as Straw sped through the last of dark New Jersey, each moment of that hour—instant by instant, purified of the spite and grudging of Hutch and Ann's long months apart—rose in Hutch's starved mind again and not only gave him the useful reminder of all he'd won in better days but also smothered for actual minutes his dread of morning. Morning, Manhattan and Wade all but gone.

*   *   *

As a dim shine began to leak through the murk in the east toward the coast, Hutch gradually woke and tasted again the nearing core of his aim and purpose—the bitter intent to save his child.

In the lingering night, Straw had got them onto the Jersey Turnpike and borne them on, by the dangerous moment, through an outrage of traffic like the silent forced evacuation of Hell. Its hard demands had him focused ahead as he'd barely been focused since his all-night lunges up and down the roads of his youth, mostly hunting for women to fold him in briefly and then fade off.

In Hutch's memory of the crowded road, it had never run through a likable landscape; but the past two decades had thrust the land, the houses and buildings deeper than he'd known into a frozen degradation or, worse, a total failure of human shame to burden the Earth and its live creatures with the active evil of outright greed and willful blindness to what the planet will bear till it recoils and wipes itself clean. *No wonder at all the country's gone mad. Let it all come down soon, one silent crash. Let the plague roar on.*

Hutch reined himself in. *You're more than half asleep. This is normal America, love it or leave it.* But then they passed the all but extraplanetary miles of oil refineries, fuming and hung with a million red lights, and then the final poisoned gray-green marshes; and Hutch was literally speechless with anger at an idea—America—botched very likely past redemption by the knowing hands of men no stronger than himself.

Only Straw could manage the adequate words as they plunged on through the lifting dark, toward the still-hid west bank of the Hudson. "Don't you hope old God turns out to be *just?*"

Hutch said "Oh no. I'm banking on his mercy."

Straw waited a whole mile, then managed the tired start of a grin. "Old-maid alarmist that you are, you *would* be in the mercy market. What have you ever done that could upset even the crankiest God?"

Grogged as he still was, Hutch turned and took in the full sight beside him—not the blasted world but the one man driving. "You say I failed you."

Straw faced the road. "That's my complaint, not God's."

Through their years of friendship, Hutch had often misplaced the rock-ribbed fact of Straw's undamaged conviction of God, a thoroughly handmade spacious God with rules that resembled no other creed's but that kept a present and active hold on Strawson Stuart. Hutch said "You think old God ever minded the times we had?"

Straw calmly turned his eyes from the road. "Of course he did. I loved you, Hutchins. Nobody but you, not truly, not then—not God nor woman nor trees nor deer, just Hutch Mayfield. Have you lost that?" Straw faced the road again and righted the car.

Hutch shook his head at the clean-lined profile of a head that was still as fine as any, on any old coin. "Never lost it, no. I recall every time our two hides touched—right down to the look of the rooms we were in and how the light fell, how the instants tasted. They're memories strong as any I've got and I'm still grateful."

Straw said "I'm not just speaking of bodies. I'd have spent my whole life bearing your weight, if you'd said the word."

Hutch could smile. "I think you truly believe that. I think you may well believe you wanted that, forty years ago. But don't forget you were cheerfully mounting married women, virgins and spinsters by the literal dozen, in between our rare good innings together; and I was deep over my head with Ann before you ever stepped into my life."

Straw said "I can love anything on Earth with a body heat of eighty degrees, or anything higher, and a calm disposition—I *mean* it; you know it or knew it years ago." Then, unexpected, he laughed the laugh of his own boyhood—the laugh that had brought such steady rafts of excellent human bodies toward his own keen beauty and the power of his heart, well before he was grown.

Hutch saw him even more clearly again, remembered each atom of his face at its best; and not for the first time, he grieved at the choice he'd made against the boy Straw was. Even if the softer man here in the night burned slower and asked for far less worship, Straw was nonetheless a welcome presence—a tangible gift to any close watcher. Finally Hutch thought of the question he'd asked himself years ago; it was still the main question for him and Straw. "But what in God's name could you and I have done—two thoroughly opposite brands of gent, trapped there in the country in too-big a house with an old Negro man and the rest of our lives to kill while the world snickered at us at the grocery store: two old sissies, harmless as house dust?"

Straw knew at once. "Aside from the fact that you and I are about as sissy as Coach Knut Rockne, we'd have had everything any man and woman have."

"Not live babies, Straw."

"To hell with babies—since when did America need more babies? We're strangling on babies."

Hutch said "Steady, friend. We'd have never had children, which is one huge lack in any arrangement that means to last; and worse, we'd have both had male-thinking minds. We'd have run out of things to talk about or to care for in common, and then we'd have just butted skulls round the clock like exceptionally dumb bull elephants. We'd have understood each other far too well before six months passed—all our big and small testosterone traits.

"Every mystery we'd had for each other would have worn out fast— we'd be as obvious as cheap fireworks. And that would have led to despising each other, then hate, then worse. We'd have loathed what time did to each other's bodies. And sooner or later, hot as we were, we'd have been sneaking out to cheat each other with every willing youngster in sight till we got so old we were paying for sex in motels and car seats." Hutch honestly thought they'd avoided just that.

Straw couldn't relent. "What would have been worse than you killing me or vice versa? No great loss to anyone but Grainger, and he might not have noticed the absence. Or we could have made a suicide pact— more people ought to take themselves out early and not ruin other people's outlook on life." Straw was plainly earnest.

Hutch had to grin.

And once Straw glared and failed to stop Hutch, he decided to join him. Their laughter rocked around in the fast car like stones in a bowl. But once they were quiet, Straw said "We failed at our one big chance. Don't ever again, not in my presence anyhow, try to wiggle your hips and slide past the fact. The two of us together had something a whole lot better than we've ever had since; you chose to ignore it and here we stand, two pitiful starved-out men out of luck."

Again Hutch felt the need to smile. There might be more than a gram of truth in Straw's tirade, but any chance they'd have had at a life was so far gone as to look like the smudge on a summer-night sky of the farthest star. So Hutch smiled and said "I've been grateful to you every minute I've known you."

Straw said "That won't buy me a dry dip of snuff." He'd never dipped snuff and soon realized it, which caused him to laugh again. There were few better laughs on the whole East Coast.

9

IN another half hour they'd crossed the jammed George Washington Bridge and in twenty more minutes were standing in a dark narrow hallway at the black steel door to Wade's apartment. The rooms Wade had shared for a decade with Wyatt were high in a well-kept building in the upper nineties over Riverside Drive, a neighborhood that had seen better times quite recently. The scattered filth, the broken heaved pavement, the rattled abandoned men and women posted every few yards with lost or frantic or merely dead eyes were plainly the normal state of things now.

Hutch hadn't stood here in at least four years, a little longer maybe; but surely it hadn't been this rejected by all human care. *Forget it, nothing but nuclear holocaust could mend this now, do your own hard duty.* He'd even dreamed, more than once in recent months, of standing at Wade's door, paralyzed to move; and now that he'd actually come, something balked him. His hand refused to reach toward the bell.

So at last Straw touched it—no audible ring. He pressed it longer—still no answer.

They waited more than a minute. Nothing.

Then the elevator door behind them opened on a single rider, a tall young woman.

When she saw Hutch and Straw, she stayed in the elevator but held the door open. The landing was maybe twelve feet by nine. The woman was no more than five feet from Hutch, and their eyes met at once.

Hutch first noticed her height and color. She was maybe six feet tall. Her skin was the shade of dry beach sand; and her hair was abundant and strong as horsetail, a lustrous natural black and long with the deep-set waves of a forties movie star. Warm as it was, she wore a black raincoat halfway to her shoes.

A quick automatic smile crossed her lips, then she went nearly grim with her dark eyes wide. She held a paper bag of what seemed milk and bread, and she still didn't move.

Hutch said "My name is Hutchins Mayfield. Do you know my son Wade?"

That brought her out of the elevator, though she pocketed her keys again.

Silence seemed so much a part of her nature that Hutch told himself she must be mute. He asked an easy Yes or No question. "Have you seen him this morning?"

She shook her head No, then finally said "I'm Ivory Bondurant."

An appealing voice, unmistakably black in its complex harmony. And *Bondurant* had been Wyatt's family name, though at closer range this woman looked ten years older than Wyatt, the last time Hutch had seen him at least. She'd be in her early forties then, remarkably preserved. Hutch extended his hand.

She took it lightly, meeting his eyes.

Hutch introduced Strawson and said "We rang two minutes ago—no answer yet."

Ivory agreed, as grave as before. "Did Wade expect this?"

What's this? Hutch wondered but he said "Yes, I spoke with him late last night—twice in fact."

She persisted. "I put him to bed at ten last night; he didn't mention visitors this morning."

Hutch drew out his wallet, found his driver's license with the small photograph and held it toward her. "I'm who I said. We've come to get Wade."

Self-possessed as she was, for a moment Ivory was shocked and she showed it. Her eyes and mouth crouched. But she refused the license, brought out her keys and stepped toward the door.

Hutch touched her arm to slow her. "What should we know?"

"I beg your pardon?"

"We've heard Wade's blind. He mentioned Wyatt's death. He sounded confused."

Ivory's shock was relenting; she studied Hutch's face, then gave a smile that was startling in its force. "Mr. Mayfield, all the above is correct. Your son has a ghastly disease that we're all but sure he got from my brother Wyatt. My brother took his own life when that was established— shot himself downstairs in the street ten weeks ago. Wade Mayfield is on his way to being nearly as bad off as any starving child on television. But come on in; it's clean anyhow." Her sentences made a real shape in the air; she let the shape hang in place for a moment like a carefully drawn, remorselessly perfect Euclidean figure. Then she opened the door and stood aside to beckon the men in.

As he came, Hutch watched her unbutton her black coat. Beneath it, she wore a blood-red linen dress. He recalled that Mary Queen of Scots had dressed identically for her own beheading, astonishing all the bystanding henchmen of her murderous cousin Elizabeth of England.

The room was empty or it looked so at first. The spare but handsome chairs and tables that Hutch remembered—the buffalo rug, the banks of records and tapes and playing machines: all were simply gone. A few dog-eared books stood by the baseboard, a sickly fern, a worn-out butterfly chair from the sixties, a radio playing what seemed to be Handel, a huge crumbled cork dartboard still bristling with darts. Hutch had bought that for Wade's ninth birthday, a gift that had seemed to displease the boy; yet here it was, a plucky survivor. Even the wood-slat blinds at the windows were gone; and the river was plain to see—the filthy Hudson, still iron-blue and stately in the visible pace of its final surrender to the sea.

Ivory entered and locked the door behind them. When she saw the two men's baffled stares, she said "They sold the things, piece by piece, for pittances."

Hutch was speechless.

But Straw said "Surely they had some insurance to help them along—"

Hutch realized he'd counted on the same thing. He only said "Surely—"

But Ivory said "Wade has a policy that covers more than half. But Wyatt's insurance canceled him out when they knew he was ill incurably. Then they were both hard up in no time. It broke my heart."

Hutch took the three words as a hopeful break in Ivory's daunting mastery here. "I understand you've been through hell."

"I didn't know I was out of it yet"—her great smile again.

Hutch said "I'll lighten your load today." He thought that was the literal truth; but once it was out, it sounded too grand.

Ivory heard the same sound. "Are you sure, Mr. Mayfield? You don't know me—"

"Miss Bondurant, I didn't know you existed. Why did I come here so many times in the past decade and never see you?"

Ivory's voice lowered and hurried to say "They didn't want you to know about me." But then she calmed herself. "I didn't live here when you used to visit. I was married then."

Hutch said "Thank God you've been here lately. We clearly owe you a great debt of thanks. Tell me anything else I should know."

She looked to Straw. "Can you believe this?" Her eyes narrowed down to contain their fury, but somehow she'd managed to gentle her voice.

Straw said "I never believe anything my eyes or ears tell me."

She said "Lucky man. Stay put where you are. The world up here's a torture factory." Then she abruptly smiled, "Tell your boss he'd need a very long year of time if I told him half of what he ought to know."

Hutch accepted the strike; his only reply was to turn away to the window again.

But Straw touched Hutch's shoulder and said "This man is nobody's boss, believe me; he's a sick man's father. Where have you put Wade?" Straw's eyes were among the rare eyes in Manhattan that could meet Ivory's blistering stare, instant for instant.

She finally whispered "Brace both of yourselves, hard, and step through that door." She pointed to a shut door off the main room.

When Hutch balked again, Straw took the lead. At the door he looked back at Hutch, who was pale as tallow on a white plate. Straw bent, being taller than Hutch, and pressed his lips against his friend's taut forehead. Then Straw opened the door, a wall of stifling air fell on him, he stepped inside. The space was dark; a torn sheet was stapled across the one window. Straw said "Old Wade, your godfather's here."

From somewhere in the hot brown air, a young voice said "Oh Godfather, I owe you a favor. Take a chair, sit down, exterminate me." What seemed an attempt at a laugh grated out.

Hutch's hand had found the switch for an overhead light.

The white glare rocketed round the space, then gradually showed another sparse room—no chests or tables, one rocking chair that had been on Wade's great-grandmother's porch the night she eloped and started her branch of the Mayfield family, nothing else but a mattress on a rolling frame and bleached blank sheets.

It took a long moment before Hutch could see that—pale as the sheets—a body was lying on them, naked. Maybe forty or fifty pounds too thin. A chaos of bones, white skin thin as paint, tangled islands of dark chestnut hair, a skull that was helpless not to grin. Hutch thought *Christ Jesus* but he also smiled and held in place.

Straw went forward though, knelt by the mattress, took the thin shoulders lightly and bent to kiss the skull.

Wade whispered "Hearty thanks" and tried to say more, but his voice broke up. His eyes looked normal, they both stayed dry and fixed on Strawson, he'd still to meet his father's gaze.

Hutch reminded himself *He can't see this*; he stepped onward then and knelt next to Wade. His hand went out to the head and smoothed the sweaty hair.

Wade's eyes found him then and, so far as they could show feeling at all, they looked surprised and gratified. He said "I'm pleased to see you, sir." When his lips closed again, the print of the teeth was stark through the skin.

Helpless, Hutch smiled. "Do you see me?"

"Not to know who you are, but I recognize your outline." Wade stopped as if he'd never speak again and both eyes shut. Blinded, he put up a finger and traced the line of Hutch's head on the air. Then he looked out again and said "You're giving off too much light." What seemed like another try at laughter rose and quit.

And a dry unwilling laugh escaped Hutch. "Son, I'm in deeper dark than you."

By then Straw had found a tan bedspread and laid it on Wade, up to the chin.

Wade's eyes had stayed shut; he was barely breathing— asleep or in some private trance.

Straw felt for a pulse in the throat and faced Hutch. "Let's get this child packed."

Hutch confirmed the pulse for himself, then stood and followed Straw back to the front room. There they could hear low sounds from the kitchen. Again Straw led the way, Hutch behind him.

To Hutch at that moment, Straw's upright back was a sight as necessary as air, the slim last promise of a chance at survival.

Ivory, vivid still in her red dress, was warming milk on a low gas flame. She'd already made toast, buttered it and laid it in a deep blue bowl.

Hutch saw she was making old-fashioned milk-toast, a thing his father had craved when sick. It seemed another small promise of strength, the hope of home.

Ivory said "If you gentlemen haven't had breakfast, I'm sorry to say this is all I've got—I make milk-toast for Wade twice a day. There's a coffee shop two blocks due east."

Straw said "We've eaten"; and as if on signal, he and Hutch both stroked the grizzled stubble of their chins.

Ivory opened a drawer and Hutch could see a small scattering of white plastic cutlery—knives, forks, spoons. He recalled his grandmother Mayfield's silver, ornate and heavy in the hand as a club. She'd left it, dozens of pieces, to Wade when he was a child. He'd stored it at home; and it hadn't been more than eight or nine years since Hutch himself had packed it carefully and brought it north, on his normal spring visit, hoping it might help propitiate Wyatt, who was already fending off Wade's kin. Surely silver hadn't survived the great sell-off?

Ivory had seen Hutch glance at the drawer. "Sorry, Mr. Mayfield, that went also—every silver piece the two of them owned. Wyatt had some too."

In these blasted rooms, like swamped lean-to's to Wade's own fragile bones, that was no loss at all. Hutch thanked her again. Then he wondered *Why thanks? Thanks for what? Why's she still here?*

As if mind reading, Ivory said "I've been the treasurer, the past six months, for my brother and Wade. It's all accounted for in that book there, by the day and to the penny." She pointed to a composition book on the counter—blue back, green spine.

Hutch took a momentary writer's pleasure in the sight of a well-made waiting blank book; then he said "I had no idea he'd run out of funds. He told me his firm paid him disability."

"They did, Mr. Mayfield—they still do—but this plague eats money faster than people. And I told you Wyatt was completely bereft weeks before he died. Wade carried him gladly; he can still swear to that."

Hutch said "I don't doubt that for an instant." Still he rightly felt small. He'd had no thought of theft or deceit; he had none now. It was almost the only cardinal virtue he claimed to possess—a genuine despisal of money, though he'd mostly had enough. This woman had apparently kept Wade alive for the past ten weeks since her own brother buckled and quit—Wade was a likable gifted man, no mystery there, none greater than the sight of human kindness, always a shock. Hutch said "What finally got Wyatt down?"

Ivory looked puzzled.

"Did his eyes fail too?"

The milk had begun to bubble and steam. Ivory drew it off the burner, poured it slowly on the toast and looked to Hutch. "My brother never really got too desperately sick—just a long succession of small but wearisome intestinal infections, nerve parasites, then a rush of lost weight, then finally a patch of Kaposi's sarcoma in the midst of his forehead like an Indian caste mark. At first he laughed that it made him a Brahmin. His doctor said he could have survived for months or years longer. He seemed to be one of these rare lucky people who somehow manage to keep the virus at a near standstill. No, I honestly think Wyatt Bondurant died from watching what he'd done to Wade Mayfield. He was sure it was him that gave AIDS to Wade; he never said why. Wade was grown when they met. Anyhow when the parasites got to Wade's eyes, Wyatt asked me here—here by this stove—if the two of them could count on me."

Ivory took ten seconds to think her way onward. "I took him to mean would I see them through to peaceful deaths. I'd have rather been asked

to kill a new baby, but I told him Yes. Wyatt was the last of my generation.
We'd seen each other through a South Bronx childhood, losing two sisters
along the way; I couldn't leave him now. At the time I didn't know he
meant to check out and leave Wade with me. But that was his plan. He
got his own business matters in order, left a short message for me to read
to Wade—the last sentence was 'Now you're in safe hands.' That had to
mean me; there was nobody else, that was safe anyhow. Then he found
a short alley between here and the river and took himself out with a gun
I forgot our father had brought up north from Virginia, sixty years ago.
A schoolgirl found his body, coming home at dusk from band practice."

It was simple as that then, in her eyes at least. Ivory Bondurant had
made a deal with her brother; she was sticking by it now he was gone.
She set a plastic spoon in the soaked toast, took up the tray and went
toward the bedroom.

Hutch said "You're bound to be a saint."

Ivory thought about that and searched Hutch's eyes but found no
clue to what he might mean, so she said "I've had my own good reasons.
It's been painful as anything I've ever known, but I don't claim any public-
health medals. It was what I wanted to do, while I could. Wade mattered
to me too."

Hutch heard her past tense; but he mouthed the words *Thank you*,
knowing his debt was too great to pay or to speak of here in these parched
walls. When Ivory watched him but gave no answer, Hutch realized Straw
was not there with him. He turned and called his name.

"In here." Straw had found the spare bedroom.

Hutch had assumed that Ivory was living in this space now; but when
he entered the one spare room, he saw it was crammed with cardboard
boxes, crates and two steamer trunks (one of them was the trunk Hutch
had carried to Oxford near forty years ago).

Straw was seated by the river window on a solid box, and his face
was bleak. In recent years he'd wept too often, always when sober; but
he'd shed all the tears he had for this place and the sights it had seen—
his eyes were dry. In silence he reached into a shoe box beside him,
gathered a thick handful of letters and held them toward Hutch.

Hutch said "No, they're Wade's."

Straw said "There you're wrong. They're yours and Ann's—every one of them are recent letters from you two, addressed to Wade and all of them sealed, the way you sent them."

"Strawson, Wade's blind. We didn't know that."

Straw whispered hard. "That woman can read." He pointed through the wall to Ivory.

Hutch worked a slow path in through the crates and stood by Straw, looking down toward the river. A barge so rusty it seemed in the act of quick dissolution, an orange sugar cube; a big white dog like the hero of some Jack London story overseeing the battered stream, a woman with honey-colored hair who took what were almost surely two lobsters—giant live lobsters—from a pail and pitched them far out over the river. They sank like plummets, and Hutch asked Straw "Would you rather be boiled to death in a pot and eaten by humans or thrown back live to the mercy of a river of human shit?"

Straw had seen the woman. "I vote for the river. I've eaten my share of mammal manure; it hasn't stopped me yet."

Hutch said "You vote for leaving today?"

"What about Wade's doctor? We should notify whoever's been seeing him anyhow and ask for his charts to be mailed home. You settled the business with that smart woman?"

"She does seem fine—no, we didn't get into details yet. She's feeding Wade."

"Has she got a job, other than here? A few sticks of furniture can't have brought them much capital. Maybe she's well-fixed on her own."

Hutch said "She and Wyatt were from the South Bronx. Or so he told me one hateful night, and she just confirmed it."

"Then you want my suggestion? I think I should go out and get us some breakfast—a big hot feed for you, me and her. You make your final arrangements with Ivory, she tells us what we need to take, we make Wade a decent pallet in the car and head for home."

Hutch was still facing the river and the white dog. More than ever, its size and patent vigor seemed the answer to a lonely boy's prayer—a perfectly faithful creature who'd understand every thought you had. At last Hutch laid a hand at the back of Straw's broad neck. "Whose home, old friend?"

Straw reached back and briefly covered the hand. "Well, he grew up where you live; you're rattling around there in too much room. Ann's place is likely temporary. Emily and I will take him in a heartbeat—we've got plenty of room, never sleep. But you make the choice, or ask Wade to choose."

Hutch stayed quiet till he heard Ivory walk toward the kitchen again. Then he quietly said "My place, no question."

"You know I'll come there and stay to the end—just say the word."

"The end could be a long way off."

Straw said "You saw him. He's looking at the grave at fairly close range."

Hutch felt a strong need to say Straw was wrong, but quietly again he said "People do that sometimes for years."

Straw laughed. "Yes, Doctor, the human race for a start—"

The laugh had been short; but Wade heard it somehow and called out "Godfather, come laugh in here." Weak as his voice was, its youth carried well.

Straw went at once.

Hutch followed him as far as the kitchen.

Ivory was rinsing the milk pan and bowl. "I've got to get on to work, I'm afraid."

"Excuse me but are you living here?"

At first she looked offended; then she understood. "Oh no, I was in this building long before Wade and Wyatt. With my ex-husband, two floors down."

Hutch heard the contradiction of what she'd said a short while back—that she hadn't lived here through most of Wade's tenure. But at the same moment, he first saw the wedding band on her left hand—a ring at least, plain platinum—and decided not to question her story. "Where do you work?"

"Far downtown, an art gallery in Soho."

"I'd be glad to drive you."

She smiled, a glimpse of a whole other person—one not seen in these walls for months or years. "No you wouldn't" she said. "You get in morning traffic with me, and you'll never want to see Ivory again. I take the subway five days a week."

Hutch said "You know I want to take him home."

Ivory said "I've prayed you would. You know he couldn't ask."

Hutch believed her but he had to ask this last soul alive a question that only she might answer. "Why has he been so set against me?"

"My guess is, mainly pure loyalty to Wyatt."

Hutch shut his eyes and agreed.

With no sign of vengeance, still she pressed ahead. "You know Wyatt hated you and all you stand for—all he could see; Wyatt *trusted* his eyes." She was suddenly splendid as any oak tree lit by lightning.

Hutch managed half a smile. "I'm glad Wyatt knew so well what I stand for. I've yet to solve that mystery in more than six decades; and I've really tried—Wyatt may have spent, oh, twenty conscious hours in my presence."

Ivory was free to laugh in relief. She'd launched her attack on behalf of her brother; now she was free of that final duty (not that she'd ever thought Wyatt was all wrong).

But Hutch was not finished. "Was it just the fact that I'm white and Southern?"

"That was part; Wyatt was *radical* back in college. So was I but I got my edge dulled as time passed, and Wyatt never did."

Hutch said "Oh he was keen with me."

"Maybe you earned that?" Though Ivory's voice had made it a question, her eyes confirmed that she fully believed the answer was Yes.

Hutch waited "Did he think I condemned the way they lived?"

"He knew you did; you told him so."

Hutch said "Wyatt may have thought I did. We had a bad meeting, the last time I saw him—all three of us badly lost our heads on the subject of race and sex and all else. But no—God, no—with the life I've led, I've got very slim rights of condemnation over the worst soul alive on Earth."

"But you never contacted them again?"

"I didn't, no—not the two together. I was standing on form, I was Wade's only father, he was past twenty-one and he knew my address. Even so, I wrote him a good many letters that he never opened."

Ivory took awhile to grant Hutch's premise. "They were much too close—I could see that myself. They were all but Siamese twins, most days. They doomed each other, is what it came to."

To Hutch there seemed only one question left. "How did Wyatt's hatred for so many white people part and make way for Wade?"

Ivory said "My brother would pick at that subject, fairly often—right here in Wade's presence. Wade always laughed and said he was the master Wyatt wanted, deep down. Wyatt would blare his hot satanic eyes and say 'Dream on, sweet honky—little white sugar-tit. I'll get you yet.' " She held in place and watched the words pierce Hutch: and for the only time today, her eyes nearly filled.

So Hutch only waited till she'd got her grip again. "We're hoping to take Wade home today. Any reason why not? Anything or anybody we need to consult, any bills to pay?"

Ivory said "His volunteer comes at ten to bathe him. All his medicine's in the bathroom cabinet; he usually understands what he takes and why. If not, the bottles are clearly labeled." She pointed again to the composition book. "I've kept a record of all he's been through—the names of the illnesses, the doctors and dates. You'll need that with you. There's a big box of Wade's papers in the spare bedroom; better take that too."

Hutch said "You think he can stand the drive—eight or nine hours?"

"Mr. Mayfield, Wade's so up and down, I really can't tell you. Some days he has the strength to dress himself and walk with me around the block, very slowly. We got as far as the river last week, then sat down awhile and came back with even a little strength to spare. Other times he's too weak to raise his head, and I have to diaper him three times a night. His eyes are either three-fourths blind or fairly sharp, depending on circumstances I've never fathomed; and as you know from your call last night, his mind's not reliable. Some days he talks like a lucid gentleman. Other days, and a lot of nights, he's flinging way out on spider thread. No harm in him, though. Never says a mean word, not to me at least. Begs my pardon all day—"

"That's a Mayfield trait."

"He's told me as much; he's a kind-natured man. I can tell you I'll miss him—" No tears fell but Ivory's dark eyes widened further, and she bit at her lip.

Hutch said "Please don't take this the least bit wrong, but we must owe you substantial money."

"Thank you, I never doubted you'd be fair. May I write you about that later on?"

"Any day you're ready."

Ivory said "It won't be anything steep—less than three hundred dollars, little odds and ends."

"Is there anything left here that you want or can use?"

Her attention was already moving toward her job; in another few minutes she'd be seriously late. "May I also think that over awhile?"

"By all means, please. I'll just pay the rent till I can come back up and clean things out—if that's ever appropriate." Hutch could hear his refusal to face death's nearness.

Ivory looked round the bare room again. "I've kept it as neat as I knew how." No ship's galley was ever cleaner.

Hutch said "You've done a magnificent job—I wasn't complaining. If I start in to thank you finally today, I'll just go to pieces."

She was in the same fix. "Let's both of us wait till we're ready. There's the phone and the mail; we'll communicate." She'd taken her black coat off a wall hook.

Hutch helped her put it on, concealing the bright dress. "Then Strawson and I will likely clear out here before you're back. I guess we'll wait till the volunteer comes—will she know details like the doctor's number?"

"It's a he, Mr. Mayfield. Yes, he knows more than me—details anyhow. *He's* the saint you mentioned."

"What's his name?"

"Jimmy Boat—we call him Boatie. He'll be all the help you need." She was leaving; she put out a long hand in parting.

Hutch took it for maybe a moment too long. "Wade may have told you that I've spent my life writing, when I wasn't teaching college. I've seldom felt at a real loss for words—" He bowed and pressed his forehead to her hand.

Ivory held in place, uncertain of how to use the old gesture or whether to refuse it. When she knew, she said "I've read every word you've published, I think. I've had hard times of my own to weave through; you've been some help. I promise a letter in the next few weeks." She moved toward the hall door.

"Did you tell him goodbye?" The moment it left Hutch, he was sorry he'd said it.

Ivory held in place at the door a long moment, her strong shoulders squared. But her face, when she turned, was the ground plan of pain. Her mouth moved to speak but nothing came, so she shook her head No and went her way.

In his mind, Hutch barely heard his own last thought as she vanished through the door. *Wade was loved, all ways.*

10

THEY'D eaten the breakfast Straw brought in from two blocks east; and they had Wade propped up, in his robe, in the rocker when the volunteer let himself in with a key at ten o'clock. He came in, back first, carrying a satchel; so at first he didn't see the company; and when he faced the room, he yelled out "God on high!" He was tar black, maybe five foot six, built like a reinforced concrete emplacement in a World War II antitank defense; and his reddish hair was high in an old-fashioned Afro arrangement above a round face, no neck at all and a silver-gray and spotless jumpsuit.

Hutch and Straw got to their feet; but before they could speak, Wade said "Boatie Boat, this is my father Hutch and my godfather Straw."

Boat said "I thought both of you were *dead*." But he set down the satchel and strode on toward them for crushing handshakes. Then he stood back and studied Wade in his chair. "*You're* resurrected, child! I told you you'd live." To Hutch, Boat said "Wade called me last night, told me you were on the road; and he made me promise not to let you see his frozen corpse." He touched Wade's wrist. "You're still beating anyhow. No icicles yet."

Wade said "Boatie, these men are kidnaping me south. Next time you see me, I'll be warm as toast."

Boat said "South got too hot for me." He put out a flat hand and felt Wade's forehead. Then with both hands he lightly probed Wade's throat; the lymph nodes there were hard as kernels. "No fever in you today at all. Sugar, you're cooling down."

Straw asked Boatie "Where you from in the South?"

"Take a flying guess."

"Society Hill, South Carolina."

Boat laughed. "Way off."

Hutch said "Social Circle, Georgia?"

"Getting closer but *wrong*."

Straw said "Where exactly?" He was only indulging the common need of country dwellers to place everybody they meet on a map of the actual ground.

But Boat slid into minstrel-darky tones. "You honkies still hunting us runaways *down*—lay back, white man; we *free* at last!"

Straw grinned and raised both hands in surrender. He'd been involved in no such complex racial theatrics since Martin Luther King opened so many eyes.

Despite his kidding-on-the-level, though, Boat showed no malice. For blind Wade's sake, he was eager to jive. "I'm from Little Richard's hometown—who know where that is?"

Hutch said "Macon, Georgia—the cradle of rock and roll, birthplace of Little Richard, all-time king!"

Boat folded both hands. "Amen, pink Jesus."

Wade crossed himself. "Mother Mary, Amen."

By then Boat was combing Wade's hair with his fingers and neatening his robe.

Wade accepted the service as a small welcome pleasure. He shut his eyes and, for a long instant, assumed unconsciously the look of a boy-pharaoh on his gilded barge, borne toward death and endless judgment, very nearly smiling.

Boat looked to Hutch. "You taking this lovely friend out of here?" In the course of eight words, his voice had changed again—realistic now and sober.

Wade's eyes were still shut; he still looked serene but a wiry snake's voice came from his lips. "Don't let this bastard here lay a hand on me."

Boat laughed. "Which one?—there's three bastards here."

Wade's eyes found Hutch. "This main man, grinning like nobody's gone."

Hutch thought *That's me—he's struck the truth finally: Wyatt Bondurant's truth.*

Boat only continued stroking Wade's hair.

In ten more seconds Wade spoke again, the same cold voice. "We'll *cut* if we have to."

Boat brought two knuckles around and rapped lightly on the crest of Wade's forehead. Then Boat looked to Hutch and Straw; he shook his head sadly and mouthed four clear words—*Out of his mind.* But what he said was "Wish *I* was traveling toward green trees and water."

And Wade's head moved to sign *Come on*, though he said no more.

So Hutch turned to Boat. "Please come on with us." It was not an idle offer. He'd sensed at once that Boatie would be the perfect help.

And Wade moaned confirmation of the offer.

Boat couldn't bear to turn Wade down, and he said it to Hutch. "Don't *both* of you break my heart. This friend Wade here means as much to me as the rest of the friends and miserable boys I've helped up and down this town for a long mean time. Wade's got his own people though—you fine gents and his mother's live, right? A lot of my boys don't have blood relations, and a lot that have got whole *housefuls* of kin get turned down by them as hateful as rats—but I see you're strong enough to take what's happening."

Hutch said "I guess we'll know soon enough."

Wade turned to his father. "I doubt I'll be all that much trouble."

It nearly downed Hutch; he literally swayed as in a wind.

But Boat leaned to Wade's ear with a secret, though he said it plainly. "You going to live till the man says 'Quit.' That may not be for long years to come if you got loving care around you, steady like you need. You been here alone; that'll kill a big horse."

Wade's eyes were still shut; and his voice was thin again but cheerful. "I may not make it to Maryland."

The three strong men considered that.

Then Straw said "No, Wade, your godfather's driving every mile. You'll make it. I promise. I never failed yet."

Wade said "You never saw me this far gone either."

Straw had to say "Right."

"Then promise me we'll make it again." Wade was in earnest.

Straw said "Wade Mayfield, you're golden with me."

Wade said "Is that safe? What does *golden* mean?"

Straw said again "*Golden.* You wait and see." He had no clear idea what he meant, but in his mouth it felt like the nearest thing to usable truth.

11

BY noon Boat had bathed Wade, diapered him and dressed him in what seemed like too many clothes for a mild spring day. Then he laid Wade back on the bed to rest while he packed everything they'd need or could use in the way of clothes and medical equipment. He'd helped Hutch reach Wade's doctor by phone to learn any vital details and procedures— the main advice was simply to continue all medicines till Wade was back in the hands of another AIDS specialist; and when Hutch thanked the brusque man and said goodbye, the doctor suddenly lowered his voice and said "You must have had a fine son." Then he was gone.

So while Hutch and Straw made several trips down to load the car, Boat sat on the floor by Wade's bed, near his wavering eyes, and worked in silence—as he'd worked so often, near so many young men—to call death closer.

Though he'd been raised in Georgia by his mother's mother in an African Methodist Episcopal church and had sung in the choir till the day he boarded the train north to Harlem, these hard recent years Boat had been forced to go his lone spiritual way. Now in the room where Wade Mayfield and Wyatt Bondurant had known good hours for actual years, a room that Wade was leaving soon and surely forever, Boat called up the face he always pictured for death itself—a thin dark woman, very much like his mother who'd vanished long since on a bus toward Chicago—and he said a silent respectful prayer as that tall woman answered his call and stood in his mind at the foot of Wade's bed here, eight feet from Boat. *Keep this child from messing his pants on the road. Let him get back far as his home and his mother, and let him see her face someway. Put him on whatever bed he slept in when he was a child and let him breathe easy till you're ready for him. Then come on into his clean safe room and lead him while he's picturing Wyatt in the days when they didn't know they'd killed each other like this and deserted a child.*

WHEN the packed car was ready and they'd got Wade up onto his feet, Boat stood on Wade's left with the boy's arm around him. Then he told Straw to stand on the right. Once they got their balance and Hutch was standing with two hands free, Boat said to Wade "You got everything?"

Wade signified Yes.

"You sure you got all your papers and things—your picture albums?"

Wade said "Oh yes, I'm well stocked with pictures. I plan to meet Jesus in northern Virginia and get my eyes healed."

Boat said "You hold your tongue about Jesus. Be sweet to him, baby. He got us in this fix we're in."

Wade said "I don't believe that a minute and neither do you."

Boat said "All right. I was racing my lip." Then he was satisfied they could head down. He asked Hutch please to bring the satchel of soap and lotion and natural sponges he'd use on the five men he still had to see today; then he said "Let's boogie on down the road."

They'd gone three steps when Wade said "No—"

Each of the able-bodied men had privately thought that Wade might balk at the fence. Now they faced one another in blank disappointment.

Wade tried to think—not a good day for thinking. So he said again "No."

Hutch thought *Wyatt's got him and is hauling him back.* It seemed more credible than what his eyes saw—a splendid man, crushed and all but gone.

But finally Wade could recall what he wanted. "Hutch, please step in the bedroom and bring that frame that's over the bed."

Hutch couldn't recall a picture there, but he quickly obeyed and took the silver frame off the dark wall. Only in the window light of the main room could he catch a glimpse of what he held—a landscape he himself had drawn near his mother's home in Goshen, Virginia when he was a boy and visiting there with Alice Matthews, his dead mother's friend: in the summer of 1944. Now was no time to think of meanings or omens in the clean-lined picture of a spine of mountains cloaked in dense evergreens. *Why this of all things?* Not thinking of blindness, Hutch showed it to Wade. "This what you want?"

Wade's right hand came out and sized up the frame. Then he nodded Yes hard and took the next step to pass through the door into the dimlit hall. In those last inches Wade told himself *This vanishes now. Never again.* It felt worse than all his life till here, worse than the prospect of oncoming death.

Nobody spoke as Hutch double-locked the door, called the elevator, and they all rode down in its weird light to cross the lobby into strong April sun—the morning of Passover, though they didn't know it, the night when God killed the firstborn son in every Egyptian overlord's house not marked with the blood of a slaughtered lamb.

In the light Wade looked even more devastated, gaunt as a flail. Not having seen himself for weeks, still he understood that and rigged a taut smile on his face, a try at pleasantness that looked like famine. So if you'd watched him every inch of the way toward the loaded car, you'd have seen no outward sign of the pain that went on tearing him like a tattered doll—leaving the site of most of the good he'd tasted in his past grown life or would ever taste: the walls that held the memory of Wyatt Bondurant's beauty, his sudden ambushes of a stunning kindness, through long nights of juncture and mutual joy.

Hutch silently tried to tell himself that the source of all the strange elation he'd felt these past two days was finally shown to him as he led his son, his only child, toward the only home they'd had or would ever have.

As Hutch and Straw worked to lay Wade out on the pallet they'd made on the long backseat, the passersby barely slowed their headlong pace through the day, though some of them veered a little aside from a face and body as near gone as whoever this ghost was.

At the final moment of stillness at the curb—Straw had cranked the car and was turning the wheel to enter traffic—Wade somehow managed to raise himself and look to the street. No one heard him, even his father, but he said "Adiós." Then he sank again and, before they were back across the great bridge, he'd drowned in the misty fatigue that lapped him constantly—the main mercy now.

T W O

HOME

APRIL–JULY 1993

April 23, 1993

Dear Strawson,

    This will be just a quick line from campus to keep you posted. I'd have phoned before now, but with Wade in the house—even when he's asleep—I somehow can't discuss him with anyone. He's so wholly dependent that I won't risk beginning to think that he's, above all, somebody to manage—even if I say it to my oldest closest friend, which (despite your doubts) God knows you are.

    I've told you that your presence on the trip north and through those first days with Wade at home was much more than a practical help, but the truth bears repeating. More even than I could, or Ann in her visits, you let Wade know that he's still very much alive and a pleasure to know. Your ease and good humor and steady attention set the pitch for us all; and I won't forget, if and when the time comes, that you've promised to come back and stay when we need you and until we're done. Meanwhile, by the way, the hospital bed you ordered is here and makes a real difference. Wade raises and lowers himself with ease and sleeps through the night almost upright—it helps keep his lungs clear and maybe his mind, which is much less likely to streak off into meanness or nonsense or self-punishment than it was at first.

    Also in the past three weeks, he's recovered more strength than I expected. I'm trying to tell myself it's the outcome of being at home with reliable care, regular company and sensible food, though he still barely eats any more than the liquid protein you found and sometimes a small dish of frozen yogurt. That seems to stay with him when nothing else will. Even so, he can't stand any flavor stronger than vanilla—it's odors apparently that trigger his nausea.

In any case I'm also trying to remind myself that whatever strength Wade regains is bound to be brief. The graduate student that I found to sit with him, when I teach or run chores, is also a big help. His name is Hart Salter. He's a good-looking, huge—not fat but muscular—twenty-six-year-old medievalist; and he knows more dirty jokes than Chaucer. He already seems to have known Wade forever, and they actually manage to laugh a good deal. Hart's marriage has apparently been rocky lately, so I think he actually gets a real benefit from cheering a fellow creature up— Wade that is; the wife seems to be one of those black holes for love, incapable of the simplest trust. If only Hart weren't due to leave us soon—he's finished all his course work and prelims and will need to travel to London this summer to start his research, but for two more weeks he'll still be available. Once he's gone, I'll be in the lurch if I can't find an honest substitute soon. That's when I may need to call you back.

Which reminds me that I've told a few of my colleagues the truth and have got only genuine concern from them and offers of help. Not that I expected otherwise. Life in an English Department can often feel like a bad day at the beehive; but the few times I've ever let it be known that I needed help of the human variety from my colleagues, they've laid it out with generous tolerance, unstintingly.

The woman doctor you said you trusted when we took Wade to Duke— Dr. Margaret Ives—she's become his main doctor and has even been out to the house for a visit. Entirely out of the blue last evening, she phoned from the hospital and asked if we'd give her that drink we'd offered. I put it to Wade, who was napping on the sofa while I watched TV (the Court channel, to which I'm addicted). Wade said "Bring her on"; so out she came and stayed past nine—Wade awake the whole time, participating more than he has till now in the talk and laughter.

Just being with people and practicing words has likewise helped to clear his mind, though his vision has definitely not improved except for brief spells when he'll suddenly be facing the window and say "There's an eagle surely" (he was right, a male golden eagle; the first I've seen in all my years out here and, according to my bird book, way off course). Or *he'll suddenly ask "Where's Mother's portrait?" (I'd stashed the picture he drew of his mother in grade school; it had hung in the kitchen till Ann went her way). Ten seconds later he won't be able to find me in the room.*

Anyhow Dr. Ives's visit was the first house call I've heard of from a doctor since steam was invented; and though we all pretended it was social, I knew that she was watching Wade closely and with more sympathy than may turn out to be good for her peace of mind and soul. It turned out she's an avid reader of poetry and has known my work since high school in Utah. We didn't talk too much about that; I didn't want Wade to feel he was her alibi for knowing me—I don't think I was that, by the way. I long since gave up feeling like anyone a sane modern reader could want to meet.

As for Wade's health, she's sticking to what she told us that day you were with us in the Infectious Diseases clinic—the same medications he was taking in New York, as much exercise outdoors as he can take, and as many meetings with people he likes as we can arrange and he has strength for. She puts special emphasis on the inhalations to prevent further bouts of parasitic pneumonia, so we're loyal with those.

Last night, when she was close to leaving, Dr. Ives turned to Wade in my presence and said "If you want us to, we can try to treat this blindness. We might even stop it before it goes further." She understands that he still has a certain amount of sight which goes and comes unpredictably, and she went on to say she could give him a fairly high-powered drug that would likely clear out the parasites and keep his eyes from failing any worse. The drug however is given through a permanent tube implanted in a hole in the chest.

I was ready to take her offer on the spot, but I left it to Wade; and once he'd thought for twenty seconds, he said "Thanks, I've known about that for some time. I decided against it."

She seemed a little rebuffed but hardly showed it. When she left she did say again that she'd be at Wade's disposal for whatever she could do; and he said again "Thanks, I'll try not to crowd you." When she still looked puzzled, he said "I'm letting it come on now." Neither she nor I had to ask what he meant. And then Wade confirmed it. He said "All I want is enough morphine when the howling starts." She said "We keep it on hand, all hours. You let me know when you feel the need."

He gave a short wail on the spot, then laughed and said "Not yet." And she left us smiling. Remind me to ask for all-female doctors when my time comes, if I don't pitch over cold-dead in class or at my home desk like a lucky man.

Ann has stopped by at least once a day; she phones Wade frequently, which he seems not to mind. I pretty much leave them alone when she's here; but when Ann and I wind up in a room, we give our best imitations of civility. I'll have to say I've genuinely enjoyed the food she cooks and brings every few days and the laundry she does almost every day for Wade. The other night, when Wade had us both in his room, he cranked up the head of his bed and said "Am I right in thinking that you two will stay here under this roof when I'm bad off and see me out?" Ann and I said Yes and faced each other. I could see she meant it. I'm not sure I did; but time will tell, I guess.

I've got to run. Today's the final day of classes before exams, and I'm risking a good deal by going through with my long tradition of having the writing class out to the house for a final discussion and a rough-and-ready supper. Last week I told the students that my son was now with me and was seriously ill—no more details. Wade knows they're coming and that he can either ignore them completely and rest in his room or be entirely welcome if he feels up to joining the students at any point. Two of them really mean to be writers and may not be deluded in their hopes. If they see Wade at all, I can hope they'll see him and his situation as life anyhow, the Great Subject.

I don't doubt Wade can handle what comes. Christ knows he's handling himself and me with a grace and strength I've never had to summon. He feels like the purpose of my life till now, even though he's ending in this blocked alley. I mean that very seriously. Slim or nil though his chances are, I feel fairly sure that whatever Wade and I have throughout these weeks will outlast us both. It'll be our good-will effort to get something right in a family that's never engineered a right thing yet—an open-eyed, willingly paired walk on to the grave in dignity if nothing better. So I'm working to give Wade all I've got while he can still use it—and the all includes whatever I've held back from him in the past. If he wants it, that is. I'm sure you won't grudge him your role in the story, if he probes that far. We almost certainly owe it to him.

None of which means that every hour of this doesn't blast on through my head like a cold jackhammer that's somehow silenced but pounds on still. The sight of this boy alone in deep water, far past my reach or anyone's apparently—well, you've seen him and know the worst.

I'll phone you this weekend. Wade will likely call you too—he says that's his plan. But I wanted you to have this much in writing first. Drive down to see us as soon as you've got the planting in hand—let me know if the business account is too low. I trust Grainger's upright and running the world still. Wade mentioned yesterday that he meant to see Grainger soon somehow. I can't be sure such a plan is realistic, and I certainly can't ask you to bring Grainger down here—even if his body could stand the trip, he very well might not recognize Wade when he got here, changed as Wade is. But we'll talk it over soon, you and I. Love to Emily and thanks for her care, love to yourself and unpayable thanks.

> Ever,
> Hutch

That same night, after Hutch was asleep, Wade managed to reach the operator and ask her to place a call to Grainger. On the third ring, the old man answered. *"All right."*

"Mr. Grainger?"

"Him."

"This is Wade, your old friend."

"Younger than me. Everything else alive is younger than me."

"Well, except for a few trees, I guess you're nearly right."

"You said you were Wade? Don't sound much like him."

"It's me—guaranteed. I'm just getting younger."

"Your eyes improving?"

"I think maybe Yes. Some days anyhow, minutes at a time, I can see moving things."

"It's the still ones that kill you."

"Don't make me laugh please. I'm sore all over."

"Somebody beating on you?—I still got my gun; just say the word."

"The word? The word. Grainger, I can't think of but one word most days."

"Your mind failing on you?"

"No, never been clearer. But all I think about is one word, Wyatt. Wyatt Bondurant—remember him?"

"Can't say I do, thank Jesus Above."

"He was hard on you, I well recall—hard on most everybody but me."

"Ain't he killing you now? Ain't that fairly hard?"

"He thought so at least—Wyatt thought so. It killed him to know it. But no, I blame nobody, live or dead. I walked, eyes open, into one big set of blades, grinding live meat. Still I liked my time on Earth, short as it's been."

"You lucky as a racehorse."

"Want to tell me how?"

"You leaving on out while you're still yourself."

"You're who you've been since the day I was born—that long anyhow."

"No, child, Grainger Walters turned into this warm corpse, oh, fifty years ago—when did Gracie Walters die?"

"I never knew Gracie, I'm sad to say. Recall she was gone well before I came."

"You missed a good sight."

"I'll miss a lot more."

"Child, you've seen every bit of the story. Nothing much to it that you hadn't seen once you tried your body on one other soul."

Wade took a long wait. "I thank you for that."

"And it's true as a knife—" Grainger hung up then, high in midair.

                                                            April 24, 1993

Dear Emily,

I was so grateful for your kindness and sympathy in phoning last evening; be assured I won't speak of it to anyone. The whole situation here is harder than anything I've been in, except for the long months of silence from Wade when he was in New York, refusing most calls and accepting nothing by way of help. Those months were the nearest I've ever come to losing all grip. Now that Hutch and Strawson have brought him back south, what the new problem comes down to is terribly simple.

Hutch wants as little of me as ever. He lets me stop by with food and clean clothes for Wade and, those times, he mostly manages to be polite. But I know he'd rather I vanished today and left no traces, surely no claim on Wade.

Even more painful, as I tried to tell you before I broke down, I can't be certain Wade wants my visits either. Oh he thanks me for favors and answers small questions; but more than not, he's silent and pulled back— dozing or pretending to, though I well know he's tired from the moment of sunrise onward.

All I'm trying to do is keep my loving presence in his mind. I tell myself that's my minimum duty, however much less it amounts to than I hope for. I try to believe that, somewhere in his mind, there's a memory of having a mother that cherished him above all others and, that if I keep up a gentle persistence beside him, he'll connect who I am with the memory of me in his earlier days. I'm the same girl anyhow. Do you feel that as strongly as I do—that you don't get any older inside but are always who you've been since birth? I generally feel like me at the age of about eleven, smarter some ways but the same general girl; and it's only when I wander past mirrors and see the changes that I shiver and think "Who's that old stranger in here with me?"

I've got to get back to work right now, but let me just ask one thing in closing. I think you know that, all these years, I've never asked you to press Straw for help with me and Hutchins. And I wouldn't today, if time weren't almost certainly short. But if you can find a natural way to say to Strawson that Ann is Wade's mother—and never was less, in spite of his refusals—then maybe Straw could find it in his heart to see Hutch and ask him to find a way to give me natural rights in this sadness. If you think it's too awkward, then thanks all the same. I wouldn't want to tread into tender ground.

Any chance you could ride down here one day soon and eat lunch with me? I hate myself for still needing food; but I do eat lunch, though very seldom dinner.

Keep us three in your prayers.

                                        And love from,
                                        Ann

April 25, 1993

Dear Ann,

Your letter is just here. Since I'm heading into town for groceries in a minute, I'll jot a quick word and mail it myself, to prevent suspicion.

Rest your mind on one subject at least. Strawson has said to me at least once daily that Hutchins is walling you out of this and that that's less than fair. I've told Strawson that fair is not the word, and he agrees to that too. But you know how much he reveres Hutchins Mayfield and all H's plans, so I cannot hold out a great deal of hope that Strawson knows any way to help right now.

If he forgets that he saw your writing on the envelope an hour ago when he brought in the mail, then tonight I'll slip in a word along the lines you suggested. The sooner the better but I can't let S think you have coached me in this—you understand.

What I don't understand is, where are you finding the strength to watch the sights you are watching? You asked for my prayers and, Ann, they are yours. The last thing Strawson would admit to me is that he prays too, but I know he does, and you are high on his list. He has always said you were "Very top-grade," which is far as he goes in human praise!

I will phone again soon. Till when,

The best love,
Emily

April 29, 1993

My dear Ivory,

I am dictating this to a man who is helping me come to life the best I can hope to. His name is Hart and he has plenty of it—heart, I mean. He is working on his doctor's degree in English literature and has studied with Hutch, so this will all be spelled correctly and in proper grammar. Not that it needs to be all that proper to say what I mean. Not that you don't know all I mean already. Or so I trust, God knows, God knows. I asked Hart to write those words down twice.

What I mean is, you have been better to me for nine years now than anyone else ever was in all my time. Everything I ever did to hurt you is clear in my addled brain this instant as any needle stuck in an eye. You

*said more than once that you pardoned me, and I more than half believe
you have. But since I've been down here, I wake up in the night—most
every night—and see your face that awful day I turned on you, when you
were needing help I didn't know how to give. Or so I thought. I was full
grown though, as you pointed out and had nobody but me to blame for
the preservation of terminal adolescence.*

*Don't feel like you need to call me up and say any words. Don't think
I'm asking for written forgiveness. But sometime soon, when you find
yourself in a quiet place and the light feels right, see if you can manage
to say inside your head "I wish a peaceful rest for Wade Mayfield, I and
my kin, through all time to come." Just those few words, between you and
the air, will very likely reach me and help me on, wherever I'm headed,
however soon or late.*

*Again, dear friend, you are matchless in the world. Long love to
yourself and all you care for*

> *From your hopeful*
> *Wade*

2

WHEN Hart had finished transcribing the letter and addressing the envelope, he brought it to Wade who signed it the best he could, folded it
carefully, then gave it back to Hart and said "You lick the envelope
please."

Hart laughed. "Lazy dude, your tongue still works."

Wade said "Too true. No, my spit's infected—I already warned you.
I try not to export the virus to friends."

Hart said "Eureka!"

Wade pointed a finger in Hart's direction. "Everything you write for
me's a deep secret—swear to that please?"

"Absolutely," Hart said. "I'm the dark grave of secrets."

Wade said "I'm glad I've met him at last."

Only then did Hart hear the tactlessness of his metaphor. He laughed.
"I'm sorry to bring up the grave!"

"That goes without saying" and Wade laughed too.

They were in Wade's room in strong morning light, Wade was dressed in a sweat suit and lying on his bed, Hart was at the small desk Wade had used in childhood. When the letter was sealed and stamped, Hart said "I'll walk this down to the road and leave it for the postman." He stood to go.

Wade agreed, then quickly said "No, wait." His hand came up on the air like a painter's, and he drew a complicated line that copied the outer boundaries of Hart—his head and trunk at least. When it was finished, Wade lapsed into silence.

Finally Hart said "Wait for what?"

Wade said "Just stand still another ten seconds—I can suddenly see you." In fact he could. Wade's eyes had slowly clarified as they wrote the letter; and now Hart Salter was here before him, the first entirely visible creature that Wade had seen in three or four months. Only at the outer limits of Hart, a kind of flickering silver aura that clung to his outline with small explosions, was there anything less than honest facts. Maybe six foot five, with a full head of thick chestnut hair and a long ingratiating face with a Jesus beard—all so real and pleasing to the eyes and mind that it sent a terrible bolt through Wade, like a single blow from a battering ram. *I'm leaving this. I'm worse than dead.* He even shut his eyes and spoke the knowledge aloud, in a whisper. "Let me be really blind."

Except for occasional shaves and trims, Hart had never spent more than an hour, all told, in front of a mirror, regarding himself. Like most well-put-together creatures, he'd been told often he was no eyesore. In fact everybody important in his path, except for his wife, had sooner or later praised his looks. But the news had weighed very lightly on him; he'd all but never relied on his looks in any exchange. So now he was mildly puzzled by Wade's wish. "I'll stay, sure, if you're hurting any."

Wade said "I am. But you can't help."

"No, try me. Say the word." Since Hart got here at nine o'clock, he'd already helped Wade bathe and dress.

Wade's eyes opened and saw Hart again almost as clearly, blurring slightly at the edges like a spirit materializing before you or slowly leaving. After a long time Wade grinned and took his biggest gamble in maybe three years. "Would you just strip and stand right there—oh, for one whole minute?"

It took Hart less than five seconds to find sufficient permission. *I'll be four thousand miles from here in another few days. Before I'm back, this boy will be dead* (he'd always thought of Wade as a boy since the first day he saw him). So Hart smiled slightly and said "You bet." Then he laid the sealed letter on the desk, briskly slid off his frayed jeans, T-shirt and underpants and stood in place where the sun was brightest. In general, he was always at home in his body—no excess modesty, just a real ease in the amplitude of the irreducible skin and bones in which he'd met the world from the start.

There were no more than ten feet between him and Wade; and after a moment when Hart felt a little more like a target than he'd planned to feel, he shifted his weight to his broad right foot and hung his right hand like a hinge at the crest of his massive left shoulder. Unthinking, he'd assumed the stance of a thousand athletes—dead for two thousand years— in shattered Greek and Roman marble, unthinkably generous in offering the world their private portion of eternal perfection.

Wade took in the sight in full awareness of both its blessing and what he guessed was its bitter finality. The splendor of the pale taut skin of the chest and belly, the smiling wings of muscle suspended from the corners of the groin, the full heavy sex—strong as they all were, they looked alarmingly fragile to Wade: one more thing he'd failed to protect and now must abandon. One more last thing. Even as he thought it, Wade's eyes were clouding. Hart's arms were already swimming in a vague light. *Ask to touch him once quick, only one touch.*

At the same instant Hart thought *Take the four steps forward; put his hand on your chest.* For the first time, Hart saw the face of Stacy his wife, who was four miles from here at her greenhouse job, still hungry for far more than Hart had to give—he or any man he'd yet known. *Well, she'll never know anything that passes here. This is between just Wade, me and death.* Hart took two steps.

Wade's hand came up, palm out toward the shield of his new friend's chest. *New friend and last.* Then the hand drew back of its own accord; and Wade told Hart "There. Many thanks but no, just there forever."

Nothing had ever looked finer than this—worth a whole life's service—
and Wade well knew that he'd watched the world more closely in his
three decades than anyone he'd known, maybe barring Hutch. Nothing
had ever looked farther away than this present goodness. Nothing—that
Wade could recall at least—had ever brought his mind more joy or the
weight of more desperate loss than this sight here, this kind young man.
Wade's hands went flat on the sheet beside him; and he lay on watching,
still saying "Just there."

So Hart stayed there, entirely at ease in the unblocked light of a day
in progress far beyond them on the actual Earth, till Wade's eyes shut
and he fell back to sleep—gone quicker than any feverish child.

3

THERE were fourteen members of Hutch's class in Writing Narrative
Poetry—eight men, six women. The oldest were two postgraduate rene-
gades, moonlighting from the Law and Divinity Schools. The youngest
was twenty-one, named Maitland Moses, a senior burdened with talent
and a mind as attentive as a small threatened creature, though he seemed
fearless and undownably cheerful. By four that afternoon they'd all assem-
bled at Hutch's place in Orange County, four miles from campus in the
evergreen fringes of Duke Forest. The forest itself was eight thousand
acres of pines and cedars, streams, lost ponds and the odd deserted farm-
house biding its time with plentiful deer, foxes, crows, hawks, wild turkeys
and herons, the raccoon and snake and indomitable beaver, even the
occasional Madagascan lemur escaped from the high-fenced Primate Center just up the road. And Hutch's twelve acres abutted the woods on three
sides.

The late afternoon air buoyed itself on a unique slanting amber light
native to Hutch's corner of the county, a ridge that his oldest neighbor
called Couch Mountain, the highest point for many miles around. Hutch
and Ann had built the house in the 1960s on an outcrop of rock at the
ridge of Couch Mountain. It was ten spacious high-ceilinged rooms, a

small greenhouse, an old-fashioned basement stocked with nothing more valuable than prehistoric paint cans and exhausted appliances, and a wide brick terrace facing due south from which on clear days you could see farther than Chapel Hill, which was ten miles away beyond the broad pasture where a neighbor's cattle still grazed in monumental stupor broken only by unpredictable mountings, couplings and outraged bellows.

By five o'clock, four of the pleasant but talentless members of the class had read their final installments of verse. Hutch had listened quietly through the criminally flattering student comments on one another; then he'd offered his own slightly keener observations and was near to calling on Maitland Moses to end the session with what promised to be the concluding part of either a long verse memoir he'd been writing all term or a newer attempt at a truly bizarre tale. Hutch had even asked Mait to start reading when it came to him suddenly that he'd failed to tell the group about Wade—the details anyhow; he knew they'd heard the rumors.

Earlier in the day, Hutch had told Wade to join them outdoors at any point if he felt up to it; and now through the open door behind him, Hutch could hear Wade shuffling somewhere inside. So he faced the students, kept his voice down and briefed them honestly. "My son Wade Mayfield moved back in with me three weeks ago. He's been an architect in New York for some years but has been ill lately and is resting up here in the house where—strangely for a modern child—he was actually born. His mother went into fast unexpected labor; and yours truly birthed him on the living room sofa, not ten yards back of where we're seated. By the time the rescue squad arrived, he was wailing strongly. I've told Wade to join us if he feels the urge, so at least you'll know him if he chooses to join us." Hutch ended even softer. "His eyesight is bad."

And while young Mait was clearing his throat and giving his usual abject rundown of what he'd reached for and failed to grasp in this final installment, Wade chose to appear. He'd dressed in a pair of his boyhood jeans that fit his narrow waist again and a long-tailed black shirt that swallowed his shrunken shoulders and chest; and as he came toward them, Wade paused in the doorway to brace himself against the full light.

Mait saw him first and, with premature courtesy, said "Join the firing squad." When Wade was plainly confused by that, Maitland tried again. "I'm about to spill my last mile of guts here. Listen at your own risk."

By then Hutch had risen and gone toward Wade. "You and I'll sit over here in the shade where it's cooler." Hutch made his elbow available for guidance.

But Wade had been seeing better all day, never so well as he'd seen Hart Salter but snatches of what seemed visual fact. He said to Hutch "Let me try the sun first" and took slow steps on toward a broad flat rock that rose in the midst of the paving bricks and took the steady light. Wade sat there carefully and looked round the smeared and jittering faces. By some kind of instinct he settled on Maitland Moses' face and said "I'm the dying homo son." Then Wade gave a grin to the whole wide circle. In the light he looked a good deal less thin—he barely weighed a hundred pounds—and in three weeks of short sunbaths, he'd replaced his pallor with a yellowish tan.

Hutch heard the self-introduction calmly with no sense that Wade meant to cause a stir. As for the students, Hutch thought only *All right, they claim they're adults; let's see them take this.*

But in fact only Mait and two of the women had heard Wade's words, and only Mait had taken the next step—*This man's got the plague.* He looked to Hutch.

Hutch told him "Read, Mait."

Whenever Mait read his rough drafts aloud, his voice was still subject to the woozy pitch of adolescence—steep climbs and plunges, hilarious yodels—but he'd long since mastered a way to read blank verse and make it sound like the pulse of a curious heart, a life that was not quite human but benign and entirely reliable. Though he'd only finished the lines last night, Mait already all but knew them by heart; and in a situation where most young poets read like whipped dogs—head down, avoiding eye contact—Mait read fairly straight at Wade's face.

What he'd brought today was the weirder of his two unfinished poems, one that had started four months ago as a kind of Browningesque dramatic monologue—the first-person and unintentionally comic account of a young husband's first adultery. In Seattle on a business trip, and exhausted at midnight, the husband goes to his hotel bar. There he meets a friendly and mildly exotic woman, whom he winds up taking back to his room.

Only at the end of lengthy foreplay does the errant husband detect two faint crescent-scars beneath the woman's breasts. He politely asks if she's had breast cancer. She says "Guess again." He says "Implants?" The woman then gives an account of her sex change five years ago. As a man she'd been a successful yacht builder with a wife and two daughters; as a woman, she goes on building yachts but is very much alone. Tonight is the first time she's dared herself to find a man, and her success quickly reduces her to sobs which the husband is powerless to console, though he goes on trying throughout the long night. It was an allegedly true story that a young computer salesman had unloaded on Maitland, in urgent confession, on an airplane high over south Georgia last winter.

But before Mait had forged far ahead with his latest draft, the class lost its professional composure and collapsed in mirth. More than half of them were exquisitely trained in the taboos of political and social correctness, but till now they'd never been challenged by a story so fraught with the heartbreak of various minorities—men-made-women by courtesy of knives and chemicals, adulterous but sensitive husbands, the vagabonds of business life in contemporary America, the unseen but surely downcast wife and whomever the man/woman had abandoned in his quest for fulfillment.

After two minutes of restraint, however, the whole class took a genuine dive into helpless laughter. The dive included Hutch as well, a teacher who always tried to obey Ben Jonson's advice never to tell a young poet all his faults. Finally he managed to sober himself. Then he calmed the group and asked Mait how conscious he was of the laughter implicit in any such tale when told in a such a flat-footed fashion.

At the first hilarity, Mait had been stunned—irony was not his strongest suit—but in twenty seconds he'd seen the point and joined the laughter. Then he literally ripped the pages apart in the class's presence and promised them better. The promise amounted—on the spot—to the final installment of another slow but quite different confession, one doled out in pieces through the term, of a fact he'd kept to himself till now—that he was both a virgin at twenty-one and "queer as a pink hairnet" (it was Mait's own simile; he dodged the demeaning label *gay* by saying he felt far more nearly *glum* and that *queer* was something he was glad to be if the world was *normal*). And the final pages he took from his notebook and read to the class now were cast as a letter from Mait to his father, a career marine who'd died in Vietnam the year the boy was born.

Right off, Hutch heard the resemblance to a poem that he himself had written for his own father Rob, thirty-seven years ago, as Hutch left America after Rob's funeral and flew back to England and his graduate studies.

At the end of Mait's second poem, three of the students tried valiantly to feel their own way into its naked heart. The lines more or less conveyed a child's awareness, at the age of seven, that men were the magnetic pole of his mind and would always be—mind and body eventually. All three of the well-intentioned students failed in their try at understanding (they'd have bedded with wolves quicker than their own gender, though they didn't quite say so). One of the law students was repulsed, though he managed to hide it in a rambling attack on iambic verse as being un-American—one of the oldest critical chestnuts and one that Hutch demolished in a sentence: "The only American line, if there were one, would be in the rhythm of an Indian heartbeat, whatever that was four centuries ago."

One student, Nan Benedict, had made her own version of Mait's discovery in her freshman year and had yet to tell anyone but the roommate who'd accepted her love as a mildly pleasant matter of course, due to end now that both would graduate next month—the roommate called herself "a four-year dyke." As Nan responded warmly to Mait's lines, she unloaded her own brisk confession onto this last class as a kind of tribute to their four-months' closeness in the crowded dinghy of a writing class.

The others heard mainly, in Mait's lines, a single message—nothing to do with eros or oddness and nothing that meant to be proud or cruel. Both Nan's lean confession and the sound of Mait's lines, in his frail voice, joined to tell the talentless watchers that *We can do all we want with these words while the rest of you'll fall further and further behind as you choke, in untold feeling, through the rest of your lives.*

It was only toward the end of Mait's poem, however, that a genuine strength broke through to Wade. In mildly archaic but dead-earnest lines, Maitland's hand reached toward his own father who'd fallen, shot through the temple, at the edge of a boatbuilder's hut he'd burned in the mouth of the Mekong River near Vung Tau.

"Sir, this untried unused hand has traveled
Worlds, or half this Earth, and guards you now.
Replay the fatal moment for me. My innocence
Can helmet, shield and glove your life—that
Life which gave me mine and which, even here,
I taste by night in dreams, your fleecy pelt."

When the word *pelt* brought a hush behind it, and no one spoke, Wade jerked upright to his feet and said "Christ-in-a-rowboat! *Thank* this man." His eyes were dry but the skin of his face contorted in pain when, still, no one spoke.

Hutch waited, then chose not to break the standoff.

Mait finally said "Thank you, Wade."

Wade stood on in place by his rock, a little rickety. He was suddenly baffled—where was he, why this crowd of voices, who were these blank faces? Then he found what seemed to be the head of his father, a head that seemed to be facing him knowingly; so he said to Hutch "I dreamed about you, old handsome sir, most nights of my life" as though his life was far behind him. Then he sat again on the sunny rock.

Hutch said "Thanks, Maitland. I share Wade's feeling—you've come so far in four months, I'm pleased. All of you know I almost never push anybody to try publishing anything, verse or prose, till it's smoking on the desk with sullen impatience or felonious narcissism at least; but I think Mait Moses has an actual poem that—once he's let it lie awhile to purify its diction, which is still a little crusty—others should read. Mait, plan by late summer to send it to *Poetry* magazine in Chicago—they might well take it. If not, whatever you do, keep it moving."

Mait flushed scarlet and his eyes had a life he'd hid till today.

A few others murmured "Excellent," "Write-on"; "Good luck, man."

Wade said "I'm just glad I lasted to hear it." By then the late light had deepened in tone, and Wade's eyes just barely registered the change. All the air around him this minute was a rich brown as deep and virtually narcotic as the shadows prevailing at the edges of late Rembrandt self-portraits. Slowly the shade was mounting round Wade like a strange welcome fluid in which he could breathe with a freedom he'd seldom known till this moment. He even turned his head through a long arc, hunting for west and the sinking sun. He discovered it finally and fixed on its brightness, then lifted his chin toward the vanishing disc. It hadn't crossed his mind that others were watching him; the light and warmth felt like a brief health, for eight or ten seconds as his eyes dimmed again even further toward blindness.

Hutch was watching though and, to him, Wade looked like one appalled face in a Rodin bronze of teeming Hell or like a rescued drowner. From eighteen or nineteen till two years ago, Wade had struck Hutch as one of the three great stunners he'd known, among men at least—that handsomely formed and carefully tended and moved by an open generous heart. Much of the beauty survived here today but only as the fragile planes and struts of a crumbling building, struggling to hold off a barely arrested downward fall. To change the present feeling, Hutch was compelled to stand and speak. "I need volunteers please to help with the food. It's all in the kitchen, thanks to the caterer, waiting to be spread."

Wade said "Wait." When everybody faced him for final orders, Wade said "Nobody's asked to hear *my* poem."

Most of the students exchanged doubtful glances.

But Hutch sat again and said "Tell us, Son." In adolescence Wade had written some genuinely likable short poems; so Hutch was curious and, for the first time since they'd left New York, he smelled again the elation he'd known when he found Wade willing to come back south. *This boy is going to surprise us yet.*

At first it seemed Wade had only been joking; his face was tranquil again but empty.

Hutch finally moved to stand.

Wade motioned him down and laughed. "Lost my mind for a minute—" No poem came though and finally Wade noticed the circle's discomfort. He rigged a broad grin. "Anybody want to ask me a question?" When no one spoke, he said "I hope you're not scared; I'm not contagious, not in formal relations." He laughed a dry note.

It dawned on Hutch that Wade might want to tell his own story, some part of it anyhow. He said "Wade, these are very thoughtful people. I've trusted my own new poems with them; they were smart and too kind. Want to tell them about what you're living through?"

Wade took the suggestion like a starved man, snagging at the word

Yes fiercely with his chin. Then he found a voice much like his old voice, deep and affable. "I'm thirty-two years old and almost surely can't hope to make it to thirty-three. Once I completed my apprenticeship, I worked six years as a licensed architect; so I have some feeling for what you people try to make in poems—there's a sturdy serviceable building in Brooklyn, a three-story brick night-college for immigrants; it's got my name on the cornerstone. Barring nuclear war, that'll probably last somewhere between fifty and a hundred years till some real-estate mogul in the twenty-first century tears it down or blows it up. Who gets much more, when it comes to lasting? What killed me though was not hard work—" Wade stopped, looked straight in Maitland's direction and laughed. "This sounds more like a bad song from the forties than anything else, but *I died for love.*" He stopped there; it seemed to be all he meant to give.

Hutch said "You're *alive*; don't use the past tense. It's hard on your pa, not to speak of the poor old English language."

Wade smiled. "I stand corrected, Doctor. No, all I'm meaning to say to you people—all I know now with my brain ruined—is that I represent a few hundred thousand Americans of a certain breed who're dead or dying or doomed but don't know it yet for no better reason than the fact they trusted their bodies with each other when nobody guessed that love or rut could kill you. For a short thirty years there, starting in the forties, penicillin cured the clap and syphilis. A vaccine fixed you for hepatitis B, they had killer lotions for crabs and fleas, and other drugs killed off intestinal amoebas. That didn't leave much but herpes and murder to worry about in the love bazaars, whatever your pick of species or gender.

"Since I never went with more than two men—honest to God, I never had sex with but three women and two other men; and the men were plainly not psychopaths—I knew I was safe. Turned out I was wrong. What you're seeing, this minute, is a young man that ought to weigh 175 and be looking at least as presentable as anybody here and who ought to be ready to build good buildings for forty more years. And what this fucked-up poem of mine says is not that you should prowl around sex, scared cold to death, or not to have sex unless you're wrapped in some stainless steel condom. No, what I mean is, if any of you wind up being writers or even just competent witnesses, then tell

the world what it means now to live—till some cure's found, if a cure
exists—in a whole new world where, for the first time since penicillin
dawned, the acts of love and the best kind of pleasure, the only good
acts most humans get to do, can kill you dead in this slow dreadful way."
By then, though Wade hadn't seen himself clearly for some four months,
he knew he stood as his own best example, in the students' eyes at least—
his broad flayed skull in setting sunlight. In that many words he'd burned
all his strength but the last few traces which let him say "I better lie
down."

Hutch looked to Maitland.

Mait stood, and together they walked Wade in to his bed.

4

FROM his decades of teaching, Hutch well knew that American students
never leave a party of their own free will. Even self-possessed graduate
students must be given strong hints that it's time to leave; most undergradu-
ates won't think of budging before sunrise unless the host specifically
orders them out. Tonight though—once they'd ravaged the spread of
sandwich makings, baked beans, wine and deep-dish pies—they trailed
off quietly into the evening. Some parted with the classic student vow to
stay in contact through the years when Hutch understood he'd likely never
hear their names again and would never miss them individually, despite
his pleasure in their brief company and the things he learned in their
presence still, after so much time.

WHEN the last car had gone down the drive, Hutch thought he'd check
on Wade first—the students had pretty well cleared the mess and washed
the few dishes. Wade's light was out, his door was open, Hutch stood at
the threshold long enough to hear his son breathing slow and raucous as
if each breath was a separate achievement. For an instant Hutch felt his

own heart shut, a desperate fist; and a wild thought racketed through him in words. *I'll get Rob's pistol and finish this*—he meant Wade and him both. *But Ann would find us.* Hutch almost grinned to think that would stop him if nothing else could. Did he mainly want to spare Ann the shock or deprive her of a grisly moment she'd dine out on the rest of her life? *You're not this vicious, Hutch. Go do some harmless work.*

As Hutch turned toward his study, Wade spoke from where he lay flat on his bed. "You ashamed?"

"No more than usual. Did I do so badly?" Hutch walked to the bed and switched on the lamp.

Wade turned, with open eyes, to face him. "You were smart as ever, smart and the soul of Dixie hospitality. No, I meant me—are you shamed by me?"

Hutch sat on the edge of the mattress and laid a hand on Wade. "I'm as proud of you as I ever was."

Wade waited so long he seemed unconscious; then he laughed two notes. "That's begging the question, Doc—how proud of me have you ever been?"

"Son, that's one rap I really won't take. You well know what you've meant to me."

"Tell me again—I must have forgot."

Hutch said "You're my beloved son, you're a good human being, a superb architect, you've carried our family's line on in style."

Wade shook his head. "I'm crashing with it now." His right hand imitated an airplane crashing to Earth; and for the first time since he'd been home, his eyes were full.

Hutch couldn't speak either.

Finally Wade said "No, what I really meant was, I'm sorry I gave that lecture to your class—that and my sizzling true confession."

"They're certified grown-ups, legally at least. They took it in stride."

Wade said "That's a lie."

Hutch said "I watched them; maybe two or three flinched. But it did them good—welcome to life."

"Amen to that. Now say you forgive me."

Hutch said " 'You forgive me.' "

"I'm serious."

"Forgive what?" Hutch truly knew of no grievance to pardon, not here in this room.

Wade's eyes focused so precisely on Hutch that anyone watching would have sworn they could see as keenly as a condor's. "Pardon me for running my life in the ground—" Again Wade gave his little airplane gesture.

"You haven't done that. And anyhow, if this monster virus had been around four decades ago, I might very well be sicker than you." That was an opening he'd never quite offered to Wade before.

But Wade was fixed on his own rail. He put up a hushing finger; *Let me finish.* "Pardon me for choosing. and loving forever—you've got to know I'll love Wyatt Bondurant forever: a man that flat-out hated you."

Hutch said "There are whole broad pieces of me anybody in his right mind would hate."

Wade said "Amen" and waited.

Hutch wouldn't object but he wouldn't ask for clarification. *What does he hate in me?* Hutch still couldn't ask.

So Wade pointed past him. "Just say the word *pardon*. It's a good English word."

"Pardon. Pardon."

Wade's hand fished around, found Hutch's and pressed it.

Hutch said "You say it too. Say it to me."

Wade's lips barely parted and made the motions that might have been *pardon* if he'd found the strength. In a moment he'd slid into sleep like a week-old infant. Sleep closed around him.

Hutch sat for two minutes, then quietly rose, switched off the light and was halfway toward his study again to read a few last papers from his seventeenth-century seminar when he thought he heard the front door close. They'd had several break-ins out here in the seventies, but he didn't feel scared. He quietly walked toward the hall to investigate.

There, with the door half open behind him, was Maitland Moses— big eyed and edgy.

Hutch said "Did you try to ring? The bell doesn't work. I was checking on Wade."

"No, I'm afraid I just walked in." Oddly Mait's voice was under control; had some new hormone just kicked in and anchored his yodeling?

"Well, you're under arrest." Hutch almost meant it; he was private to a fault and had always been. But the sight of Mait's collapsing face brought him around. "You forget something?"

"I'm pretty sure I did."

"Run find it; I've got a million papers to mark."

Quick as a burned child, Mait turned toward the door. His shorts (a pair of hacked-off jeans), the poisonous green of his baggy T-shirt, the rosy face of a Dickensian chimney sweep completed the picture of an innocent hapless Chaplinesque clown—a genuine orphan bound for the night.

"No, find what you lost, Mait."

"Sir, it's nothing I lost; but my bike and I were halfway down the drive when it just came over me that soon I was leaving this good place forever, and we'd never really sat still and talked—not off campus at least, you and I. Not in a real home."

Tired and dejected and busy as Hutch was, he had all the teaching instincts of his family still in him, ticking infallibly. Every student plea that was not plainly fraudulent demanded his attention. *You can't turn this wet dog out yet.* So he told Mait "Get yourself a drink from the kitchen and bring me that last 7 Up I saved. I'll wait in here."

While Mait found a beer, Hutch sat in his main chair and actually dozed for ninety seconds (the ease with which he could nap anywhere was a lifelong boon). When his eyes reopened, Mait was in the opposite chair, looking whole years older than he had in the afternoon—older, calmer and somehow wiser across the eyes and brow. Hutch had a sense that decades had passed or hours at least. But he looked to his watch and saw it was just past nine o'clock, same day. Near him on the table, his 7 Up fizzed in a silver goblet he hadn't seen for years—the first prize he'd ever won for poetry, in high school. Mait must have gouged deep in the cabinets. *What's this boy hunting?* Hutch took a long swallow of the cold tart drink. "You want to just start in and see where it leads?"

Mait was puzzled.

"I believe you said you forgot to tell me something—please don't confess you copied your poem from an Urdu original of the fourteenth century."

Mait gave a good imitation of *You caught me!* "I did copy, sure, but just from you. You're bound to have heard it."

Hutch smiled. "I may have detected an echo of olden days in the vaults of the Hutchins Mayfield canon, but I meant what I said. You're very possibly the thing itself, if you need to be—a live working poet. I'm fairly sure of that much, or I'd never say it." Through the years Hutch had always told his writing students that he wouldn't manhandle them in class for being less than geniuses; but if they cared to hear his honest opinion of their poems at the end of term, he'd give it to them privately so long as they knew it was just one opinion, subject to error.

None but the really good students ever asked—maybe a total of six in all the decades, and four of them had published volumes by now. Mait hadn't asked yet; Hutch had told him anyhow this afternoon and in front of the others. What was left to say? (Hutch tried to wean students once they'd left him—no lifetime correspondence courses. He and every honorable writer he knew had made their own way with bare hands through granite; he thought others should.)

Mait sat forward and gave an oddly formal speech of thanks—he was from rural upper-class Virginia and a little hypercourtly. Once the speech was past, Mait said "Next I need to know if you despise me."

Hutch was surprised. *Is this some penitential feast tonight?* "Despise you?—absolutely not. What gave you that notion?"

Mait was agonized and blushing again, and his voice broke loose. "This endlessly prolonged initiation of mine into the sodomite tribe. You've had to put up with a lot of navel gazing—or is it weenie gazing?— and I've got the sense every now and then that you'd have liked me better if I was a functional lumberjack with a ring of dumb girls hung round my studly shoulders."

Hutch laughed. "That might have been picturesque; but no, you're who you are, my friend. That's been enough for me. I'll miss your avid mind and kindly wit, but I know I'll see your work in print in the next five years."

"That still doesn't say you don't despise me."

Hutch said "For *what?* What I know about you is what I've seen, none of which repels me. Granted, I haven't trailed you around with a night-vision scope, spying on your murky secrets. But in any case, 'Nothing human is foreign to me,' as some Roman said." After nearly four decades of teaching, like most workers at any trade, Hutch was finding it nearly impossible to produce anything like a fresh reaction to a youthful question. However well-meaning he meant to be, he'd hear his words limp out from his face and creep like tattered tramps toward the young; or he'd pick up an imaginary needle, set it down precisely on his mental record and play them a paragraph or two from his greatest hits—home truths, convictions, lines from old poems: things Hutch had mouthed a thousand times.

Mait was not satisfied with secondhand wisdom, and he winced hard. The sudden age and depth of his face were holding up. "Then I need to ask you a violent question."

Hutch laughed. "What's a violent question please?"

"I feel like, deep down, you understand everything I've ever felt. You've done everything I want to do—that's made you mighty awesome to me."

Hutch smiled to think he'd at last understood. "Are you asking me if I'm queer too?"

Mait's eyes looked doused in welcome relief. He was plainly heartened by the opening, so much so that he doubted his luck. "What makes you think that?"

Hutch said "You're claiming I understand you, to the shoe soles and sockets. All right then, my world-famed understanding tells me you're feeling like nothing *but* queer; and you're hunting down volunteers for your little lifeboat."

Mait said "Bingo!" in a scooping yell.

Hutch pointed behind him toward Wade's room and whispered "He's sleeping." Then he drank the rest of his drink and faced Mait, working with more than a little amusement to drain the chalky professor from his look. "Queer—me? No, not now nor any other night—not that pure a label, no one pigeonhole." That seemed truth enough.

Mait leaned in. "Bisexual?"

And Hutch thought it through but finally laughed. "No, every man I've met who claimed bisexuality was a full-time queer in under six months."

Mait agreed. "Me too. But you understand loving your own cut and kind?"

With no trace of compunction, Hutch grinned and agreed. "Still there's never been a slot or group or club I was comfortable in. God— for instance—I voted as a yellowdog Democrat at every election since Jefferson ran; but I've never once worn a campaign button, never confessed in a telephone poll, never felt a hundred percent like a donkey. As for love and rut, I can freely tell you I've loved more than one man—oh Christ yes, loved men in every practical way from stem to stern, plus a few ways that strained the laws of physics; and I enjoyed the hell out of most of those nights.

"I can even say that, looking back, those days and nights were my main pleasure—the height of the pleasure my body's known anyhow, actual joy down the length of my skin. Men do know how to ring men's bells. And I think of those few men, all my time near them, with a lot of thanks and very slim regrets. The only regrets are for my own skittish meanness when people leaned on me. Somehow I couldn't bear another man's weight for long at a time—maybe because I bore a lovable breakable father right through my childhood. But I can't recall an act I've done with my bare body that I'm sorry for—I say that with full awareness, I think, of the moral codes of most religions.

"Still when I was only a few years older than you tonight, toward the end of my years of study in England, I honest to God felt my mind undertake a wide slow turn westward. It felt like some strong gyrostabilizer moving a ship onto some new course and locking it there. Whatever, I gradually found my mental, spiritual, sexual needs homing in on one certain young woman—my girlfriend for years, whom I'd mistreated on more than one continent. Her name was Ann Gatlin. We married once I was home from England, we had our son Wade, and I thought we were doing as well as old yoke-horses after decades together; but Ann thought otherwise a short while back and went her own way. You met her two years ago, when I first knew you—"

Mait said "I did. She's a striking lady."

"I'll tell her you said so. She's fine all right."

"So you see her still?"

"She comes by regularly since Wade is home."

Mait said "Don't answer this if I'm out of line, but surely you were tempted hard after you chose her."

"To go with other men? I can tell you this much and it's simply the truth—you may not believe me; I barely believe myself in the matter—but though I've looked at a good many men and imagined my way into their hid places, I've literally never cheated with anyone, male or female, since the day I married Ann."

"How much did that cost you?"

Hutch had never calculated. He paused to try. "Not more than a few thousand dollars a year—to translate it crassly. Nothing I couldn't fairly easily afford."

"But now you've been alone out here for—what?—at least a year."

"Longer. And I've kept to myself. I've never been a barfly or bus-station hound. Still, just when I might have looked elsewhere to feed my mind, Wade Mayfield got dreadfully sick and that grounded me."

Mait said "I hate to ask this too, but isn't it the plague—Wade's thinness, his eyes?"

"Didn't he tell you outright this evening, you and the others? I thought that was clear."

"He never said the word."

Hutch said "No but he drew a stark picture. All his life, Wade's been a poor liar."

"Did you know he'd talk the way he did out there today?" Mait pointed outside as though Wade were still there, confessing in the dark.

Hutch could see Mait was back on his best calm stride; his eyes were drinking up information like a ditch of dry sand. "No, but once he'd started, I knew I was glad."

"Glad of what?"

Hutch studied this boy before him intently. *Why should I tell this raw near-stranger?* But he knew this stranger was at least as magnanimous as any captive dolphin so Hutch went ahead. "I guess I'm glad because what Wade confided to you and the class tonight means I'll get to talk to him now myself and tell him all—he knows next to nothing about his father."

"—Which is you, his blood father?"

"Absolutely. Can't you see my eyes in him and the shape of his head?"

Mait said "Oh yes sir" as if caught in some implication of bastardy. When Hutch said nothing, Mait said "I told you I'll be around this summer, right?"

"You got the grant then?"

"Three thousand dollars to live, eat and scribble on."

"Will you keep your apartment?"

"I doubt I can. My well-heeled roommate's leaving for a year in Japan next week, and four hundred dollars a month's mighty steep for an unpublished poet. I'll get something smaller or move in with the Poufs— they've got a cheap old barny house just off east campus." The Poufs were an ongoing, only mildly embarrassing, pair of near-transvestites in sequins and pumps and Joan Crawford shoulder pads.

Hutch said "Do yourself a favor—find an ex-convict or a nice axe-murderer, but don't stay long with those painted queens."

Mait grinned and mugged. "They speak well of you." But Hutch was in earnest. "Don't narrow your choices sooner than you have to. Just because your miserable Poufs have cut themselves a path one micron wide and a millimeter deep through the whole of human feeling, please Mait, don't you. Drive off in every direction you can manage, and crash if you must—you likely won't die—but don't slim your choices down too soon. Not to feathers and lizard bags. You've got a real chance to under-stand the world, not just one tribe and its rhinestone blinders."

Mait's face assumed a generic expression Hutch knew too well—the universal muscular response when a student hears the teacher babbling outdated nonsense and seals himself off without saying so, least of all contradicting: the eyes go glassy and the lips beam thinly. In Hutch's silence the boy said finally "I came back mainly to say I can help you any way you need me all summer long, maybe longer than that."

At first Hutch was puzzled. *Help, what help?* "With Wade, you mean?"

"It's the least I can do, much as you've given me."

"But I've hardly seen you outside class."

Mait said "In my work, in the way I'll try to live."

To hear that was harder than any sympathy Hutch had got lately. All the others—Grainger, Straw, Emily, Ann, Ivory, Boatie—had blood or near-blood stakes in Wade's life. This tenderfoot poet at hand here tonight, with his naive offer to enter a tunnel as bat-lined as any since the black death killed a third of all Europe, seemed a sudden return on Hutch's years of teaching, a trade that amounts to work in the dark with almost no immediate rewards (it was after all a teacher's long dream, to know he's connected and moved a young mind a few yards forward toward a sane useful life). At least Hutch managed to say what he felt. "That's as welcome an offer as I've ever got."

Mait said "I mean every syllable of it."

"But, friend, we'll be in black water soon—right here in this house. This will get truly awful. I already diaper that dignified, powerfully accomplished young man, who only happens to be my son, six or eight times a day."

"It'll teach me a lot I need to know." Mait's face had taken on an old-fashioned fever of righteous ambition.

"Is that your main reason?"

Mait said "God, no. I liked Wade immediately. I've loved you for four years—a fifth of my life."

Hutch was genuinely ambushed by the claim. "Me? I'm more than forty years your senior, a scarred old walrus."

"You know you're magnetic."

Hutch said "I feel as magnetic as lint. But thanks anyhow." He thought of a necessary stipulation. "We'll work out a way to recompense you fairly."

Mait looked struck across the eyes; he shook his head. "Not a penny, no sir. I've thought about this for more than a week, thinking I might meet Wade here tonight; and I'm sure as a bullet on one main point— this'll be my first contribution someway to a world I've barely visited yet. I guess it's also a partial payment to God or whatever for who I'm turning out to be."

At that moment, out the window on the lighted terrace, a female raccoon made a fearless appearance. Surprisingly tall in the arch of her back and magisterial in cool neglect of the house behind her, she smelled her unquestioned way round the bricks and the rock where Wade had sat. *Nothing of any serious interest in the fading scents of an irrelevant species*, she seemed to say. But then at last she faced the wide window; and whether or not she saw Hutch and Mait, she raised her nose in a comical snub—a dowager's proud dismissal of a sighting unworthy of notice. She ambled off.

But a dry voice behind them said "What day is this?"

When they turned, there was Wade again in the hall door. He'd somehow slipped out of his diaper and waited, naked and stunned, just beyond them.

For eyes trained like Hutch's and Maitland's, Wade seemed to be two things—a young man suffering intolerably, far past their reach, and also a likeness of hundreds of images in Western art. All of them were young men tortured toward death—the lynched dying Jesus, starved desert saints, impaled rebels in Goya's *Disasters*: all long past help and as pure as new light in their unearned agony.

Hutch stood in place and smiled toward Wade, though the eyes were plainly blind again. "It's the same night you fell asleep in, darling." He realized he hadn't called Wade *darling* in ten years, maybe fifteen. When Wade said nothing, Hutch said "You been dreaming?"

Wade was sure of that much. "I haven't dreamed for two years." It seemed to be all he had to tell them. With his arms out stiff from his sides for balance, Wade slowly steered himself around and back out of sight.

Mait said "He'll freeze before morning; it's chilly out."

Hutch said "I'll cover him up in a minute."

"I could sleep in his room tonight, if you need me to."

"I'll need you more later on," Hutch said. "Get some rest while we can. And deep thanks, Mait."

They parted in a silence that felt to Mait like actual music, sober but useful.

5

By half past midnight Hutch had slogged his way through four more papers from the daunting stack. As ever he came away from the task numbed by a question—*What can have happened in America, in the past hundred years, that a people who readily speak to a friend in a room with human force and directness will seize up like an oil-drained engine when they try to commit those words to writing?* Why do so many—most of them veterans of long years of schooling—melt down, when they attempt to write, into a gummy mass that not only lacks grace and economy but, worse, conveys no legible message? Any half hour's look at a volume of eighteenth or nineteenth century letters or diaries by ordinary frontier Americans—from semiliterate riverboatmen to newly arrived East European immigrants and escaped African slaves—will show a sweet or searing intensity of feeling and a taken-for-granted trim eloquence that passes from writer to reader with no smoke or flame. Why are those qualities as rare today throughout the nation as wit and elegance? And what huge, or silent, disaster does the loss predict? For surely no republic unable to write its chosen tongue with lean precision can do its civic and personal business for long, not in clear-eyed justice and compassion.

It can't all be charged up to TV or miserable schools that can't even babysit murderous kids, much less teach language. What broke loose and why? In recent years Hutch had sensed the breakage in his own life and poetry. His emotions came and went with the same force as ever, but his writing hand could seldom move now in the close shadow-dancing it had managed before, the near-perfect fit of feeling and word. And despite a run of good new poems —some angry as hornets—just after Ann left him, Hutch had pretty much surrendered serious hope that the tide could be turned in the visible future, not for himself or for other balked Americans, not by human intervention. Now with the savage plague on hand, and the human body threatened with death at the mere touch of pleasure, wouldn't language itself only go on withering and vanishing within us?

Yet somehow the prospect hadn't soured his teaching, partly because his students selected themselves for competence and partly because—despite his age—Hutch had never quite lost his family's daily reborn taste for a given stretch of predictable hours, the time from here till tonight's oblivion. No one he could think of in all his past, except his great-grandmother Kendal, had chosen to die (she'd swallowed lye and foamed to an agonized death on the floor). But no, that same great-grandmother's father—Thad Watson—had shot himself and fallen on his young wife's just-dead body (she'd died in childbed).

That of course led Hutch irresistibly to Wyatt, Wade's companion. *A family member? All right, call him that, posthumously anyhow—a third family suicide, less grisly than the first but still an unpardonable wound to the living, the kin and friends.* The next thought had to be *And why not Wade? Has he thought of quitting on his own schedule, not waiting for agony?* At that Hutch shook his head to clear it, then stood and walked quietly to Wade's open door.

At some point in the past two hours, Wade had waked, raised the head of his bed still higher and switched on the lamp; but now that he was far gone into sleep again, there was no sound of life. He was still uncovered, his body still carving itself to the bone from instant to instant. *Let this be it, in his sleep, this easy.* Hutch stopped at the foot of the bed to listen closely. Still nothing.

Thank God. Hutch went to the edge of the narrow mattress. He freed the bruised feet from a tangle of cover (they had no more flesh than a hawk's dry claw), and he drew the blue sheet up to Wade's waist. Then he sat, his hand settling on Wade's left arm. *Warm, still soft.* Hutch lightly touched the pulse in the neck. It was there, weak but game. *Then it's all come down to this, here now on a single dry bed.* By *all* Hutch meant what he knew of his family, from old Rob Mayfield his great-grandfather and his grandmother Eva, till tonight—this young man tortured to death in sight of his father, the end of a line.

Wade's eyes stayed shut but he said "I'm just playing possum; ignore me."

Hutch's thumb stroked the ridge at the crest of Wade's eyes. It was handsome as the arc of a Chinese bridge in the mountains or the brow of a silver-backed gorilla, wiser than man. When Hutch stopped finally he saw that, gentle as he'd tried to be, his thumb had uprooted lashes from the dark brows. He carefully brushed them into his handkerchief and folded them neatly. They seemed worth saving; he didn't think why.

Then he slid a hand beneath the cover and felt Wade's waist—still no diaper. *Can I put one on him and not break his rest?*

Wade said "I'm giving you an incomplete grade."

"Sir?" Hutch chuckled.

"You're the only class member who didn't recite."

"They've heard too much of me all term."

Wade said *"Incomplete."*

Hutch said "Pick a poem then—quick, as long as it's not by me— I bet I can say it."

This tack was peculiarly urgent for Wade. *"I* told your class a very true story; so did young Maitland Moses—I could tell."

Hutch said "Did you like Mait?"

"I thought he was bold for his age, yes sir. And he's got good eyes, the best I could see."

"Mait'll be calling on us this summer."

Wade said "You're changing the subject, O Bard of the Pines. Recite me a story." His voice was thin, high and drifting, as if he was teasing a child or had gone insane since sundown.

Hutch had read stories to Wade, and reams of good poems, all through his boyhood. And through long repetition together, they'd painlessly memorized hundreds of lines. By the time Wade was nine or ten, he and Hutch would sit or lie most nights in this room and recite in unison a poem that one or the other had chosen as fit to close a particular day. Tonight as Hutch faced what had become of his son, the only lines he could hear in his mind were John Keats's last poem, written in unflinching knowledge of the fact that Keats was dying of TB at twenty-six. Oddly the poem had been a favorite of Wade's in adolescence. *Maybe not so odd; adolescents are morbid. But we can't say those lines, not tonight.*

Merciless, Wade raised his own left hand from the cool sheet and held it up in the air between them. Even in dim light it was nearly transparent; the fingers looked endlessly long and fitted with abnormal extra joints, knobby and bluish.

Hutch reached to clasp the hand.

But Wade took it back and hid it in cover. His eyes were smiling with a high glitter though; and in the new thin voice, he said " *'This living hand'*—"

It had never seemed strange on the frequent nights they'd stumble on the same poem at the same moment, but to have Wade read his mind this closely here was ominous for Hutch. He said "We couldn't get through that tonight" and reached again to stroke Wade's forehead.

Wade rolled his head aside, then looked back at Hutch with the punishing smile. "Sure we could; we're both realistic as apoplexy." Wade started Keats's poem again; and after three lines, against his better will, Hutch joined him to the finish.

> "This living hand, now warm and capable
> Of earnest grasping, would, if it were cold
> And in the icy silence of the tomb,
> So haunt thy days and chill thy dreaming nights
> That thou wouldst wish thine own heart dry of blood
> So in my veins red life might stream again,
> And thou be conscience-calm'd—see here it is—
> I hold it towards you."

It took them a moment to weather that powerful shudder of words from a century when words served gladly, in utter perfection. Then knowing the gesture might seem soft or lurid, Hutch searched in the cover and found Wade's hand.

It was hot as a small fire; and this time Wade let him hold it, unflinching. Finally Wade said "More, please sir."

"More?"

"Father, *Father*—I can ask for more now, and you can tell me safely." His voice took on the conscious creepy tones of a ghoul in a forties horror film. "I'm beyond the grave, I keep all secrets, you're safe with me." Wade laughed but still he waited for Hutch to agree. When he got that permission through pressure to his hand, Wade went for the throat. "Hutch, I'm as grown as I'll ever get. Tell me as much as I told the class."

So Hutch thought awhile and convinced himself that now might well be their last chance before Wade went past comprehension; then he gave Wade the story. And though he gave it for the second time tonight, to someone in a world as far from Maitland's as the star Arcturus, it came more easily and felt still truer as it moved into words. "What you're looking at, Son—whatever you see—is a sixty-three-year-old man who's hauling a hundred and seventy-eight pounds round the world on a six-foot frame. He's finishing up his thirty-fifth year as a college teacher and trying to write a few last poems for his fifth lean volume, a *New and Selected*. He's well thought of in the minuscule world of American verse, a few of his poems have been translated into French and Spanish and Japanese; and he's been tapped into most of the right self-congratulating clubs and academies, though they tend to give him attacks of the creeps if he goes to many meetings. But if he'd give you his honest guess, he'd reckon that not more than six of his poems have a chance of being read, much less memorized, fifty years from now."

The strain of distancing himself from the story broke Hutch's pose. When he started over he spoke as himself, in his naked intent. "Wade Mayfield, you're still set to be the main thing I bequeath this starving planet; and whatever happens in the time we get, I know you'll go on being that, among a lot else—a man that started life as a pleasure for everyone near him and who only gets better and better with time."

Wade said "Tell the truth."

"Wait—I am." Hutch lost his grip briefly. "Hutch is hard up for knowing the whole truth tonight, not with his wife far off on her own and his son in trouble—"

Wade said "Say *I*, if it's *you* you mean."

"Am I telling this story or you?"

"I'm starting to wonder." Both their voices had veered into harshness, so Wade kept silent from then on and focused his mind to guide his father's account toward what he'd wanted to know in all their adult years together and then apart.

Hutch sensed the guidance and was all but relieved to bow to it finally. "You asked the class to witness this world we're caught in here, where love can kill you as sure as gunfire. I think close watch is the main thing my work has tried to offer since nearly the start, once I'd given up trying to draw and paint things anyhow. And if I've really seen anything at all in these years, and passed it on, it's been just this—the only thing that matters a whit in human life is using your mind and body, *throttle-*

out as long as you last, to spark the gaps and to hook you to people you
need and can give to.

"I well understand I'm the ten-billionth watcher that's seen as much
and said it legibly, but I'm fairly easy these days with the fact that I'm
not Wordsworth or even Frost and likely won't be. I know this though—
the single really good thing I've done, apart from helping get you underway, is to tie myself to a few human shapes too beautiful to resist for long
and then to give them at least as much nourishment as they give me. All
but one of them are still dear friends—as near as Strawson, you're bound
to know—and the only one I've lost is dead, not abandoned by me: a
likable baffled young man named James, an Oxford stonemason with a
prison record who treated me kinder than a convent of nuns in swansdown
gloves. You surely must have known for years that, before you were born,
a reasonable number of my intimates were men."

Wade's eyes were still shut. "I've estimated as much, yes sir."

"Since when?"

"More or less from the first, I guess, when I was maybe eight or
nine—soon as I looked out and really knew I was watching other bodies
too."

Hutch laughed. "Whoa here, I resisted you at every age. I've been
many things but no child molester—"

"Easy, I'm not on the vice squad yet. I *wanted* you to touch me
more ways than one, but you were a gentleman round the clock always
and a knockout to boot."

"I'm a blighted cabbage leaf to what I was. You're pretty grand
yourself."

Wade said "—If you're drawn to the human skeleton." But he smiled
at last before he went silent and lay still so long he seemed asleep. Then
in a thin voice, he said "You're saying you're the worst thing of all—the
unhappiest anyhow?"

Hutch said "What's that?"

"One of the all but nonexistent genuine bisexuals."

Hutch laughed. "I was talking about that mythical species earlier
tonight."

"Who with?—the walls?"

"No, Maitland came back once the others left and stayed awhile— you remember you walked in on us, in the living room?"

"I don't," Wade said. He let that pass. "You weren't telling Mait you'd been bisexual, I pray to Jesus."

Hutch laughed again but gave the question a minute's thought. "Not at all, no. I honestly think I've always been *sexual*, nothing any more focused than that—though for more than thirty years, I was aimed at no one but your mother."

Wade's eyes were still shut. "What was the one thing you liked to do most—whoever you loved, wherever you were, whatever hour of day or night or sun or snow?"

Hutch thought *Wade's far past dead; tell the truth.* But then he half hedged. "Without getting down to the sweaty home movies, I always aimed to *give* real pleasure to who I was with. That was always the best reward for me. Remember what Blake said?

> "What is it men in women do require?
> The lineaments of Gratified Desire.
> What is it women do in men require?
> The lineaments of Gratified Desire."

With his eyes still shut, Wade hacked out a chuckling that lasted longer than his breath. When he'd eased again, he said "Billy Blake was the craziest coot; but he hit that one, didn't he? For me anyhow. I could look, a whole year, at a body I loved and the mind that drove it. Then all I asked was to let my hand do the necessary pleasing on that loved body—my hand or some other piece of my skin that wouldn't repel or sicken my love." Wade waited, then abruptly turned to his father and tried to see him. When he failed, he asked Hutch a genuine question. "Still, where does that leave the Poor Local Blind Boy?"

It went more than halfway through Hutch's whole body, but he smiled on the chance Wade could see him at all. Then he told him "Like me, I guess, you've got your memories." He'd sung those last four words like a sob song from a twenties operetta.

Wade eventually shook his head, a firm No; but he offered no more explanation.

Hutch thought *He's blind in his mind as well.* It was so hard to think, he smoothed the cover and moved to rise.

Wade looked out and found his father's face, a momentary milky patch on the air above him. "Wyatt told me, the first night he met you, that you'd cut your heart off from the world the day you got married— he knew it on sight." Before Hutch could answer, Wade grinned out wildly to the room in general. "You're worried about my diaper, I know. I promise if I mess up these sheets, I'll wash them myself." Both of them knew Wade could never manage that; he was weakening daily.

But in spite of the posthumous thrust from Wyatt, Hutch agreed, smiling; then gave a slight wave as he faced the door.

Wade wasn't done. "Hutch, you know it was Wyatt between us, don't you? You and me—nothing bigger than Wyatt?"

"Wyatt loathed me, Son; I mainly knew why—partly at least, though I knew he was wrong: half wrong at least. Some of his reasons were understandable, though he distorted my meanness unfairly. I had very little to do, you must know, with importing black Africans to these cruel shores or fueling the torture machine built for them. I was honest to God, never Simon Legree; not even a genial white-country-club member." Hutch knew it was too late to add the other fact—that Wade had let Wyatt *stand* between them and had never once tried to wave him aside or bring him to heel, not so far as Hutch or Ann ever knew. Before he could go on, Hutch heard his own thought—*Bring Wyatt to heel.* But Wyatt was dead, cold dead underground. *He scares me still; I'm not cured yet.*

As if eavesdropping, Wade said "Wyatt's reasons were fairly sound, yes sir" as calmly as if he'd said *Evening* or *Rain.* He took a long silence, though his eyes stayed open. Finally he said "You understand I'm totally blind now."

Hutch said "You were seeing this afternoon, out on the terrace. I could tell you were."

Wade said "I get little spells of sight—somebody's outline, the taste of the light as it's dimming for evening."

Hutch said "Surely you saw Mait Moses."

"I could tell he was lively; he was giving off streaks like the northern lights—mostly blue and blood-red."

Hutch said "But you're not seeing me here with you?"

Wade's face slowly sought out his father, and the eyes moved slightly as if they were stroking a welcome object. Finally he said "You're there, I can tell."

Hutch had returned and was standing at the foot of the bed. He took two steps back, farther away, and said "How can you tell?"

Wade said "I'm not sure—just some sort of radar that I've slowly got as my eyes went out. It's an interesting skill, one I wish I'd had in my architect days. Things almost seem to be playing a music nobody can hear till they're blind as me; even now it's faint, but I mostly can hear it. I bet you could lead me to the strangest room right now, stand me on the threshold; and I could tell you where they've placed the bed, where the windows are, which chair is the oldest inhabitant's favorite."

Hutch had stayed in place, between the foot of Wade's bed and the door. "Do you get any feeling of me?"

"Oh sure."

"What's it like?"

Wade knew at once. "You're somehow separate from the rest of the dark. You're—what?—embossed, slightly raised from the background, a kind of bas relief but *there*."

Hutch said "No, *here*. And I'll be here as long as you need me— God couldn't make me quit."

Wade grinned. "I'll pretend you didn't say that. Friend God can shut you off like a flashlight, any instant he chooses, O Seer Blest!" The grin survived a few seconds more; then Wade was gone like a shot-down quail.

These instant vanishings were badly unnerving, maybe even too convenient for Wade. But Hutch sat there another few minutes, hoping the boy would come back again and work his way past the last low hurdles left between them to some kind of justice on both their actions in the past ten years. *There's almost no time, Son—come back.*

Wade needed rest more or was overwhelmed by the gulf still between them.

So Hutch tried to find a way into prayer, a kind of thinking he'd more or less ignored through the past four decades. How does a sane human being address the mind that conceives—and goes on conceiving—

the walls or infinite reaches of space, the real or unreal nature of time and the purpose, if any, of a species as infinitesimal as *Homo sapiens*, not to speak of a single man, woman or child? Quite aside from the mystery of whether any such speech could rouse that unimaginable mind and hold its attention for a private request smaller (say) than the hydrogen atom, for Hutch the quandary came down to words as most quandaries did—what words in what order? The Buddha says only *Consume me utterly*. Jesus says *Your will be done*. Dante says *In your will is our peace*.

All Hutch could think of saying here was *Spare Wade Mayfield*. Or again *Take him now*. But he wouldn't say either. And he'd never given a moment's thought to anything as ludicrous as cursing the sky. As if the sky gave a good goddamn—the sky or its veiled shut-mouth endless boss, eyeless as any fish in the back of a mile-deep cave, afloat in pure black oakgall ink.

For the first time clearly, Hutch knew he needed each conscious hour this boy might get. And he needed them for both his own and Wade's sakes—to finish their lives and ease them out with a clear-eyed dignity, blind or not. So Hutch said to himself *Heal him someway. Bring him back*. Then he held his palm over Wade's shut face as if a father might raise the dead with nothing but skin and a weight of care that was all the greater for being reclaimed from years of silence.

THE phone rang two rooms away in the study (Hutch had muted all the other phone bells). He checked his watch—past one in the morning— then walked toward the rings and waited till the message machine clicked on and the caller spoke.

"It's late, I know, but I need to talk if you're hearing this." When Hutch didn't answer, the voice said "Hutch, it's Ann. Do you hear me?"

Hutch thought Forget it. But Ann didn't quit; she was waiting him out, as she'd almost always known she could.

He took up the phone. "I'm here. What's the problem?" Ann was silent.

Hutch thought she'd hung up. Only when he said "Good night" did she speak.

"The problem, ex-friend, is our son's on his way."

Hutch said "No, he's sleeping quite peacefully. I just this minute left him. He's had a strong day."

"You had your class supper?"

"I did. They're long gone. Wade enjoyed them."

"When will you be done with your chores?" Ann had always referred to his teaching as chores.

"I should finish reading my last exam by the 28th."

"Then you make your annual May trip north?"

"The Academy shindig? No, I'll bypass that, this year anyhow."

Ann said "I was going to offer to spell you that week."

"We're covered, thanks. Hart Salter is excellent help when he's here, and just tonight one of my seniors offered to help us this summer."

Ann said "I talked with the doctor again, just today. I like her, on the phone at least. She says Wade's stronger since the first time she saw him. I wish I agreed."

Hutch couldn't resist a knowing lie. "You're wrong. Wade's come a good way since getting home." He hadn't purposely chosen the word *home*; but as it passed, he felt its weight in Ann's lone mind. *We know too well how to maim each other.* Even after so many months apart, Hutch and Ann had fingers poised on one another's prime destruct-buttons and could trigger a mauling with the merest flick.

Ann let *home* pass. "I've just pulled a pork roast out of the oven; can I run it by before work in the morning?"

"You've got your key; come in and leave it."

"You know I don't like to use that key."

Hutch said "Remember what the sheriff said after that last break-in—'Locks are just to keep your friends out.'" Hutch laughed a little. "No, come on in."

"Will you be there tomorrow?"

"Most of the day—or have you forgot your old contention that college teachers are underworked and overpaid?"

Ann sidestepped the taunt. "I'll run by then about seven o'clock."

"You're rising early in this new life." With Hutch, Ann had always slept like the floorboards.

"We're starting a big case—the man that carved up his trailer-park neighbors near Hurdle Mills."

"So all paralegals are scrambling day and night to save his precious hide?"

Ann said "Why does that disturb you so? I thought you valued all forms of life."

"That was years ago. I'm a seasoned killer now." His voice went cold and metallic as a psychopath's. "I'm *fascinated* by your taste for crime, madam."

"It's not my taste—you're the neighborhood vampire; you hate me saving a single warped soul." By the end of that, she was half joking too.

"On the contrary, madam—I'm delighted your hands are occupied. Just don't get left alone with the defendant—you're still too well-knit to undergo whittling."

Ann chose to hear a small compliment. "Thanks, Doctor. I need that."

"It's the visible truth. That student of mine said so tonight."

"Do I know him?"

"Maitland Moses, the one that's not just gifted but rolling full tilt already."

"The one with the choirboy frog in his throat? I liked his red cheeks. I'll send him a jar of honey for his vocal cords with my sincere thanks, if he really said that."

The thought that Ann could even doubt that much—a student compliment—reminded Hutch of how much lighter his days were now without that infinite pressure of waiting from Ann: *Award my life your consent to proceed.* But all he said was "Hold off on the honey. We may owe Mait more than any honey made, if he does what he's volunteered to do."

"What was that?"

Hutch said "I told you—he offered to help out all summer long, as much as I need."

Ann took a wait. "You moving him in?"

"Not any time soon, far as I can see—though since you mention it,

I do have space. Maybe I'll take in boarders soon. No, we don't know what we may need down the road; but Maitland's offer is a bankable asset."

Ann said "Who is *we*?"

It had been the main question of their years together. Hutch smiled, but not ironically, to hear it. "It's our son and us—the Mayfield-Gatlin ex-family alone again, against all odds: remember them?"

"Why is it *ex*?"

"You made it so." When Ann took a pause to work through that, Hutch said "Ms. Mayfield, I'm whipped—turn me loose please."

She said "Don't you conk out, for God's sake."

"I love this, Ann."

"You *love* it?"

Hutch said "You know I do."

"Our son's pain and death?"

In some huge way the answer was Yes, but Hutch didn't say it. He said what was also true—"I love this chance to help him when he needs me. He hasn't needed you or me for nearly twenty years."

"Wade was not a grown man at twelve years old."

Hutch said "He was. If you and I had vaporized, Wade would have lived."

"*Lived* maybe but not much else."

Hutch said "He had you and me here squarely behind him till he finished college. Then he lit out, put a long distance between us, found a crazed mate and signed us *off*. So much for *us*."

"I always thought they were right about us—Wyatt anyhow. Wyatt Bondurant wasn't crazy, Hutch; he saw too clearly."

"Ann, if that's the case, Wade and Wyatt were also right about ninety percent of the American populace who'd find it exotic—to say the least— if they were cast as the main in-laws to a mixed-color monosexual union with the new in-law as vicious as a mongoose."

Ann laughed. "If Wyatt Bondurant was a mongoose, that makes us cobras."

Hutch said "Oh right, great hooded viperess."

"No, I grant that Wyatt was from a very different world. But he had good sense when we weren't around; he looked like a Congolese river god and could smell racism through ten feet of concrete and five hundred miles."

Hutch said "You and I are were indictable racists then?"

"At times, sure—were and are. So is every black, white, red or yellow American—"

Hutch stopped her. "I lack your trained legal mind; but if one sin's committed by all live citizens, who the hell's got any right of condemnation?"

In the face of his logic, Ann rushed ahead. "I don't think you and I are abnormal, Hutchins—not in that one department."

"But our son bought Wyatt's whole blanket indictment on Caucasoid man for nearly ten years." Hutch had calmed a little. "I think Wade's quietly letting it go, as he settles in here. I haven't heard a mean word from him yet, and we've had several crises already that might have provoked him—I told you he passed out on me in the bathtub?"

"You did, yes." Ann took a seamless breath and held it. It gave her the force to say "You know you're walling me out of all this."

"What's *this?*"

"Our son's tragedy—yours and mine."

"I'm still not sure it's a tragedy," Hutch said.

"A young man dying in agony, for no just cause, is not tragic to you?"

"It's horrific, Ann—no question whatever. No question it's the worst thing I've ever witnessed or tried to bear, and I've borne at least a normal load of hard sights. But I guess I'm starting to see it Wade's way. He's so completely uncomplaining, so ready for whatever slams in on him next. So maybe he feels like a tall lean hero at the end of something like Shakespeare's *Tempest* or Sophocles' Oedipus near his own death."

Ann said "Wasn't Oedipus a very old man when he died?"

"Fairly old, yes. But he just disappeared, no corpse at all—remember?"

She took a long wait. "Hutch, listen to yourself. This is no seminar for dazzled sophomores. A very young man is dying blind in agony, against his best will."

"Wade doesn't act that way."

Ann said "Wade's sparing you. He's spared you forever."

"Then I thank him profoundly."

"Can I come back?" If Ann had phoned with the news that an asteroid would crash between them in the next thirty seconds and atomize the world, she couldn't have made a firmer impression.

Hutch felt almost assaulted and robbed. *This thing is mine now.*

"Did you hear me, Hutch?"

"Yes ma'm, I did."

"Could I have an answer soon?"

"It was you that left, Ann."

"I quit our marriage or what was left of it. I never meant to quit all care for my child."

"*Our* child," Hutch said. "Wouldn't that be fair? No, I never said you quit on Wade; but if you've discovered this intense need to nurse him, then why didn't *you* go to New York and get him? You can drive; some junior lawyer would have ridden up with you. *I* went; *I* rescued my son—" The words were still in the air between them when Hutch heard their self-love and cruelty. He could neither call them back nor ask Ann's pardon.

She let them pass her by. "Hutch, I wrote to Wade with numerous offers for the whole past year. I never heard a word."

"That's because he never opened a single one, yours or mine. They're all here beside me, in a box he brought home, each one still sealed. Come get them when you're ready."

Ann said "I couldn't stand to see them again. And please don't you."

Hutch was suddenly exhausted—the long day, the class, this familiar arm wrestle over a son's life, a life that was leaking through their actual fingers before their eyes. Hutch said "Let's talk tomorrow then. I'm past thinking clearly."

"*Thought's* not required—just average human feeling."

Hutch said "Tomorrow please."

At that Ann was gone, not a slam-down but a silent disappearance.

People are vanishing on me by the hour. But Hutch was safe again in his house with his son; for a sweet moment he tasted the fact. Then as he moved toward bed and sleep, he thought *Cheap and stingy* and he meant himself.

6

May 9, 1993

Dear Wade and Pops,

I know it's Mother's Day not Father's Day but I've been meaning to take pen in hand ever since you two left me up here and I've been so busy that this is the first slow minute I've had to tell you both "Hey!" like they say down yonder in the cotton fields and to gripe about how much I miss my friend Wade but how glad I am that he's with you Mr. Mayfield. Happy Mother's Day to both of you—Dad and son—from your pal The Boat.

I was so glad, Wade, to get your call the other night and to know that you been gaining strength with the good homecooking and personal doctor care. Like I said I watched more than one miracle happen in my days. Just don't overdo it with the fatback and chitlins, your belly is tender, but if you get a chance just ship me a thermos full of warm pot liquor from your next turnip greens. That'll heal some bodies and souls let me tell you!

Speaking of which you don't want to hear my news, it's so pitiful. Two of my boys passed on last week, Sellers and Larry. I don't believe you know either one but I'd been tending to them since back at the start, back about '82, and they had worn themselves deep in my heart. Larry especially had been doing so well gaining a little weight and hadn't been badoff sick since winter. But he hit the ice, let me tell you, and went.

Don't let that get you down a bit. Every boy in this mess, and every man, woman and baby is a whole different thing and you can't foretell. You remember, Wade, I've still got Monte that's had a full case of it since '83 and has still not missed a day of work, never has any trouble that's harder to fight than a summer cold or a little athlete's foot from swimming at the gym. I wasn't ever too good at the books but Monte amounts to a miracle in my book.

Haven't run into Ivory to speak to since you all left but I saw her crossing the street this morning with a white flower on toward the subway station looking fine as ever. I wonder if it means her mother is dead or if Ivory's still in mourning for Wyatt? Let me stop right here or I'll get you both down and let me end with a cheerful hope. You both invited me to visit you. I may be planning to ride the bus to South Carolina for July 4th.

My grandmother is leaning on me for one more look at my homely face before Jesus calls her. I told her in that case she was safe. Since she's deaf as a post, she couldn't hear Jesus with a bullhorn no how! If you two gentlemen are not too busy it would do me good to stop by and see you. Don't let me get in the way of your plans though and don't let me weigh on your mind at all. I couldn't stay more than an hour or so or maybe one night if you got an army cot. You know my number so if the word is Yes just call me collect. If not I won't think you mean any harm.

Lord bless and keep. Pray for Boatie and the world. He is watching over you

*Like a friend
Jimmy Boat*

May 9, 1993

Dear Mr. Mayfield,

You asked me to send you a list of what I might have spent on Wade's behalf. I've finally had a chance to sit down with my receipts and add things up. It comes to even less than I thought—$217. If you'll check me against the composition book you took home from Wade and Wyatt's kitchen, I believe you'll find me accurate. If there's any question, don't hesitate to write me. One reason I spent so little on my own was that, after Wyatt's death, Wade gave me check-writing privileges on their joint account. I terminated those, in writing, at the bank last week.

I got your kind letter after you reached home. Everything you say about my time with Wade is thoughtful of you, but don't fail to know that I did it because I wanted to. Tragic as things have been in my family lately, it meant something to me to help Wade when needed. He has done me more than one kindness, and I will never forget him, I or the remains

*of my kin. Tell him please that I went out to see my mother this morning
in Sea Cliff, that things are going well out there with everybody and that
Mother sends him her love and prayers. She thinks Wade will "live a long
life" and she's only been wrong half a dozen times in the years I've known
her. She will be seventy-six next month and is strong as she's ever been
but still grieving for my brother.*

*Please keep me informed on how things go and don't hesitate to call
on me if you need anything sent from the apartment or if Wade has any
unfinished business up here I can handle. As you requested, I check the
apartment two or three times a week and water the fern. Everything except
what you packed up and took is still right there where you left it and will
wait for your plans long as you pay the rent, which I hate for you to keep
doing.*

With many good wishes from me and my family to you and yours,

Sincerely,

Ivory Bondurant

May 16, 1993

*Hello to you, Mr. Wade Mayfield. This pretty get well card hits the spot
with what we are feeling about you today. You just keep your mind set
on strength like I told you to and keep your blood purified with lemon
and water hot as you can stand it plus your doctor medicine and we
will look for you back up here at work and visiting us before much longer.
Call us on the phone late some afternoon, we are always home with the
TV on so let the phone ring awhile till I get to hear it. It would be a
real tonic for me and mine to hear your voice. You recall I grew up in
Virginia and I still get homesick when I think of the beautiful land down
there near my dear grandfather's place and all of us children running
round outdoors in the old times not scared of a single thing. My oldest
brother Bankey is still alive, by himself in the family home, last I heard.
I would dearly love to see him once more, a serious boy that could read
all night if you left the light on. I take fresh flowers to Wyatt's grave
every Sunday after church and I always tell him your name to remember,*

*Wade. Please give my good thoughts to your mother and father. They
raised a good boy.*

Respectfully yours,
Mrs. Lucy Patterson Bondurant and Raven

May 19, 1993
Dear Emily,
    *You're good to keep bracing me up with calls and letters. I wish there
were other causes for cheer from down here today, but no there are none.
Wade goes on more or less the way he's been since the day he arrived in
early April. Hutch and even the doctor try to claim he's stronger, but a
mother's eyes and intuition say no. As I told you, I take everything Hutch
will give me—daily visits with food and clean laundry—but when I'm
there with just Wade alone and Hutch not trying to hide the truth, I
generally see a steady decline.*
    *Wade's vision is pretty much completely gone; and again when I'm
alone beside him, he'll say occasional things that show he's not entirely
sure who I am or where he is at the moment and why. Just this afternoon
I sat there by him through a ten-minute nap; and when he woke up and
turned toward me, he said "Take a pen and write down this instruction."
I thought he might have some important request, so I got stuff to write
with and told him to tell me. He put all ten fingers up to his temples,
rubbed at them hard, then finally said "Wade Mayfield plans a fair
distribution of all he owns to any child under fifteen years old who grew
up an orphan like him and can prove same in writing." When he finished
he asked me to sign it for him. I continued obeying but he suddenly scowled
at me quite wildly and said "You've forged my name all your life." I begged
his pardon but before he could give it, he was out again, another feverish
nap.*
    *Without going deeper than you could stand into this domestic trag-
edy—I'd just be repeating—I have to report that Hutch goes right on doing
it all and refusing help, except for a student that sits with Wade for brief
spells some days. Otherwise Hutch is cook, bottlewasher, trained nurse
and constant companion. I'll give him this much—so far he's got the*

endurance of a mountain. He's never looked stronger; he's literally thriving. In meanness the other day, I told him if he'd been an undertaker and frequented the dead a lot earlier in life, he wouldn't have a gray hair to show, even now. He laughed and said "Maybe."

Every offer I make—beyond the two chores—is coolly rejected; and I can't ask Wade, bad off as he is, to enter the fray on my behalf. I understand Hutch loves Wade in his own way as much as I do, so I'm straining every nerve to be fair. But still I know Hutch is paying me back by the bitter minute for saying I wanted a separate life, when I moved out. When I left, though, my son was still strong—so far as I knew. Now I'm forced into what amounts to practical abandonment of the main thing I've cared for in my life. I honestly think if I turned up on the doorstep with my bag, saying I meant to stay to the end, Hutch would call the sheriff to escort me out.

I know that sounds like trailer-park news, real white-trash behavior. But that's where I stand and, even with a good deal of legal advice, I don't see any way to reach my son for more than quick drop-in visits, with Hutch standing by and checking his watch. You and Straw mean the world to him—Straw means more than ever to him these days—so again if either of you can think of a word that will gain me greater natural access to my sick child, I'll be your debtor till Judgment Day—which feels a lot closer than it has till now.

Meanwhile, love from

Ann

7

THOUGH it was only a two-hour trip on such a clear day, they were almost surely the bleakest hours Hutch had known on the road. He'd tried for days to resist Wade's wish to see the old Kendal place again, his great-grandmother's ancestral home, and Grainger there still. Hutch had told Wade lies about Grainger's poor health, he'd told Wade how busy Straw and Emily would be in the growing season, Hutch had finally even said to Wade "Don't make me do this."

But at that, Wade had shut his eyes in silence and made the wish an unmistakable demand. Though Wade could no longer see Hutch's face, he said "I want you to scatter my ashes up there by the creek where I used to go with Grainger. I want to pick the spot."

So Hutch called Strawson with the ultimatum; and Straw suggested Sunday, May 30th. Emily would make up a daybed in the dining room where Wade could rest in the course of the day without climbing steps. Straw wouldn't tell Grainger till the day itself; the old man would only dwell on it too hard and be confused when, and if, they got there—he'd already spoken more than once of Wade Mayfield as a friend of his childhood, ninety-five years back.

On the morning itself Hutch lost whatever nerve he'd had and lay on his bed just after dawn, thinking *This is the first thing I can't handle— can't and won't.* But then he heard Wade awake down the hall, coughing and feeling his way round the room to dress himself. Hutch sat up, put his glasses on, found Maitland's number and called him—ten or twelve rings and still no answer. Hutch recalled telling Mait last week that he wouldn't need him over the weekend. *Go calm Wade down; tell him you're feeling sick—whatever it takes.*

But by the time Hutch had put on his robe and walked to Wade's door, the boy had finished dressing and sat on the edge of his bed, waiting silently.

Hutch stood there, looking.

The boy did seem a little stronger this morning; and though his face was mostly blank, it wore a new kind of unanswerable demand. He said "You're trying to fail me, aren't you?"

Hutch said "Pardon?"

"You've thought of a way to cancel my trip."

"I have been feeling pretty awful all night—some stomach bug."

Wade said "I'm the host to every bug species on Planet Earth and *you're* feeling poorly." He grinned; by now the sight was appalling, all teeth and white gums. "Go lie down then. I'll call Ann Gatlin." It was the only time Wade had used his mother as a threat between them.

Hutch said "Now you've turned mean."

"Not mean at all, Hutch—just realistic. I'm making this trip, by car or taxi, alone or with one of you. I know Ann's ready."

"You call her in the night?" Wade's late phone calls usually waked Hutch; more than once he'd had to get up and go in at three in the morning and hang up the phone after Wade had dozed off in the midst of a call.

Wade said "No sir, but she asked to come with me."

"When?"

"Every second since I told her we were going."

All right, use this. You'd rather drink lye, but call and ask her. Hutch gave Wade a last chance. "You're serious now? You want Ann to join us?"

Wade said "I seem to remember a girl named Ann Gatlin brought me to life. Am I wrong on that?"

"Ann Gatlin Mayfield—you were no way a bastard."

Wade said "She's *Gatlin* to me these days. She did all the work, to the best of my memory—I know my mind's failing."

That was as near to a direct strike as any Hutch had taken since Wyatt's first days on the edge of the family, sighting and firing on social occasions with the lethal arms and precision of a renegade African guerrilla. Hutch thought *Take it gracefully; his mind is weak. Just call Ann and tell her you need her help.* But he said to Wade "You're making me do this."

"I know I am." Wade tried to laugh, then broke up coughing. At last he could finish. "You made me *be.* You started all this."

Hutch said "You just now said Ann did it all."

In the black bass voice of Hattie McDaniel in *Gone with the Wind,* Wade said "Mistuh Rhett, Lord, you *is* bad. I nevuh told you no such of a thing." It was a voice Wyatt had used more than once on his visit here, kidding on the level with his fine hot eyes.

It felt unnecessarily cruel but Hutch turned and went, with no further persuasion, back to the phone in his own room.

Ann answered on the second ring; he could tell he'd waked her, though she denied it—her role in the trial of the Hurdle Mills Strangler was pressing her still.

Hutch said "You know about this planned trip to Strawson's?"

"Wade told me, yes."

"Can you help me with it?"

Ann said "Are you sure?"

For the first time in weeks, Hutch's throat shut down; and what he said was audibly painful. "This is something I just can't tackle alone."

When Ann finally spoke, there was no sound of gloating. "Are you and Wade ready?"

"I'm not, God knows. Wade's dressed himself in a strange mixed getup; I've still got to shower. They're not expecting us till late morning anyhow."

Ann said "Shall I be there by nine-thirty then?"

"I'd be grateful, yes."

Ann hadn't spent long months with lawyers for nothing. She'd always listened closely to words; now she heard them like a radio telescope. "*Grateful* but not *glad*. I feel the same way. Anything I should bring?"

Her voice was milder than Hutch had heard lately. He lowered his own, "Bring an extra handkerchief. This'll be hard."

When Hutch hung up, Wade was standing in his doorway, smiling still in a shrunk knit shirt that said *I'm The One Happy Homo* and khaki trousers from his Boy Scout days, five inches too short. He grinned toward his father. "Nothing on Earth that can happen today will be any harder than being *me*." It was only a fact, no trace of self-pity.

It was, and would be, the only time Hutch ever heard Wade confess to the horror that was clawing him down. Hutch carefully led the boy back to his room to help him change the clothes he'd chosen blind at dawn.

8

STRAW and Emily were as ready as they could be for the visit. In the old front parlor, the daybed was made up and ready for Wade when he needed rest. Beside the cot they'd set a china slop jar and a pitcher of water with glasses on the table by a small ice bucket. Emily had gathered a cold spread of food for whenever they were hungry; and when Hutch phoned to say they were starting the trip and to look for them somewhere around midday, Straw had walked down to Grainger's to break the news as clearly as he could. He'd already made his early morning check to see if the old man had lasted the night and to cook his breakfast, so he had some confidence that Grainger was up and watching TV—Grainger liked Sunday morning political shows such as "Face the Nation."

Without knocking, Straw opened the screen and stepped into the heat which Grainger had needed year-round for decades.

The old man was immaculately dressed in his stand-up chair at an awkward height, nearly half stood up and plainly awake. The TV was off and the air around him was all but crackling with the force of his ancient patience and readiness.

Straw said "Where you headed?"

Grainger said "You tell me. Been thinking all night I'm going somewhere. Sitting here ready."

Straw leaned to the switch and lowered Grainger's chair. With his hand he stroked the polished top of the enormous skull. Any touch of Grainger was likely to make Straw feel the scary power of his own long loneliness—this life that had burned on, unpaired for so long, gave off its strength like a tangible radiance. Then Straw took the straight chair opposite. "No good news on the TV this morning?"

"Nothing but white folks trying to preach. Blond-headed strumpets and pitiful-looking sissified men in light blue suits with red hair dye."

"I thought you sent those preachers contributions."

"Do," Grainger said. "Some of them, I do; but that don't mean I got to watch them talking. I just pay them to pray for me every few months."

Straw said "I thought you could do your own praying." Grainger and churches had seldom seen eye to eye.

The head shook slowly. "I gave up praying after Gracie died. Can't see prayer ever helped me anyhow."

Straw said "*Somebody's* been looking out for you."

"You."

True as it was, that came to Straw as a considerable surprise. He'd lived in close touch with Grainger Walters for near forty years. He'd hardly felt scorned or disvalued by the old man; but no, Straw had never heard him come so near to thanks before. He said "I've enjoyed every day we've had."

Grainger said "You been short on stuff to enjoy."

Straw waited for some expansion of that—he'd had his disappointments and persistent aches but no long bitterness, despite his drinking. Still Grainger had shot his bolt for now. Straw had to move on. "You're feeling all right this morning then?"

"You can see. How I look?"

Straw said "Three or four years younger than me—you look first-rate. But we've got a problem here. You know how sick Wade Mayfield's been; you know Hutch and I brought him home last month. He's feeling a little stronger, and Hutch is driving him."

Grainger said "Wade called me up last night on *that thing.*" He still called the telephone *that thing* and often wouldn't answer it, claiming he could tell from the ring whether a call was long distance or local— he honored long distance.

Straw said "Hutch called you up last night?"

"Wade called—I told you."

"What time; what did he say?"

"In the dark sometime. Said he's coming today. That's why I'm waiting, fool."

Straw felt the need to test for Grainger's clarity; he feared the old man might upset Wade through misunderstanding. "How old was Wade last time you saw him?"

"Saw him this past spring; he come here with Ann."

"Did he look full grown?"

Grainger bowed his head deeply. "Son, I know who Wade Mayfield is. And he told me plenty about what's killing him. When he comes, lead him down here and leave him with me. Don't want you or Hutch or nobody else—black or white—hanging round, tuned in to what we say."

Straw said "Yes sir, Mr. Walters. But understand—last time I saw Wade, he was very confused. His mind's badly affected by the illness, and he's totally blind most all the time. He may not really know what he's telling you."

Grainger shook his head again. "Wade's called me plenty of times in the past year, crazy as a cat. I've known crazy men all my life, some women too—they've been good to me; I can talk every one of them down to being peaceful. Wade gets peaceful with me every time, once I talk him down some. Known heap worse fools than Wade in my time."

Even a short conversation with Grainger almost always set Straw, who still read mountains of history and lives of the great, to thinking of the scale of human time—how short it is and how long it feels. Now Straw thought of a question, entirely off the subject of Wade, that his mind had raised in a dream last night. If he didn't ask questions when he thought of them now, he'd likely forget; so he said "Mr. Walters, who was the oldest person you met when you were a boy?"

Grainger knew at once and, leaning back, told it to the ceiling. "I met an old woman in Washington, D.C. when I was changing trains on my way down to Virginia from my father's in Maine—coming to stay with my great-great-grandmother, old Miss Veenie that you never knew: something else you missed. I was sitting in the station, scared to death— eight years old and heading to where the slavery times were scarcely over, in spite of what every calendar said—when this old colored woman, size of a sparrow, come up to me and asked me would I take her somewhere to 'do her business.'

"*Old*—she looked a lot older to me than any burnt-out chimney by the road. She had to be somewhere near the age I am today. That would have been around 1900. She was near blind like Wade's going to be; so I took her hand and led her to the only place I knew about, the big men's room—a gray marble place about the size of this county. She looked like a man, bald as me now; but she wore a long dress. Still nobody stopped us and she got her skirts up and set herself down like she'd been using indoor toilets all her years. Then she held my hand while she did her business—her skin was drier than mine is now, worse than gator hide.

"It took her a long time; but when she finished and stood back up, she said 'You a mighty respectful little man.' I thanked her for that, and she said 'You bound to know who I am.' To hush her up I said I knew her; but she said 'You lying' and hit me a lick on the head, not hard. By then I'd led her back to the bench for colored people, hard as a rail; and when she sat down, she said 'Tell your children you know old Lacey.' I said 'Who's Lacey?' and she said 'One of Miss Martha Custis's niggers— Miss Martha Washington at old Mount Vernon.' Said she was a slave on the Washington place out by the Potomac when she was a girl, born a little bit after 'old General died.' That made her younger than I am today—like I said maybe just by a year or so.

"Course she may have been lying, bragging on herself; but if you sit down with your history book and do some arithmetic, you'll see she could have been telling me the truth. I thought she was then, I still think she was; she looked like the truth. I see her right now. Ugliest old woman I ever watched; but she knew her story, old as she was—less she was lying."

"And you think she was?"

Grainger said "I told you No. She was too old to make up something that hurt that bad to hear and still be smiling."

Straw had heard most of Grainger's stories many times through the years but never this one. It made him want to stand and wail to the open sky—the fact that one man, a man you'd known and watched all your life, could ram you back that far in time through direct knowledge, hand-to-hand. And here this morning they were all torn up and grieving for one particular boy who'd killed himself by strowing his seed where the ground was poison. It made Straw long, as he longed so often, to walk out of this room and keep walking straight through woods and creeks till he found the one safe place on Earth where he could pause—it had to be there, though he'd yet to find it—and then to take a dry seat on the ground, shut his eyes and never leave, never retrace his steps, never see his home and kin again.

Grainger said "Don't let this get you down."

Straw came to himself and touched the old man's knee. "I'm trying hard."

"Try harder then—this many people leaning on you, you can't cave in."

Straw said "Don't worry. I'll tend to you."

"Not me I'm thinking about, not now. You could go on and stretch me out today and I'd be glad. Hutch and his boy though—they driving up here right this minute for me to save; and I can't walk ten steps to meet them, much less ease their misery."

"They know that, Mr. Walters."

"Why else they coming then?" Grainger's eyes were crouched and gleaming with the helpless need to do a duty he'd felt all his life to a few white men that were his blood kin, though they'd let him live like a whole

different creature in a parallel world that ran—when it moved at all—
beneath their feet, never higher than their knees: a world that was generally
either ice-cold or blistering hot, furnished with big-eyed hungry children
and men and women old as Grainger, harder than ironwood and wild in
their minds. All the same, a great part of Grainger's pain rose from the fact
that all he wanted to do and give now was far past giving. He understood he
was nothing on Earth but eyes today—useless eyes and a wakeful mind
that, he well knew, came and went like daylight.

9

With all his failings Straw's body was still as strong as an engine—arms,
legs and back. So in late afternoon when Wade had rested from the hard
trip and managed to eat two slices of bread, and Hutch had put a clean
diaper on him, Straw solved the problem of how to bring the two frail
men on the place together. Grainger could never have walked to the main
house and climbed the porch steps; today Wade couldn't have made it to
Grainger's. So Straw led Grainger out of doors and sat him on a chair by
the nearest hickory in cool dry shade. Then Straw went back to the main
house and, with Hutch beside him, took Wade in his arms and brought
him down the steps and over the seventy yards of shadow and sun to
another chair three feet from Grainger. Then Straw and Hutch left the
two men alone and waited on the back steps, in sight but not hearing.

Grainger had seen Straw set the boy down and help him get his
balance in the chair. By the time Wade had faced him and said "Old
friend," Grainger's morning memory had faded to where he had no recollection of this starved face or who lived behind it; but he answered politely
"Fine, thank you, sir. How you making out?"

Though Wade knew that his smiles were frightening, he had to grin
for the first time today. "I'm bound to tell you I've seen better days. I got
carsick on the way up here and had to keep stopping along the road. I
can't vomit though; there's nothing left in me."

"You're slimming down all right—scarcely see you."

"I told you I don't see much now, remember?" All Wade could see, even this nearby, was a darker patch on the screen of his mind where he felt Grainger's force. Wade's hand came up in the air between them and traced what he could see of Grainger, the faint tan shimmer.

"Not missing a thing, Son. Nothing left of me. Right pretty leaves on these old trees though." Grainger was still not sure who was here, but the boy seemed to know him.

Wade understood that much—the blind were leading the blind again. And he managed to wonder why he'd gone through this strenuous trip, and put his parents through it, to sit here briefly by an ancient man who hardly knew him and might well die before Wade himself. In their feeble strength though, both men were patient with the quiet calm of prisoners; both pairs of hands lay harmless on their knees. And after a while, Wade thought of his point in coming at all. He took slow care to lean toward Grainger and not lose balance (his blind sense of objects had grown even keener; the way they reflected his voice would tell him what was near; sometimes he only had to think like radar, and he'd locate things and people precisely). Now when Wade thought the old eyes had found him and recognized his face, he said "You know that place back here in the woods, down by the bend in the creek? You used to watch me swim down there, saved my life that time?"

Grainger's scaly hand came across the cold space and found the boy's bone wrist. He pressed it once.

Wade thought that was Yes. "I'm going to die fairly soon after this. I've asked Hutch to bring my ashes up here and scatter them on that pool in the creek where you rescued me. Can you show him where?"

"That drowning hole where you fell in and I drug you out—nineteen and seventy?"

Wade sat back. "Yes sir. I was nine years old."

"I know my way down yonder like my hand." Grainger stopped as if to think his way again into the woods and on downhill. Then he may have tried smiling; the muscles had forgot. "No, I fixed it for you. Safe as can be. Widened the banks and filled up the deepest hole with rocks. Bring your boys anytime."

Wade laughed. "I will; thank you. You remember my friend I brought up here a few years back—a Bondurant fellow, older than me?"

Grainger said "Colored boy with the sharp gray suit?"

Wade had forgot Wyatt's handsome suit, bought specially for the one trip he'd made south with Wade. "Those were fine clothes."

"Set him back a fair piece of money, I could tell."

"Money meant less to Wyatt than ruts in the road."

Grainger said "Me too. And look at me now—" He patted around his chest and flanks as if frisking himself for hidden cash. "I'm trusting to be a big banker in Heaven though."

"You going there?"

"No doubt about it. Any minute—"

Wade said "You'll outlast me, for sure."

Grainger looked him over as if for a written date of death. "Never happen," he said.

Wade smiled but said "I'm too weak to argue."

"Not arguing one bit at all here, Son. I'm bound for Paradise is all I know."

"And you're looking forward to that prospect?"

Grainger said "I'll tell you the honest fact—in the Bible it sounds mighty tacky to me: a whole city made out of jewelry and gold. And I doubt I can stand to sing all day or listen either, not all day, not if they let many white women sing. But no, I'm planning to take plenty rest and get some questions answered finally."

"Want to say what they are?"

Grainger said "I don't; you not old enough." But the faint start of a smile tugged at him, and he said "You drop by and see soon's you get there—I'll tell you then, everything I know."

Wade agreed to that. "And vice versa. Between now and Paradise though, do me a favor? Show Hutch the place I mentioned, in the creek?"

Grainger's slow head agreed. "Ease your mind." Then his mind hooked back to the memory of Wyatt, the sharp gray suit; and he said "That colored boy called me a house pet—you hear him?"

Wade could no longer call the phrase to mind; but he guessed it sounded like something Wyatt might have said, half whispering near Grainger. Rather than deny it, Wade said "People have all grades of pets, you know. There's people with royal tigers asleep on their beds every night, tamer than rabbits."

Grainger said "He didn't mean that but thank you." The moment in which their vague minds had met at last hung on around them, a mild reprieve.

From the faint direction of the main house steps, Wade could hear the mixed voices of his father and Straw. It was one of the better sounds of his childhood on summer visits here, the undercurrent of safety mixed with the coiling invisible scent of his early body's unspoken desire—the lives and shapes of men worth reaching for and tasting. It turned Wade's mind completely away from the old man near him; and he rose in place, facing the main house. Then he gave a wide wave toward his father and waited for guidance.

Grainger said "You're the luckiest child I know."

Wade tried to laugh; it sounded like leaves. But he said "You've known a million children; how did I win the lucky crown?"

"Win what?—you losing, Son. You fading on *off*."

Wade finally laughed. "You said I was luckier than all the kids you've known. I need to ask how."

Grainger took the time to recall his meaning. Then he lined it out on the air with a finger as if Wade could read the actual words. "You dying in trusty arms like you are. Like me and you. That's some kind of luck. I seen men die in the mud like hogs—" Grainger didn't sound finished but he stopped there firmly.

Wade barely recalled Grainger's service in France, but he said "It does beat jumping out the window."

"—And leaving young. I ought to left this world, young like you, with my teeth and good health. Would have left a better memory behind me, not this old gunny sack of gristle and bone."

Gristle and bone—Wade knew that Grainger could see him at least, whether he truly recognized him or not. There was nothing else to say except "Show Hutch the place but wait till I'm gone." Then Wade balanced himself upright for Hutch and Straw—he'd gained a little strength in the shade. When they reached him, Wade said "I better lie down awhile before the trip home."

Straw said "Mr. Walters, I'll get Wade in; then come get you."

Grainger said "Take your time."

In his old half-comic grumbling way, Hutch said "Nobody but you's *got* time."

Wade laughed. "Nobody." He put out a hand again, straight to its target, and found Grainger's ear. He slowly leaned and whispered "Adiós."

Grainger said, full voice, "I don't speak French no more."

Wade paused, reeling a little to be upright in warmer air. Then he decided against the clear word *Goodbye*. He reached for where he knew Straw stood.

Straw gathered him in again and lifted him gently in one long move.

Hutch recalled for the first time in maybe three decades how Straw had lifted him similarly one night in Oxford, as easily as if skin and bone were weightless. *He's not a bit less powerful now.* That constituted a small reward.

As Hutch and Straw took Wade away, Grainger could see them through the first few yards of gradual distance; and he thought *I finished my whole job now.* It meant he could leave any day he chose—he meant to die in broad daylight, to spare anybody finding him cold with his mouth gapped open some early dawn.

10

WADE had slept so deeply through the afternoon, even with his family moving around him, that Hutch and Ann felt able to stay on at Straw and Emily's till nearly dusk. The women had served the food, washed the dishes and gone for a long walk up the road (by then the heat of the day had broken). The men had sat on the front porch, waving toward the scarce cars of a holiday weekend, calling out to a few familiar walkers— all of them black and lifelong acquaintances. They were trying to cool their minds with small talk.

Straw as usual had just read a new and inflammatory book on the Civil War, an occurrence he still chose to call the War of Northern Aggression; and he had to give Hutch a feverish summary—some overeducated son of a bitch had published a book claiming Robert E. Lee was a mediocre general and a dishonest man.

Hutch responded with the latest foolishness at Duke—a campus fracas on the question of whether or not the all-male, ninety-nine-percent-white-and-alcoholic fraternities had the faintest right to continue existing (Hutch was sure they didn't; Straw oddly agreed). Then Hutch said his newest poem for Straw, written this year at the first sight of spring, a week before they brought Wade south. The poem was a ten-line memory of a day Hutch and Straw had spent at Warm Springs, Virginia many years back—both of them stripped in their best young bodies, suspended in thoughtless fetal ease in the huge natural spring at precisely blood heat.

Straw responded with thanks and a reiteration of the blanket request he made each time Hutch wrote any poem about him. "Don't let Emily see it."

Since Emily had never read a serious poem in her life, Hutch had always known their past was safe. Even Ann had barely responded to anything Hutch had published in the past dozen years.

On the porch after that, Straw and Hutch turned to making whatever plans seemed sensible for the time left to Wade—what Straw might be called on to do by way of help. At about five-thirty, as the light dimmed a notch and Hutch was thinking it was time to find Ann and start home with Wade, Straw leaned in closer. "Was this Ann's idea today—coming up here with you?"

"Not really. My student helper's gone for the weekend, my nerve failed me for coming single-handed; and at the last minute, Wade asked for his mother."

"I'd have run down and got you."

Hutch said "I always know that. You saying I'm wrong to give her this much?"

Straw took his time. "No, it may well be the best thing you've agreed to in years." He grinned at the road first, then brought it back to Hutch.

"What's the joke here, friend? You and Emily stage this someway?"

Straw looked back to the road. "Oh no, this has the unmistakable handprints of Fate all over it." Now the grin was a laugh. Straw had drunk three glasses of wine with lunch, but there'd been time to sober.

Hutch couldn't quite laugh but he lightened his tone. "Read the handprints for me."

"You think you can do this alone; you absolutely can't."

"I've got good help and, hard as it sounds, this can't last long."

Straw said "It'll last the whole rest of your life. How in God's name could you ever blot out the memory of your one child in a hell like this?"

"I don't plan to blot it. I wouldn't if I could. If I outlive this, it's bound to be at the awful center of anything else I ever write. You well know I've dwelt on the past too much and am too old to change."

"Then ask for Ann back."

Hutch said "I don't follow you. It was Ann that left; I never asked her to."

"Hutchins, there are millions of ways to ask. You hadn't *seen* Ann for the last twenty years till the day she left."

"That's your flaming imagination again. I loved Ann Gatlin every day we spent together. That wasn't enough, not for her anyhow; she said I couldn't make her believe it. So frankly I've learned to like the relief she left in her wake. There's a lot of things worse to live among than quiet empty air."

Straw said "You're how old—sixty-two?"

"Sixty-three on the twelfth of this month; you missed it."

"Twelfth of May?"

Hutch smiled. "Falls on the twelfth almost every year."

"Well, damn. I'm sorry. I miss a lot don't I?"

Hutch laughed. "That's all right; some of my young friends remembered." By now they were back in their old slow teasing; these days they seemed to manage it only when one of them hurt.

Straw said "I know you see yourself stumbling on to the grave like some old sourdough trapped on the salt flats; but don't plan to do that, Hutch—I couldn't stand to watch."

"Who says you're going to outlast me?"

"The handprints of Fate again—don't forget my forebears: Mother's still living at a thousand years old."

Hutch said "She's eighty-three."

"And looks a lot older than a redwood thicket."

"That's because she's chain-smoked unfiltered Camels since before Walter Raleigh brought the blond weed to white folks."

Straw said "Exactly. If she's eighty-three under all that tobacco tar, then I'm bound to last till a hundred at least."

Hutch's voice was little more than a whisper. "Take me in then. Otherwise I'll croak in a nursing home."

"Oh no, not me; hire yourself a trained nurse. Cranky as you are, set in your ways—I won't come near you. You had your chance."

"At what?"

Straw faced Hutch and, simply by thinking back, produced a strong live trace of the power of his young face and eyes—the boy he'd been. "Your final chance at young Strawson Stuart. He's beyond reach today." The power held on, at a high hot burn.

For an instant Hutch looked and saw Straw was right. It felt like an immense hot loss and worthy of grief. But he said "Look, if you're in touch with that fine boy still, give him bountiful thanks from an antique friend."

Slowly Straw let his present face return. "He accepts all gifts with shameless gratitude." In his chair Straw bowed from the waist toward Hutch.

Hutch had just seen Emily and Ann top the rise in the road to his right. They were each walking with five-foot sticks like shepherds in an old Bible engraving. Hutch pointed to them. "Lo, Ruth and Naomi come leading the herd."

Straw said "Thank Christ. You be good to yours. Emily Stuart may be a Methodist missionary, but she's saved me from drowning more times than I know." Straw waved broadly to the distant women.

They seemed not to see him, but still they came on.

11

In fact Ann had seen both men as soon as she and Emily topped the rise; and for a bad moment, she felt the chill of abandonment she'd always felt at the sight of Hutch and Straw together. Till now she'd put off asking again the question she'd asked in her letters to Emily—the second letter had never been acknowledged—so these few yards of distance would be Ann's last chance to ask for help again. She said "Do you think Straw's spoken to Hutch?"

At first Emily was honestly puzzled and creased her brow.

"About me, Em—asking Hutch to let me share in this, just a rightful share."

Emily said "Ann, I feel awful about this; but I need to tell you the local facts. When you first wrote me, I spoke to Strawson; all he did was turn his back and head down to Mr. Walters' house. So I can't say more. See, I promised myself to give up mingling in Hutch and Strawson's business, oh, twenty-five years ago. It had truly eaten me up by the day, just knowing how fully they'd shared each other before I came into Strawson's life. I finally had to step back and ease off or die."

"Can you give me the directions for *how* to ease up?"

"You've made your break."

Ann said "Making a break and changing your mind—the whole way you think—are two different things."

Emily said "But I did it." Her face was as firm and self-confident as a young reliable terrier's.

Again Ann wanted to press for more than she knew. She'd never learned the entire story of Hutch and Straw and had never asked. But she'd somehow known from the start not to seek possession of facts and mental images she couldn't use or live beside. And here with Emily walking so near, with what Em implied was available knowledge, Ann told herself *Stop her right here, girl. Spare your mind.* So she said "Don't worry yourself a moment. I'll find a way to speak to Straw, or I'll phone him from Durham."

"Strawson won't support you—you're bound to know that."

With those words, Emily's face changed again in a way Ann had never seen till now—an almost scary intensity that looked like something you'd glimpse at the scene of a bloody collision and turn from at once. Ann said "I honor Straw's loyalty to Hutch. If Hutch doesn't see his own way to decency, the next few days, I'll have to ask Wade himself to speak up."

The glare in Emily's face hadn't dimmed, but her hand moved over the gap between their moving bodies and took Ann's fingers. "Don't tear that pitiful boy any worse than he's torn already. He's plowed up my heart—I've loved him too—so I know he's ruined yours."

In all the years Ann had known Emily Stuart, she'd never had one firm word of warning from her; and the sudden freshness of this demand cut all the deeper. Ann couldn't face Emily's eyes, here and now; but as they reached the mouth of the drive and turned toward the house, Ann said "I thank you for taking me seriously."

Emily said "I guess that's my worst failing—seriousness. Strawson says I treat the damned birds in the *trees* like they were angels of God."

Ann said "Which they are." And in the sudden relief they felt—near as they were to Straw and Hutch, still there on the porch—both women laughed.

12

HUTCH and Straw had to wake Wade up to get him to the car. He sat up, fairly alert on the backseat, for the next twenty minutes as Hutch detoured them through the small and moribund town of Fontaine on a mission that Wade had failed to mention but might be glad of. Fontaine was where Hutch's own father's maternal family had lived when they moved off the Kendal land in the 1880s. The boxy two-story white frame house where they'd stayed for so long was still upright on its ample lot by the train depot at the north end of town—the actual roof and walls from which his grandmother Eva had eloped on a warm spring night ninety years ago with Forrest Mayfield, where Eva's mother had drunk lye and died in agony on the kitchen floor, where Rob had spent his peaceful but longing childhood and where he'd brought the infant Hutch when Rachel died.

The depot was long since abandoned by trains, to be rescued ten years ago as a play-and-hobby center for the old and idle. But the Kendal house was barely fazed by its new coats of paint—a glossy blue-white with firetruck-red window frames and the plaster statue of a Mexican boy with a wide sombrero and a balky donkey near the stones of a walkway that still bore all the Kendals' initials and every Mayfield's who'd ever lived there.

Hutch paused at the curb and leaned to look past Ann. The house and its old trees could still move him strongly, in the right circumstances; but now it might as well have been foreign—a small dead factory.

Wade's head turned too, for what that was worth. He recognized the air of the place but couldn't really see more than shadows.

Ann said "Who painted the window frames red?"

Hutch said "The lawyer's wife, I guess." A Pennsylvania civil rights lawyer had bought the house back in the seventies once Eva died and, however tasteless, had kept it up.

Ann said "I like it—especially the windows: a nice whorehouse touch, might wake the town up. And the sculptural ornaments are equally welcome." She was honestly trying for pleasantry.

Wade quietly said "What ornaments please?"

Ann suddenly found she could barely speak.

So Hutch said "A Mexican midget and his burro." The yard behind the sculpture was cluttered with some child's toys—a yellow tricycle and numerous pieces of bright equipment: a stroller, a playpen. The lawyer and his wife had never had children; whose could they be? But then Hutch recalled a possibility. "Maybe they've adopted a Chinese girl. The wife told me she'd been thinking that over, a year ago. You can rescue unwanted Chinese girls from death now, easy—there's a place in Seattle makes all the arrangements, door-to-door."

Wade nodded once as if any news about this house, with its outlandish weight of memory, had long since lost the power to shock. In another moment, before Hutch faced the road again and drove them off, Wade drew his legs up tight to his chest, bent himself together and lay on the seat.

BEFORE they were on the main highway, Ann had reached back and spread the two light cotton blankets up to Wade's shoulders—he was already gone.

And his deep-drowned sleep lasted through the first three-fourths of the trip home. So Ann and Hutch had a further reason to ride in silence, speaking only at curious sights by the road—a palmist's sign saying *Mother Mindy's Mysteries*, three black children driving a mule and wagon so decrepit it looked like a natural object, not made by hands; and an early moon that was literally gold.

But when they were twenty miles from Durham in the full spring night, Wade suddenly spoke in his old normal voice. "I told Grainger where to strow my ashes—they won't amount to much, just three handsful."

Too quickly, Hutch tried for levity. "I heard we amount to three *quarts* of ashes. Don't sell yourself short."

Wade said "You heard wrong again; I *know*—I've scattered more than one friend these last few years. Anyhow, old Grainger will show you the resting place, when it's time." Wade waited a long time and then said "Rest," like a long-sought name that had dawned at last.

Ann looked to the side of Hutch's face. It was the first time she'd watched him challenged for a sizable response since she left their house. *You answer him. Now.*

Hutch laughed and glanced back to Wade. "You better draw a good map and file it with me; you're going to outlast Grainger by years."

If Wade heard that, he didn't speak again.

And when Ann looked back a minute later, Wade seemed plunged again into sleep like a river too swift to touch. She got to her knees in the passenger seat and reached to his forehead. It was burning hot and his hair was drenched with an oily sweat. She adjusted his blankets, then faced forward. "He's got a fever, Hutch."

"I know. I could feel it when we laid him down."

"Then we should head straight for the hospital now." Ann hadn't delivered that strong an opinion since Wade's return.

Hutch said "No, we'll go home and check. If Wade's really feverish, I'll call Dr. Ives."

In that short time Wade's breathing had gone from quiet to grating, slow but painful to hear.

Ann lowered her voice. "You know he's had pneumonia once already?"

Hutch said "In early March—he's told me the grim details several

times. I doubt this is it. We've taken all the preventive measures." But
Hutch did silently recall the times Wade would claim to be too exhausted
for his inhalation treatment.

They continued in silence till they got to the bottom of Hutch's drive.
It had been a long time, nearly four decades, since they'd been this sad
and thwarted in one another's presence; and that had been over the
transatlantic phone lines when Hutch learned Ann had aborted the child
they conceived at Christmas in Rome during his first year abroad. They
understood tonight that the fact of their separate nearness in the car, with
their sick child behind them, was increasing the pain—a pain neither
one of them could touch, much less banish. And though they literally
hadn't touched for nearly a year, Hutch took his right hand off the wheel
and laid it on the seat between him and Ann.

Ann waited a moment, not denying the offer but meaning to brace
her feelings first and not think ahead. *No further than here.* Then she
laid her left hand above Hutch's and kept it there till they stopped at the
side door of the house.

Odd as it felt after celibate months; and in this space with a dying
man, Hutch was stirred in a way he'd only known in dreams the past
year—his cock still blindly faithful after so long, such gain and loss. Sad
as he was, he almost grinned to think it might moan aloud any instant;
it had been friendless so long.

Ann was still faced forward, unsure of how she could manage to turn
and meet Hutch's eyes.

But he turned and saw her clean profile, her finest side always. Only
just lately the edge of her jaw had begun to loosen; that and the slightly
hooded eyelids were all the genuine change Hutch could see. Finally he
could tell her "It's meant a good deal, having you along today."

That brought on her tears, the few quiet tears Ann could ever shed.
And they came always for someone else's authentic trouble, never for her
own—Hutch's feelings had always shown themselves more freely than
Ann could manage. She dried the tears with her one free hand and finally
turned to Hutch.

His eyes looked worse than Wade's, already somehow bereft of his
whole world and as far past reach as any lost astronaut.

Ann had never for an instant thought Hutch could come to this.

She'd never seen him break; he was plainly close to breaking. She pressed his hand lightly once, then left her own in place above it. "I'll be with you both, anytime you say."

"Then why did you leave us?"

"I left *you*, Hutchins. No way I could stay." Ann waited, then whispered "Let's don't start this again, not here tonight."

Hutch whispered too. "No, tell me why you'd want to come back."

"You're what I've got."

"Me? Or Wade and me?"

Ann said "Both of you. Or either one."

"Come back for good, you mean?"

"I'm an old woman, Hutch; but I'm not on trial nor volunteering for a polygraph test. I'm offering the little I've got to give; please take it or leave it."

So Hutch left his hand on the seat under hers and shut his eyes a moment. "Let's see if we can get this boy indoors. If not, I'll call somebody for help."

But the two of them managed it; Wade was that nearly weightless and easy to help, though every atom of his body hurt—one more fact he kept to himself.

13

WADE was running only three degrees of fever when they laid him down; and though he was still in the curious daze he'd moved in through the entire day, Wade told Hutch and Ann, who were by his bed, "Nobody's calling a doctor tonight. I'm just worn out. Go cook your supper and bang some pans—it'll cool me down, just to hear you in the kitchen."

While neither Hutch nor Ann had thought they were hungry, they obeyed Wade's instructions, cooked a mushroom omelet and ate every morsel with Ann's fresh soda bread and a glass of wine. When their plates were empty, it was past ten o'clock; and they each felt nearly as tired as Wade.

Ann glanced to her sensible big-number watch and said "You tell me what to do next." When Hutch looked quizzical, she said "Do you need me here tonight? If so I'll run home and get a few clothes."

Home, she says—meaning St. Mary's Road, eight miles from here. What needed Ann here and now was Hutch's body, beat as it was, and his mind that had starved itself for so long of any assurance that his skin and bones were welcome in someone else's life. But he couldn't ask to feed off Ann tonight, not in these straits, unless she flagged a similar need. *Has she stayed as dumbly faithful as me? No sign she hasn't.* Hutch sat there beside her another half minute, but all he could sense from Ann was exhaustion. He ringed her wrist with his hand. "Go rest in your own bed. Let's talk tomorrow."

She was mildly relieved that he'd made the choice, for now at least. Much as she needed to stay near her son, she knew what a thicket of choices would follow—to spend the rest of her daily life near Hutch Mayfield, or another agonized disengagement and a gypsy move to smaller quarters. "You'll call me if Wade takes a turn for the worst?"

Hutch agreed. "The minute he's worse but I doubt he'll get worse tonight somehow. The trip was just hard, seeing weird old Grainger and the house Wade loved so much as a boy." Hutch stood and gathered their few dishes.

So Ann rose too. "Does it feel like I'm asking to come back for good?"

Hutch couldn't quite face her; he rinsed a plate. "*I* never went anywhere, Ann—swear to God. I've just never been the world's most *present* man. You may well remember, I don't turn up—not fully armed—till most bystanders have given up and gone. But I somehow thought, anybody who waited, would somehow collect on his or her patience—I'd have some feeling or fact ripe to give." At last he turned with one hand raised to back his oath, his strong right hand, as if it were proof that even as close a witness as he could still drift farther off than most lone voyagers and could only signal *Farewell* or *Save me*, knowing both were useless.

"Oh Hutch, you *went*—you're out there now, on your fragile wings, insisting on bearing all the weight of a death that's at least half mine. I made that child, with this same body you're looking at here." She had the grace not to touch her own body; it stood for itself.

Hutch knew she was right. Distance was his oldest instinct, seizing what looked like the full brunt of something—death, love, failure, abandonment—then winging off with it for lone decades of slow ingestion, concoction, assimilation, then a guaranteed (if long overdue) return. He sometimes thought the tendency came from the enormous fact of his mother's death the day he was born and the ensuing fact that his lovable destitute father quickly became more nearly a son than a father to Hutch. For the first time, in his memory at least, he told Ann now "I've borne the weight till today, yes ma'm. Let's talk tomorrow. Maybe we can shift the load."

Ann agreed. "Good night." She was already moving to check Wade's room and drive home alone.

Wade's light was still out and his breathing was maybe more regular. So Ann went on.

14

But it was pneumonia, the parasitic swamping of the lungs so common to this plague and so often lethal. Hutch had waked on his own at three in the morning, dreading the duty to check on Wade and maybe find him worse than before. But Hutch rose finally and went to Wade's doorway. At first the slow breaths sounded normal, but Hutch went on in and leaned to feel the boy's hair.

It was soaked and snaky, the pillow beneath Wade was drenched, his chest and sheets were sopping wet with the desperate effort to break a fever that only descends on very young children or dying adults. When Hutch took a step to find the thermometer, Wade sang " *'Old Paint, I'm a-leaving Cheyenne.'* "

"Did I wake you up?"

"Oh no, I've been swimming laps for an hour in this cold bed." Wade gave a hard shudder as a chill wrenched through him.

Still in the dark, Hutch sat on the edge of the mattress and felt the forehead again. Surprisingly cool, if this was fever—maybe the bedtime aspirin had finally broken the heat. *Some minor bug surely.*

But Wade said "Hutch, this is pneumocystis."

"You're breathing easy—"

"I recognize the thing I've got, my lungs are filling, it's only just starting."

Hutch could hear a trace of burr on the voice—the distant warning of a real death rattle from deep in Wade's lungs. "Then I'll call Dr. Ives." Hutch stood to go to the kitchen phone.

"Wait, Father—I don't plan to fight this again." Wade hadn't called Hutch *Father* more than twice in the past decade.

"The hell we won't fight it." Hutch went to the door. Any minute or second he could add to Wade's life was a monumental gain.

But Wade found strength to give what was almost a bellow of rage in the silent house—rage to do his own will this instant, to let death in and bend to its power. When Hutch turned to face him, Wade said "We're riding this through, or out or whatever, under this roof. You, Mother and me. Please help me *go*."

Hutch came back, sat and stroked the damp brow. "You'll let me call Dr. Ives at least?"

Wade shook his head ferociously.

"Then you're asking us to watch you drown with our hands tied."

Wade said "That well may be. Many parents have done it, from the edge of the pool." He took a long wait, then managed to laugh, then coughed convulsively. At last he could whisper "How crazy is that?"

"Not crazy at all. It's *cruel* as hell." Hutch had almost whispered it; but once it was said, he wanted it back. *Any parent's volunteered for this. Stand and take your punishment.*

Before Hutch could speak again, Wade said "Cruel? To you and Ann? It's no big moonlight hayride for *me*."

"Look, Son, the hospital's ten minutes away. We'll put on your robe, I'll call Margaret Ives, she'll tell us where to go, they've got the right drugs and the oxygen."

Wade's hand fumbled up and found Hutch's mouth, trying to mute it. "Promise me?"

"Yes. Wait—promise you what?"

"—That you and Ann won't keep me alive when it stops being me."

"How will I know that?"

"Say *we*—you and Ann. Ann Gatlin's my mother."

Hutch said "Ann *Mayfield*—don't forget we're legal still. But all right, how'll we know when you're ready?"

"I'll either tell you or—didn't you used to pray every year or so? Try that again maybe; ask God or somebody in his line of work."

Wade's skin still felt strangely cool to the hand, but he was plainly skirting delirium. Hutch leaned to speak clearly. "Let me be sure I understand you. You're willing to go to the hospital, aren't you?"

Wade shut his eyes and slowly agreed, barely moving his head.

Hutch accepted the signal and switched on the dim lamp.

The skin of Wade's face and neck was purplish; his eyes were wide but fixed on a far point—the eyes of some sky god hacked out of granite five thousand years back but fulminant still.

At the edge of the commanding gaze, Hutch could say only "I make you that promise, I'm sure Ann will, we won't hang on when you give the sign." Though Hutch knew it was only the simplest humane good sense, he'd have made the vow to nobody else, alive or dead. But what else can you say to your own crushed child who begs to die? Hutch pressed the switch that slowly raised the head of Wade's bed till the boy was half upright. As it rose, Wade's face—even with the eyes shut—looked like some corpse, long sunk in peace but dragged back to life and mindlessly tortured.

Wade said "Make your plans before I start howling." By now, he couldn't have howled in a firestorm; his wind was that scarce.

Hutch went toward the kitchen to make the two calls—the doctor and Ann. He'd rather have called in nuclear ruin on the entire American continent at sunrise.

15

ON the fourth day in Duke Hospital, Wade took a sharp fast turn for the worse. He was mostly unconscious or, when he woke for snatches, he was wildly reeling through scraps of lunacy and terror. His lungs were chocked with microscopic creatures, drinking his life; and a rank web of tubes brought him full-time oxygen, drugs and nourishment. Hutch and Ann visited several times a day and stood alone or together by the bed to watch the course of a war they couldn't speed or hinder. They saw Dr. Ives at least once in the course of each day or night. Her reliable warmth and her pale clear eyes seemed a kind of outrage in the rackety life of a huge hospital, a place that was less a refuge than a nonstop foundry steeped in gloom and producing at contradictory rates of urgency and torpor some mysterious artifact, never shown to humans.

But with all her sympathy and ungrudging words, Dr. Ives never gave them an atom of excess hope for time or rescue. The nearest she came to a firm prognosis was to face them both in the hall outside and say "You might want to think about last arrangements. Wade could go any minute or fight his way back for a few weeks or months." This crisis was simply uncallable—Wade was drastically weak before it started. His kidneys and liver had suffered from the two years of toxic drugs; they were functioning far below par now and could fail at a moment's notice.

All that Dr. Ives would allude to, by way of a future, was that, when she asked Wade if he'd made a living will with his plain intentions should he lose all consciousness, he'd only smiled and said "I somehow doubt this is curtains. Don't order the coffin unless they're on sale." And she'd added that, over the past decade, AIDS patients had taught her something she'd never quite trusted before—within certain limits an adult, even a very young child, can choose the day, sometimes the instant, to let death in. Her sense was that Wade was gearing up to make that choice.

Both Ann and Hutch thanked her, silently acknowledging that almost no male American physician—skittish as they were at the risk of error—would have made that considerate a prediction.

THE night of the fourth day, Hutch had stayed well past the legal nine o'clock in the chair near Wade, in reach of his shoulder, though the boy hadn't spoken since midafternoon. And Hutch left only when the splendid young black nurse named Hannah Bertram convinced him again that he'd be no good to Wade or anyone if he didn't go home and try to rest— she'd call him if anything changed either way. As always before he left

Wade's side, Hutch bent and kissed the boy's tall brow. It was so dry and thin-skinned that it felt like actual bone to normal lips. On the chance that a single cell in Wade's mind was still keeping watch, Hutch said "I'm going no farther than the telephone. Keep resting, Son; I'll be here when you need me."

In his trance, Wade heard that. He thought *No, nobody's ever been near, not when I'm truly needy.* Drugged as he was, it was almost the truth; but even when he heard Hutch turn to leave, Wade kept his own counsel, a handsbreadth from death, still refusing to yield. *Why? Why not now?*

16

BACK home Hutch had drunk two ounces of scotch and watched the news on television—the daily butcher's bill of children shot at random and beat by their kin, women raped by strangers or close relations, dead human fetuses paraded in priests' arms past abortion clinics, men burned for their race or their choice of partner, women pounded to pulp by mates or sons. In its muffled horror, a daily dose of such meaningless leering had come to be oddly calming for Hutch—like an evening spent at a knockout production of some fifth-rate Jacobean tragedy: a feast of cadavers in velvets and lace, their chalky faces specked with the ulcers of syphilis. But toward the end of this night's news, tucked in before the zany sportscaster, came the story of a young Chapel Hill man—known to be in the early stages of AIDS—who'd burned himself, his bedridden mother, the collie dog and their gnomish bungalow all to the ground just this past morning.

It was so god-awful, if Hutch hadn't felt exhausted, he'd have laughed. As it was, when he rose to switch off the set, a clear thought pierced up through his mind like an iron spike. *Wade dies tonight.* It felt as true as any thought he'd had since childhood. Hutch stood in place, letting the shock drain off through half a minute. Then he thought *Thank God*—thank God for Wade's sake, his own sake and Ann's. Hutch felt the dazed but spacious relief he'd felt at the sight of his own father's death—*Thank Christ he's gone.* Should he drive back and sit out the night beside Wade's bed or wait here for Hannah's call near morning? *Wait here and lie down anyhow.*

Before Hutch took the first step toward his bedroom, his mind brought up a whole second thought. For the first time since they'd hauled Wade's papers down from New York, he recalled the big box and the record book that Ivory had kept in the kitchen. Far as Hutch knew, they still lay shut on the floor of Wade's closet. *Do I open them now?* What would the need be? Any will or notes about last wishes could wait till the end. But it came to Hutch powerfully, tired as he was, that there might be something in the sizable box which would clear a final block between them while Wade was still breathing—some possible light on Wyatt Bondurant, Wyatt's hatred of Hutch; or some slight clue to the unknown life that Wade concealed in the midst of all those years when Hutch and Ann had hardly seen him.

To break the seal on that box now, with Wade alive, could only be right if Hutch really hoped that the boy would last through a stretch of sane days for healing the years of silence between them—if Hutch and his son's old laughing ease could someway return. *I beg for that, yes.*

17

IT was two in the morning before Hutch had gone through all the papers. Either Wade was a neater man than the pack rat child he'd been, or he'd weeded these papers in recent months, or someone else had weeded them for him. There were none of the pointless souvenirs that litter most drawers—receipts, matchbooks, hazy snapshots of vague and inexplicably grinning strangers. Every letter that Hutch could recall sending Wade seemed to be here, a thick handful of letters from Ann; early letters from Hutch's grandmother Eva, from family friends like Polly Drewry and Alice Matthews, Strawson and Grainger. There was even a diary Wade had kept in his first stay at summer camp at the age of ten, a detailed record of thirty days that still had the power to summon a taste of the hopeless misery of a homesick child—a misery Wade had never confessed.

There was nothing from his college days and little in writing to represent his early years in New York. There was, though, an unsealed envelope of photographs of young men, all in various stages of undress and many of them naked, all taken in rooms Hutch was almost sure he could recognize as Wade's—Wade's first small apartment on Bleecker Street and Seventh Avenue, above a Greek nightclub. The faces, white and black, were strangers to Hutch; but none of the dozen-odd photographs had the musky thrusting air of real pornography. Most of the men had the startled and slightly bruised air common to undressed Americans, a people not quite at ease in their skin—surely no Mediterranean poise in the body's frank grandeur or the perky indifference of Amazon tribes who wear their genitals matter-of-factly as household implements, handy conveniences. The single other shared quality that Hutch could see in the photographs was a high proportion of striking faces and cared-for bodies, the equal of a swarm of lesser classical heroes or minor gods. *Wade told the class he'd slept with only two men. Maybe these are Wyatt's. But did Wyatt know Wade in the Bleecker Street days?*

What held Hutch longest were the letters from Wyatt. Hutch hadn't realized till tonight that the two men had been separated so often, but each had occasionally traveled in his work (Wyatt was a book designer at Pantheon), and a thick run of letters survived from their weeks and days apart through the years together. Like most modern letters, Wade's and Wyatt's mainly amounted to less than the average long-distance phone call—some quick reminder of a bill to be paid, a line of greeting on a birthday or an anniversary apart, a joke overheard or some cryptic direction like *Act your own way; do what tastes true.*

There was one long letter in Wyatt's imposing and impetuous hand in dark brown ink, pages that looked like credible news from a general pausing in the midst of battle to scrawl a command—say, Stonewall Jackson at Chancellorsville or Shaka Zulu in full lion skin. It amounted to a scorching self-justification, written in late 1984 from the opposite end of the two men's apartment, at what seemed the first big impasse they'd reached. The final sentences were only the starkest from a blistering sequence.

Wade, If you think I've agreed to go on being the sweeper-up of the dry little turds from your meager past while you glide on with an appetite at least the equal of a starved hyena's, you've got less mind than even I

thought you had. I burn my push broom, here and now. Scour up your
own shit or pack your boxes, clear out of my place and leave your key in
the vase by the door. I want you to stay but not like this—not another
day, not to mention a night.

And like the long-unsuspected Rosetta stone of Wade's estrangement
from his parents, there was one last incendiary letter, separate from the
others, at the bottom of the box. It was dated *New Year's Eve 1985*; and
even before Hutch read a word further, he knew that the letter was written
at the end of Wyatt's only visit to Durham with Wade.

They'd come down on December 27th to spend a week. Hutch and
Ann had met Wyatt several times at dinner in New York; and those hours
had seemed to go smoothly enough, though Wyatt said little and smiled
to himself too often for comfort. But in Durham suddenly on the morning
of New Year's Eve, Wade had walked into the kitchen to say that Wyatt
was having to leave unexpectedly. Hutch and Ann wondered at the time
if Wyatt had somehow taken offense—they'd spent the previous day at
Strawson's with a visit to Grainger's—but Wade said "No, Wyatt has
family duties." And Wyatt himself departed with thin smiles and thanks
for all. When Wade left a few days later, on January 4th, it marked the
end of his last really natural meeting with his parents till eight years later
when he came home dying. The interim meetings had sooner or later
turned skittish or silent. And neither Hutch nor Ann had ever seen Wyatt
again, not face-to-face.

The relevant letter still smoked on the page.

Wade,

You know I didn't want to come along on that scenic voyage through
upper Dixie, but you said you'd run interference with the Klan, the Caro-
lina Nazis etc. and I trusted you. What I didn't guess, and it's partly my
fault (I'm old enough to know when a road's booby-trapped), was that the
real roadblock would be your lovely family.

The times we'd met them here in the city, I thought they seemed a
little brittle and a little more seedy by the month. But I didn't plan to
feel like I did from the hour I entered that handsome house in the piney

woods—like the field hand buck that had ravished their darling, kinked his hair, inflated his cock and rinsed his brain in indigo till all he could want was The Negro Organ of Generation and Wyatt Bondurant's grinning eyes with the white teeth above it.

I know you think I'm criminally wrong or ridiculously off track anyhow. I can see your mother and father have never done a deed that they'd call impolite, not to mention cruel. I can see what's lovable and likable about them—they look good, smell good, talk smart and funny, and roll with the punches life throws their way. I can imagine they sit down Sundays in some well-furnished church—Episcopal, I bet—and come out thinking they stand a fair chance of eternal life near God in Glory, a dignified Paradise with no voice raised and loyal colored washerwomen for the white satin robes.

My mother, as you know, believes the same nonsense—especially since we moved her to Sea Cliff, that crumbling beachhead of the old Anglo lower middle class. But I bet you all of my life's possessions that, come Judgment Day—if Judgment comes—my mother winds up in an eighteen-karat martyr's crown being fanned by coal-black pickaninny cherubs while your two progenitors are rushed up against a concrete wall by blazing archangels and mowed to a pulp with whatever brand of automatic weapon the angels are issued for simple justice.

That doesn't mean that I qualify as a justice agent on Earth for now, and it does not mean what I know you'll say—that I see racists in every skin that's not beige-to-black. What I realized it meant last night, when we got back from that drive to the country to see poor old Mr. Grainger Walters, was that any people who could use ninety-some years of one man's life like it was a substance they could wear to protect their hands and eyes from the winter wind—and him a frail man that's your father's cousin, and yours as well, and that your family's turned into a tame crippled monkey in a dry little shed you threw up around him, a shed that's really nothing but his last cage in a century of cages— well, what it told me was Wyatt Bondurant, you are out of your element. Swim fast for the shallows.

I know I've got every fault on Earth myself, in triplicate flaming letters on the sky. I know I've asked you to live beside me and put up with it. I know we spent our adult time, before we met, living lives that my dear

ignorant mother would think lead to ruin, if she knew the facts. I know
we've already done together more than a few things that every Gallup poll
says most Christians abominate (many Jews and Muslims thrown in)—
not just with our bodies attached to each other.

You know what other act I mean and its coming result that I still
dread for my sister's sake—she's paid too much already for her life.

But I want you. From here on out. I want you free of that courteous
Murder Incorporated you grew up in and that's round your feet this very
minute like a pet anaconda crushing you to ooze as you sit reading in
their tasteful rooms. Get out while you can and come back, come home
to me. At least I love you and tell you the truth.

                    Till I see you here, or whether I see you
                         again or not, I'm nothing but
                    Take-Him-or-Leave-Him Wyatt

When he'd read through it twice, Hutch knew his first response was
right—again a focused sense of elation that boiled up through him. He'd
been found out, in one of the vital cores of his life, for the first full time
by a watchful witness other than Ann. Hutch had always known that, if
the universe was just, his and his loved ones' chances of escaping execution
in the first round of burnings were virtually nil. His sense of the appalling
poison of slavery—a freezing poison that had no antidote, in his own life,
his family's fate, and the whole nation's ruin—had been born in Hutch
and had only grown. He saw, as plainly as he saw the oak floor, the
unstemmable progress of the spreading stain of human chattel on his
home country through nearly four centuries and its outward seepage now
through the nation and the world beyond. And here in Wade's enormous
pain and Hutch's powerlessness to ease it, here surely at last was the
measured stroke of vengeance—a vengeance delivered far too late to teach
or mend.

What it came to of course was unthinkably simple. An entire people
from a vast continent had been seized by the millions, abducted, molested,
raped in every conceivable posture and forced to tend the fruit of those
unions or watch them sold into still crueler hands, worked under torture,
then freed in a cataclysmic war to live abandoned—in fact, *abandoned*—

by master and righteous liberator through all the years since. So while a great earth-movement of freedom had lifted millions in the past thirty years, hundreds of thousands of unmoved, unreached but justified sons of those dead slaves were foraging still in tight bands of vengeance, exacting their due and the unpaid loans of an impatient fate from generations that were undreamt of when the first black Africans strode in chains onto these mild shores, their endless exile.

Recalling the conversation with his seminar back in April, Hutch knew his conviction was hardly fresh—it was, spoken or not, the central theme of American life, its history and literature for nearly four centuries with no sign of flagging. Even the wound from the systematic slaughter of millions of native Indians had begun to heal almost everywhere except on the stunned reservations themselves. But the force that endured as the legacy of slavery, in every city and town tonight, had swelled to a din still unsuspected in the books and visions of older prophets who'd barely seen beyond their own moment, from John Brown and Lincoln to Faulkner and Baldwin. A whole irresistible limb of one strong race— a matchless arm, say—was moving now like a gleaming scythe to level the rows of the guilty, the great-grandchildren of the guilty, and the pure newborn.

Hutch also knew that all he'd managed to do about the horror and its constant survivals in his own existence and his family relations was pitifully small—a trim set of fairly consistent kind acts, more decorous than lasting, and a steady effort at trying to understand all the minds involved: the male and female overlords' minds, the male and female slaves and their present heirs, a single mind like Grainger Walters' or half-crazed Wyatt's or Wade's sacrifice to the wrongs of his kin or Hutch's own mind that had grown its callus early and accepted the service of a part-black kinsman who nonetheless lived in exposed solitude.

Hutch's whole life then amounted to long years of quiet assent to the most colossal act of theft and murder in human history—assent by Hutch and, again, all he'd loved except maybe Wade. But in sixty-three years of Hutch's life no one but Wyatt had pointed toward that lasting assent and called its name, an unstopped crime.

For the first time ever—with Wyatt's dead unanswerable voice aimed level at Hutch in the empty house this late spring night, and the wreckage of his son's life strewn round his feet—the chance that poor Strawson had also been right bore in on Hutch as another giant failure. *"I loved you, Hutchins. Have you lost that? I'd have spent my whole life bearing your weight, if you'd said the word."*

Hutch had leaned instead on a woman strong enough to bear six men for however long their lives might take—no, he'd never leaned; that had been half the trouble. Ann had asked for burdens that he'd never give her. Had he truly borne, in childhood, too much of his father's pain to volunteer for much of a burden from anyone else? Could he somehow have managed full trust in Straw or another man, the kind of trust he'd placed on their bodies forty years back? Wade and Wyatt plainly managed it; it killed them both. But that was the outcome of nothing more fatal than the accidental convergence of time with one especially crafty virus, no condemnation of their human bent or choice. Hutch and Ann had likewise ended each other's lives—at least their chances of usable nearness, a merciful contingency of care and trust—for now and maybe from here on out.

Hutch had worked through that to the point of realizing how entirely, with a son dying four miles away, he'd spent half a night confronting himself in one more looking glass, clearer than most he'd faced till tonight. *But there's nothing else I can do for Wade; Wade's gone past me into some new world I've never known—total silence or punishment or unthinkable reward.* The thought gave Hutch no pain or ease; he was exhausted and ready to sleep.

The phone rang; it was three in the morning.

Wade had grown so strong in Hutch's mind as he read through the box that, at first, he didn't think of Hannah Bertram's promise to call with any trouble. When he answered though, it was her unruffled voice.

"Mr. Mayfield, Wade is asking for you."

By reflex Hutch said "I'll be right there." Then he needed to know. "Is he any worse off?"

"His signs have been pretty steady right along, but frankly he's been very troubled since midnight and calling for you."

Hutch said "You could have called me sooner," then regretted his haste. Before Hannah could defend her choice, Hutch said "I'm sorry. You're the person in charge."

Hannah said "All right." Then she paused. "Mr. Mayfield, Hannah is not in charge of this, nobody else either—not on this Earth. You come on soon or send somebody to ease Wade down." Young as she was, her voice had the weight of a qualified judge's bleak instructions.

Her gravity let Hutch ask a last question. "Will he make it till morning?"

Hannah said "I wish I could promise you Yes; but like I told you, I'm not the Lord." For that last moment, she sounded no older than ten or twelve—very nearly the Lord but a year or too short.

When he'd hung up, Hutch thought next of Ann. Should he call and tell Ann to meet him there? Maybe she'd left some request of her own with a nurse or doctor. *What Hannah said was, 'Wade's asking for you.' Go on by yourself. If he's asked for his mother too, she'll come on her own.*

Hutch left the box of papers on his desk and went to his bedroom to find the keys. Beside them on the bureau was a framed photograph of Wade and Grainger in the woods back of Straw's, a small bright clearing. Wade was maybe five years old, though going on fifty with his bright-eyed somber look at the lens—eyes that were all but blazingly wide and penetrating. Grainger was already seated on a stump but in full daylight and not yet eighty; he faced whatever stood outside the frame—away from Wade and Hutch himself, who'd snap the shutter.

For an instant the picture felt like a thing Hutch should burn on the spot; its chance of giving future pain seemed too great a threat. Hutch opened the back of the frame, slid the picture out, almost ripped it longways before he stopped and—still not studying it again—brought its blank side up to his lips and touched it. Then he went toward his car, not pausing to lock the house behind him.

18

SINCE his own father's death in a small county clinic, Hutch had dreaded every visit to any hospital. In fact he'd often shirked the visits he owed colleagues or family friends—the dingy carbolic air that signals untreatable germs in every breath, the raking white glare of inhuman light from overhead tubes, the glimpses through open doors of bald distress or the unextinguished hope in eyes that are plainly hopeless. But late as it was, Hutch got through the lobby, up the room-sized elevator and down Wade's hallway without the sight of another live soul. Wade's door was shut; Hutch pushed inward.

The air was pitch-dark, and the only sound was a high hiss of oxygen flowing into Wade.

Hutch paused on the doorsill, looking behind him for Hannah Bertram or anyone sane. But no one appeared; he stepped in and shut the door behind him.

No sign of life from Wade.

Hutch stood in the dark till his own eyes opened as far as they could. Gradually through the single window there came enough starlight to show the bed and a humped covered body. Hutch all but whispered "Son?"

And at once Wade's clogged voice said "I'm dreaming."

Hutch said "Don't stop." He could just see his way to the bedside straight chair. When he'd sat there silent for two long minutes, Hutch had to say "You're sounding better."

Again Wade answered promptly. "Better than what?"

"Than when I left you earlier tonight."

Wade said "You never left me once." He seemed to chuckle. "That's been half the problem."

Hutch knew not to probe for clarity; the drugs seemed to cast a dense mental haze and then short flicks of keen understanding. "Hannah Bertram said you were calling for me."

"Oh Hannah—Christ, *no*."

"Was she wrong?"

Wade waited a long time. "I said I was dreaming."

"Remember what?"

"Too crazy to tell."

Hutch said "Was I in it?"

"*In* it?—Lord, you wrote, produced, directed, starred, sold tickets and taffy and seated the crowd." Even to Wade, it seemed a phenomenal burst of words to come from struggling lungs; at the end he was seized in a barking cough.

Hutch tried to keep the dream intact. "Glad I drew a crowd—hope I didn't fail to entertain."

Again Wade seemed to have glided away.

So Hutch stayed on in the one easy chair, trying with some success not to think or dwell on what he couldn't change. By four in the morning, he was nearly asleep when Hannah walked in and switched on the light. It brought Hutch awake and onto his feet.

Wade seemed to sleep on.

Hannah's small dark body in its starched white uniform brought with it an excess charge of hope—she looked that capable of healing. First she acknowledged Hutch's presence with a duck of her chin, then went about her tasks in silence—a thermometer into Wade's left ear, his pulse, a blood-pressure sleeve on his broomstick arm, a careful look at the oxygen gauge and the intravenous bags.

Wade still never gave a sign of awareness.

And only when she was ready to leave did Hannah face Hutch and speak in a normal voice. "His fever's down again. You managed to ease him."

"You're kind to say so. He saw me come in, but since then we've hardly spoken."

Hannah said "It doesn't take words, not with most of them. They just want you here."

"You've seen a lot of patients with this?"

"Ten years' worth," Hannah said. She barely looked twenty years old, even here. Then she glanced to see if Wade was sleeping. "Every day I feel like I need to quit. I'd rather crawl naked across an acre of rusty nails." Her eyes plainly meant it.

Hutch said "Oh don't"—he meant *Don't quit us here tonight.*

Hannah said "It's all I know how to do—this and one other thing: nursing burned children and that nearly killed me, eight years on the burn ward. I'm here with you both; no fear about that. You go on and sleep." She gave a slight smile and reached for the door.

Hutch made a sign of wanting to speak with her in the hall.

But as Hannah stepped out and Hutch tried to follow, Wade said "Don't ask that lady my secrets." The oxygen tubes in his nostrils hissed, but they also deepened the pitch of his voice.

Hutch stopped, took Wade's hand and gave a quick laugh. "They're safe from me."

Hannah was gone and the door shut behind her.

Wade said "I dreamed you were pardoning me."

Hutch pressed his fingers lightly on Wade's mouth. "Nothing on Earth to pardon you for."

"You can't be serious."

"I am, absolutely."

Wade shut his eyes. "We tried to *harm* you."

"I volunteered—your family volunteers."

"Not everybody's family, not for this." Wade's two hands indicated the length of his body; it hardly raised the covers.

Hutch had heard stories of sons rejected on their parents' doorsill and infants abandoned with this frightening scourge. He said "That's the least of your worries, Son. I'm a lifelong volunteer; count on that."

Wade's eyes stayed shut but he shook his head No. "I'm trying to get out of this thing clean."

"What thing?"

"My life. You notice I'm dying. I'm meaning to do it on my own." Wade faced Hutch then and started to laugh, but his breath gave out, and in ten seconds he was silent and gaping. Only when he'd drawn in a long gasp of oxygen was he able to laugh again. "I'm making a piss-poor job of bravery, aren't I? I'm about as alone as a bitch in heat."

Hutch had never released the boy's hand. "You're a man strong as any *I've* known. Fight through this skirmish and come on home. We need some time yet."

For the first time in weeks, Wade's eyes seemed to see his father and know him. He strained his head up off the pillow as if to reach him; then he fell back blind. "I doubt I could stand it."

"Son, you don't have to stand a thing. Get through this crisis, I'll take you home, we'll tell some stories and heal some wounds."

Wade's head came up again, well off the pillow; and he clamped down hard on his father's hand. "Pardon me, sir. I need to go on." His face said plainly that by *go* he meant *leave*.

Hutch could only say "Make your own choice."

Wade lay back, shut his eyes, slipped his hand from Hutch's and turned away. It was a long time before he said "Anything left of my lemonade?"

Hutch shook a paper cup on the bed stand—some liquid, no ice. "I'll get you some ice."

"Don't go; help me drink it."

Hutch moved the curved straw to the burned blue lips.

Wade took a long draw of the lemonade and strained to down it. When he turned away again, he said "Nothing wrong with that, nothing a shot of good gin wouldn't cure—gin and bitters."

"You want some gin?" Hutch had seldom known Wade to drink spirits stronger than wine; but if gin would ease him, he'd smuggle some in.

Wade thought through the offer like the final puzzle he'd ever confront. He whispered clearly through a withering smile. "I've wanted six or eight things through the years that history has somehow denied me till now." Then his grin relaxed over half a minute into the strongest afterglow that Hutch had seen since his own father died. Wade fell asleep there.

Or fainted or died. It took a hard minute, but only when Hutch saw Wade's throat draw the first shallow breath could he make himself leave.

19

IT was well past four o'clock in the morning when Hutch reached his car in the hospital parking deck, the scene of sporadic assaults on staff and visitors in recent years. As he opened his car door, Hutch paused to look round him in the expectation—even the chill hope—that some marauder lurked in wait, a creature starved through its whole short life and eager to spring. *Quick death by knife or a merciless beating.* Since Hutch had less than the average masochist's need for damage, the thought was as new as the duties pressed from him by a son who was literally dying of love for a man who'd loathed Hutch and Ann Gatlin with a permanent fury.

There was no one in sight, no sound but occasional cars on the street; and though Hutch knew dawn would break in an hour, he was suddenly swamped by a scary loneliness, an unaccustomed fear of being on his own in the dark. *Who's awake that'll take me in and talk?* The two or three colleagues to whom he'd confided would be deep asleep. He didn't think of trying Ann, and Strawson was more than an hour away; so he cranked the engine, paid his parking fee to a near-albino man who must have weighed four hundred pounds and drove three blocks to Maitland Moses' small apartment in a concrete wilderness of student lodgings. Mait had told Hutch only last week that he woke most mornings at five o'clock to read and write before heading off to the printing shop where he worked a full shift three days a week as a trainee typesetter and general factotum.

Stopped at the curb, Hutch could see Mait's two windows, curtained and black. *He's already left. Or is still asleep. Or somebody's with him.* Though Hutch had never felt drawn to Mait's body, in the next long minute, that third possibility felt intolerable—that Mait was bedded in with a guest, either spent from sex or ready for more. In any case, in the past thirty-odd years, Hutch had never yet tracked a student to his lair for any purpose, much less a home visit in the predawn dark with no business pending. Again he tried to think of a friend who might take him in— no, none of his colleagues, all regular souls, and still not Ann. So he left the car, climbed the outside iron steps to Mait's door and gave two firm knocks—three or four would have felt like begging. *Let him come.*

After an endless twenty seconds, the door cracked open three inches on an eye that might be anyone. It stayed in place, silent.

"Maitland?"

No answer.

"I've got the wrong door. I beg your pardon—"

"Mr. Mayfield?" Slowly the door opened farther. "Are you all right?" Mait was there in boxer shorts, his face still dazed, the skin of his chest and arms white as sheeting.

Against his better judgment, the rags of his pride, it came out of Hutch in a powerful stream. "Excuse me, friend. I need to see someone—" He broke up there; two dry sobs wrenched through his teeth, then a moan.

Mait reached for Hutch's arm, stepped aside and pulled him in.

The small front room was all but totally dark; the air had a mordant smell of rut laid over the usual fug of young-male lodgings—a slightly sour icebox, a mildewed shower, discarded sweatpants and the clean strong chlorine smell of cum. Again Hutch knew he'd bumbled into some first overnight encounter of Mait's (he knew the boy had been on the hunt since graduation); so when Mait bent to switch on a lamp, Hutch whispered "I'm sorry. Go back to your guest. I'm not really sick; I'll be all right." Even then the thought of leaving two postadolescents to root each other on a stale narrow cot felt like a grim expulsion from life, but Hutch moved toward the door.

With unaccustomed force, Mait said "Hey, you woke me up, sir. You owe me two words." The light came on and showed the boy's face again, still fogged with sleep but intent on facing this novelty—an uninvited senior professor, a poet of note, on his doorstep at dawn.

Mait hadn't whispered so Hutch raised his own voice. "Two words? Help - me. Please - sir. *Four* words, sorry."

Mait said "Wade's passed away." Despite the euphemism, his eyes were as certain as if he'd dreamt the whole rest of the day and could foretell its heavy news, this early. Except for his baggy shorts Mait was naked; he suddenly shuddered in the damp air and held himself. "I'll go make some coffee. You sit here and rest." He swept a clutter of books and magazines onto the bilious green shag carpet.

Hutch said "Wade's alive. He may even have passed the crisis one more time. I just came from him; his fever's broken. The nurse called me at three o'clock, said Wade was calling steadily for me, I rushed in and found him fairly clearheaded and breathing better. He and I managed a few sane words before he slept. Then he dropped off, I waited awhile, the nurse told me to go home and rest. But by the time I cranked my car, I felt like a drowned dog and stopped off here to see a human face. I'm all right now; you go back to bed."

But Mait held his ground and shook his head No.

The boy's short body—maybe five foot eight, bare chest, arms, legs— showed a lean compacted promise of competence that ambushed Hutch. In his clothes, Mait had always seemed underpowered; the teenaged doofus. *But none of it's one bit of use to me.* Hutch tasted the acrid stench of that but couldn't unthink it.

Mait pointed again to the empty chair, stepped to the dwarf kitchen behind them and started drawing water for coffee. When Hutch had followed him and sat on a stool, the boy smiled crookedly. "I *do* have company—can you believe it? First time in my life; let's celebrate."

Hutch's first thought was *Some brand of killer,* some guy off the street who'd already pumped the virus into Mait. But he told himself *Steady* and only smiled back.

"I met him last weekend at the new AIDS hospice. I was trying to volunteer a few hours; he's a full-time staffer."

"But he's here this minute?"

"He gets a few nights off, three nights a week and one afternoon." Mait pointed down the hall, the one bedroom. "He's out, like a coma."

Again Hutch felt not exactly robbed but thoroughly sidelined by young men living his old life near him. "I was hoping you could help me with Wade from here on, Mait. He needs young company to break the monotony of me and his mother." It hadn't been a hope till the instant Hutch said it. Though Mait had visited once or twice in the past month, Hutch hadn't called on him for serious help.

Mait said "Absolutely" with the ready surrender and eager loyalty that nobody much past twenty-one can muster.

"Just a couple of hours every two or three days. I've run out of subjects that Wade hasn't heard me preach sermons on since before he was born."

Mait was facing the coffee machine when he said "Mr. Mayfield, how much longer has Wade got?" When he turned, his eyes belied the hardness of the question. Mait had promised to help any way Hutch needed from here to Wade's death; how long would that be?

So Hutch tried to answer soberly. "My guess, from what I've read and heard, is somewhere between the next five minutes and another few months. Wade's only got so many cells of flesh to lose; they melt off him daily. His eyes are finished, as you well know; his mind's affected off and on; his lungs and kidneys are worn out from fighting."

Mait came to the opposite side of the counter, two feet from Hutch. "Do you know Wade's thought about suicide?"

It shocked Hutch cold. "I don't know that—no sir, I don't."

Mait stood in place, two cups in hand, and signified Yes.

Hutch could only say "When?"

Mait knew he'd betrayed Wade—too late though. He forced himself

to meet Hutch's eyes and said "Last time I came out to your place—
what, last Tuesday?—when you left us alone, Wade asked me if I could
find him some cyanide."

"What did you say?"

"I said I could try. At the bars I've met a couple of chemists from
Burroughs Wellcome; they seem very friendly—" Mait carefully filled
the cups with coffee and held one to Hutch.

"Do you plan to try?"

"As I said, I've got more than one chemist friend. Please say if I
should." When he'd thought for a moment, Mait said "I know that sounds
awfully flip, but it could be easy if we did it right—the dying at least: we
could bring that off, with the simple right substance, in a matter of
seconds."

Hutch waited a long time. "No soul in my family has managed his
own death in ninety years—my great-grandmother Kendal drank lye and
died on her own kitchen floor." He waited again. "But you and Wade
are both grown men."

"Is that real advice or are you just polite?" In all Mait had said since
waking today, his voice had served reliably—no highs or lows.

The scent of the brewing coffee had jostled Hutch's exhaustion. He
almost smiled to Mait. "I'm cursed with politeness, as you recall; but no,
I've got no wisdom to give you. It's Wade's life and death; he's been
through more than I'll ever imagine—far more pain than you'll ever need
to know, I hope." That last was a warning which escaped unintended.
Guard your body, whoever you're with.

Mait said "Let's talk about this later. It's still not day."

Hutch knew why he'd stopped here, not for simple company but on
the off chance that Mait might finally be old enough to give what Hutch
needed and had needed for weeks—a precocious offer of fatherly guidance,
a strong voice to say *Do this, now that, now stretch out and rest.*

And there in his shorts, Mait seemed to bend to the role with no
fear. His eyes looked wiser in an instant. But then, though his voice had
kept its firmness, his face flushed brightly; and he said "Good morning"
past Hutch's shoulder.

Hutch looked behind him at a man as arresting in face and body as
anything torn off a Roman basilica and painted again in the colors of

life—black hair, dark eyes and biscuit-colored skin. Older than Mait, he also was naked except for a towel round his hips, and he'd stopped in the hall on the kitchen threshold. Hutch gave him a brief instinctive bow.

The man came on and held out his right hand. "Cam Mapleson, sir."

Hutch said his own name and took the strong hand. "I'm more than sorry I woke you up. My son is ill in Duke Hospital. I was feeling lonesome and stopped to see Maitland."

Cam said "He's told me. I'm proud to know you, sir."

Hutch thought *You don't know a thing about me. Don't grab for more than I can give.* But he only smiled.

Hoping to revert to cheer, Mait said "Is everybody hungry?"

Cam said "Are we up?"

Hutch said "No, I'm leaving—"

Mait said "*I'm* up and a carnivore to boot. Bacon and toast?"

Cam laid a light hand on Hutch's shoulder. "Please stay. I'd welcome a chance to know you, sir."

Hutch said "But if you keep calling me *sir*, I may well drop down dead on the floor of sheer old age."

Cam said "I'm sorry—it's my marine training. My dad objects as much as you, but it's in my blood—maybe too late to change." His hand had stayed on Hutch's shoulder.

Mait was searching the refrigerator. "Mr. Mayfield, what's the difference between a marine and a queer?"

Cam's hand clamped tighter on Hutch's shoulder.

"I surrender—what?"

Mait said "A six-pack."

Hutch laughed but, by now, was resenting the weight of Cam's hand. He'd begun to sense he was being lured into some narrow trap. *What does this new boy want, from Mait and me?* And in the next minutes, as he moved at Mait's suggestion and sat at the bare dollhouse table, Hutch felt more and more like an excess wheel beside this pair who were young enough to be his sons, nearly his grandsons. They'd already shared more than Hutch could guess; and their readable faces had plainly known more pleasure in the last few hours than he'd known in months, if not years. But still the thought of heading home alone, or of waiting in his campus office till ten o'clock when he could visit Wade again, was harder to manage. Hutch said "Thanks, Mait—just toast for me; I'm giving up fat."

Cam had lifted his hand and was standing in their midst, in his towel. His eyes frisked Hutch. "You're too thin, man; keep your energy up."

Hutch thought *Your eyes are flat as a puppet's; is there anyone* in *you?* But he told Cam "Relax, endurance is my strong suit." The pompous sound of that on the air made Hutch laugh first.

Mait and Cam joined gladly in the noise.

And Cam's towel fell to the floor round his feet. His whole body, pure white in the loins and bushed with black, flared like a phosphorous fire in the kitchen.

Mait roared "Help! A *man!*"

Not rushed, Cam bent, retrieved the towel and fastened it safely.

At once Hutch took the glimpse as an omen on Wade's behalf. All his life Hutch had trusted in such quick meetings with another human's grace and worth. This strange bare man—some kind of nurse and as easy to watch as any man in Wade's sheaf of pictures—was signaling better times for Wade or, at the least, an easier death. When Maitland reached above the sink and opened the blinds on first daylight, Hutch suddenly knew and actually said eight words in his mind. *This whole story can end soon now.*

He meant the story of his joined families, all the story he'd witnessed or heard from kin whose memories ranged two centuries back—most of them burning what they called *love* as their treacherous, always vanishing fuel when what they craved was merely *time*: more time above ground anyhow to feed their dry unquenchable sovereign hearts. That story was ending in Wade Mayfield, who was hardly breathing less than a quarter mile from this room and from these two ready likable boys whose excellent bodies, a few years back, Wade might have plumbed in thoughtless safety or held and honored for long paired lives.

By the time Hutch worked his way through that, drinking coffee, Cam and Mait had dressed for the cloudless sweltering day at hand and were laying out food like a four-handed creature, with that little waste of minutes or motion.

Those smooth moves gave Hutch even more hope that someway

Wade's hurried dissolution had slowed and leveled and could now be guided or aimed at least toward a dignified close. Hutch said to Mait "Thank God I woke you."

"Don't mention it please."

Cam kicked out at Mait's butt. "Take the compliment, child; the man clearly means it." And only then did Cam look to Hutch; he thought he could see in Hutch's eyes that his own hawk-face was as fine to see as the rest of his hide when the towel had dropped.

Hutch was thinking *He's maybe eight years older than Mait, those eyes want something Mait doesn't have to give, when did they meet?* But all Hutch said was another fact. "I'd got fairly near the end of my rope."

Cam brought bacon, toast and jam to the table and said "Jump or fall. We're a good strong net; Mait and I'll catch you."

Hutch knew they were promising more than they'd give—more than they had, whoever they were to one another (and hadn't Mait said this was their first night?)—but he thanked them again and buttered the bread.

20

When Hutch turned the curve and saw his own house, it was seven o'clock and growing clearer and brighter by the minute. When he reached the backyard, Ann's car was parked in its old place—no sign of her in it. *Wade's worse; she's here to get me.* Hutch paused long enough to face due south and see the highest roofs of Chapel Hill over green intervening miles of trees. For a moment he felt he was calmed. *Life at a distance anyhow. We'll last some way. He didn't think who he meant by we.* He turned, walked around to the front door and tried the knob. Generally double-locked, it was open. Hutch entered the hall and listened—silence. He froze in place, invaded and offended. Ann had long since carried off every thread and book that was rightly hers. *She's rummaging through my desk, on a hunt.*

She almost was. Though Hutch hadn't tried to muffle his steps, Ann was startled when he got to the door of his study and found her seated near the desk. Like a child, she held her hands up empty. "I was reading this sadness—" Wyatt's long hateful letter to Wade was open on her lap.

"It isn't yours."

"You haven't read it?"

Hutch said "Wade left it here with me."

"And told you to read it?"

Hutch wouldn't lie. He shook his head No. "I read it in the night, when I couldn't sleep. I thought it was something I might need to know if Wade lasts long."

"He's better this morning; I called the ward. They said his fever's down and he's breathing better. I stopped by here to wash some nightshirts and sheets." As proof, the washing machine in the kitchen pumped and chugged beyond them. Ann gathered the furious pages and laid them neatly facedown in the box.

Hutch could see her own letters to Wade, still sealed at the side of the box. But he only said "You think Wyatt's dead right, I very much bet."

"I beg your pardon?"

"Wyatt. In his letter. About you and me."

Ann intended no harm when she said "Are you sure he included me?"

Hutch was also calm when he nodded Yes. "Everybody with eyes in the past three centuries knows that white women were the engines of slavery."

"You want to defend that wild proposition? It's new to *me*."

Hutch rushed it out toward her. "White men shanghaied slaves to America, bought and sold them, worked them to death in sugarcane fields or treated them like pet minstrel dolls you can slam up against the wall anytime you're tense or a little discouraged with your day; but unless the perpetual-virgin white wives and daughters had stood on the porch or at the field edge, broadcasting hate and fear and attraction, the worn-out men would have given up such a costly burden long years sooner—the whole monster business—and done their own work, just killing each other and occasional Indians."

Ann eventually smiled, suppressing a laugh. "That's appropriately weird."

"It's true."

She still smiled. "Some part of it may be—Lord knows, my mother and all her sisters suffered most from the simple fact that they had to have black women cooking and cleaning all day behind them while they sat idle, depressed and picking at the slightest flaw in every life near them."

Hutch said "So Wyatt was more than half right."

"Wyatt got his revenge."

"How?"

"Look, Hutchins—Christ Jesus, he's killing our child."

Hutch said "We can't lay that on the dead."

"You just laid slavery on a million dead women."

He waited to think of one more answer, then raised both open hands. "Truce. I'm too tired."

"You didn't sleep either?"

"I got scared in the night and drove in to see Wade. You're right; he's better. Very slightly better. For a day or so, till this afternoon maybe when some barely harmful germ blows in and carries him—"

Ann stood. "You want me to fix you some breakfast?"

"I've eaten, thanks. You're not working today?"

"I took the day off. I needed some quiet."

"Lucky job," Hutch said. "The Hurdle Mills Meat Man get the day off too?"

Ann said "Read the newspaper, Hutch. We're saving his skin. Last week he got his charges reduced—stands a good chance of nothing worse than life with no parole."

"Who doesn't get more or less that exactly?"

"Well, you." Ann took a step toward him and studied his eyes.

Hutch realized she hadn't been this good to see for a very long while—a new kind of force flushed all through her skin; her hair and eyes, her elegant bones. He studied her, silent.

Then she finally said "You've had a full life. You *used* yourself. You liked most of it."

"Didn't you? Sure you did—"

"The jury's still out on me." But she smiled. "Permission for coffee?"

Hutch gave it. "Permission."

Ann turned toward the kitchen and Hutch came behind.

*   *   *

TWENTY minutes later, with nothing transacted beyond small talk, Ann headed out "to mow the lawn"—she had a little hearthrug of grass by her back door—and Hutch moved toward his study in the slim hope of starting at least to choose the poems for his new selected volume. The box of Wade's papers was where Ann had left it—Wyatt's letter on top, Ann's own sealed letters untouched where they'd been. It came to Hutch suddenly. *Read just one letter; you need to know it somehow.* If the thought hadn't come with a taste of hope in it, he'd have pushed it back. All his novelist friends were abject snoopers; Hutch had seldom shared the urge.

Now with no qualm, he sat at his desk and asked himself which letter to choose. *The last one she sent.* But that was still sealed, dated *March 29.* Breaking Ann's seal was not yet allowed, not under the rules that were running Hutch here. So he rummaged carefully through the box, hunting the most recent letter from Ann that Wade had opened—Wade or Wyatt or Ivory or Boat. At last he found one, slit neatly open, and postmarked just after this past Christmas.

December 30, 1992

Dear Wade,

 I hope you're weathering the post-Yule blues a lot better than me. Don't mean to burden you with my small troubles—and not to imply that I'm standing here, armed to kill myself—but my first Christmas entirely alone was an awful idea. Oh I had three invitations to parties and one to dinner with my boss and his clan; but believe it or not, I was fool enough to sit out here with the bare trees around me and wait on the phone. I even picked it up more than once as the day went on, to see if it worked; and there Oh Lord was the healthy dial tone, saying "Yah, yah, yah, nobody needs you." The rest of the day and the whole night proved it, not even one wrong number or a pitiful handicapped lightbulb salesman.

 You're right if you're thinking "She volunteered for it with both eyes open." I did, you warned me, Hutch warned me, God warned me. But Wade, let me tell you what you already know. My last four years under Hutch's roof—and it was never my roof, not the smallest shingle from the day they were laid—I'd wake up beside your father in the night and feel the weight of every object in the rooms stacked on me. Every bed and table, the stove and freezer and washer and both cars, my own small lot of precious possessions (most of which pertain to you) and—topping the pile— your father's billion souvenirs from a rich strong life, everything from the carved-bark man with the workable penis to your father's books and pictures and the manuscript mountains. I thought I'd loved them, or been glad to live near them; but in those last four years, I couldn't stop thinking They were all meant to kill me. That's why they're here. You stand up and run, girl.

Eventually I ran; as you well know, I ran. Nobody but me; nobody forced me, least of all Hutch—not consciously, never.

So why am I sitting here moaning to you, when your outlook is what it is? I'm not too sure what the answer is, but I have learned one thing I didn't quite know. There's not much out here for any woman my age, unless she wants to take the veil (and even that convent of cloistered nuns on the Roxboro road shut down years ago; they ran out of sisters). If I'd started life as a virgin martyr and taught long division for the past forty years, I might at least get occasional cards from giants of industry that I'd helped launch on their grisly course. If I'd had real friendships outside my marriage (which all but no American mates do), there'd be somebody I could eat supper with at least or join at the movies on my day off. If I'd had a real mind (a strong imagination as opposed to a dedicated homemaking robot inside my skull), I'd have sure-God never let my private soul just die down to nothing but a warm coal or two the way I did.

You're surely asking yourself—if you've read this far—"What's she want from me?" I trust I don't need to restate my offer to care for you— here or there, any place you say. Beyond that, I sometimes pray for the phone to ring and you to be there saying "Call him up, Ann. Start talking anyhow about what's left, if anything, between you and what you could stand—you and Hutch, both alone now." Second to praying you call with the news that a cure's been found, I pray for that—a way we could all live together a few years longer.

Is that what you mean, when you think about us—assuming you do? Again, forgive this burden from me. But the Season of Hope has very nearly killed me. What I may have learned in this new life is clearer, though, after these lonely days—I'm as good a woman as I know how to be (and I'm at least normally smart for my age), and the same is surely true for Hutch. He's got a whole lot less greed and malice than the average songbird—I know; I watch my bird feeder closely.

And the absolute unquestioned truth of my life is, I love you and am yours—with whatever good I could bring—for the simple asking. A premature Happy New Year, Wade. Ignore this if you need to.

> All the love left in
> Ann Gatlin Mayfield

Hutch placed the pages back in their envelope, then buried the letter deep in the box. He'd barely thought that it might have snagged a hold in his mind.

21

TEN days later at Hutch's house, on a bright dry June afternoon, Cam Mapleson stood up to leave Wade and Maitland. Cam was due at work in the hospice; Mait was going to stay on with Wade since Hutch was in Richmond to read his poems at a summer writers' conference. When Cam had stroked Wade's forehead by way of saying goodbye, he noticed for the first time the drawing that hung above Wade's bed—Hutch's childhood drawing of mountains and trees, the one Wade had wanted at the last moment as they left New York. Cam had spent a good part of his own childhood painting and drawing landscapes near Nag's Head where he'd grown up, and Hutch's drawing of Virginia mountains struck him as fresh and oddly impressive. It had the homemade but masterful quality of certain unique accomplishments—things done just once, got perfectly right, then never repeated. Cam said to Wade "Did you draw this?"

The head of Wade's bed was cranked up high. He slowly groped back with one hand and found the picture frame; the feel of the gilded wood told him what was there. His crooked smile was a gauge of the pleasure he took in its memory. "Don't you like this a lot? But no, don't thank me—I couldn't draw, even when my hands worked. This was done by Hutch, before he wrote poems. I think he was fourteen. I can look at it more or less endlessly."

Both Cam and Mait silently noted that Wade had never mentioned his blindness to either of them.

Cam said "He had some serious gifts; has he kept up his art through the poetry years?"

Confused as Wade had begun to be lately, he treated the question with greater care than Cam intended. Finally Wade pulled his hand back off the picture and extended the fingers toward where he thought Cam stood.

Cam was nearby and took the hand, holding it as lightly as any moth wing—by now it was plainly that easy to ruin.

Wade said "My father is Hutchins Mayfield, born in 1930, month of May, twelfth day." For a long moment that seemed his only finding. But he suddenly withdrew his fingers from Cam's hand; his dead hot eyes found Cam's face—its locus at least. "My father saw through the world long before he had me. When he drew that picture, he still believed · something he'd thought of in childhood—that there was something buried, buried and worth finding—beneath the world: the part we can see, beneath the skin. Or so he told me when he gave me the picture; that was the Christmas I left home for good. The only other thing he said was he wanted me to have it as a memory of him and his mother Rachel Hutchins. She died just a few minutes after he was born, so he never really saw her, and God knows I didn't." Though still Wade hadn't acknowledged his blindness, he gave a high laugh.

It took him awhile to refocus his mind. "The picture was drawn near where Rachel lived—near Goshen, Virginia: a really gorgeous piece of the Earth. Hutch and I drove up there several times when I was a boy. That was when I got the idea of having at least one daughter that I could name *Rachel*—my favorite name, for girls anyhow. God had other plans for my plumbing fixtures. But those trips to Goshen were my best days till I knew Wyatt. Wyatt Bondurant—you've heard about him, right?— was best of all: we killed each other." Nothing in Wade's face betrayed the pain of that, though he'd stopped again. Then his hand went back a second time and pointed to the picture. "Look at how spooky the *drawing* is, all there in the middle—all those thick leaves down the side of the mountain, like some dense screen they wove with leaves over something they're hiding. I asked Hutch what was hid there in the middle—" Wade waved a final time at the picture; then he went cold silent.

Cam studied the drawing and didn't speak.

But Mait asked Wade "Did he say what was there?"

And Wade remembered; it hooked in his mind, and his skull ducked eagerly. "He said 'It's a giant that's dreaming the world.' "

Mait said "That's an idea almost all children have, through the whole world apparently. I know I had it when I was five. I thought the dreamer was a great gold dragon, and somedays I would literally walk around, light on the sidewalk, not to wake it up. I knew I'd vanish when the dragon stopped dreaming. I'd forgot till last year when I took a course in world religions; the teacher said most cultures have the same idea—we're all somebody's, or something's dream: a giant's or a butterfly's, paused on a rose in the warm sun of some perfect place."

Wade nodded, a little calmer again but earnest still. "I'm there," he said. "Believe it; I'm *there*. I'm dreaming all this."

Cam said " 'A dream is dreaming us'—who said that?"

Mait said "Me, I told you—no, an African Bushman said it to some big anthropologist, in the 1920s."

Wade's head ducked Yes again and again.

Cam thought *Oh Wade, if this is a dream, for God's sake wake up and save mankind*; but he understood Wade was past clear reason, so he told him "Dream on."

Wade said "Christ, no—oh, *wake* me please." But as Cam looked toward Mait, really disturbed, Wade laughed in a voice very much like his old voice—kind and all but endlessly pleased. As he heard the sound, Wade thought *That's my last laugh*.

Cam was late for work, so he took the laugh as permission to leave. He bent to kiss Wade's forehead and asked him the riddle he'd heard only yesterday from another blind man at the hospice, scarecrowed worse than Wade. "What's the difference between Cleveland, Ohio and the S.S. *Titanic?*"

Wade's eyes were still trying to find human faces, though they couldn't now, but his grin survived. "I give up—what?"

Cam said "Cleveland had a better orchestra"; then he scissored to the door in three comic strides as if he were seen. From there he looked back. Just those few seconds away from Wade had eased Cam's mind; and when he saw him, the sight was shocking one more time—worse than any he'd seen in five years of military service or his months at the hospice: a grown man weighing maybe eighty-five pounds, not ready to die. The eyes were still wide open and hunting. Cam kissed the palm of his own hand and held it to Mait and Wade. "You two get a very tight grip on yourselves and hold it till I'm back."

Wade laughed. "Oh Christ, a *grip!* I wish I could. It's been ten months since I touched the old rascal."

Before he thought, Mait said "I make up for everybody." Laughter covered them all as Cam left.

But Wade's mind managed to hold the thought till they heard Cam shut the front door. Then he turned to Mait. "I said ten months but I can't remember when my cock worked." It was only a fact; Wade hadn't had sex with Wyatt since nearly two years ago, and even self-service had proved impossible for—what?—long months, maybe more than a year. If the urge dug at him, he'd try to reward it; but almost always, before he could run the mental pictures to fire him onward, he'd recall that his cum was now a poison, a lethal substance; and that would down him. Oddly today, that long-lost pleasure seemed the least of Wade's problems. The better memories of his times with Wyatt seemed more or less sufficient now, the times when Wade could remember to let himself dwell on those thousands of indescribably excellent junctures with Wyatt.

Mait said "I sometimes wish my rascal didn't work at all."

That soon, Wade was puzzled. "What rascal you mean?"

"My red fire hydrant, the flaming weenie that runs my life."

"Oh child, don't let it. It's the whole wrong century for that lovely failing." Those were far more words of real warning than Wade had attempted in all the years since the plague arrived; they left him empty.

At such stalled moments Mait had learned to sit still and wait till Wade either dozed or regained his footing on breath and clarity and could speak again.

The eyes stayed open and the lips were gapped, no sign of pain or suffocation though. Finally the bony head turned to Mait and worked at a smile. "You talk. Let me listen."

So Mait took that as maybe a last chance to hear the answers he'd never got from anyone more likely to know the truth than this aggrieved man, vanishing by the instant where he lay. Mait said "You can just nod or shake your head a little, but help me please. I trust you, Wade." Mait took a long breath, then was shamed to think of his own body's ease in a room like this—his healthy ease and opulence in young skin and joint. Still he said to Wade "You regret your life?"

Wade replied at once, a silent No.

"You sorry you were queer?"

Wade said "Still queer—queer, dead or alive. The answer's No. I loved most of it; I was one strong lover. I don't just mean sex either but love—I could evermore watch the person I loved and figure his needs and set out to fill them. Damned nearly did too, till the time it really sunk in we were sick. I'd have loved Wyatt right on, cell for cell—we were past hurting each other any worse—but he called it off, stopped sex on a *dime* like it was a skate." Wade imitated a braking skate with his long right fingers. Then he shut his eyes. "You understand Wyatt killed himself?"

Hutch had told Mait that much, days ago. Now was no time to ask for more; Wade was plainly exhausted. So Mait raised a hushing finger, then recalled that Wade couldn't see it. "Are we some kind of monsters—you, me, Cam, Wyatt, whatever percent of the human race we constitute?"

Wade very slowly signified Yes.

"Truly? Actual felons?"

"Not felons, except in the idiot terrified law, just not quite *Homo sapiens* either but mostly well-meaning monsters, I think—a different and partly benign neighbor-species. *Monster* in that sense. Better at some things, worse at others."

Mait said "Aside from this new plague, what's the worst thing about us?" When Wade stalled a moment, the boy pushed on with the Yes or No rite. "Adultery, alley-cat promiscuity?"

Wade shook his head No.

"You don't regret knowing so many men?"

Wade said "I told you—I knew two other men besides myself. Exactly two. Few lily-white martyrs were chaster than me."

Mait smiled, though he couldn't stop himself. "But all we think and talk about is sex—the queers my age at least."

"You ever sit down with two other straight guys, anywhere else but the State Department? Every coffee break is a pussy op—pussy and money: all they talk about. No classic queer that ever lived was as hipped on cock as straights on cunt. I doubt Plato told many cock-jokes."

"I bet Socrates did." Mait laughed, real cheer.

Wade joined him, the best he could—his lungs were still weak. When he'd rested awhile, he suddenly knew the answer to Mait's flat-footed question. "If straight men weren't hardwired for women, with all women's training and doubts and plumbing problems, they'd fuck as many times a day as the most crazed queer on the south side of Eighth Street. No, what's wrong with queers—the only wrong thing they don't share with straights—is nothing but children. Queers don't make children, not as a rule. I figured you'd noticed."

Mait said "Oh yes. But that didn't seem to throw too big a monkey wrench into some of the Homo Great's working plans—"

Wade shut his eyes and, in his most bored voice, reeled off a stretch from the sacred litany of queers. "Donatello, Botticelli, Leonardo, Michelangelo, Caravaggio, Handel—"

Mait took up the chant. "Sophocles, Virgil, Shakespeare, Melville, Whitman, Tchaikovsky, Mann, Auden, Britten, Barber, Copland—"

Wade raised a finger. "Mann and Melville and Shakespeare had children." Wade's blank face slowly produced a grin; he beamed it toward Mait. "Reminds me of a joke—why did God make queers?"

Mait said "I give up."

"Because he looked down at the Earth one day, well after that dust-up in the Garden of Eden; and he said to himself 'They're just getting nowhere at *all* with the arts.' "

Mait laughed but was still too riled by Wade's diagnosis of the great lack in queerdom. He said "Now back to us not having children. A good many straights are born barren as coal mines; they sometimes manage whole faithful lives together."

Wade smiled for an instant longer but then went stiller than any sunk ship. In a long wait, his eyes seemed to fill with the only water left in his body—too few tears to run.

Mait started to change his tack. "For me, the main problem seems to be—"

Wade raised his whole right hand from the sheet and moved it toward Mait, three or four inches nearer.

Mait took it, as Cam had, with serious caution not to crush the stark bones.

And then Wade agreed. "It's children, truly, most of the time—just not having children underfoot for years at a time, leaning hard on you for life itself. In general a queer's got nothing at home but one other man and him the same model as you in the head—the same age and, deep-down, the same brand of wiring: same instincts, same thoughts, same unstoppable testosterone boil-ups that sabotage a whole day or night in a flash. I'd have been a fair father to a likable child; I had things to tell."

"You could still tell me. I'm going nowhere."

Wade shook his head and withdrew the hand. "My mind's burnt up, Son."

"So I should have children?" Mait was as poised to act as any hot axe.

Again Wade was silent, refusing to face him.

"What's so urgent about more children? Children, all sizes and shades, are starving by the million from right here near us to the high snows of Asia."

Wade shook his head in furious denial. "Someway. Have children. One child anyhow."

Mait could think *Wade's crazy—keep that in mind.* But the answer caught in his mind like a gaff.

22

NEXT morning when Hutch had phoned home from Richmond, spoken with a confident-sounding Mait and even with Wade, who was weak but sprightly, he felt safe enough to pause on his drive home and run a brief errand. After an early hotel breakfast, Hutch drove toward the street in the dead heart of town where—ninety years ago—old Robinson Mayfield, his great-grandfather, had lived with the girl Polly Drewry who'd nursed him through the last days of TB and warmed his body, though he'd never married her. Polly herself had stayed on in the house, vital as a lit lamp and brave as a sled dog, when old Rob died. Then she'd stayed on as housekeeper, and eventual common-law wife, to old Rob's son, Hutch's grandfather Forrest—a Latin teacher and an amateur poet with a certain gift, however restrained by his time and reading.

Over long years Polly had proved to be the soul who could give Forrest all the love he'd failed to find in his young wife Eva Kendal, who'd abandoned Forrest when their son was born—young Rob, Hutch's father. When Polly had finally outlived Forrest, she'd lingered on in the same house still—alone but industrious, a talented seamstress and all but indomitable veteran of time. Once his father had died and Hutch was home from England for good, he'd finally done what the family should have done ages ago—deeded the Richmond house to Polly, paid her annual taxes and otherwise helped her with small sums of money and irregular visits through the rest of her days till, in her late eighties, she lost clear sense of who she was and what was expected of an elderly spinster. Even then, she generally recognized Hutch on his unpredictable look-ins till she died upright in her sewing chair in 1980, having all but finished a needlepoint cushion she was stitching for Wade, who was then a boy. It bore a plain message, threaded in green, in her own forthright script—*May You Never Know Sorrow.*

Though Hutch hadn't tried to find the house since Polly's funeral, this morning he found it easily—disheveled as it was and derelict in its tiny yard of shattered glass and knee-high weeds. He stopped by the curb and paused to think of what the actual house had been when his kin owned it (Polly had left the house to Wade; Wade had turned it over to Hutch, and an agent then sold it for less than a song). Since there was no other human in sight in the early sun, Hutch sat in his car, with some amazement, for at least two minutes in quiet respect to the several powers that had lit those rooms through nearly a century of his family's life. No single one of them had ever matched Polly for sheer satisfaction in the passage of time and for an apparently native gift of love without hunger or even demand, the love commended by virtually all the world's religions but scarce as pure water—now as forever.

While Hutch waited a few yards distant from where Polly Drewry had led a life as openhearted as any since the saints, he missed her intensely and thought *Nobody left alive on Earth can help Wade die the way Polly could have; bring her back just long enough to see Wade through.* Hutch's longing and practical need were so strong that, in the next instant, he saw Polly's likable tidy body and her intact face, here on the cobblestone street before him and clear as she was till her mind had clouded. She was dressed in black from neck to ankle; and she carried a small leather overnight satchel in her powerful left hand, ready to serve.

Hutch well understood she was not really there, not palpably, though some real part of her presence was there—her healing eyes and her readiness. He also knew this was maybe the only vision of his life, the single all but credible return of someone irrecoverably gone and lost. So he held both palms toward the warm windshield to offer the sight whatever piece of his own life it might accept in a bargain for help. *Take anything left alive in me but come here. Nobody known to me but you can send the dying out in an honor that precludes no trace of love.* Hutch knew he was nudging the thin edge of sanity; he was calm in the knowledge.

As the sight faded slowly, he thought of the only conceivable substitute—his long-dead mother's great friend Alice Matthews in Petersburg, south of here on his route (with the years, Hutch had come to assume that his mother and Alice had been some brand of lovers, before his mother met Rob anyhow). As different from Polly as Eve from Ruth in the Hebrew Bible, still Alice had meant almost as much as Polly to Hutch in his childhood and youth. Lately their correspondence had come down to Christmas cards and occasional phone calls.

Hutch hadn't seen Alice for three or four years, though she'd phoned on his birthday this past May and said she was nearly eighty-nine years old, still living in her own apartment and battling to stand on her own till she "quit." Hutch recalled that Alice often referred to death as simply *quitting*; it seemed an accurate personal banner for someone as forceful through a long life as she; Hutch hadn't told her about Wade's illness.

He looked one last time to where the sight of Polly had waited— mere early light, the start of a day that would never know Polly. He turned the car in a wide circle on the broad cobbled street and headed south.

23

As a rule Hutch never visited any friend unannounced, but a half hour later he parked at Alice's with no prior warning. He'd thought a surprise appearance might please her more, sparing her hours of sprucing the place. But once he'd knocked, he thought *Oh God, she may be cracked or bedridden too.* When they'd talked in May, Alice had mentioned her balky heart—"this tremulous pump that's seen better days." And when light footsteps came to the door and paused on the locked side, silent, Hutch thought *I've scared her.* So he said "It's maybe your oldest friend."

Another long silence; then with no hint of joking, Alice's voice said "Insert passport beneath the door." Odd as it was, she sounded as clear as she'd sounded in May.

But again Hutch wondered if she'd lost mental ground. Still he said "I'm traveling on confidential documents; give me the password."

At last Alice said the word *pearl*, then laughed a high note; then "Pearl, Pearl, Pearl—Great Pearl of the South, swim into my cave." She proceeded to throw back a series of locks and opened on Hutch.

At first Hutch thought *She's younger by years. Everybody but me gets younger.*

And Alice was startlingly like herself, for all the years—a little shrunk maybe but straight-backed still and with hair so white it seemed the source of a curious intermittent shine, harmless but unprecedented in Hutch's memory.

He bent to kiss her.

She smelled as ever of lemon cologne, and she wore an immaculate dark-blue dress as quietly costly and dignified as if she'd expected a presidential call. She bore his kiss calmly; and once she was free of his arms again, she said "I haven't been kissed in so long it feels like a primitive rite in Samoa."

"Sorry," Hutch said.

"Not a bit. I miss a little savagery now and then. Of course I could leave my door unlocked any hour of the day and stand a good chance of winding up flayed and nailed to this door in an unbecoming pose." When Hutch looked puzzled, Alice said "The neighborhood is sinking by the minute—you're bound to have noticed. Six more months, it'll be a bona fide slaughterhouse out there." She turned and led the slow way inward down the hall with its striking framed photographs of little-known statues from hidden piazzas and backstreets in Italy, Greece, Crete and the islands—all taken by Alice in midlife solitary tours and enlarged in the kitchen, just yards away.

"You planning to move?"

"Oh no. I'm considering volunteering to be the next victim. I hear if you call the police and they fail you, the county pays to repair and embalm your scattered remains."

Hutch said "I'd double-check on that. Sounds far too logical."

"Darling, I made it up—give me a laugh." Alice paused to study his eyes for the first time. "What's gone wrong?" Before he could answer, she sat in her favorite chair, blue velvet now.

Hutch sat on the forward edge of the sofa, then couldn't speak.

"Is it Wade?"

Hutch signed Yes with his eyes.

Alice shut her own keen gray eyes and turned her small sharp face toward the ceiling as if she kept hints for wisdom posted there. At last her eyes looked back to Hutch. "I've known, deep in my bones, it was coming."

"What?"

"He's got this dreadful plague, I'm afraid."

Hutch said "Has he called you?"

"Not a word from Wade, no—not for three years. But I've felt it bearing down for months."

"How?"

"I've known Wade, darling. I guessed at the danger. I've known for a decade he's been in the eye of this fearful storm."

Hutch was genuinely thrown by her foresight. "When was the last time you saw him then?"

"In New York—my last trip up there, four or five years ago. I went with a cousin older than me, and we got out with unbroken bones but not much else. Wade took us to dinner with his young man."

"Wyatt Bondurant?"

"I think so, yes—a light-colored gentleman of African extraction."

"And Wyatt didn't ruin your trip?"

"Ruin it?" Her eyes were bemused by the thought.

"With meanness; he didn't tongue-lash you?"

Alice laughed. "Lord, no—the soul of well-bred politeness. I thought Wade had freed him from some ancient spell; he seemed so much like a resurrected gallant rake from Restoration days, in pale plum satin."

"Wyatt? You understand Wyatt was black?"

"I just said as much—are Negro men exempt from elegance?" Her eyes went cold and narrowed slightly. "And what's this *was*; where's Wyatt now?"

Hutch knew he was caught in a just rebuke, but his news impelled him. "Wyatt died last winter—the same plague as Wade, though he killed himself first. He'd infected Wade; he couldn't live with that, couldn't stay to help Wade."

Alice studied her hands. As much as her face, they'd refused to age— almost no spots and few ropey veins. She finally said "My eyes are as good as they ever were, Hutchins. I see you here now—welcome as rain, which you've always been. And I saw Mr. Bondurant that one night as a beautiful Negro man straight out of my great-grandmother's parlor— the finest of manservants, perfectly trained. Of course I hated myself for the thought. I also saw he would spring like a wolf and tear my throat out if I gave him *that* much cause." With her thumb and finger she'd measured off a slim half inch.

"He sprang at us, God knows—Ann and me, throat and eyes. He kept Wade away from us the past few years, right up till he shot himself in an alley last February with Wade already bad off. That left Wade all but alone in the city and desperately weak. When I found out early this past April, I went up and got him."

"Wade's with you at present?"

"For however long. He's trailing off by the day, skin and bone." Hard as the past two months had been, in close sight of Wade, the boy's fate had seemed just bearable till now. In reach of a woman as self-contained and fearless as Zenobia Queen of desert Palmyra or Portia the wife of Marcus Brutus, eating live coals, Hutch suddenly felt done in by a judgment precisely hurled at his own private failings, a plunge dead center to the heart of his error—the secret central wrong of his life. *Which is what—what's the secret?*

Before Hutch could even start an answer, Alice said "We both need a glass of good sherry." And she rose to get it.

By the time she was back with the usual tray—a bottle of excellent amontillado, a plate of homemade cheese sticks and two glasses, Hutch had calmed himself and could watch her pour with pleasure in the sight of how little she'd lost. When she gave him his wine, he offered it up at once to toast her.

But she said "Not so fast. It's still my house so it's my first toast—to you, dear blessed one."

Hutch thanked her and drank. "I'm feeling deeply unblessed here lately."

"Of course you are. You're past sixty, aren't you?"

"By three full years."

Alice smiled. "Sure, the blues are a sixtyish burden. Once you strike eighty though, you're suddenly young. I wake up every day before daylight, full of curiosity and a whetted appetite to say what I know, to give what I've got and then get something new. Then I rise on my old feet and face my mirror, which is ancient as me but exceedingly literal and realistic. At the gruesome display, I think *Old girl, you've had your run. Lie back down and sleep.* Sometimes I do—nobody to stop me. I slept past ten o'clock this morning, a well-fed baby."

"You look very rested."

"I am—that's the horror. Nobody's used me in thirty-odd years."

Hutch said "I feel like a worn-out broom, used up to the stick."

"It must be awful—I see these deaths, by the day, on television: far more merciless than anything known when I was a girl. I trust you and Ann have got good help."

So Alice didn't know about Ann's experiment. Had he failed to tell her or had she forgot? Should he pile that onto the news about Wade? *No, spare her something.* Hutch said "Two Duke students have helped us a lot; Wade has liked them both. We've so far managed the rest on our own. I can't guess for how much longer; it's worse by the day."

"Wade's failing that fast?"

"As a matter of fact," Hutch said, "he's rallied a little this week—that's how I could dash off to Richmond and earn us a small piece of money. But the fact is, it's all an ice chute from here on. Wade's had parasitic pneumonia twice, half the microbes known to man are nesting in him, his eyes have failed to where he can only sense light from a window, and one of my students who sits with him often tells me that the boy's asked him for cyanide."

Alice had always been as unflinching as the brow of a sphinx, but she waited to be entirely sure of her ground. Then she said "Get the poison. Let Wade make his own way while he still can." There was not a gram of uncertainty in her level gaze.

And it shook Hutch hard. For the first full time, he thoroughly knew Wade would die very soon. All his frank words up to this point had merely concealed a shocked man's delusion that the lethal axe would freeze in midair, remorseful somehow, just short of his son. But of all his friends alive on Earth, Alice was the last sane one who'd never lied. Hutch said "You're serious."

"Darling child, I was never anything else, not ever; it's been the bane of my long life." And when Hutch sat speechless, facing her eyes, Alice said "You've walled Ann out of this."

"Has Ann called you?"

"Not once in her life."

"Then Wade."

"Not Wade. Give me credit for some degree of sense, Hutch. Even if it was a millennium ago, I loved your mother like night-blooming lilies; I somehow managed moderate fondness for your helpless wonderful-looking father, I met his cold mother and that little terrier of an aunt you loved—both of them powerful as iron locomotives on pig iron rails—so you couldn't hold a secret from me if you strained every nerve. I wish you could. You want all this ghastly death, I know; and you want it alone." She could even half smile.

Hutch accepted it again as her verdict, relieved that someone beyond him and Ann comprehended the need to possess—actually to *own* a son's death. He'd heard no reproof in all Alice said, and rightly so—she intended none, only simple description and the venting of a backed-up private knowledge she could seldom spend in her lonely days. He said "I'm the child of both my parents—no less, little more."

Alice said "I'm asking, not telling, but have you got their big luckless hearts?"

"I think so, yes. I'm seldom stingy or really indecent." He offered a laugh, which she barely received.

"You froze Ann out, I'd estimate."

At last Hutch knew he had and he agreed. "I never wanted all Ann had to give; she was way too gifted and starved as a snake."

Alice said "Good people tend to be. Send her up here to me. I'm vanishing alone."

"You'll outlast me."

Alice took the proposition seriously, then said "I may. Is there anything I should say in my prayers for your poor soul, any errands you might want me to run?"

Hutch said "See that I'm near Wade please—wherever he goes, however hard. See he knows me there and grants my rights."

Again she gave it careful thought. "You're not imagining Wade Mayfield in some private Hell for men who've used each other in love or even quick pleasure? You're not that evil or ignorant?"

"I'm not, no, truly. I'm just dreaming, in my weakest fantasy, of some cool place with more serenity—a place where Wade can finally comprehend his mysterious father."

Alice's eyes began to relent. "My darling, the purpose of human life has little to do with understanding your parents. In any case, I never thought you were that hard to plumb. But you're speaking of filial respect, aren't you? You still want that?"

Hutch said "Partly—maybe. I'm thinking of the after-life just now. No, what I'd really give a great deal for would be some brand of laughing welcome from Wade—not frequently but often enough to keep whatever blood's still in me alive and running."

"You're convinced we last on, somewhere past death?" The set of her eyes showed she asked in all seriousness.

"I wouldn't lay all my funds on it, no; but the last time I was in church—Good Friday a year ago—I listened to the creed as I said it with the others. I got through 'I believe in the resurrection of the body and the life everlasting' nearly as smoothly as if I'd said I trusted water ran downhill."

Alice said "Water does that mostly—" She suddenly chuckled. "I've seen exceptions. But yes, I find myself talking to the night air more often as I wade onward here; a sane bystander might call it prayer. I'll talk my damnedest for you and Wade, from today to the end—rest easy on that. I've built up a sizable head of credit, if the Maker keeps books (I assume that there's a Maker with account books). Nobody's got less love from the world than tough old me, not since your mother married at least.

"I used to bear the world an almighty grudge; but oh about thirty years ago, I saw I'd made a whole life in the famine. An enviable life compared to most of the ones I've watched, in close quarters anyhow— a Virginia Vestal Virgin of solitude who taught that virtue to decades of students, almost none of whom listened but you; and you disobeyed me. Ever since that realization, I've admired myself—within reason of course, no greatly swelled head. I took what time gave, mostly hardtack; and I came back for more. I'm ready still." With eyes as gleaming as they'd ever been, even in the long-gone presence of Hutch's mother whom she'd loved above all, Alice took up her glass and drained the final thick drop of her sherry as if the prospect of eventual welcome was a foregone conclusion, not subject to doubt.

Whether or not her certainty bore a chance of being the bankable truth, Hutch finally saw why he'd made this detour and borne this old woman's reckless honesty, straight as a javelin flung at the eye. For a last time he toasted her silently and drank.

24

ON the fast trip home in midafternoon, Hutch's car broke down near the first turnoff in North Carolina. The engine simply quit in the road—no warning, no smoke. When he'd spent ten minutes trying to crank it and gazing under the hood in bafflement, he trudged up the ramp, found a crossroads mechanic who said he could either tow it to Durham for $100 or fix it here for a good deal less by late afternoon.

Before deciding, Hutch phoned home to check on Wade.

Mait answered, said things were even-keeled and not to worry—he'd stay till Hutch was back, whenever.

Hutch asked to speak with Wade for a moment. But Mait said "Wade's been a little mixed up—not unhappy though. Should we let him rest?"

It troubled Hutch but he held to his plan, only exacting a promise from Mait to phone Hutch at the garage in an emergency and then to call Ann.

No call ever came and the sun lunged on at the helpless Earth—a dry heat, almost deadly in its force. Soon Hutch felt that the hair of his head might ignite any instant. And to find some shade beyond the reach of the voices of the mechanic and his wife, Hutch walked out through a thicket of junked cars into a stand of tulip poplars behind the station and sat on old leaves against one thick trunk. In a silent three minutes, he began to cool; and soon he'd shut his eyes and was hoping for the first time in months that a new poem would come—one line at least, what Paul Valéry called the "one given line" that comes unbidden to a natural poet (Hutch would never have called himself a large poet; but he knew he was born with the gift in his brain, a native tendency to think in rhythmic words that reached a few thoughtful souls and lodged in their memory).

To aid the hope for a start at least, he sat on—oblivious to the day around him—and tried to accomplish the gray erasure he could usually manage on his working mind, the calling up of an empty screen with no thought or message, just a patient pregnant waiting.

He could work it for five or ten seconds at a time; then Wade's face would come, not now as it hurled downhill toward disaster but as it had been on the crest of his life. A tall strong-limbed boy, twelve or thirteen, slowed for a moment by the last step to manhood and toward all the pain that closed around him once he took that final rise in the even ground that must have looked welcoming but led him on to life in a city as cursed as any since Nineveh and into however many poisoned bodies he'd plumbed in nine years. Hutch finally gave up trying for blankness and dwelt on the valuable sight of young Wade, smiling gravely at the pitch of his noon.

Only then, when a live boy yelled out beside the filling station's air pump—"Foster, goddammit, you'll bust your tube!"—did eight words come into Hutch's mind, ready-made and dressed in authority, his given line maybe: *This child knows the last riddle and answer.* Hutch said it aloud, convinced at once that the *child* was Wade and not the yelling boy there beyond him. He repeated it twice; then fished out a pen and a scrap of paper napkin and wrote down the line. Somehow it would turn into Wade's elegy, in time for his grave. It felt like the one trustworthy thing that had come free to Hutch since spring at least, and it heartened him to stand again and walk toward the boys. "You fellows traveling north today, are you?"

The older boy said "No sir, we're at home."

But the younger—Foster—said "You want a ride? I'm heading for Spain."

"Spain? Why Spain?"

"I'm an ace bullfighter."

The older boy cuffed out at his brother. "You won't even step in the field with a bull; tell the man the damned truth."

Foster faced Hutch as seriously as if this was court and his life was at stake. "I'm just who you see."

Hutch said "You look fine. What are you—eight or nine?"

The older boy said "Man, you bound to be blind. That little flea ain't but six years old."

Hutch fished in his pocket, found a dollar in change and held it toward Foster.

Foster said "What you buying?"

Hutch said "Not buying. I'm thanking you, Son."

"For what?"

"Don't question your luck; just take it."

The older boy said "Take it, fool."

But Foster was already on his bike and bound away.

The older boy said "I'll give it to him for you."

Hutch gave him the change; and as he left too, Hutch called to his back "Go straight home and *stay*." In the backwash of both boys' vanishing scorn, he felt like the primal sire of the race. It helped him smile.

25

At that same moment Wade's eyes came open in his darkened room in Hutch's house—not that he knew any name for the place. By now he could see no more than a kind of pearly light in which occasional tall or round shapes stirred faintly at a distance like hands in milk. He said "Well, I'm here"; and his left hand scratched toward the edge of the mattress, feeling for his exact whereabouts. He found another hand, warmer than his and softer, though large. The arm above it was bare to the shoulder, where he felt a soft shirt. Wade started to say "Fe-fi-fo-fum, I smell the blood—" Then he lost the rest of the saying. So he laughed. "Who's in my bed?"

Mait said "Your Mait." He was lying full-clothed on the top of Wade's cover, a handspan apart.

Wade said "Hey, Mait." Then "Who the hell are you?"

"A young short guy—twenty-one years old though: no minor, don't worry, no charges are pending."

Wade's whole head seemed to retreat a long way. He finally said "I beg to differ."

"How?"

"I'm convicted. And sentenced."

At once Wade had pushed Mait past his calm moorings. Mait laughed anyhow. "Convicted of what? Nothing worse than roadhogging."

Again Wade paused. Mait's hand was still in reach, so Wade took it again and thought he pressed it—the pressure was barely detectable. "I think I'm guilty of just one thing."

"Want to tell Father Mait?"

"If I do, will he trust me and not make the same mistake again in his entire life?"

"A promise—Mait'll give it a serious shot."

Wade's lips were so dry they stuck together and only opened when he shook his head. "I was stingy as some old village miser."

Mait said "I heard otherwise—rumor says you were truly a gent and a spender."

"Too much of a gent—way too much. But barely a spender. Oh Jesus, no."

"You failed to buy what?"

Wade knew right off. "Oh love. Fine bodies. Warm cries in the night."

Mait laughed again.

"I mean every word. Don't hoard your body."

"But Wade, your body's what's punishing you—*using* your body anyhow." Mait bit his lip to have said the word *punishing*; too late now.

The huge skull agreed. "For a few good years with one splendid man. One woman, for a few months before I actually figured who I needed, before I knew Wyatt. One tacky boy before I left home, a senior at State. God, I could have known every man in the nation, from stem to stern, and not be dying faster than this."

Mait said "You've got a point. It's scary as hell."

"It's *waste* and you know it. No, child, listen and recall this forever— remember Wade Mayfield tried to save you from stinginess, as mean a failing as anything else but strangling children." Any person with eyes, seated by Wade, could have seen he was sane and urgent in his warning. What a watcher might have failed to see was how unstoppably the whole past life of his family surged in Wade and pressed out the news he'd passed to one boy, one who might or might not have the wits and courage to use it well.

Young as he was, Mait knew to thank him, though he thought at the time *Wade's waving me on toward a death like his own.*

26

I⊤ was well past six in the evening before Hutch took the last turn in the drive and saw home, broad on its green hill, no sign of trouble, a rest for the mind. In the final twenty minutes of the trip, he'd all but panicked in the simple need to see Wade again and know that the boy had waited to see him and would recognize his face and accept his gift. Hutch had brought Wade a gift from Richmond, a small piece of staurolite, a dark brown stone that occurs in the natural shape of a cross and is mined in the mountains of Virginia.

Hutch checked his pocket for the stone cross, found it, then searched the house windows for life. The sun stalled, ruthless, above the tree line; but in every window some lamp burned. Hutch thought *They're gone and they left in a hurry.* Mait's bike still waited in the back turn circle and a strange old Buick. *They called the ambulance or Ann came and got them.*

By the time Hutch reached the door, he nearly believed it. But he turned the knob—open on cool air and the sound of laughter, a man's voice deeper than Wade's or Mait's. Hutch waited in place. *Who on Earth?*

Then Mait's voice called out "Welcome back." His undiscourageable face appeared at the end of the hall, in Wade's doorway. He was wearing khaki shorts and a green tank top.

Behind Mait, a taller darker man stood and faced Hutch squarely. He was in the act of donning a T-shirt.

Hutch failed to recognize the man; and when a surge of resentment struck him, Hutch heard himself say to Mait "You called in strangers?"

Mait's face collapsed.

The other man said "Mr. Mayfield, I'm Cam—Cameron Mapleson. We met at Maitland's." When Hutch stared on in obvious anger, Cam said "I was badly dressed at the time—it was dawn—and I'm still sorry."

Then Hutch remembered their awkward meeting and nodded curtly; but he went on feeling invaded, assaulted. *Why did Mait feel the right to bring in company?*

Cam understood. He came halfway down the hall toward Hutch. "Sir, this visit was my idea. I had the evening off, I knew Mait was staying out here with Wade, I wanted to see them both and I stopped by. I thought I might help someway, with my background." He extended his massive right hand to Hutch.

Finally Hutch came to meet him and took the plainly guileless greeting with the trace of a smile. "I'm just an old bear, sorry—guarding my cave."

Mait's guilty face was still at Wade's door, well beyond them.

So Hutch said "Who's feeding this great multitude?"

From his bed Wade tried to call out "Me," a broken syllable.

Hutch could hear it but, to Mait and Cam, it sounded like trouble. They both looked to Hutch for directions. *You deal with the crazy.*

Hutch lowered his voice. "Let me see Wade alone. Then I'll cook us supper."

Relieved, the two young men agreed and moved past Hutch toward the bright-lit front room.

When Hutch got to Wade, the boy was lying flat with both eyes open toward the ceiling. For the first time in weeks, the eyes had the look of real connection; they were almost surely seeing something beyond them in the world.

Hutch leaned to the forehead and kissed it—cool. "What're you watching, dear friend?"

Wade tried to find him but settled on the wrong place, the foot of the bed. "I'm running our old home movies by the mile."

"Which reel?" There were years of old eight-millimeter film in cans in the attic—Hutch and Ann's honeymoon in Charleston, Wade's whole childhood; Hutch's grandmother Eva in the year of her death, daunting as any Cretan priestess brandishing gold snakes; Wade's graduation from architecture school at N.C. State and departing from the airport for his job in New York.

Wade said "I'm watching, over and over the ones of you as a boy up at Strawson's." There were no such films. Any movies Wade watched were confined to the screen of his uncertain mind.

Hutch understood that, but still it set off a recollection. He'd bought the movie camera just before he and Ann were married in the fifties. To a mind as visually grounded as Hutch's, in those years even his private events had hardly seemed real until they'd been witnessed by some kind of camera and stored as proof for future reference—*We had this life, it's not all gone, I can bring it back partway.* So he said to Wade "I wish we did have some record of me. I've got no idea how I really looked or moved in the early years, just that I never smiled in snapshots. I was always posing ferociously as the Hope of Mankind or the Blazing Avenger of Sensitive Souls. There's an all but daily record of you in your first year, your first six Christmases until you told me I was Santa Claus, and I beat a retreat."

Wade said "I'll burn those."

You couldn't strike a match if your life depended on it. But Hutch said "They'll just mean more and more to me."

"You can't ever watch them again though, can you?"

"Why?"

Wade's voice slid into the high singsong he used more and more. "Go incinerate every one of them *now*. You're in my command."

Hutch said "I don't watch them more than once in ten years; but no, they'll be precious further down the road."

Wade said "They'll kill you—on sight—you well know that: watching me young and well, in my right mind."

Hutch agreed in silence, then quickly moved the subject aside. "Enjoy your break, your two days with Maitland?"

Wade waited a long time, then ducked his head hard. "They stripped buck naked for me, let me feel skin. Mait and Cam—they mainly let me listen while they did it." Wade was plainly not joking, he seemed clearheaded, then he faced Hutch and smiled the first abandoned smile he'd managed in months. "I'd forgotten *hair*, Hutch—sweet private hair. Don't it heal your heart?" It sounded like unimpeachable thanks.

And it took Hutch awhile to process the news with no resentment. Finally he granted the truth of Wade's question. "Hair's one of the absolute good things, true—the right kind of hair." He reached for the bones of Wade's hand on the sheet, lifted them gently toward his own dry lips and barely brushed them—the withered whorls that had been fingerprints.

Wade said "Don't stop. I'm living for pleasure entirely these days." Then he gave the strongest laugh he'd given since before Wyatt died; he heard it himself and wondered at his strength.

Hutch laid the cross-shaped staurolite in the palm of Wade's hand. "A little gift from Old Virginny."

Wade's fingers felt it hungrily, then took it to his lips, forced the long teeth open and the lips sucked it in.

Hutch thought *Oh Son, don't swallow a brown rock.* But he only said "It's not candy, boy. Don't break a good molar."

Wade said "I know it's the Holy Cross. I'm draining it dry. It knows my name." In another five seconds he'd sunk into sleep.

Taking a clean rubber glove from the drawer, Hutch carefully opened the clenched jaw and teeth, felt for the staurolite with his finger and fished it out. He set it on Wade's bedside table, went to his own room and washed the trip from his face and hands, then went to see if Mait and Cam were gone.

No, they were silent, back in the kitchen, well into cooking clam sauce for pasta—their own idea.

Hutch was too tired to feel resentment.

27

BUT an hour later, with the food and wine and low-keyed laughter, Hutch was partly restored. The ache for Wade was a steady presence, sure to last as long as Hutch lasted and to blare out unpredictably in solitude. Yet the nearness here of Cam and Mait had worked to remind Hutch of time's persistence and the hell-bent course of every life except the self-haters who circle, slow-motion. Finally, when the dishes were washed and the two guests stood to leave, Hutch confronted them, smiling. "You gave Wade a brief *exhibición* I hear?"

Mait didn't know the word.

But Cam had heard it years back from his father, a U.S. Navy vet from the days when Havana offered sailors a wealth of booths and small theaters where women, men and assorted animals supplied their starved eyes with live exhibitions of mammal flesh at the outer limits of its will to join, delight or torment other flesh. So it was Cam's turn to look trapped and sheepish. Still he tried to put his best foot forward. "Wade remembered and told you?"

Hutch said "Long enough to tell me he'd felt skin again."

Mait understood at last and went through his full regulation response—flushing, stammering at various pitches. "Sir, Wade asked *us*."

But Cam faced Hutch. "Not truly, no, he didn't. It was my idea and it went a little further than I intended. You feel insulted?"

When Hutch kept silent, Mait said "We just sat lightly on the bed by Wade and talked—in our birthday suits for half an hour."

Not glancing to Mait, Cam said straight to Hutch "That's a lie, sir. We made flat-out love in easy reach of Wade."

"On that narrow bed?" Hutch was asking Cam.

But Cam looked to Mait and gave a slow gesture. *Over to you.*

So Maitland said "Wade asked us to—"

In a calm whisper Cam said "No Wade didn't. We offered it to him—*I* made the offer. I'm his age, I can feel his loneliness, I had the right."

Hutch bridled. "The *right?* Where's your half of the deed? This is my house, Cameron, while I draw breath."

Cam held in place at the table and took it, eye to eye with Hutch.

Mait's face had reddened to the point of real danger. He nodded to Hutch though. "Wade liked it, right off."

Cam leaned forward finally. "Sir, I don't think we harmed your son in the slightest. He's been so far gone from life and caring, I'd all but guarantee we did him a kindness—a service at least."

Hutch said "I'm sorry you can think that simply." He didn't feel puritan outrage or envy, just one more taste of bone-aching regret that once again Wade had been forced up against a human pleasure he'd never share again.

Cam said "Don't be sorry. And think how wrong you may well be. Whatever Mait says, I can tell you this—I never did anything any more intimate with anyone else, male or female, than what the two of us did for Wade. I'll never forget it."

Hutch said "You both took precautions?—Wade's a very sick boy."

Cam said "Rest your mind. I work with the sick."

Then oddly, for the first time in years, Hutch was ambushed by concern for Ann's rights in this. *Ann would hate this; she'd blister us all, the moment she knew.* He even said to Mait "Did his mother drop by?"

"This morning early. Then she called up again in midafternoon."

"How much did you tell her?"

Mait said "Cam wasn't even here that early. I told her the truth— Wade and I were fine; you'd been delayed but would be here by dark."

Hutch had to say "But what if she'd walked in on you?"

Mait looked to Cam.

Cam said "We'd have stood up and acted polite."

Hutch imagined the scene and couldn't think whether to laugh or howl. "She'd have shot you both dead—she packs a pistol" (Ann did,

quite legally in her purse, ever since she moved to the deep sticks alone).
By then Hutch could risk a smile.

Mait said "Mr. Mayfield, I'm apologizing."

"To me?" Hutch said.

Cam said "I'm not."

Hutch said "I wouldn't accept it if you did." He turned to Mait, who
was still humiliated. "Friend, thanks for the time, if not the sideshow.
We may need more of your presence yet; I'll make it worth your while,
as I told you."

Mait said "Your money won't work with me."

Hutch was stumped.

Mait said "I owe you anything you can ask—you gave me my life.
Don't even say *money*, sir."

Cam was standing by, behind Mait's chair. Now he leaned and folded
Mait into his arms, rubbing his chin on the crown of Mait's head.

And to Hutch, Mait's outburst felt like as good a reward as he'd ever
get for his years of teaching; the sight of Cam's eyes and face were a gift
too. So Hutch said "My friends mostly call me Hutch—please no more
sirs, not from either one of you." When he'd shaken their hands, he felt
so empty that he nearly begged "Better let me go rest."

But Wade's voice sang out through his open door yards away, a high
soft line from "The Last Rose of Summer"—"*Left blooming alone.*"

Frail as the sound was, Hutch knew the voice well enough to know
that Wade's lips were grinning.

Everyone chuckled and Mait and Cam left, not turning back on their
full day.

28

By half past nine Wade was washed and diapered and back asleep. Hutch
had locked the house and was in his own room, ready for bed, when the
telephone rang. Two rooms away, the message machine broadcast Ann's
voice. "Hutch, can you hear me?"

He badly wanted to ignore her, but he knew she'd panic and drive straight over to check on Wade. So slowly he took up the nearest phone. "—Just barely. I'm exhausted."

"The trip was hard?"

"I had some car trouble; but no, I'm just not the wandering bard I was."

"You're no worse than tired though?" Her time among lawyers was telling on Ann; she sounded relentless as any prosecutor.

"Christ, no, lady—I'm no worse than beat. Not to the best of my knowledge at least."

"You can't fail, Hutch."

"I don't plan to fail. But I need to rest." He was rushing her. "What's on your mind?"

She balked. "You're conceding then that I've got a mind?"

"Games, Ann, games. I resign; play solitaire. Sincere good night."

"Wait—it's been a rough two days."

"It's been a rough life." When she didn't agree, Hutch briefly heard Alice back this morning—*You've frozen her out*—so he said "What's the latest?"

Her voice moved through it like a memorized speech, with pauses and feeling but clearly practiced (which made Hutch despise it, from the first word on). "I need one promise from you, just one. I'll even pay for it—don't hire young Maitland Moses again to sit with Wade. I'll pay for a nurse if you have to leave. When's Hart Salter coming back from England?"

Hutch said "Hart's gone till the fall at least. No, save your cash; young Mait worked fine—he's honest and careful. Wade told me so."

Ann said "Give me this much."

"You've scarcely seen Maitland; what's so bad about him?"

"You'll say I'm a bigot, but I'm also Wade Mayfield's only mother. He's dying of the kind of life he chose; it seems very wrong to me that, in these straits, we should leave him alone with one more man who's made the same blind and killing mistake." It was literally the first time Ann had broached the subject with Hutch in all their years. For all the recognition she'd conceded, Wade and Wyatt might have been blood twins or orbiting astronauts, chosen by lot.

Instantly Hutch felt bathed in the lights of a television panel show of idiot simplicity—*Our Sexual Roles: Genetic Fate or Adult Choice? Choose one and justify.* All he might have learned from Alice that morning flushed through him and vanished. He wanted to tear the phone from the wall; but he finally said "Yes, Counselor Mayfield, you're right as always—your son and mine chose his own life and death exactly the way presexual children choose brain tumors or pediatric AIDS, just that freely— so has Maitland Moses. Christ, wake up, Ann. Or *wise* up, at least. You're too smart to mimic some nineteenth-century Baptist deacon who thinks Jonah spent three days in a whale and that women who lie with donkeys must be stoned. I fear you've spent a few hours too many with the criminal element—or is it just Christian TV you're watching? Whatever, it's plainly dulling your mind and damning you to Hell."

Ann said "I haven't mentioned a donkey yet, though the word *jackass* does come to mind often. But no, just because you ruined your and my life through cowardice doesn't make me wrong."

"Cowardice?"

"Hutch, I trust you've known for decades—God knows, I have— that you made a choice and made it wrong. You loved Straw Stuart but married me."

To his surprise, and shocked as he was by this delayed charge, Hutch had a ready answer. It came so smoothly that he thought, as he said it, *This has waited for years.* "Ann, I've loved Strawson nearly all his life. He's a lot more loyal than the average collie—not to speak of humans including my mate, who abandoned me for nothing worse than the normal atmospheres of a marriage that's lasted awhile. But I couldn't have lived with him forty-five minutes—Straw or any other man I've known. So your brilliant diagnosis of my wrong turn is so inaccurate that I won't dignify it with a full answer. From somewhere around age fourteen and onward, I've steadily done what I meant to, in my main choices, with you at least and in starting our son on his way to life.

"I reached out and tried for a sizable life with a woman as different from me as a panther. And up till last year, I thought we had a life—a good-sized existence, give or take normal failures—till you skipped out for your experiment in radical secular hermitage. Anyhow, whoever ended our marriage, the main result of what we did is dying now, way past our help. That much is tragic; what's left of you and me is ludicrous—you just made it so."

Ann held a long moment. "I told you the truth, and you well know it. What you wanted was wrong—and it's caused our pain, all ours and Wade's—but I wish to God you'd gone with Straw and left me free. There ought not to *be* anything left of us."

If Hutch could have found the energy for one more speech, his actual fury might have caused Ann harm, even at a distance. That at least would have been a true sign of what he felt. But finally he only said "Good night. I'm gone." And he was; he hung up. He sat still a minute, in case she called back. No call came and, in ten minutes more, Hutch was on his own bed—stripped and out like a smothered child, desperately unconscious.

Over again, till Wade called for him a little after dawn, Hutch dived and surfaced in a tangled continuous dream of paralysis. In all its parts, Hutch could see his real body, laid here on his bed and frozen to stone in every cell. On a straight chair against the wall beyond him, he could sense Wade's presence—huge now and strong again but still blind and stunned. The one great need was for Hutch to make a simple request, a single demand of Wade, requiring an answer; but his lips couldn't move. And a spot on the surface of his locked brain, the size of a stamp, was all that could think. In that small spot, on through the night, Hutch repeated the single request in silence, trapped in his skull but meant for Wade—*Will you give me an answer?* Whether or not it ever reached Wade through the air between them in the dream, no answer came, not all night long, though Wade sat on in reach of his father and had sufficient strength to free him.

29

AT five forty-five in the morning however, the actual Wade called Hutch's name between their rooms; and Hutch came at once, not pausing to put on more than his briefs. In the doorway he paused and tried to see Wade's shape, trusting he'd still be down in bed, weak as he'd been since the last pneumonia. But when Hutch's eyes came open in the dimness, the bed was only a tangle of sheets.

Wade had somehow got himself up and dressed in a flannel robe from his childhood, a remnant that fit him once again. He was crouched on himself in the one easy chair. When he sensed his father, he said "I've been up a very long time, sir, waiting for you."

Hutch said "I'm sorry; I must have been even tireder than I knew. You should have called me."

Wade said "I did, about five hundred times. You never heard me and I couldn't walk closer."

By then Hutch had moved to the bedside table and switched on a lamp. The boy looked no worse than yesterday, but Hutch said "What's wrong?" and sat on the bed.

Again Wade took slow time to decide. The message would sink, then rise and hook at the base of his brain, then vanish again. Finally it rose for long enough to let Wade say "I'm a whole lot stronger suddenly." To prove it, he did a physical trick the neurologists had taught him—shutting his blind eyes, extending both arms, then finding his nose with his straight forefinger—first one arm, then the other. Each time the finger found its way with no detour.

Hutch said "No doubt about it; you're better."

Wade put a silencing finger to his lips. "I know this means I'm close to dying. No, don't shut me up, Hutch. I've watched it in others—we get a few of our faculties back, like a small tip from fate." Wade chuckled deeply. "There's something I need to tell you soon, before I'm gone." He stopped and wiped his dry blue lips as if they were wet. He'd lost his subject.

Hutch said "I'm listening."

Wade ran a hand down the length of his face as if clearing cobwebs but nothing more came. So he finally smiled. "Remind me every day from here on out. There's something in me that you need to know."

The announcement of death was all Hutch heard, and he knew at once that Wade was right. He went to the bathroom, filled a pail with water, brought soap, a rag, and a small soft towel; then he went back, stripped and bathed his child where he sat in the chair as dawn progressed at every window.

30

THAT morning Ann drove the ten green miles to Hillsborough, the small
county seat with its pillared old court house, the town green where the
leaders of a protorevolutionary force called the Regulators had been cere-
moniously hanged by the Royal Governor in 1771, the airy home of a
signer of the Declaration of Independence, and a small jail that still looked
like a holding pen for cutthroats dragged from a pirate hulk off the Outer
Banks, which had been a bolt-hole for the dreaded Blackbeard, Edward
Teach.

Those facts—and the strata of pain they implied—were hardly fore-
most in Ann's mind as she paused at the first stoplight in town; but the
peace of the place, its slow air of entire self-confidence and serene faith
in its chance of enduring centuries longer were parts of the ease Ann felt
as she parked just off the main street. Today she and a younger woman
attorney had had an appointment to talk with the law firm's most urgent
client; at the last moment, the attorney got sick; so Ann had come on her
own, unruffled, to ask more questions of that dire client—the young man
whom Hutch called the Hurdle Mills Strangler (Hurdle Mills was fifteen
miles north, a quiet village).

The man's name was Walter Wilk, called Whirly or simply Whirl
by all; and what he'd done—unquestionably, this past Easter morning—
was strangle his mother with a Donald Duck necktie, a gift she'd brought
him from her Thanksgiving trip to Disney World with the women of her
church. Then two days later when no one had yet discovered his mother,
who lived alone, Whirly suffocated his passed-out alcoholic brother-in-
law with a pillow in the early hours of a Sunday morning as the drunk
snored on beside his drunk wife, who never heard a peep, in their double-
wide mobile home in the woods.

In the weeks that Ann had worked with the killer—taking his increasingly hair-raising confessions and his simultaneous fevered mission to win
her and all her colleagues to Jesus—she'd developed an undownable
sympathy for what Whirly had endured in his thirty-six years (a father
like something from the Brothers Grimm, a runaway wife as ravenous for
love and money as any debutante, a string of early felonies involving drugs
and break-ins, and the sight of his sister delivering a stillborn baby in her

kitchen with nobody present but Whirly and her husband's deranged pit bull).

The day Ann had first seen Whirly in jail, three months ago, she'd noticed—as he turned to leave their cubicle, chained hand and foot—that the back of his head with its thick black hair beginning to curl, the wide level shoulders and rail-straight posture all but made him a twin to Wade Mayfield: a lost twin mangled by the hands of his kin but waiting still for some hope of rescue, a hope as surely futile as Wade's.

Now as the jailer led Whirly in to the same green conference cubicle, he still wore handcuffs but no leg irons. His hair was even longer, he'd thinned down further in the week since Ann had seen him, so even his eyes were now moving in Wade's direction—the blank and unbearably helpless stare of the volunteer martyr, oblivious to his crime.

Since Ann was part of Whirly's defense team, the jailer was forced to leave them alone—checking at intervals through a glass slot to see if she was staying alive in such proximity to a known madman.

As the madman faced her across a three-foot-wide oak table, Ann saw that his face had gone on clearing in the past eight days—a well-shaped landscape, purging itself of mountainous waste and a lowering sky. Ann opened her notebook, reminded herself *He's not Wade, Ann; he's killed his own mother; you're not his Aunt Jesus;* and then she amazed herself by saying a thing she'd never mentioned before, not in this death house. As each word came, it sounded more unprofessional than the last; but she gave in and told him. "Whirly, my son's at the point of death; so talk plainly please, fast. I need *out* of here." At once she felt like fleeing in shame. She'd never so much as acknowledged being human, much less a sad mother—not in this awful room—but she begged no pardon and waited for his answer.

Whirly said "It's AIDS, right?" His eyes were as flat as aluminum washers.

That he'd gone for the throat like that, in an instant, barely seemed strange to Ann. *Somebody from the firm is bound to have told him. But surely not.* "Who told you that?"

Then slowly Whirly's eyes went hot as an ermine's at the throat of a mouse. "Mother Mary, in the night. She tells me a *lot*."

Whirly's strain of Christianity, from what Ann had gathered, was a holy-rolling Protestant sect with a self-anointed woman bishop weighing three hundred pounds and called Sister Triumph. Sister's theology, oddly, included a few Roman saints and the Virgin Mary in exotic doses— Whirly wore a black rosary around his neck every time Ann had seen him; he claimed to use it hourly at least. Now Ann said only "Ask her to pray for him then."

"Who?"

"Mother Mary."

Whirly's eyes were puzzled. "What's your boy's name then?" When Ann balked, Whirly said "I got to have his name—she don't take nameless requests nohow." Then he smiled broadly; his teeth were calamitous.

"Wade—Wade Mayfield, Raven Wade Mayfield. As good a man as breathes." Even more certain she was on crazy ground, Ann glanced to the window in the door—no sign of the jailer. *I've crossed completely over, someway. I'll never leave this room, not today.*

Whirly's voice stayed level. "Young Wade's a queer?"

Of course it all but stupefied Ann. *Now, like the rest of the hateful Christians, he'll damn him to Hell* (Ann's own youthful Christianity had been scorched out, long since, by her notice that groups of Christians bigger than three, tend to grow scornful fangs and dream at least of executing God's vengeance on their neighbors). But since she'd constantly stressed to Whirly that he needed to tell the full truth at all times to all his defenders, she couldn't lie here. "Wade lived for some years with a man in New York, a black man that hated his father and me. No girlfriend ever, not that I ever saw—not since his college years at State. But nobody I ever met or watched in any brand of news was a kinder soul. Wade could watch you every day of the week and still act kind."

Whirly said "*Was?* Nobody else *was.* Ain't Wade alive? You just said he was." Whirly's hands had joined on the table between them, making a flat empty pyramid against the dark oak. Big as they were, they could easily suffocate a Doberman, an ox.

"Wade's hanging on, yes, by the thinnest strand. Nobody yet has rounded a curve with AIDS and come back." Ann could hear that, already, she'd said the word AIDS in this dim room more times than elsewhere. But then these walls had heard the worst the human race could dream or do, for well over two hundred years and counting.

"There you *go*," Whirly said. "Ain't that everybody's boat? Who gets
back alive?"

Helplessly honest again, Ann said "Well, you're hanging on, my
friend, in fairly good shape."

"Hold your phone here, lady. Everybody's warming up the gas chamber—ain't they?—making little signs that say 'Whirly Wilk, *die* in your
own shit and stink'; but I'm swimming for *land*." Whirly raised both giant
hands and stroked at the hot air, an Australian crawl.

Ann pushed back a little from the table, tried to smile, and stroke a
few yards of her own beside him.

Whirly said "Where to?"

"Pardon?"

"Where are *you* headed?"

Ann said "You tell me *your* destination."

Whirly likewise pushed back, some six feet from her. In a full minute's
wait, with his eyes shut calmly, what he came up with was "A piece of
high ground. Plenty light, a cold spring, shady groves and music—deep
banjo music all night and noon, not too near to drown you or upset your
rest. No in-laws present, no blood kin but maybe a deaf old aunt, a few
distant cousins—beg your pardon on that." He smiled thinly but looked
as sane as any magistrate, exercising pardon on a room of young children.
"I'll wait for him there."

"*Him* is my son, Whirl? *Him* means Wade?"

Whirly smiled an entirely new credible smile, then ducked his chin
in a fix-eyed surety. "Wade Mayfield, sure. He'll be safe as trees."

Mad as she understood Whirl was, Ann half chose to trust him. *Even
so*, she thought, *that leaves me lost.*

31

Two days later at the end of work, Ann came to the house, knocked at
the front door and waited while Hutch put down his book and answered.

His first sight of her, in the late oblique light, was the same fresh
shock she'd given him often in the past forty years, the most reliable gift

she gave—the jolt of her beauty even here, this far along; the depth of her eyes, her lustrous hair that was more than half white now, the delicate and tacit promise she'd always offered to join him in private acts of pleasure with a steady daring grace that could bring down immense rewards. It took Hutch a moment to raise his resistance to such a body and its intricate, forbearing, feral mind. Then he said the first two words that came. "Lose something?"

Ann had lectured herself all the way out here to turn his first thrust, not to flare and explode. So in a low voice she answered him literally, then said what she planned. "I'm losing the same son you are; and, Hutch, I need to move back."

"Back where?"

"My home, the legal address of my child and the man I'm still married to."

In its single blast, it nearly thawed Hutch; he was startled again to feel how hard he wanted her—not *for* anything but her frank handsome presence and the matrix of shared time and acts they'd laid down beneath them as food and shelter precisely for this late time in both their lives: the chance at a peaceful evening glide before full desolation and age. But he said "I can't fall down here, Ann, and let you walk right over and past me suddenly. You dug this whole bizarre canyon between us; I can't just ignore it and—"

"*I* dug the canyon?"

"We both did—sure, I dug along with you—but you chose to move to the far rim, right?"

Ann yielded his point with her eyes, her best argument.

So Hutch drew back from blocking the entrance and stood as she walked in.

She went up the hall to the living room door and paused there, looking back for further permission.

"You can go on to Wade's room."

In her normal voice, not whispering to spare Wade, Ann said "I'm asking for the back bedroom—not for life, understand, but just the duration." She pointed toward Wade's room—the term of Wade's life, she plainly meant. When Hutch failed to answer, she said "I'll pay rent, my share of the groceries, the phone and lights, anything else you say." By the end, when she understood she was begging, she'd begun to whisper. She was whispering now, though few other humans could have yielded so much and still looked upright and straight as an elm.

Hutch pointed to the kitchen and also whispered. "Let's talk back there."

For all their problems, neither one of them ever had leaned on alcohol. Generations of drunks in both their families had warned them off it. So Hutch knew not to bring out the wine or Ann's preferred brand of unblended scotch; they'd need full clarity. There was ready-made coffee on hand by the sink. Hutch poured that out into two tall mugs, sugared Ann's her way, heated the mugs in a microwave big enough to roast a grown pig, then sat opposite Ann at the breakfast table. When they'd each downed swallows, he said "You know it nearly killed me when you left?"

She shook her head No. "You never said."

"It did—the pure truth."

"Hutch, if that's meant as flattery, I can't take it here." Yet his deepset eyes met hers—unaged, undimmed—the one part of him that could always reach and, most times, hold her.

He shook his head No and again said "The truth. I thought I'd die for the first few days, flat-suffocate. It's still like another great rock on my chest."

"Then I'm more than amazed." There was no keen edge or burr on her voice; she was aiming at honesty buffered by the years of sympathy she hoped they'd laid down, a hanging bridge between them.

Hutch met that offer with his own precision. "You know I've had trouble all my life telling people I love them. I'm afraid it'll spook them, maybe even kill them. It killed my mother."

Ann said "Hutch, your mother died of a hemorrhage."

"—Caused by me."

"Not *you*, never you. She'd loved Rob Mayfield and wanted to bear his child—plain as that. She was grown when she chose to bring you to life; her eyes were wide open. The doctor couldn't stop her bleeding the day you came; it was plain as that."

Maybe it was. Hutch had never seen it that way, not that simply. It might even serve as a skeleton key to some old locked gates. But he still owed Ann more explanation. "You and me though—I couldn't convince you we were barely two people. In forty years we'd grown into being all but one thing, one thing with two minds. I was fairly content. You seemed to need proofs of love, on the hour—proofs of how separate we were but how needy—and I couldn't give that. All I had to offer was a visible fact, the homely fact that *there I was*. I couldn't and wouldn't, not two years ago and maybe not now."

Ann said "Let's don't even mention love yet, not between you and me. What I'm asking for is a room in this house, whosever it is, and the right to do my duty to our son. I can't love Wade one bit less than you; grant me that much, Hutchins."

"It's not up to me to grant you that. I've never doubted your care for Wade."

"Then let me near him, any hour of the day or night."

Hutch said "I remind you you've got a key. I've never once bolted these doors against you."

"You bring people in here that I can't face—"

"They're not yours to face, Ann. They're my trusted help."

Before her lips had closed just now, she'd heard her mistake. *I left this house; it's his to fill—or torch if he chooses.*

Hutch gave no sign of hearing; but he took a second draft of his coffee, then got to his feet. "Wade's waiting. He's called your name all afternoon."

Ann heard the small compensation in that, the tidy offering—*Wade still knows you*—but as Hutch turned from her and moved toward his study, she knew she wouldn't be sleeping here soon.

32

AT nine that night Hutch phoned Ivory Bondurant. There were nine or ten rings, then a silent pick-up; then nothing but the distant weaving of music, Debussy or Ravel on a harp. He finally said "This is Hutchins Mayfield. Is Miss Bondurant there?"

After five more seconds of music, Ivory said "Good evening"—no trace of surprise or welcome.

Hutch had to say "Are you all right?"

"I think so, yes"—very cautious and slow.

She's drugged or sick. But he said "I'm afraid I've waked you. Sorry, I'll call another time."

"No, no, Mr. Mayfield. How are you?"

Only then did he realize *She must think I'm calling to say Wade's dead.* "Thanks. I'm well, Miss Bondurant. Wade's had pneumonia but is back home again and a little stronger maybe."

Ivory said "And his vision?"

Hutch had noticed, from the start, how everyone's dread at the thought of Wade went straight toward his blindness (as recently as two weeks ago, Dr. Ives had repeated her offer to treat Wade's eyes with the single drastic remedy at hand, however late). So Hutch lied now, to ease the news. "He sees a little, odd times of the day; but no, his eyes are a good deal worse than when you saw him last—I think so at least. He's confused more often, and of course he's thinner still."

Ivory said "That's expected," then waited for more. Behind her the music solved its way toward a tentative ending, followed by silence.

Had a radio died? Had some live harpist been in another room of Ivory's apartment and shut down this moment? In the calm Hutch couldn't remember why he'd called, and his uncertain wait stretched out like tension.

At last Ivory said "Mr. Mayfield, what has Wade told you?"

Late as it was, Hutch heard nothing strange in the question. It even triggered the memory of his purpose. "Wade mostly lives in the here and now—I think his memory's almost gone. But today he did bring up the apartment; he asked me if we still had Wyatt's portrait. I can't recall seeing any such picture. I thought you might."

"I have it, yes. It's safe with me."

"Is it a photograph or a painting?"

"A painting—the absolute soul of Wyatt Bondurant."

"Who painted it?"

"I did, years ago, when I still painted—when my hand could still do it. I gave it to Wade once Wyatt died; but even with his failing vision then, Wade told me he couldn't stand to have it in sight—he regretted

Wyatt so grievously. It's been here with me, turned to the wall. I can't watch it either. Wade can have it anytime."

"I'll tell him that you said as much. If he wants it down here, I'd pay of course for your gallery to crate it."

"Just let me know."

"Did you ever paint Wade?"

Ivory paused. "I did, eight years ago, but now that's gone."

Hutch was interested. "Sold?"

"No, it's with my mother out on Long Island. She cherished Wade and asked me for it."

Hutch said "Thank her for me, over again. She's written us kindly."

"She's far more than overqualified for a saint—my sainted mother. I wish I had a tenth of her grit." Ivory waited again.

So Hutch came to the point. "You're getting the rent checks I send on time?"

"No problem with that, except I wonder if you don't want me to clear out those rooms and let them pass to a new set of people. I could ship everything that matters on down; it wouldn't fill up more than three more boxes. It may be a crime, paying this much rent on useless space."

Hutch said "It's useful to Wade, I believe. Shutting it down might actually kill him."

"Would Wade have to know?"

"I couldn't lie to him; he grills me occasionally, to be sure it's there; that we haven't ended his old life without a sign at least from him."

Ivory said "I didn't know his mind was that clear."

"*Clear*'s not the real word. But even now he sometimes speaks of going back up there to work again. He knows the last drawing he left on his desk." Hutch hadn't quite understood he felt that till then, though he knew he'd never grudged the steep rent, both Wade's and Wyatt's shares (Ann's absence from the house had freed up some cash).

Ivory said "Then I see what you mean; that might well throw him. I know my brother's empty space in this building keeps *my* hurt strong."

"I hadn't considered that."

"Then don't—Lord, don't. I can last it out. It's a small task compared to yours and Wade's mother's."

Hutch couldn't recall that Ivory had mentioned Ann before, and he wondered what contact they might have had. Had Ann ever phoned her or vice versa? *Stay out of that.* So he only thanked Ivory.

She politely denied that Hutch bore her a debt; but when she could hear he was near hanging up, she said "Mr. Mayfield, is there something else?"

"No, not really. Nothing but the sadness, and you share that. It doesn't slack, does it? I thought it would."

"You're terribly right. No, I just thought you might have something on your heart or mind."

Her tone was so gentle Hutch couldn't imagine she meant Wyatt's hatred of him and Ann, but he said "You mean about Wyatt's refusing us?"

"No, sir, I didn't." With that she went silent, plainly finished.

Hutch heard it. "Would you say the name *Hutchins* once please?"

Ivory said "Hutchins" in her richest voice.

For a moment it gave Hutch his old childhood thrill at hearing his name, two syllables of noise that were somehow him. "Thank you, Ivory— if I may call you that." For an instant he thought *God, she'll think I'm playing massah*; but he said "I'm almost old enough to be your grandfather. Please call me Hutchins or Hutch from here on." Awkward as it felt, Hutch wasn't embarrassed. He'd suddenly needed a woman's kind notice; it might help him through one more restless night.

Ivory said "I'll try, if we meet again."

Just as the phone moved down from his ear, Hutch thought he could hear her music renewed—one wide and darkly chromatic chord.

33

BUT well after midnight Hutch still hadn't slept, so he reached out into the dark and dialed the operator. For some odd reason he lied to the woman and told her his lights had suddenly failed, he couldn't see to dial, would she please connect him to a long-distance number?

That late, the woman took time to be pleasant. "In the dark all alone, eh? *I know* how you feel—believe you me." She assured him he'd get the cheap rate all the same, and the number rang twice.

Strawson answered *"Late,"* sepulchrally. No one alive could be far off and still establish, with voice alone, the vivid sight of his physical body and the air around him quicker than Straw.

"It's nowhere near late for you, old watchman."

"I was just lying here awake thinking of you."

Hutch said "Much obliged; your thoughts must have reached me."

"They do that, yes. It's the last of my powers; all else has failed me." But he laughed around in the lower reaches of his deep bass register for a good while longer.

Hutch had not spoken with Straw in ten days, not since Ann's night-time phone attack; and he suddenly needed to mention that surprise and hear the effect on whatever Straw had meant last April when he said Hutch had failed to request his life—Straw's own young life as it sped through its brief prime. Now was almost surely not the right time to ask; still Hutch said "Where are you at present?"

"Lying beside my legal spouse, who's snoring nicely."

Hutch said "Good" and felt he meant it.

Straw said "Wade"—more a hope than a question.

"Wade's about where he was when we talked last."

"Would he know me if he saw me?"

"Pretty surely," Hutch said. "For part of the time; he still goes and comes."

"Then I'll be there soon." Straw had never been prone to guilt; for once, he sounded caught out and sorry.

"How about tomorrow? Come spend the night anyhow." Hutch knew that Straw had the countryman's aversion to spending a full night away from his groundings; he'd never spent a night in Hutch's Durham house.

"I'll do it soon but, no, it can't be tomorrow."

"You busy watching weeds grow?"

Straw's wait was so long Hutch thought he'd hung up or drifted to sleep. Finally he said "I'm drunk at the moment. Been drunk five days. I'll be there when I can face you and Wade."

"You sound clear to me."

Straw laughed. "Cast your mind back through the slow centuries, friend; the pageant of S. Stuart's profligate course—when did you ever hear me sound less than clear as the evening lark at dusk?" By the time he'd reached the end of the sentence, he was more than half serious.

Straw Stuart, soused, was several notches clearer than the average air traffic controller; and Hutch well knew it. "Then come on here. I've weaned you before."

"You weaned me from you—that's absolutely all. No, I'm tapering off my usual way, a half pint less a day. I don't want Wade to smell a drop on me; he never has yet."

That instant, Hutch felt painfully single. *I can't see this thing through alone.* He could think of nobody else alive, since Grainger was ancient and Ann disqualified, whom he'd trust to watch Wade's last days with him. But he also knew Straw meant what he'd said—Straw had always kept his drinking from Wade. Even in the worst times, twenty years ago, the surest way to sober Straw was to tell him young Wade was on the way up for a few country days (Wade had literally never seen Straw high, much less drunk). So now Hutch only said "Hurry please. Wade's all but gone. I'm running out of guts."

"You're not and you know it. You watched your father die, hard as this; and you helped him right through."

Hutch said "Not so, old friend. I watched Rob, sure, for a few long days just before he went; but even lung cancer's a moonlight walk compared to Wade's plague."

"You mentioned—who was it?—young Jimmy Boat awhile back. He seemed like a truly old-fashioned gem. Is he still coming down from New York for the Fourth?"

Hutch had forgot the letter from Boat; the thought encouraged him. "Boatie wasn't really young and anyhow the Fourth is still a good while off."

"Call him up. Speed his plans. You could put him on salary as long as you need him."

"Straw, Boatie's got his hands full up there."

"Boat's taking the Fourth off somehow—remember?—to bus himself to—where?—Macon, Georgia and his old grandmammy in her cabin in the cotton. Call him tonight and tell him you'll pay his substitute to work a while longer if he'll help you out."

"Did Boatie say he'd arranged a substitute?"

Straw said "Bound to. He's an angel of God; wouldn't leave his boys to starve alone."

"You got his number then?"

Again Straw lingered as if paging slowly through a universal phone book. At last he said "You do, in that book you brought from Wade's kitchen—Ivory wrote all the numbers down there in the back."

So she had. And Hutch had not called one, not since New York. He'd barely ever cracked the book open; it threatened to unleash its piece of the past. But even before he finished with Straw now, he reached for the lamp on his bedside table. The clock said twenty minutes to one. *No, Boatie works hard; let him sleep till day.*

34

STILL Hutch couldn't wait. When he'd hung up on Straw and gone to Wade's door to check on his breathing, Hutch went to the study, found the composition book and Jimmy Boat's name with a number beside it. After eight rings Hutch was ready to quit.

Then a woman said "*All* right," an old black voice more native to here than the heights of Harlem.

She repeated herself before Hutch could ask for Boatie or Boat. "Nobody named that."

"Is Jimmy Boat there, please ma'm?—I'm sorry."

The woman said "Man, I'm sicker than you'll ever know, to get woke up here, dark as this place is; but hold your water, I'll try to get James."

It took three minutes and Hutch would have quit except for the fact that, right through the wait, he could hear the old woman shuffling through rooms and muttering sentences to what seemed cats or maybe dogs named Arthur and Pepper before she finally knocked at a door and said "James, some sick man in trouble out here."

Eventually James picked up the phone. "Boatie's awake. Can he help you please?"

The way Hutch felt, few questions could have been more welcome. "Boatie, this is Wade Mayfield's father—Hutch Mayfield—in North Carolina. Wade was Wyatt Bondurant's friend, remember?"

"Mr. Mayfield, sure. And Wade—Wade's on my mind every other second." Boat felt a reflex moment of cheer before it dawned on him that Hutch's news could hardly be good. So he rushed to say "Jesus, say it's not so."

"No, it's not, not yet. Not tonight anyhow. But we need you, Jimmy."

"Well, I'm hoping to see you—like I said—round the Fourth of July. That still sound good?"

"What would sound like manna from heaven tonight would be you saying you could fly down here tomorrow morning. I'd make all the plans, make it well worth your while."

Boat seemed to be considering the plea.

Behind him the old woman cranked up again with cries at her cats and loud swats with what seemed like an old slapstick.

Then Boat said "Mr. Mayfield, excuse my aunt; she's crazy as me. Fact is, we're no kin on Earth; but she took me in when I was a raw kid up from Georgia with no more sense than to know I should *run* from where I'd been. She'd fold now without me—eighty-six years old. And don't you know I got men up here counting on me, by the hour and minute, for air to breathe? I can't cut loose. These boys up here would strangle alone, and then I could never forgive myself."

The voice was mild and stripped of the blackface-comic growl it had by day, but Hutch felt a sting of shame. *Marse Hutchins givin his orders to de hands.* "I understand that," he said. "Forgive me, Jimmy."

Boat said "No sooner said than done. But listen, you haven't got no help at all?"

It felt like a dead-right diagnosis. *No help, no. Not a soul I truly want, anywhere near me.* Hutch's throat dried on him; but finally he said "I'll get by, sure. I was just feeling sorry for myself in the night."

"Every reason on this wide Earth to feel sorry. Go on and bawl, sir; I'll sit till you're through."

The thought of Jimmy—the size of a jockey—waiting through long-distance tears in a room with a cracked old aunt and her stray cats was a palpable relief. Hutch said "I'll try to spare you tears. Truly though, if whoever's spelling you in early July can help awhile longer, I'll gladly pay him for all his time so you can stay longer with Wade and me. Of course I'll pay you too." Even laid out meekly, it sounded too grand. "Jimmy, help me—I sound so goddamned rich. I'm not, not in *nothing*." Hutch had never confessed that much bankruptcy to anyone before.

Boat said "Course you're not. Everybody's broke now, everybody *I* know or want to know till this nightmare's over."

"Say it's a dream, yes."

"Child, I wish I could." Boat heard himself and said "Mr. Mayfield."

"*Hutch*, please—just Hutch."

"All right, sir, next time I see your face. But is Wade failing fast?"

"I wrote you he had pneumonia again. He's back home from that and barely holding his own. His throat has got patches of yeast infection the size of half dollars. Just this morning an apparently healthy tooth simply dropped from his jaw and he swallowed it. His hair's lost color till it's nearly transparent and breaks at the touch."

Boat took that in, old news but still stunning. "His eyes all gone?"

"Afraid so, yes—his eyes and his mind. He drifts in and out. He'll know you though. He asks about you several times a day."

Boat said "Then tell him to hold on for me. I'm coming if God gives me strength to travel, and I love him good as ever—don't fail to say that. Tell him Boat says Wade Mayfield *deserves* it—all the love in the world. I truly mean my words."

"Will you call me collect the minute you've got your travel plans?"

"Guaranteed, sir. You'll be the first to know."

Hutch said "I don't think we've got much time."

"Course not," Boat said. "Not one of us has." But then he managed to laugh and whisper "I wish you could see my poor aunt now, here reading scripture to these wild cats—she thinks they'll talk any minute, quote the Bible. They're learning too; they're calling my name! Don't never wake her up again this late!"

"Please tell her I'm sorry."

"Mr. Mayfield, everybody alive is as sorry as you and me and Wade, or they ought to be."

Hutch said "I believe you."

35

ALL that was toward the end of June. Then the days geared down for the coming swelter of July; and when its humid hand clamped down, Wade had very nearly vanished. Confined full-time in the chill clammy house, he now had no flesh left to lose. What coated the awful rack of his bones, that had once been the armature of such welcome beauty, was more like a thin glove leather than skin. He never left bed except in the arms of his father or Maitland; he slept through most days and all of each night in a frail fast dreaming that juddered in his eyelids; and when he woke, he swung from minutes of perfect clarity—recalling his whole life in close detail—to hours of serene but unreadable confusion and long paragraphs of speech in a language unknown since Babel.

For Hutch the single blessing of the time was that he, with help from Mait and Ann and occasional generous visits from the doctor, was able to fill Wade's apparent needs. Hutch gave the medicines, replenished the intravenous nourishments, held urinals and bedpans, emptied and washed them, and fitted the oxygen tubes to Wade's face when his breathing slackened to inaudible wisps. Hutch bathed Wade's skin with the lightest touch each morning and every time Wade fouled himself—less often since there was so little of him and such slim waste to flush through his bore. Hutch sat at the bedside, long parts of each day and much of the night, to answer Wade's deranged requests, his fears and outcries of weak delight, and to tend his remains with the deference due any agonized loved one.

Often Hutch would read aloud from old anthologies of verse—the Greek anthology (its epitaphs for a world of lost boys), the silver Roman poets of friendship and loosely worn love and the splendors Hutch could tap at will from Britain's inexplicably long run of genius (Elizabethan, Jacobean, Metaphysical, Augustan, Romantic, Victorian, Modernist) on down through America's Whitman, Dickinson, Robinson, Frost and Eliz-

abeth Bishop. One afternoon, when he thought Wade was sleeping, Hutch
read out—for his own lost sake—Bishop's villanelle on the death of her
longtime companion Lota Soares, a suicide.

> "The art of losing isn't hard to master;
> so many things seem filled with the intent
> to be lost that their loss is no disaster.
>
> Lose something every day. Accept the fluster
> of lost door keys, the hour badly spent.
> The art of losing isn't hard to master.
>
> Then practice losing farther, losing faster:
> places, and names, and where it was you meant
> to travel. None of these will bring disaster.
>
> I lost my mother's watch. And look! my last, or
> next-to-last, of three loved houses went.
> The art of losing isn't hard to master.
>
> I lost two cities, lovely ones. And, vaster,
> some realms I owned, two rivers, a continent.
> I miss them, but it wasn't a disaster.
>
> —Even losing you (the joking voice, a gesture
> I love) I shan't have lied—"

Hutch had got that far, barely whispering not to wake Wade; but at
the word *lied*, Wade's voice came alive and said the final lines from
memory with all the remains of strength he had.

> "—Even losing you (the joking voice, a gesture
> I love) I shan't have lied. It's evident
> the art of losing's not too hard to master
> though it may look like (*Write* it!) like disaster."

It was a poem they'd never recited together, published after they'd
stopped their bedtime poems; and Hutch was amazed that Wade had

learned, on his own, a poem that meant as much to Hutch as any published in the past fifty years, since Eliot's *Quartets*. But once Wade said the final line, he sank back into what seemed a deep trance, maybe something deeper; so Hutch couldn't ask him how and where he'd found the poem and why he'd learned it. *What's the worst loss he's known? Losing Wyatt, or his home and us, or his body and life here now by the inch?* Lately Hutch had managed to invent quick snatches of prayer he could say with no embarrassment, though with next to no hope. So here by his son, he silently said again *Take Wade this instant.*

But Wade breathed on.

36

THEN on the Friday before the Fourth, in the midst of a suddenly cool afternoon, Hutch was in his own room for a rest when he heard a car stop near the house and slow footsteps toward the kitchen door. The steps were much too heavy for Ann, and no one else was expected to call. *Some homicidal kid out to steal TVs. Let him on in, sure.* For a minute the thought seemed serious—a young crazed killer would simplify things. Hutch got up, quickly brushed his hair and went toward the kitchen to meet whomever.

Straw was standing on the back porch, facing the hill and the natural terraces of pine and juniper and honeysuckle thicket that rose toward the crest and its unblocked view of more green miles. There'd been no word from Straw since the phone call, no sign he'd tapered off from his binge, no apparent interest in Wade.

So the sight of Straw was not really welcome. Hutch thought of hiding—all doors were locked; he could crawl to his own room and ride out the visit. He even got as far out of sight as the windowless hall and waited for the knock. But no knock came. Maybe five minutes passed and still no knock.

By then Hutch was thinking of Straw as more threatening than any housebreaker. *What's he after? He'll somehow burn the place down*—not remotely sane thoughts but they came nonetheless. *Where is he this moment?* Hutch went back then and opened the kitchen door.

No one in sight, though Straw's car was still there. Hutch called out "Strawson—"

Nothing, no reply.

Hutch stepped out and walked around the whole house.

Nothing still.

Is he up in the woods? Hutch estimated that had to be it, but he couldn't leave Wade long enough to check. He went back indoors and tried to proofread the typescript of his recent poems, with very slim luck. None was more recent than the one for Straw, written months ago; and they all felt feeble with repetition of his own trademarks and his disconnection for criminally long from the brutal present.

It was past four o'clock when Hutch finally heard a tap at the front door. By then he was more than ready to answer; and there was Straw, unshaven, gray-faced and looking years older than when Wade had visited Grainger in May. Hutch said "What's wrong?"

Straw said nothing but stood facing Hutch, looking for a while as if he couldn't speak.

Some kind of stroke? Hutch reached for Straw's arm and drew him inward.

In the dim hallway Straw drew two long breaths, as if he'd run a hard race to get here. Then he bent at the waist and laid the palms of both hands on the floor—he was still that supple.

Hutch said "Your *joints* work at least—"

"Every goddamned thing on me works, and in spades." Straw faced Hutch and grinned. "That's the awful thing."

Hutch could smell Straw's breath—no trace of liquor. "You been on a nature hike?" When Straw looked baffled, Hutch said "My woods—you took a long walk." His tone was edgy with the threat of impatience.

Straw ignored the swipe. "It's *all* nature, Hutch, everything I do—all natural as humping. But yes, you could call this a nature trip."

Hutch motioned to Wade's open door and signed that they should lower their voices.

"Is Wade asleep?"

"Most of the time. He'll want to see you though." *But aren't you half drunk?* Hutch stepped forward to where he'd smell the bourbon if Straw had had a drink today. *No smell at all.*

Straw said "I doubt Wade ought to see me."

Neither one of them had heard himself use the word *see.* But Hutch said "You're sober. What's on your mind?" Whyever, it was plain that Straw was far off his stride.

Straw turned and led the way to the kitchen.

THEN only when they'd each drunk swallows of coffee, ten minutes later, did Straw speak again—nearly whispering now. "You remember Charlotte Armfield?"

"Afraid not, no."

"The girl that owned the wolf—from Virginia, right after you got back from England. Recall her?—tall, stunning girl, eyes that could fell you at two hundred yards."

Hutch said "Fell *you.*" But then he recalled the wolf at least, only a small cub yet already fitted with the gimlet eyes that were meant to see him through a lifetime of killing every morsel he ate. "I remember the wolf but not the owner. Weren't you and I at that steakhouse in Roanoke, and didn't the manager make one try to evict the wolf and then beat retreat when it stared him down?"

"You got it—Roanoke. And Charlotte was there. I spent a lot of nights beside her that summer. She asked me to save her from a fate worse than death—something to do with her awful father: all hands and assorted appendages. I let her give me the wolf and walked out like the virtuous gent I was in those days. You recall those days—"

Hutch remembered Straw bringing the wolf to the old Kendal place as a Christmas gift to Grainger. Hadn't Grainger set him free in the woods in a matter of days? "Where's Charlotte these days?"

Straw turned to the window.

"You seen her lately?"

"All of last night, just up the road." Straw pointed west, the germ of a smile at the edge of his mouth.

"She live in Durham?"

Straw said "Pittsburgh. She's visiting her daughter, a Latin professor at Chapel Hill."

"Charlotte called you up after—what, thirty years since you walked out on her?"

By then Straw had decided to tell it; he faced Hutch again and laid it out. "Charlotte called me at home yesterday morning. Emily was outside, digging up weeds; I was reading *Nostromo*—the final book on that reading list you gave me last fall—and I just tried to ignore the phone. It finally stopped but rang again at once; so I thought it might be you, needing help with Wade. I hadn't heard Charlotte's voice in—right, thirty years: more like thirty-five. Soon as she said my full name though, I knew her and saw her. Even on the phone, keen as ever, I could see her face and her whole long body; and I wanted to hold her. She said she'd found me through Information and was calling on a hunch—she'd be at her daughter's in Chapel Hill for another two days, any chance we could talk? I told her I'd get to her somehow by dark."

From Wade's room there came a high yip like a dog's.

Straw watched Hutch wait for a second call; but when none came, Hutch said "You're referring to dark yesterday?"

Straw nodded. "And I kept the promise. I told Em and Grainger I was coming to you and Wade; I'd see them by bedtime. The minute I laid eyes on Charlotte though, and realized she was just baby-sitting her daughter's parrot while the daughter left town, I suspected I wouldn't head home for a while."

A taste of rot was spreading in Hutch's mouth, yet he felt compelled to know the whole story. "She looks that good still; she's what—fifty-six?"

"Fifty-seven going on thirty-five. She looks like she's slept inside clear amber every night since I saw her. She never was exactly beautiful—was she?—more like haunting, with those slate eyes that never shut and that amazing mouth. They're strong as ever, and everything else that mattered about her is with her still."

"So you spent the night?" It was not said harshly. With Wade down the hall as light as a locust—a locust in flames—Hutch hardly cared where Straw laid his head.

"As a matter of fact, I didn't, no. We went to bed, all right, naked as minnows. But those few hours were shocking as hell—I haven't been used like that for years."

"You look a little used—like a car wreck really." The taste of rot was fading in Hutch.

"No complaint, God knows."

Hutch managed to smile. "I trust you took precautions against the lover's plague, for your sake and Emily's if not for Charlotte's."

"I did, thanks for asking."

Hutch said "So you went prepared?"

"As a matter of fact, Charlotte saw to that before she called me." Grim as the details felt, spelled out, Straw's excitement was undiminished. He actually seemed thrust back through time, some thirty-five years— that ready and rising, that eager to fling himself on his sword for an abstract cause: his right to feed his mind and body whatever it craved, and damn the torpedoes.

Hutch had always, and rightly, seen Straw as a sexual mystic. Since boyhood, Straw had always tried to use his body, at every chance, as an instrument of knowledge—the nearest implement any human possesses for truly exploring the limits of knowing his human companions and maybe the angels. Hutch himself had got many powerful signals from the same dark notion—moments and hours with beautiful others in whom he found real ease and reward, whole unexpected islands of knowledge surpassing speech and as unmatched as music—but long ago, for whatever reason, Hutch had agreed to a simpler life than Straw would settle for. So now, facing Straw on fire from his meeting, Hutch could only say "Where've you been between your thrilling night and this dull minute?"

Straw looked as if he'd been struck broadside.

"You said you didn't spend the whole night with Charlotte."

"Did I? I guess not—I left before dawn. But when I tried to aim the car home, it wouldn't go."

Hutch said "Where does Emily think you are?"

"She's guessing as usual." Vicious as it sounded, it wasn't meant to be. Again Straw was speaking from the core of his hunger, a lifelong need that no one person had ever filled—never volunteered to fill. By his own lights, he'd mostly tried to treat others fairly. They were all adults, they'd watched him well before they'd joined him, then they'd chosen to know him and stay beside him, they could only accuse him of so much treason when he turned elsewhere. In fairness he'd always accepted that brand of betrayal from others with slim resentment.

Still Hutch knew what Straw was asking. "I'm guessing you want me to phone Emily for you."

"That had crossed my mind, yes."

"And tell her what?"

Straw said "You're the poet—call up your muse."

That rubbed Hutch wrong. He knew he had no earthly right to judge Straw for cheating. He'd lied for Straw many times in the past; and he'd perpetrated cheats of his own, though never adultery—but the thought of inventing excuses here for one more dingy pelvic cheat collided with the sterile but vehement concentration of his care for Wade. Hutch said "I'll gladly pay for the call, but you do the talking." He pointed to the wall phone three steps away.

For most of a minute, Straw was angry; but in real exhaustion he finally thought his way into Hutch's mind, its scalding white light. Then Straw rose quietly and placed his call.

Hutch was nearly out of the room when he heard Straw say "Grainger?" He paused and looked back.

Straw said to Grainger "Old gentleman, you feeling all right this afternoon?" Apparently the answer was Yes. So the rest of the conversation consisted of asking who Grainger had seen today and whether Emily had fed him on time. Was Emily there with him by any chance? No? In that case Straw would see him by dark. His voice had the sound of saying goodbye; Straw said to Grainger "Say hey to Hutchins" and held the receiver out to Hutch.

Hutch shook his head No and thought *I've never refused Grainger yet, and he'll die any day. Make it up to him soon.*

Straw gave the old man a few more words, hung up and quickly called another number.

Hutch stayed in place in the kitchen door, disgusted to think Straw had left his tawdry errand to Grainger. Emily would come down with Grainger's early supper; the old man would tell her Straw was on his way home.

But the number answered and Straw said "Emily?" Then with few words from Em, Straw begged her pardon for his absence—no explanation, false or true—and said he'd see her well before bedtime.

By then Hutch was half hoping Emily would strike back. It showed in his face.

When Straw hung up, he said "You hate me."

Hutch all but agreed. "Almost."

"Where's your license to hate—hate me anyhow?"

Hutch shook his head at the flagrant nonsense, the foul idiocy of Straw's self-defenses.

But Straw said "You've told me some of your cheats. I don't recall they smelt sweeter than mine. Hell, you dealt your biggest cheat to me, when I'd offered you nothing less than my life. What have I done worse?"

Hutch knew the accurate answer was *Nothing*, but he couldn't say it. He knew Straw deeply believed he'd offered his entire life on the threshold of manhood, and Hutch had refused him. Maybe Straw was right. So Hutch went on watching Straw's disarranged face, baited as it was with remnants of his shine from years ago.

Straw sensed that Hutch was aimed at the past, and a splendid piece of it rose up in him. "Forest Hill," he said. "Remember us at Forest Hill?"

At first Hutch didn't and shook his head No.

"The church where you said John Milton got married to his first wife; the girl that left him straight from the honeymoon, dick in hand—what was her name?"

Hutch said "Mary Powell, age sixteen; John was twice her age. I seem to recall us driving out there, yes." Forest Hill itself was barely a village, a few miles from Oxford on the London road—several low cottages, stands of old trees, a pleasant but undistinguished early church where Milton and Mary had recited their vows, a disastrous union that maimed them both—and, yes, Hutch had driven Straw there in the three days they spent together in England, July '55.

"You don't remember the offer I made?" Straw's eyes were clearing by the moment, firm in the memory they were still seeing.

"I know I've got a snapshot of you, in the churchyard, pouting."

Straw said "Surely a famous American poet can tell the difference between a pout and a bruised damned heart." No one else could have made that sentence sound almost sane.

"We were happy those days, in my mind at least."

Straw said "You refused to take my hand."

"Beg pardon? When?"

"In Forest-damned-Hill that hot afternoon. We had that dim church all to ourselves, you were up by the altar, I came up behind you and reached for your hand, you let me take it for one cool second, then pulled it away."

Hutch thought *This is more than mildly crazy*. "We'd held a lot more than hands, the night before."

Straw said "Amen—I feel every minute still. But in Forest Hill I offered you my time, my whole life to come."

"In the form of a handshake? You were eighteen, friend; your mind and your cheerful cock were headed off in six or eight directions—no hint whatever of a real destination. And I was in no state, psychic or otherwise, to give or take anything or anybody, not anybody that threatened to last." When Straw's eyes heated and fixed Hutch in place, Hutch said "I'm sorry I ignored your gesture."

Straw held stock-still. "Get it *straight*, here now where it's past too late—it was no gesture, Hutchins; no offer to shake hands and pledge blood brotherhood. I *wanted* all of you."

Hutch quickly said "*All* of it would have killed you—it killed Ann Gatlin; it may be killing Wade." At once Hutch thought *What the hell do I mean? I'm crazy as Straw*. But as he watched Straw's face respond to the wild outburst, Hutch understood fully—and for the first time— that, in the raddled mind Straw brought here today, he believed himself. Straw fiercely believed in his right to have borne this mammoth grudge through four decades, minus two years and counting.

Whatever the buried facts of that summer afternoon in '55—lazing through a musty church that had seen John Milton at the pitch of his pride, on the ledge of a fall—Hutch felt he should honor Straw's maddog force: it was scarce as valor, words like *honor* and *valor* and the force they'd once had to shape whole lives. So he said "Old friend, I've loved you as long as anybody breathing. Through the years, I haven't had as much to give as you."

Straw's head ducked gravely. "You're goddamned right."

For a moment Hutch thought *Straw's the lightning rod; I'm just the rain barrel.* It snagged up a laugh from deep in his chest; but in respect to Straw's ravenous heat, Hutch swallowed it down. He thought *I can't use this; get Straw out of here, quick as you can.* Then he turned his back and went toward Wade.

37

Two minutes later Hutch was sitting by Wade, who seemed asleep, when Straw came to the door and stood. Hutch didn't speak or even look back. He was aiming a powerful thought at Straw, a thought that was very nearly an order. *Leave now. I'll call when I'm calm.*

Straw understood but wouldn't leave. He had a strong sudden knowledge that this would be his last sight of Wade. He'd always liked the boy, had always felt at least partly his father; but not till today had he felt that Wade's leaving would tear his own heart, which Straw dreaded tearing. The least he could do here was have some sober last word with the boy. He came forward quietly and whispered to Hutch "Can I wake him a minute?"

Hutch leaned toward Wade; the sleep seemed genuine, though dreamless. In his normal voice Hutch said "All right," then stood and moved toward the door. "I'll leave you. Don't wear him out, don't beg him for pardon, and call me when you leave." Then he went to the study.

Straw stood awhile longer, moving the last few inches to the chair and sitting beside his young friend's bed, among the futile defense equipment of tubes and wires against a death manned by ten billion enemies, visible to nothing but electron microscopes. Straw slowly shifted his mind off the shock of new life he'd got in the hours inside Charlotte's body and her avid mind; and eventually he was reeling back through pictures of Wade from infancy on through late boyhood to the time when Straw had ceased to see him often, the day Wade took his degree at State and headed north.

Straw's own child had given no tangible cause for offense—a pale tall smart girl, now a married woman in suburban Atlanta, certifiably successful, though barren as sand and with less family feeling than most third cousins. Wade had won all hearts from the day he was born, a child with each of his parents' strengths and no great weakness except his constant aim to please every soul around him. After maybe five minutes, Straw actually said, in the lowest whisper, "Take what's left of me and let Wade be." By *be* he meant *live—Let Wade live on past me, years longer. I've had too much; I've used up me and too many others.* Warmed as he'd been by his hours with Charlotte, Straw was intent as any threatened creature longing to last in the wild—the black rhino or the snowy egret. He literally hoped to die in this chair here and set Wade free into new healed life, a calm eternity or pure oblivion.

And Wade's head finally turned toward Strawson. In the past two weeks, since shaves had proved painful and dangerous, the boy had accumulated a beard—short and patchy, as if the hair itself were exhausted, but still a surprise. Now his eyes opened as if they still worked; and when he'd sensed what lay beyond him in reach of his hand, Wade put out his arm and said "Thank God."

Straw took the hand and said "What for?"

Wade had to decide. At last he said "For somebody happy to be here now."

Straw thought at first *You couldn't be wronger;* but as he felt the chill fingers heat in his grasp, he knew Wade was right as he'd mostly been. After they'd got through minutes of silence, joined that closely, Straw finally leaned to kiss Wade's wrist and replace it carefully under the sheet. He told the boy "I recall every *hour,*" and he felt that was true—all their hours at the Kendal place, in the woods and fields, whole years of laughter and ten thousand stories.

When the words were out in the air between them, Straw suddenly hoped for the least hint that Wade had heard him and halfway agreed. But the glazed eyes held on Straw's face, unblinking; and the dry lips were set. Then after a long time the lips said "Minutes. I know all the *minutes*—" Nothing else came.

So at last Straw stood and forced himself to turn his back on the vacant face and its awful eyes. Then he left the house in total silence, without so much as a sign to Hutch, and was gone toward home.

38

ON the fifth of July, a blistering Monday, Hutch met Jimmy Boat at the Durham bus station. By then it was past eight o'clock in the evening, and the heat had relented, so Boatie could say as he came down the steps "Ocean *breezes!* This is cooler than Mama's."

Hutch told him not to get his hopes up; they were locked in a drought. But the sturdy refusal of Boat's short body to show discouragement cheered Hutch enough to let him laugh for the first time in days. He made Boat let him carry the suitcase; and all the way to the car, they talked about nothing but Boat's family and the feast they'd offered him yesterday in rooms as hot as any brick kiln.

Since Wade was sleeping at the house with Maitland reading beside him, Hutch took the chance to drive Boat through both halves of Duke campus, locked in their annual chaste summer daze.

Not till they'd passed the chapel tower did Boatie speak of why he was here. He'd talked on the phone with Hutch yesterday, so he felt fairly safe in saying "Our boy bearing up all right?"

"He's been a little stronger all afternoon, I'm glad to say. I honestly think he's waiting for you."

Boat looked to Hutch's face; any trace of the jockey or clown had leached from him. "For me to do what?"

Hutch could only laugh again. "For your kind face."

"He won't see that." Then after they'd left the campus gates, Boat said "You mean he's waiting on me to die, Hutch?" It was the first time Boat had said only *Hutch*, and it didn't feel right.

Hutch said "May be." The chance implied in Boat's last question had not quite dawned on Hutch till he heard it. *Boatie's his last bridge to Wyatt and that world.*

Boat's head moved slowly. "Lord Jesus, again. You know I've been to forty-eight funerals in the years since this thing took real hold—eleven years?" Though he managed to hide it, Boat felt a sudden longing to open the car door and fling himself out, anything now but the fresh sight of Wade after three more months of a pain and wasting more savage than any locust plague in the Bible—a book which Boat read nightly in his narrow room, a room Boat scrubbed on his hands and knees nightly and loveless as any field of chalk.

39

BUT when they reached Wade, he was propped in bed on a thick nest of pillows; and Mait had shaved him and tamed his long hair.

Boat had learned, in the years of the plague, to freeze his face against the ambush of a person's changed body or the air that clung round him. He'd learned to scent, sharp as any deer, the distant signs of a new assault—bacterial, viral, parasitic—or the inevitable rush to surrender, after years of drawn-out hope and fight, to a matchless foe. Now Boat kept his smile at full white blast as he faced Wade and thought *You can't weigh eighty pounds*. He saw right off that Wade had passed through the narrows at least toward the broader water that would be his death soon, and the first thing he said was "If you get any handsomer, baby, I'll call the cops." In a strange way, he meant it.

Boat's voice and the crisp charge of his attention reached Wade quicker than most things lately. In under five seconds he also grinned. "I'm out of the running, I lost the bikini competition, save the public funds."

Boat said "Naw, boy. You're too hot to handle—Mr. America in Technicolor!"

Wade said "I've settled for the Mr. Congeniality prize." His hand pointed to the bedside chair where Mait was sitting.

Mait stood at once and Hutch introduced him to Boat. Mait said "Boatie, sit here. It's the best seat we've got."

Boat said "Keep your place. I been sitting all day. Anyhow I need to hug this child." He went to Wade, touched the dry hair lightly, then bent to his forehead and kissed him there. Boat glanced back and—quick, while no one saw him—he made a short sign of the cross on Wade, where his lips had touched the disappearing child.

As Boat leaned back, Wade said "You scared to kiss my mouth?"

Boat understood at once. "Come on—you know me better than that. I just didn't want to be overfamiliar after so long apart and give you all my big-city germs."

Wade looked like Death on his cold white horse, but he said "Nobody's kissed me head-on since I left New York."

Hutch knew it was true and felt rebuked.

Boat bent again, with no hesitation, and met Wade's thin lips—dry as clean cloth.

Wade said "Many thanks."

"My pleasure, all mine." Boat took the chair then and laid a hand on the bone of Wade's arm. "Tell me all the trash you seen since you left me. I'm starving for news."

Mait and Hutchins left him there.

40

It didn't seem strange to Hutch that—once Wade fell asleep and he and Mait fed soup and sandwiches to Boat, who was finally showing hunger from his trip—Boat said "You mind if I sleep in yonder with Wade?"

Hutch thought Boat meant to sleep in Wade's bed with him; even then he could think of no objection except the chance that a healthy body might bruise or break Wade, but he said "If you think that can help him any—it's not a wide bed."

Boat could hear, in just those words, that Hutch had watched this death too closely; he was losing grip. What Boat had meant was a cot or a pallet beside Wade's bed.

And there was an antique folding cot. Hutch and Mait brought it up from the cellar, opened it in the kitchen to check for mice or flying squirrels' nests, found it clean and dry, and rolled it into Wade's room where Boat insisted on fitting it out with the sheets Hutch gave him—Wade had long since drifted off.

That got them to nearly eleven at night; and though Boat was plainly tired from his trip, Hutch offered him and Mait a drink. So the three men sat in Hutch's study and drank small quantities of good apple brandy, atom by atom, making it last. They were that slowed down by the weight and heft of oncoming death which was pressing now at all the boundaries of the house and at every window. There was no sense of fear or dread in anyone, only the mild hope to huddle down with reliable friends and see death work its final will.

Exhausted as he was, between sips of brandy, Boat went on responding with pleased surprise to this or that picture on the walls or the odd arresting object nearby—an ostrich egg brought from Africa by a cracked old missionary woman Hutch had known in boyhood, a framed lock of what claimed to be Thomas Jefferson's hair (given to Hutch by a student years back, a red-haired boy who was Jefferson's great-great-great blood nephew); a brass bugle that had sounded taps in France on November 11th, 1918 (a gift from Grainger, who'd blown the call for his own black contingent and could guarantee it). Boat touched, then stood before each object as if each one were giving off rays—invisible power he could feel but not see. Wherever it came from, Boat sensed it was good; so he let it flow through him, hoping it had some strength to give, some guidance in moving this house toward its end.

Watching Boat stand in such mute patience deepened Hutch's trust in the small burdened man. All Hutch's life he'd noticed with puzzlement the fact that ninety-eight percent of his visitors never gave a moment's attention to any manmade or natural thing in the house. They were not only legally blind, like most Americans in a swarming television-blinded century; they were likewise trapped in the tunnel vision of self-absorption or were swaddled to the ears in the devastatingly barren legacy of a puritanism that refuses all worldly pleasures to the eye, not to speak of the mind or the lonely body.

When the three men had gone for ten minutes more with very few words, Boat walked a straight line toward the mantle. Most of the rocks Hutch had gathered through life were laid out there in long months of dust—flint arrowheads he'd found in childhood at the old Kendal place, an almost perfect Indian axe-head Grainger had found when he dredged out the creek, a stained shard of marble from the days Hutch spent with

Ann in Rome when she met him there on his first Oxford Christmas; and a flat white pebble from the town of Capernaum on the northern shore of the Sea of Galilee, Simon Peter's home.

What Boat picked up though and held toward the light was something Hutch had almost forgot. A primitive carving in thick pinebark five inches long. It was all Hutch had of his great-grandfather, old Robinson Mayfield, the family starveling who'd consumed so many lives, white and black. Well over a century ago, Rob had whittled it brutally into the rudimentary shape of a man and had hung in its crotch, on stiff copper wire, a half-inch cock you could flip up or down. (Polly had persuaded old Rob to remove the prong; Hutch had restored its full flagrance, in his childhood, when Polly gave it to him.)

Boat worked the toy cock up and down twice, then shook his head. "One piece of skin has killed all my boys."

Hutch smiled bleakly and agreed.

But it struck Mait wrong—a small attack on his own person; the choice his body had made, whenever. He said "Skin is mainly what's killed men always. And women have certainly used theirs for harm."

When Boat looked embarrassed, Hutch defended him calmly. "I don't think Boatie's indulging in blame, Mait. That's just an old carving an ancestor made—my great-grandfather. He all but killed four or five of my kinsmen with the works of his cock—the acts it led him to anyhow. Nothing new about that—right—but don't take it personally."

Boat set down the carved man and came to his chair. "Some nights I get back to my room late, after spending fifteen hours or more with boys that are dying in shit and shame just because they ran their cock into one wrong socket or got run into; and all I can think to pray is 'Lord, let people just cool off from here out; let em stop hunting skin like skin is *coal* or oil for their fire.' "

Hutch accepted that, then turned to placate Maitland. "Mait, this hard time is not really new. Sex has been part-time lethal almost always, especially to artists. Syphilis alone killed half the best male writers, composers and painters of the nineteenth century." It was not quite true, but it rang true enough for Hutch to brace it with a partial roll of the actual names. "Maybe Beethoven—that's not quite certain. But definitely Schubert, Donizetti, Flaubert, Schumann, Verlaine, De Maupassant, Wilde,

Nietzsche, Van Gogh (whom it drove to crazed suicide), Gauguin, Hugo
Wolf and a whole slew more, including Rimbaud almost surely, Scott
Joplin, the female Isak Dinesen, and that great painter in gore—Al Ca-
pone.

"Just lately here I read in the *Times* where they've found the remains of
syphilitic skeletons thousands of years old in the Middle East, so Columbus
didn't invent it at all. No, the simple act of rubbing your joy knob—to
make more babies or soothe your mind—has always been subject to slow
awful death. Sometime in the next decade or so, we may well find a
treatment at least for this latest plague, then we'll pull out the old skin
throttle again and go at it hard; then eventually—when our poor successors
expect it least—death'll stalk back in through somebody's cock."

"Or cunt," Mait said.

"Not mine," Boat said. "I'm the first male Afro-American *nun*."

Mait said "I know I'll die of it too."

Hutch and Boat looked toward him, in real surprise.

Boat leaned to lay his hand on Mait's mouth. "Take it back while
you can."

But Mait shook his head free. "I know it, that's all. It's in my bones.
I can't use myself and love anybody else without this plague slamming
in on me soon."

Hutch said "Mait, it's not that easy to catch. You're taking precautions, right?"

Mait said "Not really. Oh condoms, sure, and spermicidal jelly; but
Jesus, who can even think about love—not to mention pleasure—when
you've got to suit up like an astronaut on a poisoned planet?"

Boat said "Then you're right, if that's how you're thinking. You'll
go soon, child." He put both hands up over his eyes. "Don't ask me to
watch. Don't let me even get to *know* you, not if you're bound to die like
a fool on a window ledge."

Even Hutch agreed.

They all sat a moment, then abruptly Mait stood. "I better go then."

Neither Boat nor Hutch could find the will to stop anybody who was
that bound to die.

Mait stopped at Wade's door to say good night—Wade was deep
asleep—so he was actually out on the front stoop before Hutch caught

up and hugged him close. "You're the best young writer I've known for a long time. Even better, you're a good human being, Mait. You need to last; I need you to last."

Mait stepped back and thanked him, but the smile was false; and for the first time in Hutch's presence, the boy's face bore a trace of hot despisal.

41

It was one in the morning before Hutch was in his room, ready for bed. He'd seen that Boat had all he needed and thanked him again for being here; they'd quietly checked the sleeping Wade and smoothed his covers. Then they'd signed good night to one another, though no doors would be shut between them. So Hutch was mildly startled when he threw his own covers back and suddenly noticed Boat there on his doorsill. "Whoa, man, you scared me."

"I scare nice people everywhere I go." Boat was barely joking; he knew that his dark knotty face, his short bow-legs had either scared or tickled strangers from the day he was old enough to walk outdoors and meet the public.

Hutch could see that his guest's eyes were wide awake and troubled. "Something on your mind?"

Boat's head shook. "I know Wade's not a praying man; but you are, aren't you—being such a big poet?"

Hutch smiled and sat on the edge of his bed. "Oh sure, I pray several times a day—more often than that, with Wade on board—but I don't claim to know God's full name. I don't offer guarantees he hears anybody."

"You a Catholic, I bet."

There were several Byzantine icons in the house, an ivory Spanish Corpus Christi on the wall by Hutch's bed; but he said "No, I neglect my soul. I never found a church that didn't turn my stomach."

Boat agreed. "Me too. Oh I got drug to the Methodist church with my grandmama two times every Sunday; but once my body struck out on its own, all I could hear in church was meanness—old women dry as navy beans, old men limp as dishrags and all of them shipping us young ones to Hell for doing what our minds *made* us do."

Tired as he was, Hutch had heard all he needed about sex tonight, sex of whatever brand; and he guessed Boat's was queer. He smiled to try to seal off the subject. "You sure it was your *mind* making you act up? It's time you put that mind to rest."

"It is, I know it—mine and yours. But you got to be the smartest man I ever been near."

Hutch said "Much obliged; you've got the wrong man. I'm your average jackass."

Boat shut his eyes tight. "Most educated man I'll ever meet, I can swear that to you." When he looked out again, Boat raised his hand to stall Hutch's clear will to send him to bed. "Tired as you are, please answer me one thing. I come all this way for just two things—to see Wade a last time and ask you one question."

So Hutch said "Thank you. Fire away—one shot." He pointed to an easy chair beyond him.

Boat came two steps into the room but stopped in the pool of pale light from a single hanging lamp, centered above them. More than ever, Boat knew he looked like a creature you beat when you're mad, a troll in the one book he'd owned as a child—*Three Billy Goats Gruff*. He nearly laughed, then recovered his bent. "I need you to tell me where Wade and I are bound—in your best opinion."

"Where you and Wade are *bound*?"

Boat nodded deeply. "Which way are we headed, do you think—up or down?"

Hutch guessed, on instinct. "Heaven or Hell?"

"That's the two choices, right?—so far as we know."

"If choices exist at all, maybe so."

"You're bound to believe in God and the Devil." When Hutch kept silent, Boat rushed ahead. "You been watching Wade in all his shit and poisoned blood and pain; you *bound* to believe."

Hutch said "Boat, I'm trying to trust one thing—" His voice failed him there.

"Tell Boat; get it out."

"I'm trying to trust that pain as hard and long as Wade's—pain that

I know could crush rocks in the road—leads to something at least a little better than a blackout: numb darkness forever."

Boat's face went hot as any iron stove. "Boat *knows* it does."

Hutch was nearly as serious. "Then tell me how, how you know anyway."

Keeping his distance, Boat searched Hutch's eyes—could he trust this man with his chief secret? He soon saw he could. "Hutch, don't tell a living soul I shared this with you; but see, I talk to Jesus every night— that's how I *know* Wade's bound somewhere better."

"In prayer you mean, you and Jesus in prayer?"

Boat said "Not prayer exactly. See, when this mess started ten years ago, I was scared as most queer boys—scareder than most, praise God on High; so now I'm well while my friends are dead or dying by degrees, black and white together, no prejudice at all. Scared as I was before they found the name of the virus and I tested clean, I got into coming back to my room every night in my old crazy aunt's apartment and scrubbing my skin, my nails and mouth, the soles of my feet and every square inch of the floor in my room. I'd push back my pitiful furniture and mop with Lysol every night. I could *hear* germs dying to left and right; but it wore me out, hard as I worked daytimes.

"So I kept asking God Above to give me a break, let me calm down and take his lead through the trouble, let me trust he'd keep me healthy to lead his miserable boys on into their peace—some few of them anyhow, if he'd accept them. I didn't hear an answer for the longest time, so I kept my job delivering prescriptions for a big drugstore.

"Then maybe two months before they found out the test for AIDS, I was washing my poor floor again one evening—now I scrub it every night of my life—when up in the corner, up in the dim ceiling, this man's voice said to me 'You be my help.' I recognized it was Jesus' voice from the movies I watch on late TV; I never doubted that—he's got a good voice, even deeper than yours. So then when, two nights later, he said 'You help me but first get your own soul free,' I asked him 'Lord, get free of what please?' " Boat stopped in midair, with his voice pitched firm on a clear tenor note. He held there silent for maybe half a minute; then he took another step nearer Hutch, who was half laid back across his wide bed.

When Boat didn't speak again, Hutch said "You think he meant free of being queer? You asking me that—did Jesus mean that?"

"A lot of people say so, left and right—church, TV, radio, nuts and crooks in the gutters and some powerful people I used to respect: bishops, you know; big senators."

Hutch said "A lot of such people claim white is green too, and day is night. Walk down the street, doing your level best to honor the Earth and all its creatures—a fourth of the people will think you're an asset, another fourth will think you're an ass or a rabid felon, the other half won't even know you're there. You can't pay that much attention to people. I seriously doubt that whatever God or force of nature made an infinite universe, with endless zillion stars, cares a lot about the whereabouts of my pee-pee at any given moment, long as I don't rub it on the skin of a child or ram it into someone that's told me plain No."

"You don't see nothing at all wrong with queers?" Boat's whole face expected an answer at last.

So, while he laughed one tense dry note, Hutch had his answer fast. "Nothing deeply special, no; and I tell you that quick since—to be honest, Boat—I've played long innings with fine men's bodies and never felt a trace of guilt, except for occasional stingy meanness that I laid down in other departments besides my cock." Hutch paused to hear how far he'd gone. *Be true; you can't lie to this kind man.* When he faced Boat again, Boat was patiently waiting. "No, Boat, I don't claim to be pope; but I've really never seen anything especially wrong with queers, nothing that's not wrong with everybody else I ever met—self-love, planned cruelty, ignorance and greed."

Boat's head half consented, though his eyes were dubious. "You don't object to us not having kids? Preachers always talking about 'God made Adam and Eve, not Adam and Steve.' "

Hutch quickly thought of his talk with Strawson back in the spring—how with no child between them, they'd have never made a life. He felt the strength of that barrier still. "I strongly suspect that most queer couples run out of ways to feel and act to one another; they're likely to perish for lack of anything else than them*selves* to think of or do for. But think of this too—and tell it out loud to the next flip preacher that lowers his boom on Adam and Steve: I heard the clear fact on the news this morning—250,000 children were born on the planet Earth just today, these twenty-four hours.

"A great slew of them will die starved or agonized, a scary part of all the survivors will grow into monsters, even the balance of law-abiding citizens will almost surely pollute the planet with their trails of waste and excess kids. No, thank Christ for queers." Hutch could suddenly hear Straw's voice speaking through him, edging him off his old objections. In sight of Boat's near smile though, Hutch recalled one objection that needed making. "I will say this—for the past twenty years or so, queers have been turning way too fundamentalist. Few country Baptists are as shut to the full truth as many young queers—such flaming evangelists."

Again Boat half agreed. "You're saying you got the full truth on your side?" If he meant sarcasm, he'd flushed it from his eyes.

Hutch smiled. "I didn't mean to claim full truth, no—just that I loathe any self-anointed team of two or more humans who claim they're righter than any bystanders in the range of their voice."

Hutch had gone past Boat; and to show he was lost, Boat raised both hands, shut his eyes, sealed his lips and shook his head wide. When he looked again, Hutch was waiting, still and silent. So Boat changed his tack. "See, I search the scriptures fairly steady, most nights. Old Testament gets right rough on the boys; St. Paul throws *fits* every time they come up."

"You notice how Jesus never turns on them once?"

Boat said "You notice too? Why don't people preach that on the TV?—not one word from Jesus anywhere in the Bible where he damns queers."

Hutch had noticed long since. "And he surely knew some—roaming round Palestine with those twelve lonely men, those rich young rulers with big crushes on him and all those clerical lawyers and priests."

Boat wanted to grin but wrestled it back. He also felt an official reluctance to take any views, just because they were white. Yet Boat was held by this talking man who made more sense than he'd dared to hope for.

Hutch said "On the contrary, come to think of it, Jesus may well bless queers by name, in person. Remember where he says 'Some men are born eunuchs, some make themselves eunuchs, and some are made eunuchs for the Kingdom of God'?"

"A eunuch's cut off his own balls, right?"

Hutch laughed. "Cut off? No balls at all." Then bleared as he was, he remembered a song from the Oxford pubs and sang a quick chorus.

> "No balls at all, no balls at all;
> She married a man who had no balls at all."

Boat was frowning by then. He was still in earnest. "I wish more of my boys had cut off *something*."

"No you don't."

"You see Wade dying like a dog in the road. You don't wish he'd of stopped using himself that way with Wyatt?"

Hutch said "No I don't."

"So you think Wade and me got a chance at Heaven yet?"

Hutch saw that he owed this anxious man—an undoubted angel of tireless heart—one serious answer, late as it was and dazed as he felt. He finally said "Boat, if there's any Paradise, with any crystal river, you'll be there in *hip boots*."

"And Wade?"

"You and Wade."

Boat waited. "And Wyatt?"

It took a long moment, but at last Hutch agreed. "I'll let Wyatt argue his own case in Glory."

Boat's face had eased slightly; he'd waved good night again and turned to go, then wheeled around. "What you mean by *hip boots*?"

Hutch laughed. "Nothing special—the word must have poured out of what I feel. Unlikely as it seems, if there's any place where good is repaid, Jimmy Boat, you'll need hip boots just to breast your floods of reward."

"You're not fooling me? I've read less than ten books in my whole life, except for some filth—you wouldn't confuse me?"

Hutch said "I've told you the absolute truth, so far as I can guess it. *Guess* is all I can give you, this late and this beat."

Boat said "I may ask you again in the morning then."

"Help yourself, friend; but morning or night, your host is a fool next to you; and he means it."

Boat couldn't bring himself to thank Hutch for that, but he looked to Hutch with a trace of fear. "You really want to know what I think about all this?"

"I'd be glad to know."

Boat said "I been thinking here lately—God's bound to love queers; he's killing them so fast."

Hutch guessed there was more than a trace of discovery buried in that; he was too beat to pursue it. "You may well be right."

Boat left with that one sentence clear before him. He said it over more than once to himself till he slept at last on his cot next to Wade. Several times he replayed Hutch's voice just now, laying out broad calm answers like a banquet, not spilling a morsel; and he thought *Boat, you know as much common sense as him. Make up your own mind.* Then he'd tell himself *The man respects me.* Boat was right about that too, as his whole life was right in its unstinting gift of all he owned and could do with the hands his tireless mind freely offered to boys in howling need, boys from his native country on Earth.

42

WELL before daylight Wade woke and lay on his back a half hour, silent and still. He could hear the sound of another creature breathing slowly, off to his right. Wade had barely registered Boat's arrival, hours ago, or the setting up of a cot by his bed; and he had no memory at all of who was with him, asleep at his side. By now his mind was mostly a sheet of clouded glass, an undamaged but thickly frosted window. He understood that much—how the plague had brought him one kindness at least, a calm blank mind most waking minutes. And though he knew he was safe from external harm, that he had guards around him, whatever their names, still he wondered who was here with him this instant.

And he strained to guess the name and the reason. The main thing he guessed was, it couldn't be Wyatt; Wyatt was almost certainly gone from the Earth. *Don't count on it though.* And the sound of the breathing was too high and easy to come from Hutch—Hutch struggled through sleep like a distance swimmer. *Maitland maybe?* But Wade couldn't think why Mait would be here unless Hutch had gone again and not left word. *Ann, surely Ann.* Wade thought he recalled that his mother was still alive and strong, though mostly out of sight for some reason he'd long since forgot. Not Ann then, no. Not Strawson nor Grainger. Not Ivory surely.

That really left Wade with only one choice, the most unlikely guest of all—the only one he'd actually wanted. *Wyatt after all. Bound to be. How'd Wyatt get here?* Despite his blind eyes Wade turned to his right side, careful not to detach his intravenous needle—he was down to a single needle tonight. On his side, he was facing the regular sighs that came from maybe a yard away and—*Christ*—came surely from Wyatt, here.

Wade forced back a smile and tried to whisper "When did you get in?" The words came stronger than he intended. *Careful here.* He'd wake Hutch and start some painful scene—he still recalled Wyatt's scorn of Hutch. So next Wade only wrote the words out on a scrim in his mind, a nonexistent surface. He and Wyatt had long since reached the point where words could pass between them in silence, intact on the air of a quiet room. *Move closer to me. You won't catch anything you haven't had. I'm safe to hold—easy though; these bones are sharp and every joint aches.*

When no one moved—to come or go—and the sighing breath went on at the same rate, still Wade's hope survived. Wyatt Bondurant was here again, wherever he'd been these last hard months; no one else knew. *He'll see me out of here before day anyhow. Now we can go.* At last Wade allowed himself what felt like a final smile, and in another minute he slept again.

BOAT's exhausted trance, not six feet from Wade's skull, never wavered but kept him locked in a dream of swimming and walking deep beneath the surface of a broad stretch of water—a warm lake, clear as any glass, that was secret to all but Boat and his brother who'd died years back: a funny boy named Bloodstone Boat, named after the stone in their mother's ring, a ring that had come her way through the family from a great-grandfather who'd been born a slave in the flooded rice fields of coastal Georgia—fields that were as lost as he today, choked with marsh grass, cottonmouth snakes and the houses of idling doctors and lawyers.

In the dream Bloodstone would swim beside Boatie, then dart ahead out of sight for a while till he'd suddenly come back smiling through the murk and always holding out, as a gift, some precious thing he'd found alone. In the course of the night, Blood offered Boatie numerous seashells made out of silver, broad purple flowers that grew underwater and a palm-sized carving in pure white rock of a child that had to be Wade Mayfield in the days before he'd bowed to his death and all but pared his body to bone.

43

AT ten that morning, after Hutch drove into town for supplies, Boat sat down alone by Wade and began to read him one more chapter in a book he'd asked to hear for some reason, Sir Walter Scott's *The Heart of Midlothian*. As always the act of reading soon lulled Boat toward the edge of dozing.

Wade could hear Boat's oncoming torpor, so every few minutes Wade would lift his right arm and say "Please wait."

Boat would wait and, after three waits when Wade asked for nothing, Boat finally said "You need the bedpan, baby?"

Wade's head shook hard and his face went dark as if a great vein had burst in the midst of his stark-white forehead. Then both his eyes focused square on Boat and seemed as clear as they'd ever seemed (Boat would have sworn Wade could see him plainly). At last Wade said "You want to try to persuade me I'll meet Wyatt Bondurant again?"

"No, baby, no. I'm no big preacher."

That helped clear Wade's mind for a moment; he gave a wide smile. "You told me you were a shouting Methodist—passport to Heaven."

"Recall I told you that years ago. What I've seen these past years, baby, I'm flying blind as you, every day."

"Then you're not much of a navigator—" The sentence dissolved in a deeper grin that cut across Wade's face like a slash.

"Never said I was nobody's navigator; won't claim to be neither. I'm just an old boy that empties the slop jars and cheers up his friends."

Wade darkened then. "Christ, man, I'm aiming to get *out* of here. Lend a hand or *leave*."

Boat sat till he had the start of what might constitute real help. "Baby, I haven't had your education—I quit the eighth grade—so I've missed a lot of the world from not knowing what to look at or what I was seeing if I did look at it. And I didn't know you all that long before you and Wyatt hit onto each other and left me swinging at the north end of Harlem like a cat on a string; but what I've seen you turn into through the past mean years is a lot better man than most I've known, maybe any other man since my brother died when him and me were kids. Bloodstone Boat, his true exact name, was some kind of magic. I miss him every day, sweetest man God made—beside you, like I said. I mean, just the way you set up Ivory and her little child was a lot damned further than my dad went for any of us. Ivory knows it too—I made sure of that, told her nobody I've known has had better luck."

Wade held up his arm again; and when Boat stopped, Wade said "You seen him lately?"

"My dad? No, baby, my dad's long gone to Hell. Thank you, Jesus, for that."

Wade said "—Ivory's child." Then he found the name. "Raven."

"Haven't laid an eye on Miss Ivory's child since she moved him on out to her mother's on the Island. When was it?—five or six years ago."

Any power to gauge the passage of time had left Wade by now. The things he recalled stood separate in his mind, untouching inside the bounds of a narrow hoop in his shot memory, all paler than they'd ever looked in life but stiller as well. Wade tried for a moment to answer Boat—had the boy Raven lived in Manhattan ever? Didn't he go straight to his grandmother once Ivory left the clinic? Or was it months later? But the idea slid like water through Wade's hands and soon was gone. He faced the general direction of Boat and gave a short lift of his naked chin to whatever Boat had just asked or said.

Boat gathered courage from the sign and eventually felt he had the right to say "Is there anything on this Earth you want me to know while I'm here with you?"

Wade stayed blank.

"Any business you want me to do for you, down here or up yonder, whatever comes next? Any message you got for God or man—I'm a first-rate messenger boy, remember?"

Wade nodded again, then thought through his needs. At last he said "I want you just to remember how Wyatt looked in his prime."

It was not the errand Boat had hoped for. Still he said "That won't be no big problem. I see Wyatt this minute, fine as wine." And he did— young Wyatt, the finest-looking black man he'd ever known, though *black* was not the name for the color of Wyatt's skin: more like some kind of expensive beige cloth with good blood streaming behind it in sunlight, giving the surface a high fast life, like nobody else ever seen on land.

After that Boat gave up asking for more about Ivory's child. And in a while he was more than glad that Wade had stopped him there, for whatever cause. Those questions anyhow were things that Boat would never have asked a stronger Wade—young Wade before this terrible hand struck him broadside in every cell and left him nothing but coated bones with a smoky candle lit in his skull in a wind as hard as any tornado. So in the next minutes, as Wade went quiet, Boat also drifted peacefully off in his straight-backed chair.

At one o'clock when Hutch returned and looked in before sorting groceries in the kitchen, he saw Boat asleep upright in his chair, though Wade was watching him steadily with eyes that still were clear but useless.

44

THAT evening at half past eight, Hutch and Boat were back in the kitchen, cleaning up after their light supper when the sound of a nearing car broke through their mild but pointless talk. Entirely separate, the two men thought it was Ann Mayfield. Hutch felt annoyed—he was nearly exhausted from the long day and couldn't imagine another round of tilt and shove. Boat felt the slight dread he'd come to expect at the prospect of meeting any white mother of one of his boys—he'd seen so many monsters, nearly ten in ten years.

But when the car showed, out back in the dusk, at first it was strange to Hutch, a deep green color he hadn't seen on a new car in years. This was surely not Ann, but a single woman turned the wheel and stopped. She'd opened the door and taken a step before Hutch remembered the car and the standing woman's outline.

It was Margaret Ives, Wade's chief physician. A tall thin woman—maybe forty-two, black hair to her shoulders—came briskly forward in a lapis blue dress and managed to touch the back door knocker before Hutch opened on her. A wide and all but heart-easing smile broke out as she saw him; it nearly concealed her own bone-tiredness. She hadn't slept in nineteen hours.

Hutch said "Oh welcome. You need a good chair." He hadn't seen her since Wade's pneumonia, though they'd talked on the phone every three or four days. As ever, he scented a whiff of hope in the fact of her nearness—young enough to be his own daughter, still she seemed so patently dauntless. So worthy you'd seek her out in any disaster scene, knowing she'd last and lead you onward.

Her smile endured. "Welcome? Truly? Sure I'm not interrupting?"

Hutch said "Never. We were just drying dishes."

"This is flat rude, I know. I should at least have called you; but I had to drop off a friend's cat farther down the road—I've been cat-sitting the past two weeks, an antique Persian demanding as an empress—so I thought I'd see how you and Wade are faring."

Hutch stood aside and waved her in; then looked for Boat, to introduce him. He'd vanished or fled. So Hutch lowered his voice. "A good friend of Wade's from New York is here; he was Wade's best help in the hard last days—not quite a practical nurse, I guess, but still a godsend. He's in with him now."

Though the smile she'd launched at the door had faded, Margaret's face still literally beamed; some innate unquenchable power worked in her steadily.

Hutch had never quite registered her beauty and its elegance, its veiled but potent strength—even this far from Duke Hospital, she seemed to have damped her fineness quite consciously. *Does she think it's irrelevant or an actual hindrance?* He gestured to a chair at the kitchen table. "We've got some fairly sinful homemade ice cream a neighbor hand cranked—fresh Sand Hill peaches, make your last artery clamp down and die for joy. Let me fix you a dish."

"I just ate, thanks."

"At the hospital?—ugh."

"You're looking at a hardened soul, Mr. Mayfield."

"It's not your soul I'm hoping to feed. And call me Hutch. A drink, some wine?"

Margaret shook her head No. "I need to get back to a patient by dark; but if you think this is not too sudden—too sudden and bald—and if Wade is strong enough, maybe we could ask him a question or two about his own wishes."

With a silent thud like a great fist descending, Hutch understood; but still he said "Wishes?"

Her wide eyes shut for a long two seconds. "For treatment. Last wishes. We both may need to know Wade's intent, when he can't really tell us."

Hutch said "This soon?"

"It's not really soon, if you think about it. I don't know how he's living this minute; he's long past exhausted in every cell. But not if you think it's premature tonight, no. I've just admired Wade's spirit right along; he asked me to see him through to the end with the absolute barest minimum of brakes."

"Did he say 'the *end*'? Did he truly say '*brakes*'?"

Margaret gave it a careful moment's thought. "Those two words, yes."

Hutch said "Then that's all I need to know." He signed for her to proceed him toward Wade.

As they moved up the dark hall, well apart, a whippoorwill in the thicket to the east was turning out its manic cry like a stuck organ grinder.

*   *   *

IT had taken Hutch a slow ten minutes to introduce Boat, who was deeply abashed near an actual doctor; then to wake Wade carefully and help him know who was here beside him—his father, his New York guest, his doctor.

Wade held his left hand out in the air toward Margaret Ives. "You do me great honor, ma'm."

Margaret took the hand and stroked his forearm. "Your trust honors me, Wade, kind sir." When he stared on at her, with no further words, she said "Please say my name, if you would."

Only silence.

"Wade, I need you to say who I am—"

Hutch longed to coach him but knew that Margaret was working to establish his sanity for the last decisions.

Wade's eyes searched her face as if they were floodlights hunting a killer. Then his lips jerked up in a wild grin. "You're the Queen of Doctors, from the flatlands of Utah."

Margaret stroked his arm again. "Right, the Utah part anyway. Recall my name?"

It turned out he did. "Mag, Meg, Maggie, Margaret. Margaret Ives."

She said "At your service, sir. You've had a fair day?"

In a stage whisper Wade said "Wait right there." Then he waved his right hand out toward Boat; it could barely stir air.

Boat came up and took it.

Wade shut his eyes and held a long moment. "Hutch, aren't you down there near my feet?"

"I am, exactly."

"Then lay your hand on my feet. Please, Father."

Hutch lifted the sheet and obeyed.

Wade held again, with his eyes still shut, till all the others thought he was sleeping. Only when Boat squeezed the right hand a little did Wade look up—at the ceiling, no face—and in one sentence, dispel the weight of dread above them. "The instant I can't draw my own breath, the instant you can't recognize Wade in who I am, then cut me loose—wave me on off."

No hand released him, none of them pressed, and no one answered.

So Wade said "*Swear—*"

In Hutch's head, he could hear the ghost of Hamlet's father compel-
ling Hamlet's balky vengeance. "*Swear, oh swear.*" But Hutch couldn't
speak, though Boat's eyes waited.

At last Margaret Ives bent and kissed Wade's arm at the elbow hinge.
Her voice said "*Swear.* Every one of us swears. You sleep on that."

Boat said "Amen."

Still amazed that a live American doctor had earned the grace to
greet a dying man so closely, Hutch could only go on looking, silent. He
knew his own eyes had little time to see even this last shadow of his son.

45

THAT was the Tuesday after the Fourth. Boat had said he could stay till
the Thursday night bus, then would need to head north and resume his
duties before another weekend. So with that slight reprieve, Hutch took
the chance to leave the house for the long afternoon and do neglected
chores in town. He told Boat he'd phone every hour or so; Boat said not
to worry—things would likely be fine. To his own surprise by then, Hutch
agreed (he hadn't expected ease again till Wade was gone). So he left
Ann's office number on the table beside Wade's bed.

And Boat spent the second half of Tuesday cleaning Wade's room
and the nearest bath. He'd hoped he could wash all the clothes and maybe
cook a few things that Wade could eat. Boat had long since learned how
to cook soft foods that some of his sick men, men who'd barely chewed
in years, could swallow at least—mostly childhood food: warm, bland,
mouth-crowding. But when Boat found that Wade's mother washed the
clothes, and Hutch was firmly in place in the kitchen, he chose to fill
the only other need he saw.

Wade's room was reasonably clean and neat; but with Hutch's permission, Boat moved the small furniture into the hall, swept the floor quietly,
then mixed oil soap with scalding water, got down on his hands and knees
and scrubbed the oak boards to an unaccustomed shine. Asking Wade no
questions at all, Boat sorted clothes in the jam-packed closet, culling out

stacks of moth-eaten sweaters saved over from grade school and trousers and coats from Wade's college days. With every piece he touched, Boat thought something like *This jacket would look good on poor Sam Butler* or *A sin in this world to leave stuff here while so many creatures are wrapping their sores in stinking rags and walking barefoot.*

As each of his New York boys died off, Boat took every chance to ask the heirs for any old clothes to pass along—the homeless gave him genuine nightmares, the thought that a country rich as America still was throwing people away like old rags and paper. But he knew not to mention such thoughts here. *Never strip the dead; you'll die cold yourself*—he'd heard his grandmother say that when they found an old man cut down by the train one Sunday dawn.

Though Boat had got short glimpses of hope, throughout this plague, that some kind of miracle might intervene—some one boy anyhow might rise up from his bed, healed and whole, to prove some human at least could outlive it; some few might silently die in their sleep, not looking like husks of ancient monkeys—he'd learned to spot the angled glance, the flaky dryness in the hands, the lank brittle hair that meant a boy was ready to die. *Wade's ready. Good Jesus, let him go while I'm here.* With some of his boys, Boat had actually bent to their ear when he saw those signs and whispered permission to let go and leave. He thought he'd wait till late tonight and then give Wade that last encouragement.

But when Boat had finished the floor and closet, when he'd sorted every drawer and shelf and dusted each souvenir of Wade's past, he saw he'd come to the end of his chore and that Wade, who'd slept through most of the day, was awake again.

Wade's eyelids were shut but his breathing was smooth; and once Boat noticed him, Wade put up a hushing finger and beckoned him closer. When Boat had bent almost to his lips, Wade whispered "Much obliged."

Boat whispered "What for? I'm just your old pal."

"For getting me ready."

Boat couldn't deny that. "Baby, I'm not doing nothing for you. I wish I could. But you know that."

Wade's hand found Boat's mouth and muffled it. "One more thing—"

"Name it, anything the Boat can do."

"Bring Mother in here."

Boat had never seen or met Ann Mayfield. All he knew was that Hutch had told him Wade's mother dropped by every day or so with laundry and food, so Boat surmised a local minefield that Ann took only one pathway through. Through all his nursing, he'd run up against a hundred kinds of family trouble—parents who flatly refused to bring a sick son home, some who even refused phone contact; others who'd send no more than checks and only appear after their son died, just in time to confiscate his property, denying his loyal mate so much as recognition. Boat was hardly likely to plow in here and raise the dust. He said to Wade "Your dad'll be here shortly, baby. You tell him you need her."

"I never said that."

"You just *want* her, don't you?"

Wade took awhile to agree to that. Then he persisted. "Tell Hutch you think he ought to call her. Not later than now. Hutch worships you."

Boat laughed and tapped his own brow. "Nobody ever worshiped *this* fool midget."

Wade shook his head hard, and splotches of color came to his cheeks for the first time in days. "My father literally worships black people."

"He's been kind to me—"

Wade's color stayed bright; he was oddly thrilled to find again and say aloud here what he'd always known but never quite faced. "Hutch thinks black people, all bound together, are the angel burning to fuel human time. His words exactly. And wild as it sounds, I think he's part right. I've thought at least that much, since my own childhood. Black people have burned—truly *burned*, I mean, for more than their share of all known history, them and the Jews (though Hutch never knew many Jews as a boy, not here in the South)—but also odd bands of most other people in various ages: brown, yellow, red, white, queer as coots, straight as rails. It's nothing else—is it? all this old history—but a permanent bonfire, maybe a holocaust if that means anything, old at least as human time and somehow the literal oil it takes to turn the big wheel."

"What wheel?"

"Oh the world, like I said. The poor old world. What African country

is it today?—every month it's a new little desert or valley where millions
of children, gorgeous as ebony carved by saints, are starved to bones or
hacked to ribbons in their dead mother's arms: all burning, burning. For
me and you."

The smile that spread on Wade's dry lips was as awful a wound as
Boat had seen in all these years. He laid cool fingers on the lips to smooth
them, then told Wade "Baby, you rest your mind. No need for you to
be this far gone, in this fine house with your own people, not if you'll
rest more."

Wade frowned to warn off any break in his frail line of thought.
"Hutch tries to convince himself he's a Klansman—see, he let Wyatt
ruin his self-respect, when all of us knew Hutch bowed down deep in his
mind to every black face he passed."

By now Boat was used to most kinds of dementia. You listened and
patted their hand and said Yes. He tried that here.

But Wade's voice hardened. "Listen to *me*."

So Boat tried his next trick, changing the subject or reverting to
an old one. "I'm listening, baby, but I'm not God Above. If your folks
don't want to be here together, Jimmy Boat can't force them—can't and
won't."

In all the years that Boat had known Wade Mayfield, in all the
months he'd seen Wade through this hard slow fall and Wyatt's brutal
death, he'd never seen the trace of a tear on Wade's face. Boat himself
was a regular fountain of tears—he'd weep at television commercials
where grown men phoned their fathers on Father's Day—and more than
once he'd felt real pity for Wade's refusal or inability to vent his stifling
grief.

Now, though, the sockets of Wade's blind eyes were brimming water.

Knowing that even tears could carry the plague virus, still Boat leaned
again and wiped at the tears with his bare thumb. He stood back and
listened for Hutch's presence—no sound from the kitchen or elsewhere
near—so in almost a normal voice, Boat said "Oh baby, I'll ask him
someway or other between here and dark. Maybe your mother will even
drop in."

Wade waved away the thought of any drop-in. He said "*Tell* Hutch.
Get Mother back here tonight. I'm ready to go."

Standing that near a face as wild as Wade's, Boat thought *This boy can still do a good many things but no way left for him to stand up and call his mother in here for the final end.* And all he could think to tell Wade here was that, yes, Jimmy Boat would find a chance to relay the message between this minute and tonight someway.

46

AT seven o'clock though, Hutch was still in town; and Ann stopped in on her way home. By then Wade had been asleep for hours. Boat had long since finished his cleaning and was in the kitchen, making rice pudding and vanilla milk junket when Ann let herself in through the back door. She'd known that a helpful friend of Wade's would be there from New York, but she'd never met Boat and was startled to find a tiny black man busy at the stove. She thought she managed to cover her fear and at once went toward him, extending her hand. "I'm Wade's mother, Ann."

Boat had seen her clearly from the moment she left her car, walking toward him; so while he seldom thought of himself as the kind of black man always harping on how white folks have ruined the world and him in particular, he went a little cold and reached for a dish towel to hold in his hand. That would ease this rich-looking woman right off—him being an old-time kitchen boy. Still her sudden smile and hand were unexpected. Boat put down the towel, accepted her hand and said "I'd have known your face on Mars or in Panama." The moment he spoke, Boat thought *Crazy fool*—he'd seen Panama in his navy years.

Ann went on smiling; she well knew how much Wade was like her. "Mr. Boat, I don't think we can ever thank you."

Boat wondered who she meant by *we*. He'd gathered that she and Hutch were as far apart as parents get. *She means her and Wade.* So he told her "Wade's been good to me ever since we met long years ago. If I didn't have my duties up north, I'd be his main help."

"I know you would." A quick look showed Ann what Boat was

cooking. "That rice pudding smell takes me back a long way. I hope Wade can eat it."

"No doubt about that. I fixed it for him up in New York every chance I got. He loves the raisins mainly." Boat pointed north as if the city were closing on them and would be here soon.

Ann had long since forgot Wade's childhood love of raisins. She'd tried every other food she could think of and failed to rouse Wade's appetite, and now Boat's memory rebuked her own, but she didn't say she doubted Boat's chances. She said "Is Wade sleeping?"

"Last time I looked. He's barely been awake all today."

"I'll just tip in then and get his laundry."

Boat pointed again, toward the washing machine and dryer in the pantry. "Every stitch is clean." Ann's face looked so forlorn to hear it— he wished he'd thought to save her a chore. "The dryer just finished; clothes'll still be warm—you can fold them easy."

She washed her hands at the sink and went to sort Wade's clothes. Only at the door of the pantry did she look back. "Is Hutch all right?"

Boat said "As all right as any of us can be in these mean days. He's in town catching up on things. Called and said he'd be back soon as they changed his oil at the shop."

For Ann that sounded like a short reprieve. To her own surprise she folded a few of Wade's white briefs and a green T-shirt, then came to the door and said to Boat "You understand I want to be here?"

By then Boat was seated at the worktable, reading a story in *TV Guide*. "Yes ma'm, I do."

Ann managed a slight smile. "No *ma'm*—please, sir. I answer to *Ann*."

Boat smiled and agreed.

"The reason I moved out of here had nothing to do with Wade."

"I doubt he knows that. He wants you back. Told me so just now."

Ann took a long wait. "That means he's near to—"

Boat said "It mostly means that. I've seen it a lot, even when their mothers have shut them off. I've seen boys' natural parents shut them off like rats in the walls; slam the door in their face and them as harmless as day-old pups, just needing attention—"

Ann said "Do you understand Wade's father has made me keep this distance, ever since he was home?"

"Mrs. Mayfield, I can't touch your business—Mr. Hutch's and yours. All I know is, Wade wants you. When he told me this afternoon, it burned me bad. I couldn't see a way."

Ann's face was wan in the late sun that broke through the windows beyond her, but it also looked remarkably young and as strong as she'd ever been. With Wade's green shirt still warm in her hands, she came halfway back toward Boat's chair and told him plainly "Hutch'll have to call the Law to make me leave here tonight."

Boat thought *The mothers, even the monsters, always smell death coming first.* But he said "No way Hutch'll do that much."

Ann said "We'll never know till we test him." When Boat was quiet, she said "Will we now?"

"Let me say it one more time, polite as I can—this is your business, lady. Don't make trouble for me. I'm just here to be an invited guest."

Ann said "You claimed you were here to help Wade—"

"I wish to God I was. If you'd seen that sad boy today, you'd know nobody in this weak world got help for him—not where he's at."

Ann's eyes flared up. "What a thing to say—"

Boat stood in place and shut his magazine. *Leave out of here, Boatie. Call a taxi and run.*

But as distant sounding as if it came by satellite, Wade's voice called out a long high "Ann?"

She held in place, still facing Boat.

Wade called again. "I heard my mother's voice."

When Ann held still another slow moment, Boat called "You did. She's on her way, baby." When he finally faced Ann, he said "All yours. Go fix him please."

That broke the lock on Ann's last restraint. She laid the green T-shirt near Boat's elbow, smoothed it carefully, then said "I'm sorry. I'm not my best self."

"Few of us ever is." Boat reached for the green shirt, opened it out and folded it again—a neater job.

So Ann went toward Wade, whoever he'd be when she got there.

47

WHEN Hutch phoned again a few minutes later to say his car was finally ready and he'd be home soon, Boat answered in the kitchen, said things were steady but didn't mention Ann's presence. She'd stayed on in Wade's room. Boat had heard no words or moves; so when Hutch came in through the kitchen door, the house was still. Boat was reading *The Farmer's Almanac* in a chair by the table and copying down the full-moon schedule for the rest of the year.

Hutch set two bags of groceries on the counter, quickly put a few things in the freezer and washed his hands.

Boat said "I'll shelve the rest of those."

But Hutch said "I see my wife's car. How long has she been here?"

"Maybe half an hour. She's in there with Wade." Nothing on Earth made Boat feel weaker than family strife.

Hutch could see the misery, so he tried to smile. Then he gave his arms and legs a mock hand-frisk. "We don't pack guns, Boatie. We can be civil."

For all his unease, Boat knew he had to speak. "Mr. Mayfield, she's back here for good."

Hutch said "How's that please?"

"Your wife told me she's staying here till Wade passes on. She knows he's close—"

"Close to what?"

Boat said "You know—to passing."

"Who told her that?"

"Mr. Hutch, that woman's his natural mother."

"And that makes her magic?"

Boat well understood that the answer was *Yes*, but he held out his two flat palms—empty-handed.

Hutch kept his voice calm, but he said "No she's not." He stepped off in the direction of Wade.

So Boat stopped him with a powerful whisper. "Mr. Mayfield, Wade needs her with him here."

"Did he tell you that?"

Boat's head shook hard. "Right after you left."

"How did he say it?"

"He told me he was ready to go; so he wanted her by him, along with you."

Hutch was in the doorway that led to the hall. He stayed there, both arms raised and pressed to the doorframe. Again he meticulously gentled his face. "Were those his words?" When Boat hesitated, Hutch said "About me—wanting me with him too?"

Boat knew what he said was a technical lie; but since he'd heard Wade in New York talking so often about his dad and their good times together so long ago, he compounded his lie. "Yes sir, he asked for both of you with him."

"You think Wade's right?"

"About what?"

"Dying soon."

Boat whispered again. "Maybe tonight, around four in the morning. No later than sundown tomorrow for sure."

The odd precision somehow convinced Hutch. "How many of these boys have you watched die?"

Boat said "Mr. Mayfield, they were all grown men. To answer your question, I believe it's twenty-three I actually watched. I may have lost count, it's hurt so bad."

An old high wall of Hutch's pride crashed silently down. The nearness and service of this stunted young man, here at hand in the kitchen—apparently some kind of valid angel—was the strongest rebuke Hutch had met with in years. Boat's face and level voice alone were a justified and fair reproach to feelings that Hutch still thought were his due, his right to rancor in Ann's abandonment. But any will to usher Ann back to her car tonight, to refuse her presence, seemed not only petty but an actual evil. And Hutch believed that very few things were evil in the average life—the normal run of men and women being seldom awarded the chance or the force to make mistakes with enormous outcomes. He felt a new and deep-running relief, so he brought his arms back down to his sides and said to Boat "This kitchen smells better than it has in years. Anything ready to eat for supper—just the three of us: you, Ann Mayfield and me?"

Boat said "You brought in a big load of food, looks like. Go in and check on Wade and his mother; I'll have something ready in, oh, twenty minutes. Any special requests?"

Hutch had heard Wade praise Boat's kitchen skills, and he tried to think of something quick and good. Nothing came. "You choose, please sir. Maybe a little surprise would help us."

"That's exactly my intention, Doctor."

But before he left, Hutch had to explain. "I understand you're here as our guest and ought not to work as hard as you're doing. But if you wouldn't mind cooking a little, I'd be much obliged. So would Wade if he could thank you clearly."

"Don't give it a thought, Mr. Hutch. Not a thought. I'm here to help any way I can."

"*Hutch*—call me Hutch."

Boat smiled. "Sure—Hutch. You leave this to me."

Hutch said "I wish I could leave the rest of my life to you." Then he knew he meant it.

48

ANN was sitting by the side of Wade's bed, her hand on the bones of his left hand, lightly riding the pulse that was only a feeble transmission. The main light came from the desk across the room, Wade's old student lamp at its lowest power.

Hutch waited in the door, trying to gauge Wade's rate of breath. It was all but inaudible, so wide spaced and shallow it barely moved the sheet that covered the leg bones and ribs and on to the chin. The eyelids were shut on eyes that had shrunk inward so far they seemed no bigger than the waxy fruit from chinaberry trees or healthy blueberries.

Ann didn't turn; she hadn't sensed that Hutch was there. By now she felt almost a part of the house again; and though she'd heard Hutch's voice at a distance, talking to Boat, she'd heard none of their words nor Hutch's steps toward her. As she sat on motionless, she was only fixing the line of Wade's profile deep in her mind by gouging it again and again on her thigh—just her long dry finger on the cloth of her skirt.

At last Hutch cracked the joints of his right hand.

Ann looked round, then got to her feet and stood by her chair.

Hutch came on to the foot of the bed, touched both of Wade's feet beneath the cover. "Son, I'm back." Though he'd said it as a final claim on the boy, Hutch understood that Wade might not hear him—*You're mine; I'm with you.*

But slowly Wade heard it. His head raised an inch from the pillow toward Hutch. The eyes stayed shut and he said "Aye, aye, sir."

Ann was still in place; but she said "Sit down, Hutch, and rest a minute. I'll go help Boat" (the sounds of work were coming from the kitchen). The set of Ann's eyes and mouth left no question that she meant to eat, and stay, here tonight.

And Hutch raised none. As Ann came past him, his hand went out of its own accord and brushed her wrist.

She gave a slight sound, nearly a moan, but never broke stride.

So Hutch went on to the chair and sat in Ann's narrow warmth.

WHEN her footsteps faded off, Wade's eyes opened, though his head still didn't move toward Hutch. His mind had given up trying to see. When Hutch's hand touched the crown of his skull, Wade drew his right arm out of the sheet and held it straight in the air above him like a lightning rod or a white antenna. Finally he got whatever message he waited for, and he said to the ceiling "Call Ivory and tell her."

"Tell her what, Son?"

"That this whole tour is still underway, and I'll be seeing her and her family any week to come. Soon."

That seemed the first guarantee of dementia Hutch had heard—all the other strangeness, he'd half suspected of being intended for various reasons—but he said only "Fine, Son, I'll call Ivory later this evening."

"Remind her I want to be buried with Wyatt."

"You told me you meant to be scattered on the creek behind the old Kendal place, on Grainger's pool where he rescued you." When Wade stayed silent, Hutch said "Remember?"

Wade appeared to try, then said "That's not the first thing you've got wrong." When the words had faded on the air, Wade laughed—a parched chuckle, the first in days. He turned his blind face in Hutch's direction.

Hutch was compelled to turn aside.

"Don't take this personally—you're my good friend—but you know less about me than these birds here."

Hutch tried a short laugh. "Aren't the bluebirds especially smart this summer?"

Wade said "I'm talking about these birds that are helping me travel."

"Then thank them for me, Son. Many thanks."

Wade lay on, facing his father; and his eyes stayed open. But long minutes passed before he said "Big tall brown birds. Maybe storks but taller." Then he said nothing else.

Hutch sat on, determined to bear the sight. The sounds of peaceful work came from the kitchen, the mingled voices of Boat and Ann. Hutch could feel no objection; he knew he was far too tired and sad to fight old battles and lick cold wounds—those scores could wait. What chose to rise from the depths of his mind was that single line he'd got, days past, as he waited for his car to be fixed in the country—the possible start of a poem for Wade.

It repeated itself two clear times in Hutch's head. *This child knows the last riddle and answer.* The line had come to him an instant after he heard the distant voices of two boys on their bicycles at a country cross-roads. Was the waiting poem meant to be about them?—they were brothers, the younger one named Foster who claimed he was bound for Spain, a bullfighter. Surely the poem had to be about Wade, the only child Hutch had really known or wanted to know.

But the dreadful pitiful husk of a body that breathed beside Hutch seemed drained of any question or answer that a living creature could hear or use.

Almost unaware that his voice was audible, Hutch said the only thought he had, as natural as air. "Pardon for any harm I caused."

The word *harm* snagged Wade back from his daze. His skull signed Yes and he said "Sure. *Harm.*"

The single word in Wade's voice, weak as it was, tore a hole in the

air; and in a stiff rush, Wyatt Bondurant pierced the wall of the room—
his presence and force undoubtedly plunged in from whatever place they'd
lingered for so long. The force went straight to Hutch and poured all
through him instantly, freezing him deep. Though Hutch was a man
more susceptible than most to the unseen world of the lingering dead,
only one other time had he been in touch with the actual power of a
vanished life; and he'd kept no memory of that benign visit. (The night
after his father Rob died, Hutch had slept alone in the old Kendal place;
and the thinning shape and fading force of Rob's vanishing spirit had
searched the house one final time, touching Hutch's unconscious body
lightly as it left for good.)

Here beside Wade, Hutch knew at once whose ghost was in him.
For a long minute he sat in calm terror, thinking his own death was
maybe at hand. All he could ask was *Let me outlast Wade just long
enough to see him buried the way he wants.* That freed him to think *I'll
take his last wish and put him by Wyatt.*

If the promise somehow reached Wyatt, his cold strength gave no
sign of mercy.

So Hutch sat on for another minute, breathing carefully and trying
to quiet his thudding pulse. With all he'd felt and thought in these
moments, he'd never questioned the hard-eyed sanity of his gut knowledge. *Wyatt Bondurant is here in some form, real as the one I knew.* As
a kind of amulet against that certainty, Hutch repeated his single line
many times—*This child knows the last riddle and answer.* No other lines
came, Wade never roused to speak, but slowly Hutch felt his own chill
body reclaim itself from Wyatt's assault. Only then could he start to
wonder *Does Wyatt mean us harm?* Before Hutch could think, he heard
steps behind him and turned to the door.

Jimmy Boat stood there, small as he was, a welcome sight. "Hutch,
you go eat a little something please. I'll sit here with Wade."

Hutch tried to say No.

Boat shook his head and pointed to the kitchen. "You need all your
strength. We got a whole night, maybe some bit longer."

Hutch agreed, then wondered if he should mention Wyatt. *No,
Boatie knew Wyatt. Let Boat deal with him if he's truly here someway.*
But before Hutch stood, he leaned to Wade's ear and said he'd only be

back in the kitchen—call him if needed. Then he thought he should say "Son, your mother's here too. For as long as you need her."

That seemed to reach Wade. The boy didn't rouse but he took what looked like the first painless breath he'd had in more than a week of long nights; and he made a sound like the liquid hum that escapes some sleeping birds, mysterious as to meaning or purpose. Then as Boat stepped forward and Hutch reached the door, Wade said "My mother died the day I was born."

Boat's eyes went to Hutch.

Hutch frowned, unable to think or speak an answer. Wade was imagining some new path through Hutch's own story, Hutch's own mother's death. *Is he somewhere already, forced to relive it?* Hutch wanted the words to clarify that much anyhow. "No, your mother's here, Son."

But Wade was still again.

So Boat came on past Hutch on to the bedside, touched the cover above Wade's chest and said "Baby, everybody you love is here."

Hutch thought *Then Boatie's felt Wyatt here too.*

But in a stronger voice than before, Wade told Boat "That's a lie. Thanks anyhow." They would be his last words.

Hutch thought *Then somehow Wyatt hasn't reached Wade yet.* But he knew he couldn't describe his own meeting, not to this fading mind that was maybe half elsewhere, in some further life. Hutch thought it wasn't his duty even, weak as Wade was. *Wyatt Bondurant can tell his own news.* Hutch was also ignorant of what Wade was dwelling on when he called Boat a liar.

Boat said to Hutch again "Please keep your strength up" and pointed toward the kitchen.

So Hutch went to eat.

WADE heard his father's footsteps leave; and when they were gone, the grip of Wade's mind slowly released its hold on the world. The few remains of his body went weightless, no anchor or ballast to hold him back. The eye that had stayed alive in his mind through all his trouble went entirely clear again—Wade could see all he needed to see. And what he saw was a tall narrow room maybe twenty yards long, with beechwood floors and smooth bare walls that showed all the colors of pigeon wings—gray with shifting blues and purples. Wade was standing at one end of the room—the west end, he thought. He also thought *I'm on my feet for the first time in—when?—oh, years or days.* And then he knew, for the first clear time, that in his dreams he'd never been sick. *But is this a dream?* The answer came in his own strong voice, *No, no dream.*

And in that moment a live companion suddenly stood at the room's far end. By now, all human names were leaching from Wade's new mind. What he understood plainly was that this guest here was a young man, maybe twenty-five years old, in the nearly perfect body and face that made him a bare strong manifestation of all Wade had hoped for, ever on Earth—an entirely admirable welcoming man, at ease in both his mind and body and eager to give both freely without stint.

As Wade made a slight courteous bow toward the guest, the dazzling body took the first step toward him.

Wade thought *He'll reach me in maybe ten seconds.* He still tried to think it was Wyatt, renewed. But it took the guest well under ten seconds; and when he'd arrived at the edge of the bed and held out open arms and hands, Wade felt the pouring out in his chest of unthinkable joy. By then all human names were wiped from his mind—Wyatt's, whosever—so he never quite learned that the guest wore the ageless face of his dead grandfather Rob Mayfield, young again, a man Wade had never seen alive above ground. Wade stepped on forward into the harbor of powerful arms, and the light was blinding.

49

ANN was already seated at the kitchen table, under the hanging light. Boat had thawed two quarts of Brunswick stew that Hutch had bought at a roadside church sale back in the fall, and he'd somehow managed to make real corn sticks in an old iron mold that Hutch and Ann had forgot they owned. When Hutch walked in, Ann was staring at the clean empty bowl before her as if it held answers she'd need before day.

Hutch sat across from her, unfolded his napkin, then suddenly surprised himself. His right hand, of its own volition, went out and covered Ann's hand on the table.

At first she flinched and nearly retreated; then she held in place, though she didn't look to meet him.

Against his better judgment, Hutch said "What's wrong?"

"It would only ruin your night to hear it."

"Ann, this is not one of my good nights."

She went on drawing a tall abstract figure on the table, but she finally said "—How awful it is that you and I sit here, in fairly clear sight of three-score-and-ten, and our son's leaving with no remains. Nothing we can hold hereafter."

"What exactly do your hands want?" His voice was not hard.

"Oh Christ, Hutch, look."

When he looked he saw, not the worn woman here but the girl he'd loved in Rome and Richmond, more than half their lives ago, forty years—the girl who'd gone to a back-alley kitchen (on her own, uncomplaining) and ditched the first child they conceived when she thought Hutch had left her. He said "We ought to have covered our bets, yes. Is it too late for you to adopt a grandchild?" The moment he heard it, it sounded cruel and crazy.

Ann let it pass but her eyes still searched his face and eyes. "I want you to know that never—never, I'm thoroughly sure—can I agree that Wade chose rightly: Wade nor none of these miserable men that choose each other."

Hutch only said "You know I think you're tragically wrong. You know I'll never understand why you punish yourself with simple lies about the human race through all of history—you're smarter than most Supreme Court justices; *use* your mind, Ann."

She let that settle around them in the stillness. Then, smiling a little, she took up her spoon and clinked on the bowl. *Food, nothing but food now.*

After fifteen seconds Hutch drew back and stood to serve the stew.

"Just a mouthful for me." Then conscious that the food had been bought by Hutch, Ann said "It looks fine; I'm just barely hungry."

Hutch repeated Boat's warning. "We may need extra strength through the night."

Ann waited, then managed the start of a smile. "I think I've got the strength—"

Hutch said "I can't remember when you didn't." With a full bowl of stew, he came back and started to eat.

He'd finished a corn stick before Ann said "You think it's safe for me to run home and get a few clothes?"

"Boat could go; he told me he drives."

"Boat wouldn't know where to start with my mess."

So Hutch said "I think if you tell Wade now that you're going out for less than hour, he'll wait for you."

"You think it's that easy?"

Hutch said "About as easy as chewing barbed wire. But no, I think Wade is running this thing. He's in some kind of temporary control. He'll tell you if you shouldn't leave."

Ann reached for a corn stick, buttered it slowly and ate a small bite. "He's told me, Hutch. You know he's asked for me."

"I do, yes. We'll make up the guest bed."

"I can't move Boat."

"Boat sleeps on a pallet by Wade—he asked to."

Ann said "I doubt any of us will sleep for days to come. Wade's got a timetable. I feel it in my bones."

Hutch could only agree. "It won't be days." Before his throat cleared, the wall phone rang with startling force. He scrambled up to prevent a second ring. "Hutchins Mayfield."

"Hutch, it's Maitland. How's Wade this evening?"

It was the first time Mait had phoned since his coolly threatening departure on Monday night; and Hutch was constrained, not just by Ann's objection to Mait but by his own recent knowledge of what seemed Mait's fool recklessness. "Thanks, Wade's about the same as he was."

"Is Boat still there? I'd like to see him again before he leaves."

Hutch was trying not to say Mait's name. "Boatie's got his hands pretty full tonight. We both have, in fact."

Mait smelled trouble if not the precise kind. "You can't talk now or you're mad at me—which?"

"Neither one, truly. Wade's on his last legs. I'll keep you posted. Thanks for calling."

Mait said "I've hurt you—"

"No, you couldn't do that." Hutch heard his own words; what they really meant was *You don't matter enough in my life to* hurt *me now*. So he tried to blur the message a little. "I'll call when I can. Take care of yourself." When he got that far, he realized Mait was no longer there. He'd hung up somewhere in Hutch's last words.

With all the other causes for pain, still this slight impasse was the one that chose to fall on Hutch and bring him down. As he hung up the phone, tears flooded his eyes. To hide them from Ann, he went to the sink and ran cold water.

Still, when he turned, she said "Oh please don't give in yet."

That rubbed Hutch wrong—he'd borne up at least as well as she. But strangely no hot words came to him. And stranger still, his next move was slowly to walk up behind her, lay both hands on her shoulders and press. They'd barely touched in more than a year, and in those months she'd lost no serious trace of the fineness she'd borne all her life—all the years Hutch had known her. Even here his hands only touched Ann's blouse; but when she didn't shrug him off, Hutch extended his thumbs and found the bone at the base of her neck. He'd only begun to rub there gently when he realized Boat was standing in the door, in the stillest air Hutch had seen in long years. Again Hutch couldn't speak.

Finally Ann said "Mr. Boat, here, let me fix you some stew."

Boat shook his head and gave a slow smile that darkened the whole room—nothing in sight was as bright as his eyes. "Thank you, Ann. I'll wait a little while on that. I just came to tell you Wade's gone on off."

Hutch didn't understand at once. "Off?"

Ann knew. She only said "No—"

But Boat's head signed Yes over and over, and his smile burned on. "Yes ma'm, he's passed. Peaceful as any child asleep. I was two feet from him and couldn't hear him go. There was no time to call you."

Hutch's mind lunged hot into anger. *Of course there was time to call us, you fool.* But he kept his silence for the moment it took to search

Boat's face and confirm his good intent. Hutch stood in place, his eyes bone dry.

Ann didn't face Hutch but, as she stood too, her right hand came up and found his hand behind her. Separate as that, they held each other a long minute till Boat turned and led them on in to Wade.

IN death what was left of Wade Mayfield seemed the absolute proof that life is a power that fills real space with its mass and force. The cooling bones and hair and skin were hardly enough for a ten-year-old boy harrowed to death, much less a grown man whose shape had contained ten billion memories of life lived and stored, for reward or fear. Though Boat had shut the eyes before calling Hutch and Ann, they'd opened slightly. Through the long dark lashes, the enormous pupils had set at an angle like the angle in portraits whose eyes can follow you round a room. But they showed no threat now and made no plea.

Ann reached out and carefully shut them again.

This time they stayed down—they and all the rest of the body.

Though Ann and Hutch and Boat were silently sending out the last of their care and the start of their grief like a final healing or at least a balm, the abandoned body was already past such negligible wants. In Boat's word, the substance of what had been a life—a life with serious weight and reach, and with numerous thousand unmet hopes—had plainly *passed*.

50

BY ten o'clock they'd done what they could. Hutch, Ann and Boat together had washed Wade's body and dressed it in a clean nightshirt. With very few words they all decided the body should lie in its own bed tonight; early tomorrow Hutch would call the undertaker and gave him instructions for a simple cremation (they'd plan a memorial service for later). Then once they'd each touched Wade a last time—each kissed his forehead—

and left the one lamp burning by his bed, they still had to find small tasks for their hands, tasks to numb their minds. They were wide awake, and no one had mentioned Ann's leaving again.

Hutch felt compelled to pack every bottle of pills, every dressing and diaper and intravenous tube in a single big box and take it to the laundry room, out of sight.

Boat helped Hutch root out the last signs of illness; then he turned to the kitchen and swept and scoured the floor and counters as if nothing but the sight of unvarnished wood could satisfy him or ease Wade onward—Wade and Wyatt, whom Boat knew was with him.

In the dim bedroom, ten feet from Wade, Ann sorted the clothes in the old chest of drawers. She'd meant to set aside for burning anything that was frayed, and give the rest to the Salvation Army for needy children. But then she got to the bottom drawer and found the one old sunsuit that had lasted, a sole survivor from the year Wade was five—a white sailor shirt with navy piping, a whistle on a lanyard and short white pants with a button-front flap. Though it was cotton, some bug had got to it and made lace of the middy shirttail. There was no way Ann's hands could discard it though, not here tonight. She folded each piece meticulously and laid them all back into the chest. There'd be time for them later. Then she went to the kitchen to make strong coffee. Never in their lives had coffee ever fazed her or Hutch's chance of sleep.

Boat followed and stayed with her there, finally eating the supper he'd missed. They said no single word that didn't pertain to food or washing dishes.

Hutch spent twenty minutes alone in his study, turning through handfuls of pictures (his long-gone mother, his father, Grainger, he and Ann near Rome in the fifties with a lanky American airman they'd met in their semi-whorehouse pensione, a homesick stunner; then dozens of views of Wade in every year of his life till he left for New York). It came to Hutch that, here tonight, he should find that cache of naked men he'd discovered in New York, the small stack of snapshots—whosever they'd been—and burn them in the fireplace before Ann could find them and turn them against herself. *No, not tonight. They're genuine relics, not mine to destroy.* So Hutch stood and went to join Boat and Ann in the kitchen.

They were still seated at the center table, quiet as animals stalled for the night.

Boat was darning a knee-length argyle sock of his own (his crazy aunt could still knit).

Ann was reading through papers from a full briefcase—the pitiful strangler, committed to paper, still mad as a breakaway threshing machine.

When Hutch had poured a cup of coffee and found the box of dry saltines, he sat between them.

No one met anyone else's eyes, and the better part of two minutes passed before Boat spoke. "Mr. Mayfield, is it too late to call Ivory?"

Hutch glanced to the wall clock—just past eleven. He'd forgot his promise to Wade to call her, but it seemed late to disturb a working person with desolate news. "I guess we'd better wait till morning."

Boat said "Wade asked for Ivory several times today, while you were out."

"And Strawson," Ann said. "Straw never sleeps."

Hutch had forgot Straw too. Well, it had to be unmerciful to rouse anybody for news they couldn't act on, not tonight. "I'll call them both first thing in the morning."

Ann agreed.

But Boat met Hutch's eyes a long time.

Hutch said "Am I wrong?"

"Mr. Hutch, this is your business to run. But if I was up in Harlem this minute, hearing nothing but garbage trucks in the street and men killing kids, I'd want you to call me soon as you could, any hour of the dark—I loved Wade that much. I could anyhow get down on my knees and beg God to ease him passing over and guard him from worse than he's known already."

Hutch looked to Ann.

She said "The same for me." No tall sycamore in late December was ever stripped cleaner.

So once they'd each lapsed back into silence and Hutch had drunk the last of his coffee, he said "I think I'll say good night. I'll try to phone Ivory and Straw from my room. If anybody needs me, don't hesitate to knock." He pushed back his chair to stand.

But Boat leaned toward him across the table, both hands extended.

Hutch reached to take them and press them hard. They were tough as new leather and nearly dry as Grainger's.

Boat freed one hand and held it to Ann.

Hutch met her eyes and mouthed a silent Yes.

So she gave her own two hands to make a full circuit. The three of them held there, quiet together, for maybe ten seconds. Still no force moved among their hands—none but their own alert exhaustion, their bone-deep sadness.

Hutch stood and left them.

51

THIS time a machine answered Ivory's number, a deep strange man's voice. "Please leave a message."

Hutch almost hung up but then chose to gamble. "If this is Miss Bondurant's residence, I'm Hutchins Mayfield in North Carolina." He waited a moment.

Then Ivory's voice said "Good evening, Mr. Mayfield."

"I'm sorry to wake you."

"You didn't. I was lying here, knowing you'd call tonight."

"And so I have."

"Wade's gone then," she said.

"Very peacefully, yes. Jimmy Boat was with him in his old bedroom; his mother and I were just a few yards off in the kitchen—no sound or struggle."

Ivory took a long wait. "Well, God, now we can all stop hoping."

Though plainly not harsh, it struck Hutch as a very odd thing to say. "I guess I'd given up hope way back."

Ivory said "You had to. I'm just a fool. But then I guess I need to be."

Again the words seemed so unlike her, Hutch wondered if she was drinking maybe or confused from sleep; and who was the strange man's voice on her answering machine? "Whatever, Ivory—you helped Wade live as long as he did. He mentioned you today."

"How was that, Mr. Mayfield?"

Again he asked her to call him *Hutch*.

"That doesn't seem right—not yet at least."

So he answered her question. "Wade said to tell you his tour was finished—he may have said *trip*, but I think it was *tour*. Then he said he'd see you and your family soon."

Ivory said "Wade Mayfield was one gentle man."

"That he was, to the end."

"Do you believe he's ended then?" Her voice made it sound like a genuine question.

Hutch said "How do you mean that exactly?"

"Do people outlast death, as themselves somehow?"

He said "I've got a lifelong hunch they do, no personal proof though. One of my old college philosophy teachers used to say 'The human race in general has believed in immortality; the opinion of a whole race is worth consideration at the least.' " When Ivory was silent Hutch said "And you?"

"I pretty much gave up faith, back in college; but lately I've had strong feelings again, like messages almost."

"From Wyatt or who?"

Ivory said "As a matter of fact, my brother, yes."

"You've felt him near?"

"Just twice," she said. "Both times *strong* and close at hand. The second time he brushed my hand, along the back, barely raking my knuckles."

So Hutch had to tell her. "I felt him today—Wyatt, *strong*, yes. I was in Wade's room just before he died—just Wade and I in the space alone—and I'll swear Wyatt's presence swept in on us."

Ivory took the report as a credible fact. "He's furious, isn't he?— still, poor child."

"Frightening, yes."

"He'll start to calm." Her voice was free of tears.

"How's that?" Hutch said.

"Wyatt has all of Wade on his side from here on."

Hutch couldn't think how to go further than that. *Can't and maybe won't ever need to.* He said "I'll let you sleep on then—deep thanks again. Wade's asked to be buried up there by Wyatt. When we've had our memorial service among his friends down here, in a week or two, I'll bring the ashes north and shut the apartment. Then if you and your mother don't object, we'll bury Wade with Wyatt—I think you said Wyatt's buried on Long Island?"

Ivory took a long wait. "He is, in Sea Cliff next to our father. Mother and I won't object, no sir. Not if that's your wish."

"I'll call again when I've got clear plans. But get some sleep."

Ivory balked at saying goodbye. She said a long "Ah"; then "Would I be welcome at Wade's service, if I could get off?"

"You'd be welcome as the day, absolutely. We'll have it on a weekend if that will help. Please come."

"If I can," she said. "I owe him that much."

"Ivory, you've paid any debt many times with the care you gave him. But I'll call the moment we have a firm plan."

For all her self-possession, Ivory said "Promise—"

"A strong promise, surely."

Then she was gone, no word of goodbye.

That chilled Hutch a little; but before he could dwell on Ivory's strangeness, he punched Straw's number. Two rings, then Strawson's deep "All right."

At the sound of that voice, Hutch's own throat shut again.

In his deepest bass, Straw carefully and politely said "If you're the psycho son of a bitch that's been calling here and scaring my wife, you've met your match tonight, hot stuff. Here comes ten thousand rads of pure X ray down the wire to your ear." He made an ominous crackling sound; then "There, your brain is hopelessly fried."

At least Hutch could chuckle. "It's nobody but me."

"Hey you. You holding your own tonight?"

"That's the point," Hutch said. "My hands are fresh empty."

"Since how long ago?"

"Three hours maybe. We've all been busy, doing small chores."

Straw said "You're saying he's already gone?"

"Wade died tonight. In a good deal of peace."

Slowly Straw said "Please understand me. Is Wade still there at the house with you?"

"His body, in his bed, clean and ready, yes."

"I'll be straight down there then, all right?"

"We've got a full house—Ann's here and Jimmy Boat."

Straw said "I won't lie down; I won't press on you. I just want to see that boy on human grounds, not in some creep's embalming parlor."

"No chance of that. Wade asked for cremation."

"But you said he's still there."

Hutch said "Till morning. Then the undertaker comes."

"I'm leaving this minute."

Hutch couldn't pretend he wanted Straw's presence this late in the night, but he knew Straw had true rights in this—all his care for Wade through the years. He said "Don't knock. Just tap on my window."

Straw said "I'll sleep in the car till dawn."

Hutch knew he meant it, no point in a quarrel. "I'll see you at daybreak; watch your step on the road." Then "Thanks, old mate."

"None older," Straw said. "Lean on that at least."

In under ten minutes, and fully dressed on top of his sheets, Hutch was deeper asleep than he'd been in weeks.

52

AT four forty-five in the sounding dark, Hutch's eyes clicked open. The moment he knew he was truly awake, a thick shaft drove right through his body from head to feet—*You are utterly alone.* In fact, he was. With Wade gone, there were no blood kin to whom Hutch felt remotely close except old Grainger at the end of his century. No friend any nearer to hand than Strawson. And Ann had made her choice to leave, a choice Hutch still couldn't make himself fight. So a fairly enormous story had ended, as human stories go at least—a story whose long path was visible for ninety years anyhow, from a night in the spring of 1903 when his young grandmother had abandoned her family to flee with her high school Latin teacher and start the line that ended here in Hutch.

All his adult life he'd been a namer, a man whose trade was an effort to transcribe the living and dead in durable words—the minimal words that can summon an essence before the eyes of distant strangers and leave them better endowed for time than they presently are, alone in the solitary cells of their own lives—so now Hutch lay on flat in the thick dark and tried to name his family's journey. All he could find, here anyhow, was a single word—a word he'd dreaded most of his life: unmitigated *waste*. What was left of ninety years of Kendals and Mayfields, them and all their close dependents, but the barely phosphorescent trail left by the burning of what they'd all called *love* as their fuel?—their treacherous, always vanishing fuel, their craving for time. With Wade's abandoned shell of a body just yards away, that finding seemed unbearably right to Hutch and too hard to live with, this close to daybreak.

Hutch got to his feet, found his robe in the dark and quietly made his way to Wade's room. In the doorway he paused and listened for Boat—Boat had chosen to sleep again on the floor by Wade.

And there was faint breathing, steady enough to indicate sleep.

So Hutch stepped in. The chair that had sat by the bed was gone. With slow care to make no noise, Hutch sat on the edge of the mattress at the level of Wade's sharp hipbone encased in the dry nightshirt and the sheet.

At first he felt he shouldn't touch Wade; the skin would be cold and the rigor of death would have surely set in. But as Hutch sat on, working back toward pictures of a live smiling Wade—ten, twenty years ago—he soon was silently telling himself *This is truly the end of the best thing you made; touch him one more time for memory at least*. Slowly again Hutch ran his left hand under the sheet toward Wade's upper arm.

It was cool, not cold, and still yielding to the touch.

Hutch's thumb tried to brush the skin lightly.

Only then did a force as repellent as high wind pour out of Wade into Hutch's own body.

Tired and grieving as he was, Hutch still could think of no name but Wyatt's. Ivory, nearly five hundred miles north, had known that Wyatt owned all of Wade now. Hutch kept his thumb in place and tried to tell the source of that power how thoroughly he ceded his rights in the last remains of his only child. In his mind he said three times *Take him, yes*.

But the force became an actual blast of silent demand, as strong as loathing.

Hutch bore it ten seconds more—it was surely reaching Boat's sleep too. What would Boat do or say?

When Hutch couldn't stand it any longer and drew his hand back free from the covers, Boat spoke plainly from his mat on the floor. "You know who it is here this minute, don't you, Hutch?"

"I do. And I've given Wade up to him—"

Boat waited so long Hutch thought he was gone into sleep again; but then Boat said "Excuse me, Mr. Mayfield, but maybe you still need to know—Wade hasn't been yours to give for long years."

Hutch thought *I've known that longer than you*; but he had the grace in the dark to thank Boat, then stand and leave.

53

WHERE he went was toward Ann. She'd shut the guest room door and no light showed; but the last few minutes had left Hutch gravely in need of a presence that stood a chance of welcoming him, tolerating him at least. Without a knock he turned the knob and entered dark air. A good deal of starlight fell through the one big window that Ann had opened beyond her.

Her body was clearly outlined on the bed, a wide double bed. She was on her side, facing the window, apparently wearing only her slip. Her legs were covered to the knee by an afghan.

Hutch went to the near edge of the mattress and waited long enough for Ann to send him out if she wanted, if she sensed his presence. What felt to Hutch like a long time passed, a stretch of minutes in which his right hand burned on still with the memory of Wyatt. Finally he couldn't make himself wait longer. With gradual care to lighten his moves, Hutch laid his body in the tangled space on the near side of Ann. She was still turned away, though she'd silently waked; Hutch was on his back.

Separate but near, they each soon thought of their bodies' long denial.

Neither had touched another body, not in intimate need, since Ann left here. Alone on their own beds, they'd fed their bodies the best they could manage in their first weeks apart. Then as Wade came home, and his desperation gripped them, they'd silently lost all secret need and lived in their own skins, chaste as clean linen. Now with Wade bound outward, Hutch and Ann lay on, wondering if some kind of trusting union might come down on them in a new natural craving, for partial ease. But neither one's mind could raise itself to that pitch of want; neither one's voice had the modest daring to speak in this quiet room and own up to what had become for each a slow starvation.

Eventually, as the starlight dimmed for the endless minutes before sunrise, Ann turned to her back and lay, facing upward, a handspan from Hutch. When she could hear he was still awake, she said "You're thinking of Wyatt, right?"

"Right, as ever."

"He's been all in here, all night, hasn't he?"

"In my mind at least. And Boatie's felt him."

"God damn his soul then." Ann plainly meant it.

Hutch waited till he felt he had the full right. "Oh no. Wade's his."

"I understand that, yes. It hurts worse than Hell."

"It'll pass," Hutch said. "Hell doesn't exist—not for Wade Mayfield, not after tonight."

"You can't promise that." Ann's voice was level but still firmly convinced.

"No, I can't—no promises ever again. But both of us need to believe we'll outlast even this."

Ann said "I'm sorry to repeat myself; and Hutch, I'm half glad you think I'm so wrong. But still I very much doubt I'll outlast my soul's deep suspicion that, if there's a place of long damnation, then Wade is in it."

That stopped Hutch for minutes. He finally said "You're *willing* Hell, listen. That's all Hell is—pure human sadism: you want Wade to burn, for your wild reasons."

"I've got no choice; my whole life believes it."

Hutch had always known that the unseen world—of gods and fate, yes or no—had come to him much more strongly than to Ann. The simplest child's prayer was a trial for her; was she telling the truth or sucking sweet lies? So he knew he couldn't press harder tonight. But he found what felt like a sizable fact and offered that to her. "I've known a big lot of smart women in my life. Not one of them ever out-ran you for smartness. You can't scald yourself in ignorance forever; trust your mind. Wade died a good man. Teach yourself that at least. Two people as bent on life as we've been are bound to survive, so we owe Wade simple justice at least—intelligent memory."

Ann had no answer, or offered none. Like Hutch, she'd lost too much through the years to doubt her own adamant strength—the child she'd aborted (that still came at her in dreams, begging life), her long-gone parents, a dozen or so dear missing friends: none of them had downed her, deep as they hurt. So she lay in reach of the warmth from Hutch, not speaking or touching, till daylight first pierced the wide east window. Then she quietly rose and went to look out. It took her awhile to understand, but then she turned and said to Hutch "Strawson is waiting out there in his car."

In the threatened night, Hutch had forgot that Straw was coming; but he only said "He's expected, yes." What he hadn't expected was the hope that suddenly shot all through him from the sight of Ann's face.

Even this early, and her hair disarranged, the strength she'd promised last night to bring was visible on her, in her face and eyes. It even seemed greater than ever in her life. And to Hutch that strength felt almost ready to open again and offer him anything he could use. He thanked her simply for being here; but when she only nodded and moved toward the door, he thought the prospect of Straw had troubled her. He said "No way we can wall out Strawson. Straw was in at the start of Wade's life, and you well know it." Then Hutch got up too and went toward his friend, the first hope of ease.

Ann reminded herself that she'd urged Hutch to call Straw last evening. She had no grounds for real complaint then; and for the first time in more than a year, she felt none at all. Age and loss—she'd started to see—were the normal acids in every life, eating away the iron spine of anger and greed and unjust demand. She'd wash and dress in yesterday's clothes and offer to cook a big breakfast for all. Even she was hungry. So what she said was "Bring Straw in, any time you're ready."

54

July 7, 1993

Dear Professor Mayfield,

I'm extremely sorry I crashed in on your privacy today. I was feeling two strong emotions at once—homesickness and pleasure in my findings over here in the British Library—and since my father had sent me a check for my birthday last week, on a whim I decided to place that call to you and send my greetings and thanks in person. Thanks for all your encouragement in everything, life and work. Then you told your news, and I've been regretting my impulse ever since.

Of course I'd known that Wade was bad off before I left. And my wife has kept me posted at intervals on his progress—you recall that she knows Wade's mother who shops at the greenhouse where Stacy works. But hearing he's gone, in your controlled voice this afternoon, has struck me harder than I'd have guessed, even with all the liking I felt and all my admiration for his courage and remarkable cheer in the times I was with him this spring—that long ago.

Because I've been the receiver so often of your own kindness and openness to—what?—human failings maybe, I want to risk a few words to you now that may prove a surprise and a gift, I hope. I mean them anyhow as my main gift in Wade's honor here, all I can send you from as far off as London.

The gift is one fact. Almost the last day I sat with Wade while you were on campus, he told me his eyes were having a good day and would I please strip off my clothes so he could see me—altogether me. We were out there, alone as any two hawks on a thermal updraft; so I thought "What the hell?" and gave him his wish. He watched me closely; I felt like it helped him. I can honestly say I know it helped me and bucks me up still when I get low. You recall I was having problems just then with my

scrappy marriage, so any word of a hint that I or any part of me was of
serious use to another live creature—well, it came as a help.

You understand that I'm aimed at women like a heat-seeking missile
of the most abject kind; but that day with Wade, I even stepped near
enough to take his touch if he'd felt up to that, but he turned it down—
all very polite on both our sides, and a memory that gives me the little
comfort I feel, here at this distance with the weight of his death on my
mind and your grief. He'd said I was something worth watching with the
eyesight left him by then. I've never felt nearly watchable enough, despite
my mother's praise.

That's meant of course for nobody but you. Even though I've invested
in express postage here, please burn these pages, to spare any hurt it might
cause another, if other eyes see it. And if learning that fact has anyway
deepened your present pain, I send you my deepest apology ahead of time
to say I'm thinking of you by the minute, with the best hopes for strength
and that somehow your own work will see you through again, as I know
it has before. I'll phone again soon. Meanwhile,

> Yours,
> Hart (Salter)

> July 9, 1993

Dear Hart,

That news means a very great deal to me. I thought Wade had died
in an unbroken drought. Now I know I was wrong. I've burned your letter
but the picture it gave me will last, I'm all but sure, the rest of my life.

I'll look forward to your call.

> Grateful affection,
> Hutchins Mayfield

> July 10, 1993

Dear Strawson,

A bright cool Sunday morning here—the first chance I've had to draw
a long breath for what feels like weeks. And first on the list of people I

*need and want to thank is you of course. I only wish I'd had the foresight
to ask you to stay another day or so and answer the phone, distribute the
excess food and flowers, and in general stand between me and life till I
got a little better balanced on my pins.*

*It turns out that even the simplest plan to cremate a body and scatter
the ashes, as directed by the dead man, is mined with traps of various
sizes—none of which is your concern, so I'll spare you the moan of a father
aged sixty-three who had to stand helpless and watch his one child vanish
this awful way (I have to remind myself I can say that awful way now,
that it's finished at least—it died with the boy).*

*There is one sizable dilemma I failed to mention while you were here.
You know how Wade insisted on visiting Grainger in May and that he
asked Grainger to oversee the scattering of his ashes on the creek behind
the house. He went on to stress that intention to me on several occasions
afterwards. Just before he died, though, he told me twice to bury his remains
with Wyatt Bondurant in Sea Cliff, Long Island.*

*Confused as he was those last few days, I couldn't take an oath that
he was demented when he changed his plan—my guess is, he understood
what he was asking and had weighed it sanely. In fact the only credit I
can take from these last weeks comes from promising Wade I'd follow his
wishes. I even phoned Ivory the night he died and let her know that Wade
would be on his way north as soon as I could bring him. She calmly agreed.*

*The hitch of course lies mainly with his mother. Ann didn't hear Wade
express a last wish, and now she's all but dug her heels in and defied any
thought of taking him farther than those backwoods and the creek Grainger
dredged. You'll understand what a concession she's making, just in agreeing
to that first plan—spreading him on my own family's ground, not a neutral
cemetery plot in Durham or in southside Virginia with her own gruesome
clan.*

*I suspect you're straining to suppress a grin. Sad as it all is, as
quandaries go it does sound a lot like the unholy wrangle over D. H.
Lawrence's ashes in the thirties. In his case—Frieda Lawrence (the spouse)
and Mabel Dodge Luhan (the patroness) had decidedly separate plans for
the remains, and Frieda finally resorted to mixing every particle of the
ashes into wet cement and letting it harden. In no time thereafter she had*

Lawrence safe in a ton of concrete that Mabel with all her millions couldn't haul.

I'm nowhere near that desperate yet, and I won't claim to like Wade's last idea, but I feel a deep loyalty to a deathbed promise. So I may yet ask you and Emily to speak about the matter with Ann and help her see what's understandably all but as painful as the loss itself—that her son, in his right mind, chose to leave her again in a choice she loathes, and this time for good.

Whatever, we're planning a small service here for Saturday afternoon, July 31st. If the weather's good we may try to have it right here at the house where Wade after all lived two-thirds of his life. I guess I could get Duke Chapel for a half hour—Ann seems to want that—but I'm not sure I can be responsible for bearing up the way I'd want to in those huge surroundings. When that great organ gets underway, in those levitating vaults, I forget that the whole place was built with the proceeds from a billion lung cancers; and I more or less instantly revert to the worldview of, say, an Anglo-Saxon mason—the ceiling peels back, clouds evaporate, I contemplate God's face at point-blank range and find slim reflection of me or my life anywhere in his eyes: slim or none at all. (I'm prepared to learn in any case that Wells Cathedral was built with, say, the proceeds from the archbishop's chain of licensed brothels and that God Itself cares nary a whit for anything but the sight of our awe, facedown on the pavings.)

In any case I'll keep you posted as arrangements are made. Ann and I both want you to participate as you think best—remarks or the reading of something you think will suggest Wade best to his few survivors. When I spoke with Ivory the night Wade died, she said she might also come down to join us. Again you can guess Ann's feelings on the prospect, but so far she's issued no ultimatum, so I'm writing to Ivory later today with full details. Should I ask her to speak?

I may drive up toward you late next week, if you mean to be home— see Grainger and you, beg Emily to feed me old childhood favorites (are the butter beans in?), maybe spend a quiet night. I'll give you fair warning. Till when, more thanks than even an aging Mayfield can send. You know we've always been big thankers, whatever our faults.

Love always,
Hutchins

July 10, 1993

Dear Ivory,

I'd never in my life seen an entire orchid plant, so the one you sent was not only beautiful the hour it arrived but is by me still as I write to thank you—even more blooms, each one more mysteriously made than the others.

I don't need to tell you that it's been a hard week, a hard three months; but just today I begin to feel that the tunnel of numbness may well end. Not that I'm eager to start responding with sober nerves to all that's happened since I last saw you—and to all that happened to Wade and Wyatt and you for months before I blundered on the scene. I hope you'll also understand how deeply I feel relieved—many hours of the day and night, to the roots of my bones—and how guilty I feel at even the chance to shut my eyes for more than ten seconds and not expect a voice to call me. I've never been much of a believer in "blessings in disguise," not even when the blessing comes as death. I've never thought any one I love should need to die. I still don't.

We have made a practical plan or two, though. On Saturday afternoon, July 31st, we'll ask Wade's closest friends to gather for a brief chance to honor his life and recall his best. I was grateful when you said you might come down for that occasion. I very much hope you can still be here. The guest room in this house is quiet and cool with a bath of its own; no one on Earth could be more welcome. I'll hold it, waiting for word from you, and will also reserve you a room in town in case you prefer. If you can be here, may I ask you to speak your heart at the time? If for any reason you feel you can't, no need to explain. Wade's family—his mother, his godfather Strawson and I—know how much you've done.

After the service, you and I can talk a little about the only two remaining problems. I need to face up to shutting that haunted New York apartment, and I need your advice on the final disposition of Wade's ashes. I told you that the last wish he expressed to me was to lie by Wyatt. Earlier he'd told an ancient cousin and his mother about a different plan, and I trust you'll realize that she's distressed at the contradiction.

Long Island's a long way to go from Durham to visit a grave. By the time you're here, we should have a solution—one way or another. Conceivably I could drive you back north, finish emptying out Wade's apartment and then inter him by Wyatt in Sea Cliff, or you might stay

*a day and drive up with us to my old homeplace an hour from here and
spread him there on a creek he loved back deep in the woods. That was
Wade's original plan, expressed in strong terms to several of us.*

*Please let me hear soon. I don't want to burden you with one ounce
more of my family's business than you've already borne, but let me say
one last word in closing—your presence here on the 31st of July would
mean an enormous amount to me.*

*Ever in gratitude,
Hutchins Mayfield*

14 July 1993

My dear Hutch,

*I never dreamt I'd have to mark French Independence Day in my old
age by learning of Wade's death and your plans to remember him. I've
been permitted, for whatever cruel purpose of fate, to outlast the ranks of
all I've loved except your good self. What else can I tell you but King
Lear's monosyllabic response to his one good daughter's murder—"Howl,
howl, howl"?*

*As for your invitation to come and speak for Wade at the chapel
service, can you understand how hard I want to refuse you flat, then to
sit right here—bolt every door and window, chink every keyhole—and
refuse to acknowledge one more departure?*

*I'm coming, though, if I live and can walk downstairs on the morning
in question and get past the Petersburg city limits sign. Don't think about
sending somebody to get me, but thanks for the offer. I've got an elderly
Negro gentleman who drives me places I can't help going, and I've already
phoned to book his assistance. I won't spend the night, so forget about
hotels. If I'm not there by the hour appointed, you'll know I'm prostrate
or have quit myself.*

*It's all I can offer you, dear boy, now or ever after. You'll never get
over this; don't even try. It will make you strong as a heartpine knot
though. You'll be minting out poems and sterling pupils when Western
Civilization is back in the hands of the wolves—speed the day! Wolves
constitute a far more admirably organized species in every way than we*

and our brethren. I even read recently that wolves seem to have a developed religious sense—their love of the moon and worship of it—but as yet they have no known TV evangelists raking in the shekels. No doubt their basic decency has spared them any such vulgarity. May your own wolf nature serve you at present.

> I send you a lifetime's love at the least,
>> not that my love ever cured any pain yet,
>> least of all my own, though I'm breathing
>> still and glad to be

                                                            Alice

                                                      July 15, 1993
Deep Sympathy in your Time of Grief, Mr. and Mrs. Mayfield,

   I am Wyatt Bondurant's only mother as you well know and I think I can guess in the pit of my chest how you are looking at life these days. I have seen both of you in pictures Wade showed me in happier times and I know you are younger than me by some years. So please don't think I am forward in saying the Lord will answer your need if you ask him in coming weeks. I have seen a lot, from old Virginia where I grew up to Long Island presently, and one thing I know about the Lord is, he may take you by the scruff of the neck and shake every last tooth out of your head but he very seldom cuts you off at the knees, or much below. Once in a great while but very seldom. To be sure, you may have to hunch down deep to bear his will. I am bent nearly double with all I watched since I was a girl in a family of nine. I have buried twenty-three loved ones in my life, including two children from my own body. But God won't press you lower than you let him, not till your time is up and he's ready. I wish we could be with Ivory at the service but will think of each of you through that day. And every other day till I am called home.

                                 Respectfully yours,
                    Mrs. Lucy Patterson Bondurant and Raven

July 15, 1993

Dear Hutch,

I'll be there to help you with the service. Won't even attempt, however, to advise you or Ann on scattering the ashes—here or Long Island. To my mind, they're ashes, no more precious than woodsmoke. Everything that mattered and will last of Wade Mayfield will hang all around us every day of our lives till we follow on. Flip a coin, I'd say—but I said I wouldn't say, so just ignore that.

Meanwhile Mr. Grainger finally responded to the news I gave him eight days ago, soon as I got home from seeing Wade last. When I sat down and told him then, he didn't move a muscle. After ten minutes when I stood up to leave and asked if he recalled what I'd told him, he looked at the TV and said "Strawson, you couldn't tell me news if you tried. I foretell every breath you ever draw." Still, this morning when I helped him dress and had made him his breakfast, I opened the door to start my day; and he said "Go post this message to Hutchins." He held out this little wad of folded paper. I have not opened it but send it on for what it's worth.

Love anyhow from
Strawson

The enclosed tight-folded plain sheet of paper with pale blue lines seemed to say in the faintest readable hand, which was all but surely the remnant of Grainger's old strong script,

Raven Hutchins Mayfield
Raven Wade Mayfield
Grainger Walters: *kin people.*

In all the years any white Mayfield had known him, since he came south in 1904 from Maine where his father (who was old Rob's mulatto son) had taken the family in flight from Virginia, none of his white kin had ever heard Grainger claim blood relation.

For most of his own life, Hutch had understood how immense the distance was between the lives the white Mayfields had led in their well-built homes and Grainger's adjacent tacit pain and solitude. But still this glimpse of the old man's spider-silk words on paper shook Hutch to the sockets like nothing he'd seen since the last glimpse of Wade. It partly braced Hutch for what came to him the following day by express mail.

July 16, 1993

Dear Mr. Mayfield,

With any luck I'll be there on the evening of July 30th, but please don't count on me to say anything at the service. I couldn't. I saw too much in this past year and felt too many feelings, being powerless to help; so anytime I let myself recall it, I seize up cold and simply can't speak. Wade knew he mattered in my life, more or less from the day we met; that's what counts with me.

Since you've been so decent to me and my mother through this, I hate to complicate matters this late. But better now than when I'm down there, in the midst of your guests. The fact is that, once Wyatt died, Wade sat down on the night of the funeral and wrote a letter to you and Mrs. Mayfield. He sealed it just as it is today and made me promise to mail it to you when he was gone.

I don't know all of what it says; but I've held off this long, trying to find a way to burn it and maybe spare you a further hurt. I'm too much of my Baptist mother's child, however, to fail a dead man if I can avoid it. If anything Wade has written makes you want to stop my visit, just leave a message on my phone machine. I will understand far more completely than you know.

Till whenever then, I send you and all Wade's people my thoughts, my strongest good hope.

Truly,
Ivory Bondurant

The letter she enclosed was sealed in a business envelope, no sign of tampering with the flap. In Wade's unquestionable script, already shaky, it said *For Hutchins Mayfield and Ann Gatlin once I am gone.*

February 20, 1993

Dear Hutch and Ann,

We buried Wyatt today on the Island, so I don't have the will to copy this twice. I trust whichever one sees this first will share it with the other, however far apart you are at the time. It's the only thing you need to know about me that you don't already know or haven't surmised.

Wyatt has a living sister named Ivory Bondurant, a good-looking, smart and admirable woman. Through my work I met her my first week up here, summer of '84. At that time she worked in the same firm as I, a first-class draftsman. She was only just recently separated from her husband, I was lonesome as a cactus and still hadn't set my big sex drive on a single last rail, so she and I got very close in a hurry and stayed that way all the slow steaming summer. So close that, when Ivory realized she was pregnant that fall, we frankly didn't know if the child was mine or hers and her husband's. They'd gone on meeting occasionally.

At the time I knew I loved her in a real way. I also knew I was built to need men, pretty much exclusively, and was headed that way at the first sign of promise. Ivory had more or less understood that from the start; and once she found she was carrying a child, we discussed her having the blood tests done to answer the question of whose child it was, but she wouldn't hear of asking her ex to participate—the last thing she wanted was for him to think he had a claim on the baby; by then they were parting bitterly. He was incidentally also white. The other last thing she wouldn't hear of was shedding the baby. Till then she hadn't felt safe to get pregnant because her marriage had been so rocky. So I stayed near her till the child came safely and have ever since helped her each month with the bills. As I say, she'd pretty much understood from near the start of our friendship that I couldn't spend my whole life with a woman, however fine, though I surely meant to honor the child if time proved him mine.

In the fall of '84, Ivory moved uptown to be near her brother in a better apartment. And that was when I got to know Wyatt. In fairly short order he and I seemed to understand that we were set for the long haul, despite our loud disagreements and crises, which mainly arose from the unavoidable fact that we were built as differently as Memphis and Mombasa. It didn't hurt Ivory, not that she ever showed, not for long anyhow *(though I've also suspected her of being the greatest actress since Eve). By then her and Wyatt's good mother had taken the child to Long Island, except for occasional visits in town. So Ivory, Wyatt and Wade became a working family of three, with a likable weekend guest on occasion.*

What am I telling, or asking, you? First, the child may be half mine. Second, you owe me or Ivory nothing by way of moral or financial support. She will be the sole beneficiary of my insurance and the money I've got in my firm's pension fund. I know you won't dream of contesting that. She's also got quite a decent job, Wyatt left her good money, and—knowing the Bondurant pride as I do—I'm certain she wouldn't accept a dime further. No, I guess all I want is for you to know that Raven Wade Mayfield may have a son to live on beyond him, whatever he's called and wherever he lives. You two may have a survivor on Earth. I wish I could leave you more than that. You'll have to lean on memories, I guess. I've done that for months.

I trust each of you will do whatever is right by your standards. I also wish I had the time and sufficient strength to admit here fully how very much pain I've caused you—and suffered for causing—how wrong I feel about all I'll never get to do for Ivory and her likable boy. The strength to tell you just is not available in my body and won't ever be.

                    So love for now—and, sure, always—from
                                        Wade

55

THAT news reached Hutch the next afternoon. He had spent the morning alone in the house, whittling through the thicket of letters he'd got since Wade died. However kind, most of them had come from fellow writers— poets, novelists, playwrights—and their guaranteed eloquence had made each one a hardship to read: the words went so unerringly straight to the core of his pain. When he'd thanked as many as he could bear in a two-hour stretch, he turned to the all but mindless job of choosing from his own lifetime stock of poems for a *New and Selected* volume he meant to publish in '95. That would be the thirtieth anniversary of his first small volume.

He worked by writing the title of each of the poems from the past forty years on a separate index card. They came to a dauntingly thick stack of cards, nearly two hundred poems. But undeterred, Hutch dealt the cards out on the desk before him—grouping, rearranging and finally winnowing. At first he winnowed mercilessly, saving only the poems he suspected would last another fifty years, maybe even a century, as useful objects for a brand of reader scarcer nowadays than clean air to breathe. That left him with less than a twenty-page book. He shuffled his deck again and started a slightly more tolerant game, one in which he worked again to forgive himself for all he'd omitted.

For years Hutch had known that, because he'd confined his work to verse and, specifically, brief lyric meditations—like the vast majority of American poets since Robert Frost's narrative prime—he'd arrived at the edge of what might well be his last decade without having dug, with words at least, into ninety percent of what he'd seen in his family and the world and what he'd learned and deduced of the past that stretched behind him and the places he'd known. If, forty years ago, he'd tilted toward the novel and learned to convert his gift and his findings into sizable stories—and one of his teachers had urged that on him, fruitlessly—he might have something more to show now than what felt like a few dozen bright chips off enormous, deeply socketed stones that were long past his reach.

In the midst of that, Maitland Moses arrived a little early for lunch. So Hutch gladly broke off and made colossal sandwiches which he and Mait ate with cold beer in the kitchen—it was far too hot to sit on the terrace. Neither of them mentioned Mait's behavior the last time they met, his volunteering for an early doom; they kept to milder subjects. Mait claimed that his friendship with Cam was strengthening steadily, and Cam was looking for a less demanding job than the hospice. As it was, they had so few nights together. They were homing in on the thought of sharing a larger apartment than Mait had presently, if they could afford it—after Wade's death Mait had taken a job in the Duke Library, the manuscripts collection.

Hutch began to tell Mait about his plan for a *Selected Poems*, asking his advice on what to exclude. And soon that had them moving to the study and fiddling again with the index cards. Finally Hutch asked Mait to lay out his own idea of a volume. "Keep all you think you'll want to recall from an old friend's work when you're sixty years old and discard the rest."

Mait faced him squarely. "You know I don't think I'll get to be sixty?"

"Don't depress me again. Just do what I ask."

So while Hutch shelved a few dozen books that had come in the mail when Wade was dying—most of them new poems by friends and ex-students—Mait stood at the desk and played out the white cards carefully. In twenty minutes he turned to Hutch, grinning, and gestured to a wide star of rescued titles. "I gave you sixty-five, one per year for the age you'll be in 1995."

From across the room Hutch said "Way too many."

"You haven't even looked yet."

Hutch said what he suddenly felt in his gut. "I couldn't bear to. So many dead little dinghies in the shallows."

Mait laughed his old high-low croak. "*Now* who's being reckless? These are all trim craft, all still at sea; a few of them qualify as dreadnoughts at least."

Hutch shook his head in honest rejection, but he walked to the desk and studied the titles. In another two minutes he felt a quiet surge of surprise. There seemed at least an even chance that Mait had built, not simply a star of cards but an honorable—maybe better—showing for a lifetime's witness and silent labor. Hutch knew it might all crumble in his mind in the next ten minutes, but for now he looked up. "Don't let me destroy it."

"Sir?"

"Remember it, Mait, just the way it lies. Don't let me hack it up in self-loathing."

Mait was smiling still but he spoke, quite firmly, "Not on your life."

Before Hutch could ask him to gather the cards in order and keep them, the sound of a truck moved up the hill; and a Federal Express man brought Ivory's letter with the separate news from Wade.

Hutch asked Mait's permission, then sat across from him and read both pages in a deepening calm. The peace surprised him more than the news in Wade's few lines. *Is it news at all? Have I always known it?* As the words passed through him, Hutch knew he'd partly dreamed or guessed them—when? *Ages since.* It likewise strangely raised his spirits to meet, head-on, a fresh and surely insoluble mystery (Wade's death had seemed such a terminus to questions of hope). When Hutch scanned both pages a second time, he held them toward Maitland.

Mait grinned but stalled. "Secret dispatches?"

Hutch shook his head No but insisted "Please read them."

Mait took what seemed like abnormal time; then looked up, solemn. "Is this as big a shock as I suspect?"

"Strangely not."

"But it's really weird, right?"

"*Weird*—as in what? In a country as hopelessly sick on the subject of family as ours, with the whole millennium speeding down on us, this sounds like fairly old-time human news—surely nothing weirder than what goes on behind barely closed curtains in middle-class houses down every street *I* travel anyhow."

Mait said "You've got a point."

"I've got a lot more than a point, young pal."

"I guess you could do some DNA tests, if the mother would let you."

As calmly as he'd tracked the sight of the news, Hutch said "No, never."

"Won't Wade's mother really want to know?"

Hutch waited. "Ann put up with me for four decades; I think she's earned her spurs in the dire uncertainty department."

"But will you tell her?"

Hutch hadn't yet thought there might be a choice. Ann's name after all was plain on the envelope, no smaller than his. But he wondered if he might not wait till after Wade's memorial service, when Ivory and the others had come and gone, and then tell Ann. That way she could respond in the slow aftermath, with no threat of panic. So he said to Mait "I may hold off a day or two; but no, clearly Wade meant his mother to know."

"Then hadn't you better tell her before the child's mother comes down? She may have her own plans to tell both of you her side of the mystery."

Hutch saw Mait was right. He'd need to reach Ivory tonight, no later.

56

IT was nearly midnight, and again the mechanical man's voice answered; but when Hutch spoke his name, Ivory picked up the phone. Her voice was tired but not unwelcoming. "I'm sorry I've missed your calls more than once. I've been at a friend's."

Hutch said "Your message got here this afternoon."

"There were two separate messages, Mr. Mayfield."

"Both arrived, clear as day."

Ivory took a long moment. "No sir. Wade's message to you is uncertain."

"How's that?"

Again she waited, this time for so long that Hutch thought she was gone. Then at last her voice came, with more life in it. "I'm assuming he told you about my son. Whatever else Wade said, the name of the father has *never* been clear—not to me at least. And if I don't know, nobody else can. Nobody ever chloroformed and raped Ivory Bondurant."

"What's the child's last name?"

"My name—Bondurant, as I just told you. I never gave it up."

"But you know Wade and I both have *Raven* as part of our names."

Her voice came like a speaking statue's or a sleepwalking child's. "I well understand where *Raven* comes from. Wade and Wyatt and I chose it together. All that meant to us that long summer was, we liked the name. It may seem odd from this far along; but we also thought it was mildly funny since, either way, the boy was half white—more than half; Wyatt and I are both quadroons."

Hutch said "Will it feel right to you and your mother if you bring him for the service?"

"Young Raven? No, that hasn't crossed my mind. He's in day camp out on the Island, at Mother's. He's well settled in and has been for years."

Hutch saw himself barging through pitch-dark water with his eyes half blind. *Why am I more lost, here with this creature who seems at least kind, than anyone near?* But he told her still. "Wade's mother and I would surely value the chance to meet Raven."

"That's kind of you both. I've thought more about this than you've had a chance to, and I'll have to say you'd be complicating your lives a good deal."

"How?"

"Raven's that fine a child."

Hutch said "How old is he, Ivory?"

"Eight, going on eighty." She managed a smile that colored her voice.

Hutch could hear it. "Eight is one of my favorite ages. I honestly think I knew more good sense at eight than ever since."

Ivory said "Oh, me too—maybe nine with me.

If you told me at nine I'd be sitting here tonight, having this talk with you ten thousand years off, I'd have no doubt said 'Girl you're stark-raving nuts.' No, at nine I knew that the world was divided into *Fair* and *Unfair*, forget *Good* and *Evil*—"

"And of course you were right. The average child is."

"I was way past average, if I do say so. I'd have never sat still while this whole mystery around a fine child turned half rank and fishy."

Hutch said "Well, no. Far stranger things turn up every day on the evening news or the afternoon talk shows—children waiting in pain for long decades, then crawling through fire to find a lost parent, cascades of tears."

"Mr. Mayfield, listen—I've never been lost. Neither has my son." She was peaceful and still self-possessed as a heron.

"Ms. Bondurant, I have never doubted that once, not one hot instant." With that, Hutch suddenly felt he'd lost some final chance at continuance: another tack for a dying story, the telling out of his and his family's path on the ground, which was otherwise what now?—Wyatt's dry ashes in a bowl.

"Then thank you, sir. I'm glad you know."

"Shall I call you *madam*?"

"Pardon?"

"You're calling me *sir*. I'm a U.S. citizen, nothing grander." But for a harsh instant, he thought *I've paid mine and many others' way. That's fairly grand.*

Ivory said "Sir, suh, oh suh. Maybe I'm just an old-timey girl—my mother's child from old Virginny, one of the Pattersons from Patterson Hall." No trace, though, of a smile or a sneer.

"Remember I asked you to call me *Hutch?*"

Again Ivory paused for a long breath, then "Hutch, Hutch, Hutchins."

Torn as he felt, in her rich voice finally, it sounded to Hutch like a chain of long-sought hopes amply rewarded, partly earned but never entirely—decades of pardon and boundless bigheartedness, the promise of rest. He understood he was hearing too simply. No human voice could give that much in that little time to any live soul. But for some reason, gently, he told Ivory "Thanks, sleep now, good night." Then he suddenly found he'd said all he knew. Not waiting for an answer, he hung up quietly.

THREE

BOUND AWAY

JULY–AUGUST 1993

From fifty yards' distance, the child was as striking as a palomino colt, a privilege to see; and he watched the car from the moment Hutch turned at the stoplight and drove through the greenery toward him.

The day Ivory's letter came, in mid-July, Hutch had reserved a room for her at the Washington Duke Inn, ten minutes from his house. She'd arrived by plane on Friday night and gone, at her insistence, straight to the inn. Now it was Saturday afternoon, a quarter past two, as Hutch came down the drive to the inn and saw them both, already waiting at the curb. Good as Ivory looked in a dark purple dress and a wide-brimmed straw hat, Hutch naturally focused at once on the child who stood beside her peacefully—a little small maybe for eight years old, in a tan summer suit with an open-necked white shirt, a face the excellent color of his mother, and with eyes as dark as any polished onyx.

Hutch felt a swift flood of expectation—Ivory had never promised she'd bring the child—but he knew he must rein himself in hard. He thought firmly *This child's real, Hutchins. Get one thing right in your life, starting here.* He stopped at the curb, got out at once and stepped toward the two.

For a long moment they looked like the sudden embodiment of all Hutch had lost in his life till this moment—his own young mother whom he'd never seen, young Wade, young Strawson and even Ann herself in her own best days. As Hutch neared them though, they were only themselves, not echoes of others; and that felt like enough of a bounty. He knew not to rush the boy at once, so he put out his hand to Ivory. "You're a friend to be here. Wade's mother will meet us at the chapel."

Ivory shook his hand, then touched the boy. "Hutch, this is Raven Bondurant, my son. Raven, this is Mr. Mayfield—Wade Mayfield's father."

At close range the child was almost too good to see. Hutch refused the urge to hunt for Wade in the flawless skin of the face, the eyes, the black hair and lashes, the silent poise of his whole body in its raw linen suit and starched white shirt. Hutch bent a little and offered his hand. "That's a handsome suit, my friend. Welcome down."

In general, children shake hands like the dead; but Raven Bondurant took hold of Hutch with surprising strength, though his eyes were fixed beyond him. "Brand new," he said. He stroked both palms down his wide lapels.

So Hutch opened both doors on their side of the car and stood while they chose the front or backseat.

Ivory took the back.

Raven slid up front; and when Hutch had joined them, asked the two to buckle their seat belts and then moved out, Raven said "Mother, this place is all green woods."

Ivory said "More trees than you've ever seen. Or may see again. This is how the Earth was meant to look, Son, on weekends at least. You remember it, hear? It's vanishing fast."

Hutch thought *It's vanished already, long gone. These are stage-set trees. But remember me.*

Raven said a single word.

Hutch said "Pardon?"

The child's face was pressed to the window on his side. He took his time before repeating the word. *"Hideout."*

Hutch said "You're in hiding?"

Again the child waited; then still not looking round to Hutch or Ivory, he said "This whole place is some kind of hideout."

From memories of his own childhood and Wade's, Hutch had to assume that the child liked the sight of so many trees—what child doesn't dream of the perfect concealment, the invisible ambush, the cave with two exits? But when he asked whether Raven liked the idea of hiding out here, he got no answer but a shake of the small head. By then they'd reached the first stoplight and could see the chapel tower beyond them. Hutch pointed. "We're headed there."

The boy turned back to his mother and laughed. "Looks like a big old funny church, see?"

Ivory smiled; Hutch saw it in the rearview mirror. "It's a big church, baby. You know what I told you?"

"To hush up and sit."

"And you promised me?"

Raven said "I know it."

"You know it *what*?" Ivory said.

"I know it, yes, Mother."

In the rest of the three-minute drive through campus, none of them said another word, though the boy pointed silently to tree after tree— enormous cedars, pines and huge water oaks. On the air, his finger would trace a whole outline—trunk, branches and leaves—then start another.

Hutch couldn't help thinking the boy was hunting some trace of the sleeping giant who dreams this world and its contents, and he nearly asked. But then he knew *If I'm wrong, it'll be too big a disappointment*; so he drove on in silence.

Only then when he'd stopped in front of the great wide limestone steps to the chapel did he look back and meet Ivory's face. "My wife hasn't seen Wade's letter, the one you sent me. I haven't found the right time to tell her yet."

Ivory registered the fact serenely. "That's entirely your business." Then she and Raven waited in place, still as soldiers, till Hutch came around and opened their doors.

2

HUTCH and Ann had planned the memorial service days ago; and early this morning, Hutch had come in and checked on the flowers and pro- grams. But as he walked in now, twenty minutes early with Ivory and Raven, and felt the chill of the steep gray walls, it seemed as foreign a place as the pole. *What are we doing here, in so much peace? And who are we kidding?—Wade Mayfield died in agony.*

Ann was standing in a corner of the narthex. As Hutch and the Bondurants moved toward the final steps and the long nave, she joined them quietly and met both visitors. Then she looked to Hutch. "Strawson and Emily are here, down front. I told them we'd join them."

Ivory had stepped slightly back from the Mayfields. She meant to signal she'd follow them in and sit some distance behind the family.

But Ann touched Ivory's arm. "Please sit with me."

Hutch said "Yes, with us by all means."

So—Raven with Hutchins, and Ivory with Ann—they climbed the tall steps, entered the towering aisle lit only by the flaring reds and blues of the stained glass, which swarmed with blared-eye faces of prophets, saints and (at the peak of the huge altar window) the terrible bearded head of God aimed at all watchers.

Raven's eyes followed the rising vaults to the pale height of what was, after all, an upturned stone boat the length of a warship. Even a child could see the likeness, a long keel overturned.

Beached or abandoned?—Hutch often wondered; but now he silently led them past rows of maybe eighty friends and strangers to the very front where Straw and Emily sat in a shaft of brown light.

Straw stood in place, hugged Ann and Hutch and sat again after bowing to Ivory.

Beyond him, Emily smiled faintly and bowed. Despite her severe dark dress and small hat, her thin plain look seemed to Hutch like a hint that the actual country might never quite vanish—the fields and thickets and patient faces prepared to last till time relents in the speed of its pace or lifts its hand for a run of days unmarked by pain.

All of them sat but Raven. With the slow deliberation of an old man, he got to his knees on the cold stone floor, folded his hands beneath his chin, shut his eyes and seemed to pray.

If it was a new idea for the boy, Ivory gave no sign, though when he finally sat beside her, she circled his shoulders and gathered him inward. For a moment he entirely surrendered to her, and that left him seeming younger than he was—a precociously well-dressed six-year-old.

But then Ivory kissed the wiry close-clipped crown of his skull and set him free.

From that moment on, Raven sat with the grave self-esteem of a bronze head from Benin or Delphi, unconsciously giving the color and line of his unmarred face to all who were lucky enough to see him.

Behind the family, a quiet hubbub of others filed in; and then at precisely three o'clock, a friend of Hutch's from the music department started on the massive organ behind them to play a *Siciliana* of Handel's, so effortless and gravely joyful in its winning try at perpetual motion that it seemed yet another guarantee of survival. *Who could make such a sound and then die out?* When the last notes had died in the echoing space, a short line of witnesses rose one by one and spoke from a lectern at the top of the choir steps.

The first was a high school teacher of Wade's from Durham Academy, a plump-faced woman in a lace jabot above a yellow suit. She'd single-handedly noted Wade's skill at design when (as a sophomore) he wrote a term paper on the pattern he saw in the plan of George Eliot's *Silas Marner*. In under five minutes now, she managed to summon Wade's high adolescence with credible force—"a good-hearted looker, dangerously generous with all he owned" and "the most charged boy I've known till today; oh I've known some *magnetos*." She ended with a memory of seeing him walk beyond her one day after graduation, in a shopping mall. He'd worn a new "absolutely blood-red shirt," and all she'd seen was the back of his head in a crowd of others; but that live sight had come back to her the night of his death, well before she heard the news. When she'd addressed him directly at the end of her memories—"Wade, thank you for a splendid sight"—she was followed by Hutch's faculty friend who'd helped him most in recent weeks, an eminent Shakespearean.

George Williams stood in his eternal pinstripe seersucker suit and green bow tie. He'd spent more than forty years, in Charlottesville and here, teaching Shakespeare with the tireless vigor of a November cricket or a smart and willing young guide dog. Now he looked straight to Hutch and said "I knew Wade Mayfield all his life and thought it a privilege as each year passed. I know I was not wrong and not misled.

Most of you, I trust, share my strong sense of being his debtor for a long time to come. Let me bid him what I see as temporary farewell with this sonnet of Shakespeare's—number 146." Then in his crisp unsentimental voice, not looking once to the book in his hand, he recited the brief indelible poem.

> "Poor soul, the center of my sinful earth,
> Thrall to these rebel powers that thee array,
> Why dost thou pine within and suffer dearth,
> Painting thy outward walls so costly gay?
> Why so large cost, having so short a lease,
> Dost thou upon thy fading mansion spend?
> Shall worms, inheritors of this excess,
> Eat up thy charge? Is this thy body's end?
> Then, soul, live thou upon thy servant's loss,
> And let that pine to aggravate thy store;
> Buy terms divine in selling hours of dross;
> Within be fed, without be rich no more:
>   So shalt thou feed on Death, that feeds on men,
>   And Death once dead there's no more dying then."

In the pause that followed the resonant end, the next speaker—a friend of Ann's who'd likewise known Wade from his first year—had barely stood when a man strode fast up the center aisle and faced the pews. Hutch had never seen the man; and when Hutch looked to Ann and Ivory, they shook their heads too—plainly a stranger.

A well-dressed stranger, maybe thirty-five, in a well-cut blazer and stiff white trousers that looked like U.S. Navy surplus. But his face was flushed an unnerving purple; and though he faced no one in the pews, his eyes were wild as they scanned the air above all heads. Finally he said "I'm a friend of Wade's from way way back. But I hadn't seen him for more than five years, and then I saw his obituary in the Durham paper and called the English Department at Duke to find out when this service might be—I knew he wouldn't go under unwept. I felt like I had one thing to tell that nobody else would—I've heard his longtime partner is dead too—so here I am, the first human adult Wade ever slept with after high school. He told me that fact anyhow right off; and even when we parted company later, he never denied it; and I still believe him. He was my first too and the start of my luck—I'm one lucky fool.

"What I know then is the personal truth of a living witness to a life that's gone. Wade Mayfield was one enjoyable sight in any room or under the sky, by day or night. His skin was as sheer as any good silk. He never stopped laughing when the going got fast; and while I've somehow escaped AIDS myself, I know for certain I'll never love anyone as thoughtful as Wade, or anyone else that can watch you as steady or be gladder to see you just when you feel less respect for yourself than any blind mole; and above all things—" The voice failed a moment and the silence lengthened.

Though Ann had looked to Hutch's profile from the start of this unexpected splurge, trying to make him hurry it on, Hutch had stayed seated. In the man's silent falter, Hutch leaned toward Straw and signed *Get up, go stop him somehow.*

But Straw kept his seat another ten seconds.

And by then the speaker had mastered his throat. "Above all things, Wade had the best eyes south of Fairfax, Virginia—that's my bailiwick; I'm a student of eyes. Thank you, Wade. You've left a hole in the local air, but sleep on for now." He left the microphone, still nameless and flustered, and fled down the aisle on hard leather heels.

Hutch thought *Well, we're here still. The vaults haven't cracked and his speech may have been true. God's heard worse.* He looked to Ann.

She was clear-eyed but riled. Still she sketched a smile at the edge of her mouth. This space after all was a vast well of secrets—mostly from young lives, decades of students.

Ivory and both the Stuarts were calm. In the space next to Hutch, Raven's face still poised on the air, a motionless setting for eyes that surely must match any eyes between here and—where?—surely Fairfax, Virginia if not Long Island or Ultima Thule.

From that point, the service went according to plan. Ann's friend, whom the stranger had balked, spoke barely audibly about Ann's early care for Wade—how lovely they'd both been, "madonna and child."

Then another friend of Ann's rose, a colleague at the Rape Crisis Center where Ann volunteered two nights a week. She'd met Wade twice at dinner on his last healthy visit home; so she spoke only of his manners and wit, both of which she defined as "rare and delicious."

The chairman of Hutch's department spoke briefly, then a junior partner from Wade's architecture firm (a rabbity man who'd barely known Wade in his healthy days), and then the girl Wade had dated through high school. A painter with a husband and numerous children in Tennessee, she'd never lost touch with Wade through the years; and she ended by saying "Wade saw more things, with his good eyes, than any three artists I've ever met."

Then Strawson rose.

Hutch dreaded the prospect, knowing that these words were bound to cut deepest; but Straw looked sober and in full control as he reached the lectern, so Hutch shut his eyes and braced his mind.

Straw said "I've known Wade Mayfield's father since I was a child myself—he taught me the best part of what I know, if I know anything. Hutch and I spent a lot of time together forty years ago; so when he and Ann finally made their choice and started a child, I asked them if I could stand as one of the godparents once the child arrived. I forced their hand; they couldn't say No. But being themselves, they said 'Go to it.' When it came and was Wade, and they christened him soon, I bit right down on the duty I'd sworn to God to perform. All I knew how to do, though, was show him the Earth the way I'd learned it and try to tell him what seemed like to me the very few laws God means us to heed—laws about decency to everything breathing, which includes the whole planet and the distance beyond.

"I don't mean to say I set an example that Wade could learn from—I'm a reprobate. Or a renegade, more like a renegade. Anyhow he outstripped me fast. By the age of seven, he knew more about the Earth and animals than any six Cherokee medicine men; and he'd still never done an indecent, thoughtless, mean-spirited thing—excepting the normal lies and jokes involving body functions and his growing parts. That pretty much lasted, the times I saw him, till he left here and moved north to earn his keep. Up there he found out something I'd known forever—that he was not your average boy.

"It suited me fine, I never tried to stop him, I couldn't have managed if I'd wanted to stop him. He was born ready-set, I'm fairly certain. Which is all the more reason for sadness today, that the power deep in him finally thrust him out in the path of the cruelest plague in six hundred years. I don't need to tell this smart a crowd the low-down truth—that when people say this curse was sent by Fate to punish a special brand of human, we ought to ask—right back in their teeth—whether they think leukemia is sent to punish the millions of children that die of it everywhere, not to mention God's exquisite care for the children tortured by the thousand today in the Balkans or the bruised and starving everywhere from Durham to Durban."

Straw's voice stopped there; his mind was blank—he hadn't intended to say that much; anger and fierce devotion to Wade had burned him severely. But he looked to Hutch and recovered his plan. "I'd like to close by recalling a verse from Paul's letter to the Romans, chapter eight.

'I reckon the agony of this present day is not fit to be compared to the glory which shall be unveiled. For the anxious expectance of all creation eagerly waits for the last unveiling of the sons of God.'

Wade may not have known those words in his life—I doubt he admired the Apostle Paul—and I stand before you as the last man alive who can swear to the future with no trace of doubt, but I'll make you a fairly confident bet Wade knows those words and their full meaning now."

As Straw came down and moved to his seat, the organ broke into Bach's giant fugue "We All Believe in One God." Like the Handel, Hutchins had picked it himself—not favorites of Wade's but then Wade was not the one needing strength here. As the massed unanswerable statement rolled through the crowd and onward through the altar window and the baleful eyes of God on high, Hutch told himself in the wake of Straw's speech *We don't all believe God gives a damn, though.* It even seemed urgent that, here this moment, Hutch stand when the fugue had solved its conundrum and state his own sense of where Wade was, if Wade stood the chance of being anywhere more desirable than a funeral urn that was back at the house, barely full of ashes (Ann had resisted his instinct to set them here in their midst). But the fugue compounded Bach's rock-ribbed conviction through its three-minute claim with such immense power that, when it ended, Hutch could only look down to Raven beside him.

The boy had already looked up to Hutch; and when their eyes met,

Raven shook his head as if throwing off water. Then he said "Lord, Lord!" in his grandmother's voice, having never heard an organ in full cry before.

Hutch smiled at the eyes and touched Raven's warm hair. "Wait for me," he said. Then he rose, went forward, faced the crowd—more nearly a crowd than anyone expected—and said "Wade's mother and I won't easily forget that you came here on this hot afternoon to back us with your presence and your memories. Surely your generous share in Wade's death will help tide us through the daunting pictures of his last days that are still fresh with us. Wade, to be sure, is beyond us all. Or so I very fervently hope, though I'm also more than half persuaded that he's conscious, not of us and our errands but of whatever peace lies still at the hub of actual things. The final piece of music we'll hear will be the only piece that Wade requested, three weeks before he died, of his mother. It's the last great song of a band whose records he loved as a baby, early as two or three years old in the early 1960s when Vietnam had us all in despair. By the time the band scattered, Wade was nine years old; and their last song was always his favorite. More than once I've watched it move him deeply. May we leave here then to the sound of the Beatles in 'Let It Be.' "

Hutch had got permission from the dean of the chapel for such an unorthodox conclusion. So the man Hutch had hired from the sound department cued the tape perfectly; and before Hutch even returned to his row, to stand while Ann and the others filed out, the truculent-choirboy voice of Paul McCartney started the song.

Anne's face, that had hardly met Hutch's today, turned quickly toward him. Her eyes looked helpless to bear another note.

Hutch knew that she could; he silently mouthed the one word *Surely*. She chose to trust him.

As young Raven stood and entered the aisle, his head was strongly affirming the beat of a song as foreign and old to him as the farthest keening monk in Nepal, frozen in snow and adoration.

Hutch reached for the boy's hand; and they went out together back down the nave through the song's big jubilant but still sad ending, itself a claim of eventual solace as firm as Bach's. By the time they reached the steps out to sunlight, what had surprised and moved Hutch most was the sight of Alice Matthews standing beside her old black driver and turning her unblinking eyes toward Hutch. Mait's splotched white face was also a welcome sight. Then the sunlight took Hutch, and Raven broke loose to run ten yards onward into its power—the force of a guarding or killing hand.

3

It was just past eight, and dusk was rising, when Hutch and Ann saw the last guest off down the winding drive. Some thirty of them had come straight out from the chapel to the house. They'd stayed indoors for the air conditioning—with drinks, mounds of ham biscuits and artichoke pickle—and all of them had gone on speaking of Wade. But as the glare and heat of the afternoon eventually slid through gold and tan to the indigo of summer night, Wade's lingering presence likewise dimmed. And when the more watchful guests realized that now they were laughing and weeping toward his back as Wade turned his face away forever and was finally gone, the heart went out of the day at last, and they all started leaving.

The first to go had been Alice Matthews and her immensely dignified driver, bound north to Petersburg—a two-hour drive. Because Hutch had known it might unnerve Alice to see the picture unexpectedly, he'd taken down his childhood drawing that Wade insisted on bringing from New York—the landscape Hutch had drawn on a day's sketching trip with Alice near Goshen, Virginia nearly fifty years back. When he'd known for sure that Alice would come for Wade's service, he'd wrapped the picture; and now he carried it under his arm as he guided Alice's careful steps downhill to her car.

Neither one of them spoke till Alice was seated by Herc, the driver who'd napped through most of the blistering day. Her eyes went to Hutch, and she actually smiled to guarantee the truth of her words. "It won't get worse than this, old friend. They haven't got anything worse in their quiver." For years, she'd referred to *fate* as *they.*

Hutch bent to kiss her upturned forehead. "I sure to God hope not."

And for an instant Alice's certainty broke. It made her eyes crouch—

Hutch saw the fear—but then she literally waved it off. "I was right the first time. Start living again."

Hutch agreed. "Yes ma'm." He opened a back door and laid the drawing in the midst of the seat. "A bolt from the past," he said.

Alice said "Oh no—"

But Hutch had shut the door and faced her again. "It's a pleasant surprise, from our best old days." When Alice looked back, he said "Don't open it—not till you're home. Let it be a surprise."

She looked confused for the first time yet. "It can't be anything valuable, darling. I'm too old for that."

"You're younger than me—in heart anyhow. If it makes you enjoy it any better though, put my name on the back. I'll collect it someday if you quit first."

"What is it? Don't surprise me."

Hutch could somehow not tell her. "Oh"—he suddenly remembered the instant he'd finished the last branch and leaf of the scene, the last pencil stroke and the title he'd thought of in his green grandiosity—"it's nothing but the meaning of things!" He laughed a little and said it quietly.

Alice showed no sign of recognition but she managed to smile. "Then I thank you. I was short on *the meaning*. I'll write you tomorrow." Her gloved right hand made one short wave; she rolled up her window and the car moved off. She made no effort to mime through the glass, but she turned as she left and watched Hutch standing alone in the yard. *Never more than alone* was all she could think as long as she saw him. But another thought came to her clearly as the car took the first curve and Hutch disappeared. *Another soul I won't see again.* Again she was right; she'd quit by Christmas, asleep in her own bed, no pain or awareness.

THE last to leave was Maitland Moses, a little drunk but quiet and polite (he and Cam had argued last week and were split at present, though Cam had sat alone today at the back of the chapel and bowed to Hutch). Hutch also walked with Mait out to the terrace; and in the full dark, Mait suddenly took him in a long embrace.

Mait's earlier threat to court the plague still troubled Hutch. So when they were separate again, he said "You owe me a solemn vow."

Mait was already looking away, but he said "I know what it is."

"Swear to live—or at least try—or don't come back here. I can't take this again."

Mait said "But isn't that radically stingy?"

"May very well be; but Son, I'm as earnest as a fractured skull." Hutch was almost sure that would reach Mait now, in the live quick flesh, whether Hutch ever saw him again or not.

But Mait took a long look toward the dark south above the trees. Then he turned and managed to see Hutch's eyes. "I'll have to let you know about that—"

"Again, I'm earnest."

"—And again Hutch, I really can't be your son. One father has all but killed me already."

Oddly Hutch was too tired to take it amiss. He even grinned.

So Maitland finally had the nerve to say "You're scared and sad. I understand why. You sidelined yourself so long ago you've forgot how it feels to have a live body and need to use it." Surprised by his force, Mait gave a slight stage-idiot chuckle.

"I can't tell you how wrong you are." Then Hutch turned silently toward the house, no word of goodbye.

Mait took the refusal and went his way.

FROM outside, through the living room window, Hutch could see only one thing—Raven Bondurant stretched on his stomach, in his new linen suit, asleep on the couch in a deep exhaustion as pure as the night. Hutch tried to think *This child knows the last riddle and answer.* But it felt staged and false, like a poet in a movie receiving his lines from birdsong and clouds. So he moved on toward the actual child. With Ivory's permission, he'd wake the boy and maybe show him pictures of Wade's own youth, which felt like a thousand years ago.

When he opened the door though, Ann stood in the entrance,

taking down the black hat she'd worn in the chapel. She was plainly readying to leave. When Hutch looked puzzled, she said "I've got every glass and dish clean. Ivory has offered to clear up the rest. I need to leave."

"You need to leave, or you think I want you gone—which one?" Hutch had no immediate preference of an answer.

Ann managed to smile. "A good deal of both."

"Then you're at least one-half mistaken. We need to sit down with Ivory here and settle this question about Wade's ashes."

Ann's whole face tightened. "That's immaterial to me—believe it."

Hutch agreed. "I believe it. I also know you'll live years longer. Time may come when you change your mind and want Wade nearer at hand than coastal Long Island."

"I've got him all in here, for good." With one hand, she ringed her throat lightly. "I *made* him, Hutch."

"You did. With some help." But then he could smile too. He reached to take her hat. "Please stay. We need you."

So while Ann heard him avoid the claim that he alone needed her for anything tonight, she let him hang the hat back up.

Together they paused to look in at Raven, still skewed and drowned. Till now they hadn't been near him without some other adult.

In her lowest voice Ann said "Who's he look like to you?"

Hutch waited. "His mother."

"Even better," Ann whispered. "His mother and Wyatt."

It chilled Hutch to feel the words in his mouth, but he let them out at normal volume. "And maybe Wade."

Ann faced Hutch. "You don't think there's any chance of that?"

Hutch thought he detected the trace of a hint that Ann had made her own discovery, or had she been told some new fact by Ivory? He wouldn't press to know. "I've given up hunting for answers long since."

Ann took that as though it were all she needed. Then they went on to Ivory.

4

IVORY had made surprising progress in the minutes since Ann first tried to leave. The kitchen was almost alarmingly clean—blank stretches of space, the cactuses watered and draining in the sink. Who could ever bear to eat here again? As the Mayfields entered, Ivory smiled to acknowledge that Ann was back. "Oh good. How about I make some fresh coffee?"

Ann said "Not for me, thanks."

But Hutch said "A gallon—and strong as tar."

Ivory stopped an instant to let the order pass. Then she chose to curtsey to Hutch and say "Yassuh, Mr. Rhett."

In a quick recovery he said "Much obliged, Miss Scarlett—oh yes" and bowed from the waist.

Ivory turned to grinding coffee beans.

Hutch joined Ann at the bare table, both vacant eyed.

And soon Ivory sat in the one free chair, at the head, slightly dim (she was farthest from the hanging lamp).

At last Hutch said "Let's agree on the ashes."

When Ivory tucked her chin and kept silent, Ann told her "I've tried to back out of this. Wade knew I loved him like shade in August. Anywhere those ashes go is fine by me; they're not mine at all." She took a long breath. "They're not Wade either."

Ivory said "I feel very much the same way—not that I claim I shared him with you or mattered anywhere near as much through the years as you. But no, Wade's gone for me and mine."

Hutch waited through a lengthy silence. Then, not quite thinking that Ann might hear his words as insane, he risked a new tack. "Wade's either gone or he's napping in there on the couch this minute, not ten years old." When Ivory and Ann both looked mystified, Hutch pointed behind him toward the living room. "Maybe Raven Bondurant is half Wade anyhow, the only part left. At some odd angles, he helps *me* feel that Wade's not all gone."

Whatever she thought, Ann's face held its own. Nothing on Earth could amaze her tonight.

But for the first time in either Hutch or Ann's presence, Ivory flushed; and her eyes sought her own long hands laid before her. So far as she knew, Ann still hadn't read the note Wade left; but she faced both Hutch and Ann and finally said "Both of you—understand this, if nothing more. There was a time, way back, when I loved Wade and thought he loved me—in every sense of the word, I mean. That didn't turn out to last in our lives, but we stayed close friends, and he always mattered seriously. From here on, though, I make no claim whatever, now or doomsday, on Wade or his leavings or either of you. Neither will my son, who liked him too. You've been kinder than I had any right to hope for; but don't give me and my son a *thought* when you make your plans, not a single thought from here on out. We're taken care of and I'm a strong soul, my mother's real child—I'll get us through, young Raven and I."

Though Ann still knew nothing of Wade's message to her and Hutchins, she'd sensed from the moment she saw Raven's eyes and heard his name that the boy leaned her way somehow in space, not a visible tilt or the trace of a plea to her or to anyone in sight but something unbroken and strong nonetheless. What Raven cast her way—and she knew it was cast unconsciously—was more like a net or an unseen globe with a powerful draw all round his body, a draw that pulled at her mind and the stump of her love for Wade. Ann was too sad and tired to feel more than faintly warmed, warmed from a distance as if by a lantern set on a raft in the midst of a broad river she stood beside. She faced Hutch wondering what to ask—had his mind broken slightly, and what could he mean, and why more wrangling now about ashes?

Before Ann could speak, Hutch said "All right, can we do this then—the three of us and Raven? I'll call Straw and Emily so they know we're coming—I warned them we might; they said whatever we wanted would work. We'll leave after breakfast tomorrow morning, drive up there, pay our respects to Grainger and spread Wade out where he said he should be when he still knew clearly." He looked to Ann and then Ivory. "Agreed?"

Ann said "I'll be ready."

Ivory said "Whatever you believe is right—and you know I think that's the better plan—but let me just say one more thing now: Wade was in his right mind to the last, I very much believe. He phoned me, the night Jimmy Boat got here."

Nobody, not even Jimmy, had known that. Still Hutch heard it calmly. "Anything we should know, from what he said?"

"He asked me to talk like Wyatt, a last time. Since I was a child, I could imitate Wyatt and fool everybody. I played jokes on him and Wade to the last."

Ann said "Did you do it again when he asked you?"

Ivory said "Oh yes, I called his full name the way Wyatt would when he got home at night. 'Raven Wade Mayfield, show your fine face.' " Her voice had easily become Wyatt's voice.

It shook Hutch. He said "Can Wyatt bear this?" as though Wyatt stood in the doorway, assaulted and bracing to answer.

Ann said "Bear what?"

Hutch said entirely seriously "Us talking like this."

Ivory said "No question. He's got all of Wade now—but I told you that. That was Wyatt's only plan, from the week they met." Her face was pained for the instant it took to make the last concession.

Hutch covered her hands with his own.

Ivory met his eyes to thank him, then withdrew her right hand and held it to Ann.

When Ann had again closed a circuit among them, Hutch could withdraw. He stood and moved toward the inside door, meaning to check on young Raven's nap; then find Wade's letter and pass it to Ann, out of Ivory's sight, before Ann left for her own house. She'd said again just now that she was going and he hadn't objected. With Ivory and Raven here (Hutch had persuaded them to move from the inn), there was no spare bed, unless Ann wanted to sleep in Wade's room—the bed he died in or a pallet on the floor.

Hutch couldn't offer her that, not yet; and for all the help they'd given each other in the past few weeks, he couldn't yet want to fold Ann back into his own life for good—not before they'd managed a drastic coming to terms with all her own years of grievance and want, and his own cooled bitterness: his ingrained distance. She'd need to make her own choice on that, then to tell him somehow and let him decide what he could take and whether he could learn to stand in closer. For all the margin of space around him, by his own lights, Hutch had never abandoned anyone yet, not anyone who mattered in his life; he didn't plan to start this late.

But he quickly thought of a fresh exception. *Young Mait Moses. I've turned him out*. And as Hutch reached the door of the living room, with Raven snoring lightly beyond him, he saw Mait's face in his mind this evening, trailing his hellbent body downhill. *I'll phone him later; Mait's too good to lose*. Then Hutch walked silently over to Raven, got down on one knee beside the boy's head and held the palm of his hand a half inch above the damp hair. Though Hutch couldn't know it, some form of the same cloud of force that had drawn at Ann was reaching for him. Hutch brushed his chin to the warm whorled ear and told himself *This child knows me somehow. He's trusting me here*.

The child's rest, though, was fabulously deep—way past fear or hope or any plain dream. At its lowest ebb, still Raven's mind could know that it and all his body was safe as any child alive, banked with care like a fast horse with roses.

Hutch knew he mustn't turn strange here. *No plans for this child. His mother's leaving and he's going with her*. So he rose and went to find the letter that Wade had written for his parents to read. In the two weeks since Hutch had first read it, he'd felt a conscious low-grade shame, withholding it from Ann—her name after all was in the address as plainly as his. Why had he waited? *Part meanness no doubt but also maybe the fear that Ann might have plunged off on some errand of her own and pressed on Ivory for hard details, or even flown to New York and tracked down the child and blundered into some innocent harm. No way to hide it another hour though*.

Before Hutch had taken two more steps, he knew—he all but knew for a certainty—that the letter was not just the last news from Wade but was also maybe the main truth he'd left them: a last open door. *This story may not be ending yet*. No way he could keep the news from Ann beyond tonight, and no wish to keep it.

5

IVORY and Raven had been in their room, asleep, since ten o'clock that evening. Hutch had managed to stay awake till midnight, listing the names of guests while he recalled them and reading all the sonnets of Shakespeare. He hadn't read straight through the whole cycle—a hundred and fifty-four poems as mysterious as any ever written—since his years in Oxford when he'd sometimes drive the forty-odd miles between his college and Shakespeare's home in Stratford-upon-Avon just to stand on the bridge there or poke through the streets and silently think through a speech from the plays or a few of the sonnets. He'd known a handful by heart since the ninth grade; they'd clung to his mind with the hooks of young memory.

Even here when he'd read to the end of them all, and the clock said quarter past midnight, Hutch shut both the book and his eyes and lay still to run through the bristling power of

> They that have power to hurt and will do none,
> That do not do the thing they most do show. . . .

And

> What is your substance, whereof are you made,
> That millions of strange shadows on you tend?

His light was out though before he recalled, and found he still knew, the whole of the poem that—forty years ago—had seemed the flag of his care for Strawson.

> Lord of my love, to whom in vassalage
> Thy merit hath my duty strongly knit,
> To thee I send this written ambassage
> To witness duty, not to show my wit:
> Duty so great, which wit so poor as mine
> May make seem bare, in wanting words to show it,
> But that I hope some good conceit of thine
> In thy soul's thought all naked will bestow it,
> Till whatsoever star that guides my moving
> Points on me graciously with fair aspect,
> And puts apparel on my tatter'd loving
> To show me worthy of thy sweet respect:
> > Then may I dare to boast how I do love thee,
> > Till then not show my head where thou mayst prove me.

Now in the dark of his house, Hutch lay and let tall waves of amazed thanks and charred loss pour freely through him—thanks for the plentiful love he'd got, through the length of his life, from sane other souls and harsh regret for his monstrous failures to take and honor every gift of flesh and pleasure, trust and pardon, that was offered his way. The failures came to him as they always did, stark separate faces—Straw's, Rob's, Ann's, Grainger's, Wyatt's, Wade's. Before he could check the hurtling speed of his runaway guilt, Hutch had run through dozens of students, friends, loves, all the lost names of lives he'd skimped or cheated on. *Waste, grim waste in the teeth of plenty.* He was almost asleep when the bedside phone rang; he caught it at once. "Yes?"

"Hutch, it's Ann. I'm sorry to wake you—"

"You didn't at all; I'm up reading Shakespeare. Thanks for the company today; it truly counted."

Ann pushed that aside. "I've read Wade's letter and I guess I can maybe half understand why you felt you should hold it back till tonight— you were wrong; still I can't fight you now—but before we meet in the morning, I just need to know a few things."

"Me too. It's still a deep mystery to me."

"But you've discussed the details with Ivory?"

Hutch said "In about four cloudy sentences only, not a real discussion. I honestly haven't felt I had the right. And Ivory's said nothing really, not to me, that throws any further light on the boy. She's said we have no debts to her at all, but you heard her say that much again tonight."

"You think Raven's ours?" Raw as the words were, Ann's voice had its old patient candor. *I can take what comes; so can you, beside me.*

Hutch almost laughed. "He's not ours, no ma'm."

"You know what I mean—is Raven actually kin to Wade?" Even Ann heard the quaintness of her question.

"I very much hope he is—kin to us too. We may never learn."

Ann said "Don't be so sure we won't. As he goes, Wade's traits may well show in him. Meanwhile, we can't just let him and Ivory drift off and pay them no mind at all, not for the entire rest of our lives. She'll need boxloads of money through the years and practical help to raise a child alone in New York."

"She can do it, Ann. She plainly means to. She may never want us to see him again."

"And you don't plan to ask for anything—some reasonable visits, a hand in the child's life? You don't think we should contribute to his care?"

Hutch said "I want every bit of that, yes; but Ivory Bondurant owns her own mind—I've learned that well. I very much doubt she'd smile on our hopes. Never forget she's Wyatt's sister."

"Oh I haven't, not once." Ann waited so long Hutch thought she was gone; then she suddenly said "You think that Wyatt will give us some peace now?" Ann was as likely to mention ghosts as any particle physicist.

Hutch was stunned for a moment. "Wyatt? Peace?"

"You know what I mean."

I do; too well. They hadn't mentioned Wyatt since the night Wade died, when they'd both acknowledged his nearness and power all through the house. Hutch said "Wyatt's gone, I'm fairly sure; but Ivory's got to be as scorched as we by memories of him—what he thought about us as Wade's close kin, the ghastly way he chose to die."

"Don't blame poor Wyatt for that; God knows, he was not himself then."

Hutch said "How do you know that? And don't call him *poor*."

"Ivory told me that much, tonight in the kitchen when you walked out."

"How did she put it?"

Ann said "Just that plainly—you were barely out of sight; she turned those strong eyes on me and said 'You know my brother lost his mind before he died.' Since she'd been that honest, I pushed a little. I asked her how far back that confusion went, in his life and ours—"

"Oh, careful, Ann."

"No, Ivory took it calmly. I could see she knew I was fishing for hope that all he'd thought and said about us was truly insane, but she didn't stretch an inch past the truth. She said 'I date it from three weeks before he picked up the pistol. Till then he was clear-headed—wild and sure he was right but clear-headed.' "

Hutch waited for Ann to go on.

She didn't; she'd apparently finished for the night.

So he opened his mouth to say "Till morning then" but other words came. He heard himself say "Could you come back here?"

"Now, tonight?"

"Whenever, for good."

Ann said "You can't mean that."

Hutch wondered if he did. It had shocked him to say it; it could be anything from a moan to a lie. Still he said "I very well may mean it, yes."

"You're thoroughly worn out and sad like me. Sleep awhile anyhow; we can talk tomorrow." Her tone was a little too sensible.

Hutch said "Are you at the office or home?"

"Home—great God, I don't work till Wednesday."

"Till breakfast then."

Ann said "Till when. Or whenever, friend."

Hutch said "Old friend—"

But by then she was gone.

ONCE Hutch had lain on another ten minutes, asking himself to explain the plea he made to Ann—was it a plea or a hurtful probe?—and finding no answer, faces began to rise again and challenge his failure. This time the clearest face was Maitland's. Hutch remembered he'd promised himself to call Mait later tonight, after their bleak parting. The lighted clock said nearly one, but he seldom hesitated to call students anytime—they hardly slept except on Sundays. Yet it took a long ten rings before Mait answered. "Moses," he said.

Hutch said "Mayfield."

A wait, then Mait said "Morning there, Mayfield."

In a shy reflex Hutch said "You alone?"

"No, I've got Barnum and Bailey here with matched white tigers and a small troupe of midgets."

Mait seldom joked and Hutch felt shut out, so he only said "I'll leave you to your midgets then. I just meant to tell you I spoke too harshly, way too harshly, tonight as you left."

"No you didn't. You were telling the reasonable truth; I still wouldn't hear it."

"I was too harsh though."

"You were honest," Mait said. "It's all harsh news, here where I'm living. I just can't live by your fears, Hutch."

"Then by all means don't. Nobody yet ever got happy from me."

"Now you're lying. You've cheered me a lot. I told you you've given me a whole sense of life, of somewhere to go and a way to get there."

"Can I lean on that? Will you try to keep living?"

Mait said "Absolutely, for what it's worth. I just can't promise to obey you though. My body can't. Or won't anyhow."

Hutch realized Mait's voice hadn't cracked once in maybe two weeks; the boy had pushed through some final membrane and stood tall and ready for stripped-down life. In the dark Hutch's own eyes were suddenly exhausted; a kind of mist had settled on his face, a dense cold webbing. He said "Please come to supper on Tuesday."

"Cam and I both?"

"Well, if you like. I thought the two of you were on outs."

Mait waited. "We were but he came by an hour ago. Wade's service really moved him."

"He's not still with you?"

"No, but we talked calmly. I'll go by to see him at the hospice tomorrow."

Hutch said "And you want to bring him here Tuesday?"

"Do I hear a suggestion you don't want Cam?" Mait was calm at the thought.

Hutch managed a laugh. "Oh no, I've mostly been a third wheel, some sixty years and rolling."

Mait thought he heard a trace of self-pity. *I'd better ignore it.* So he just said "We'll bring the groceries and cook them. Cam's a dynamite chef."

"I doubt I can easily eat dynamite."

Mait said "No, *dynamite* means he's really good." Then he guessed that Hutch was joking after all. "You know that, right?"

"My ears can still just barely hear what young people say, yes. And sure, I'll be glad to let Cam cook—some night next week." Then Hutch thought *What if Ann's back here by then?* But he said "I'll be hungry and waiting at six."

Mait said "Adiós," not knowing he'd echoed Wade's farewell on leaving New York.

Neither did Hutch but the word snagged in him, a strong clean hook. He could only think to sign off with the simplest translation, inaudibly whispered. "Yes, Mait, *to God.*" Then before he hung up, Hutch thought he should also have phoned Straw with word of the plans for morning. *Not tonight. I'm finished. I'll call him at dawn; he'll be there the rest of his life anyhow.* The phone was barely back in its cradle before Hutch slept.

6

So in all the house no one was awake but Raven Bondurant, flat on his twin bed six feet from Ivory's in the back guest room. In the perfect dark the boy was not scared, despite the depth of stillness around him—a stillness he'd never heard, even on Long Island. He was holding in both hands, atop the sheet, a doll that had been Wade's. Hutch's father had bought it for Hutch, the summer they visited Jamestown together, the site of the first white permanent English-speaking colony on the continent and the harbor into which the first black African captives were brought and sold as things.

The doll was a well-made realistic copy, ten inches tall, of a Stuart cavalier in his doublet and soft boots, his ruddy skin, blond beard and one earring—hardly the kit for life on the rim of a country settled by six million red men with plans of their own. The doll's painted china face wore the gold-struck inner gaze of a murderous innocent, bent on triumph if it could just master the starving icebound winter ahead.

When Raven had gone in tonight, at Ivory's urging, to thank Hutch for all his attention today, Hutch had reached to a shelf by the living room fireplace, found the doll and held it out to him. "This is yours from here out, Raven. Wade used to love it when he was a boy."

Though Raven himself would never quite know it—nor his mother or grandmother, Hutch nor Ann—the lasting traits of Wade Mayfield, who was Raven's father, (Wade's merciful wit and early decency) would seep into the child's growing body through this small likeness of a body both paler and older than Raven's, the artful token of three whole peoples (two of whose blood ran in the child's veins) locked in the toils of a mortal combat still undecided but apparently endless. And while it was still three hours till dawn on Hutch's green hill in the midst of quiet woods, that nonetheless harbored their own nocturnal raptors and prey, the expectant boy took only short naps till daylight showed him this latest treasure— an unthinkably intricate potent doll, in his small hands, that would be his for good.

7

WHEN Hutch phoned Strawson at six that dawn, Straw showed no surprise and said that Emily was anticipating the Mayfields and Bondurants for lunch. So Hutch and Ann—with Raven and Ivory—headed out in a bright and remarkably dry midmorning for the short trip north. Raven sat by Hutch up front with Wade's ashes boxed on the floor at the child's feet. Very little was said by anyone, though Ann would occasionally point to a distant house or tree or a lone white horse and describe it to Raven.

They even passed a solitary mule in a huge mown field; and Ann said "Raven, remember that sight. Mules are all but a thing of the past; they used to *own* the country."

Ivory was the one who laughed and showed interest. "My mother's favorite brother was Mule—she's always saying he was just that stubborn. But I never knew Muley; he died too young." She leaned forward near enough to tap Raven's head. "Maybe I ought to start calling you Mule, Mr. Set-in-His-Ways."

Raven didn't look back but, once he'd watched the mule out of sight, he said "You talking about that boy who died when I wasn't born?"

Ivory said "Yes, he was your great-uncle."

Still watching the road, Raven said "Don't mention him dying again."

Hutch said "Why not?"

"I can't stand to hear how children die." From then on Raven faced only the woods.

So Hutch tried to think how this world looked through this boy's eyes. If Raven had watched as much television as most young children, and since he'd barely left Long Island till two days ago, these hardwood thickets and evergreen jungles must look more like the surface of Venus than anything common to New York state—some planet anyhow where men, women, children were far from the center of anyone's gaze. And surely, Hutch knew, the child who grows up watching nothing more self-possessed and reliable than people and cars, buildings and madmen is cruelly blighted from the start. *Is it too late here to let this child watch fields and trees and feed his mind every element it craves?* They were no more than five or ten minutes from the Kendal place when Hutch said at last "You enjoying the scenery?"

Raven still didn't turn and he offered no answer.

Ivory said "Son, answer Mr. Mayfield."

Finally the child said "If I tell the truth, it'll hurt his feelings."

Hutch laughed. "No you won't; I'm a tough old turtle."

Raven said "I don't see *nothing* I recognize. Lord, I feel like I'm lost for good."

Ivory heard the sound of her own mother's voice; still she said "You don't see *anything*—"

Hutch said "Trust me—this is my native ground." He chuckled again.

Raven said "That's the problem. I stopped trusting people."

Now Ivory laughed. "Don't talk crazy, Son."

Raven pressed his face to the window glass. "It's not me that's crazy. People killing children everywhere. You watch the TV, you'll learn some news."

Everybody let the child's words settle slowly; then Hutch said "Son, you're safe with me."

Raven looked round and studied Hutch like a hard lesson. Finally he said "I'm not your son."

Ivory said "What a thing to say. You mind your manners."

Hutch grinned at Raven. "You're right as rain. I'm a well-wisher though; I could still be your friend."

Raven said "Well, I'm thinking that over."

All the adults laughed.

But the child faced Hutch. "Man, I'm telling you the truth."

Hutch said "I never doubted you were."

8

It was past noon then when the car drew up in the shade of the oak at the Kendal place and Straw came down the back steps to meet them. The previous day, after the service, Raven had taken a shine to Straw and followed him up the slope back of Hutch's—the bare crest from which they could see for twelve miles south. Beyond the spires of Chapel Hill, Straw knew very little about what lay there peaceful before them; but he got the boy to join him in populating the wide sea of woods with buildings and creatures designed to fulfill their joint pleasures—horse-riding schools full of pretty girls in various shades, an ice-skating rink with giant benevolent dinosaur-instructors, tremendous rooms with women and tall men boldly dancing in long white clothes, and numerous other houses and contests: all likewise benign, though some hilarious and some fairly risky.

So as Raven was the first to climb from the car this Monday noon, he ran toward Strawson till Straw stopped midway and crouched to greet him. Somehow the unaccustomed sight of an open-armed grown man stopped the boy in his tracks till Ivory came up behind him. "That's Mr. Stuart, Son. From yesterday. He took you walking. Show him your new friend."

Raven stayed in place but slowly extended the cavalier doll.

Straw knew it on sight; Wade had brought it up here on numerous visits. But he accepted it from Raven, studied its face a moment, then handed it back. "You know who that belonged to, don't you?"

Raven nodded, silent.

Ivory said "Tell him 'Yes, thank you.' "

But Raven waited, then said "That dead man" and suddenly laughed.

Hutch and Ann had caught up by then; so everybody could laugh with the boy as Straw stood and led them on into the darkened cool house, the roof that had sheltered a sizable portion of Hutch's long-dead kin a century back and further still. Their faces hung on in the least used rooms—Straw had bothered to round up portraits and photographs, from Hutch's grandmother Eva, when he first moved here. They were all plainly marked by their own ancestors with the long broad foreheads and splendid eyes that, even in painful antique poses, burned with a heat that could still be felt—a heat transformable to love, hate, victory at a moment's warning and tirelessly ready. One by one, as Straw showed Raven through the rooms, he pointed the pictures out with histories and family names.

The boy absorbed as much as he could of an almost foreign world and time. Then at the picture of one hefty woman, swathed in black and coiled with braids, he finally told Straw "I think I need to stop doing this."

Straw said "I may agree with you there." Then he led Raven down to join the others for the bountiful meal that Emily had worked on since nearly dawn—eight vegetables (picked in the garden today), endless fresh crisp fried corn cakes, iced lemon tea and a strawberry pie with cream from half a mile down the road—a cow named Battleaxe.

Through that, Wade's ashes waited on a table on the shady back porch among the day's harvest of ripe tomatoes—maybe fifty big fruit. Thin as Wade had been on the night he died, his ashes filled the salt-glazed urn that Hutch had driven to Jugtown to get three days ago, made for him by his friend Vernon Owens there—a master potter from a line of potters that went straight back to Staffordshire, England more than two centuries past. The urn was eighteen inches tall and a high tan-gray with the figure of a dark horse running on the curved face.

The horse was the potter's own idea—he'd met Wade more than once in Wade's childhood and said he recalled the boy asking him once to make a horse's head, life-size, in clay and then bake it hard. Vernon claimed Wade said that horses knew more than people at least. That would have been maybe twenty-five years back; Wade would have been maybe seven years old. Hutch had no memory of such a request, but he'd taken Vernon's memory as true. So he brought home the urn, poured in the two quarts of Wade's grainy ashes with small knots of bone and left them to wait for whatever plan developed for their scattering.

They were minerals now and dumb to the voices that washed out past them through open doors from the dining room. The voices, though, were gladder than not to be alive—well fed and gathered for this brief pause at the edge of Wade's last traces on Earth.

9

By the time they'd got to the end of lunch, Ivory could see that Raven's sleeplessness from last night was calling for rest. They were still at the table, she was sitting by Hutch, so she asked if they had time for Raven to lie down for maybe half an hour.

Everyone present had reared a child, and Hutch said "By all means."

Raven objected seriously, though his eyes were closing.

But Ivory said "Everybody else go right on with your plans. I'll stay here and let this rascal nap awhile. Otherwise he'll be mean as a hornet all evening."

Hutch turned to Ann. "We're in no hurry, are we?"

Ann said "Not I."

Hutch said "In that case, we could all stand a breather. Let's wait in the cool here while Raven snoozes."

Straw had known, since he first laid eyes on Raven, that Wade was somehow involved in his life. And here he could sense that Hutch shared the feeling. *Hutch wants this child to scatter Wade with him.* Straw said "Raven, you and your mother can rest in the upstairs room with that fat lady's picture you loved so much."

Much as he hated yielding to it, Raven was at the mercy of his age. Like most children, his strength had quit him in an instant with no warning; and he was almost asleep in his chair. But before Ivory led him off toward the stairs, he said "Don't anybody *do* anything here till I get back."

Emily said "We won't, Son. Go have a nice dream."

It was natural enough, even for a woman who'd borne one daughter and no male child, to call Raven *son*; but Straw heard the word in Emily's mouth as a punishment on his own past and future, his silent refusal to give her children beyond their own daughter, so far off now. In the instant, his whole life stretched like a salt plain, behind and before him. All he said however was "A first-rate meal, Em. You're better by the day."

Not meeting Straw's eyes, Emily thanked him. Then she and Ann stood to begin clearing up and washing dishes.

                                    10

HUTCH and Straw went to the front room and took easy chairs for a snooze of their own. First, Hutch leafed through the day's *News and Observer*. It had been twenty years since he'd read the news daily; so whenever he came across a copy of a small-city paper, he was always surprised how full it was of possible lumber for stories and poems—vanished children, an adult male dwarf beat to a pulp in domestic combat somewhere in east Durham (the article noted that "Officer Pulliam said 'He was nothing but gristle when we got there' ") and the perennial fuming letter-writers, flashing their crank convictions like road flares with nuclear fuel.

Hutch looked up and read Straw an item on the claim of a twelve-year-old black girl that she'd walked to Raleigh from Cordele, Georgia with a month-old baby and an old bulldog to celebrate her great-grandmother's birthday. The piece made the girl seem smart and credible, despite her grandmother's stated doubt—"She may be telling the truth. I can't say. I got so many descendants, you know, I wouldn't recognize most of them stretched out on the bubbling road under my flat feet."

Straw laughed, took a long breath and said straight out "You recognize Wade in Raven, don't you?"

"Amen."

"Was it news to you?"

Hutch said "It was news all right, big news; but we'll never be sure the news is true—not short of far more tests and studies than Ivory Bondurant would ever agree to or I'd ask for." Then he wondered *Did Wade discuss this with Straw?* So he said "How long have you known about Raven?"

Straw said "The minute I laid eyes on him. First time I saw him tilt his head—Wade Mayfield's hid in his spine like a great spring."

Hutch almost agreed. "I hope that's the case. We'll never know."

Straw said "If there's any question of leaving the child any land or money in your will, you could probably get a court order for tests."

Hutch stopped him with a flat palm, firm in the air. "You, of all people, know I thrive on mystery. Anyhow what's to say I can't leave every scrap I own to the nearest bird dog, if that's my whim—not to speak of a likable healthy child that may be my dead son's only leavings?"

Though Hutch smiled to say it, Straw knew he was earnest and wouldn't budge further. Through a drowsy half hour then, they sat at the ancient rolltop oak desk and looked through Emily's meticulous records of every seed planted since January 1st, every nickel paid out for help or supplies, even the pints of bourbon Straw bought to tide his tenant through quarterly three-day drunks and recoveries (she kept no record of Straw's own quarts).

Numbingly familiar as the process was, Hutch took some comfort in Straw's hot nearness beside him at the desk and in the certainty that, at the least, they were once more performing a major rite of the human race, as old as man's descent from the trees—far older than any glimpse of art more durable than the blankets of wildflowers laid on their dead kin by roving Neanderthal bands in Asia sixty thousand years back.

When Straw gave signs of dozing again, upright at the desk, Hutch said "Put your head down and dive for five minutes."

Straw obeyed, laid his arms and head on the desk and was gone in three seconds.

Hutch took the time to rise and walk silently toward the far bookcase, lift its glass door, then choose the last volume of *Lee's Lieutenants* from Straw's miles of Civil War lore. With a glance to check on Straw's snoozing breath, Hutch reached in his pocket and brought out the wrapped small stack of pictures he'd found in Wade's papers—the nude young men: some nude, some naked as peeled raw eels. He'd thought of them at sunrise today. *Get rid of them quick, or they'll break Ann down.* Again, though, Hutch hadn't managed to burn them. Whether they were Wyatt's or Wade's brief companions or store-bought outright provocations, they still were live traces of a vanishing warmth.

With no clear plan, merely acting on the instant—half joking in fact—Hutch slid the pictures to the back of the shelf behind *Lee's Lieuten-*

ants. Given the depth of cobwebs and dust, it was guaranteed Emily never touched these books. Straw might find them, though, years down the road and think of—what? *A life I denied him, for good or bad? Or simple human pleasure in itself, these vulnerable young men—many surely dead now.*

As Hutch slid the one concealing volume back into place, Straw roused and said "Now—" He plainly meant Wade, *Now we lose Wade at last.*

11

AT the final moment Ann touched Hutch's arm and said "Friend, I'm going to wait here with Emily."

The pain in her eyes kept Hutch from urging a change of heart. So it was past two when he took up the urn and walked with Strawson, Ivory and Raven down the back stairs and out to Grainger's. By then the heat had climbed past ninety, but the window air conditioner at Grainger's was plainly not running, and every door and window was shut.

Straw said "Everybody brace yourself; here comes a brick kiln. This old gent's been a little cold-natured for the past few decades. We won't stay long." Straw climbed to the door, knocked twice, then opened it and leaned inside. When he'd said "You ready?" and got Grainger's nod, he waved in the others.

Few brick kilns could have been appreciably hotter; but Grainger was in his automatic chair, fully dressed in his usual khakis with his neck buttoned tight and a cardigan sweater. Straw had stood aside to let Ivory enter first; and when Grainger saw her, he stood on his own—not waiting for the chair lift and lurching only slightly. Straw had prepared him for a lady from New York, with her young son, and Hutch of course; but he'd mentioned nothing about the lady being colored or who the child might favor. If Grainger was surprised, he gave no sign. He did bow deeply, though, when Straw introduced her as Miss Bondurant; and he offered her his chair.

Ivory declined but introduced Raven. "Mr. Walters, this is my son,

Raven Bondurant." When Raven stepped forward to take Grainger's hand, Ivory said "Son, Mr. Walters helped raise Wade."

Oddly, Raven said "Thank you," not quite sure for what; then he felt mildly shamed and fell back silent.

Grainger faced the boy long enough to say "Pretty name"; then he had to sit—his knees were unreliable in such dry weather (his joints worked opposite to everyone else's). As he sat, his eyes found Ivory a last time. "You'll have to excuse my feebleness—no disrespect to you, ma'm."

Ivory reassured him.

But by then he'd fixed on Hutch and the urn. "You finally going to keep my promise to Wade?"

Hutch said "Yes sir, it's only right."

Grainger said "You've done a fair number of wrong things, you understand—I been mighty worried." His old dragon eyes could well have been smiling—even Straw wasn't sure—or they might have been merely pleased at their victory.

Either way, Hutch was easy. He'd mainly been watching to see whether Grainger paid close attention to Raven here by him. *Who can he see in this child's eyes?*

Grainger was done with Raven though. He'd quit liking children once Wade was grown, and was making no exception today.

So when the old man seemed suddenly gone on one of his driftings, Hutch said "I wish you could walk down with us to scatter these ashes. We better head on."

Straw said "Mr. Walters, you had your nap?"

Grainger said "Haven't had a good nap since the war." As always he meant his war—France in 1918, the trenches, cooties, mustard gas.

Raven laughed and looked to his mother.

Ivory put both hands on her boy's strong shoulders and said "Mr. Walters, we're honored to meet you. I've heard Wade speak of you many many times—Wade and my brother both appreciated you, and I only wish my mother could have been here. She hails from Virginia, a good while back, and misses the South."

Grainger didn't face her but said "She had her head tested lately?" Before anyone could decide to laugh, he said "I'm from Maine" (it was literally true; his father Rover had left Virginia in early despair and gone north to build boats in the late 1880s). If he'd meant anything by that sideswipe, Grainger gave no further sign.

So with no more to say, and no lead from Grainger, Ivory steered Raven toward the door. They'd wait outside; the sun was cooler than this stifling room.

Straw said "Mr. Walters, you better rest a little. I'll be back down with your supper at four. Call if you need us—Emily's up at the house."

Grainger raised his right arm, as if in school, to speak; but when Hutch and Straw moved closer on him, he found no words.

Hutch thought he'd simply forgot his point; he said "Just wait. It'll come back to you."

But Straw understood. He grinned broadly and slapped his own thigh. "So you're saying you want me to leave you and Hutchins?"

Grainger still didn't speak. He was facing the blank television screen as if it would, at any moment, flash instructions for his imminent departure or as if he might learn from his gaze alone a whole intelligent new brand of speech and the hard-earned power of generous judgment.

Straw said to Hutch "He wants you by yourself. I'll be outside with Ivory and the boy." As he left, Straw said "Mr. Walters, when they made you, they threw away the door—much less the key."

Straw's hand had hardly touched the doorknob when Grainger said "You let Hutch walk down yonder by himself, hear?" When Straw was silent, Grainger raised his voice. The ghost of its old self, its old bull bellow, it was still astonishing. "You hear what I said?"

Straw didn't look back but he said "Aye, aye, sir"—not harshly but whispered.

So when Strawson had shut the door behind him, Hutch went to the edge of the bed and sat. The urn was in his hands, resting on his knees. He thought *I ought to be pouring tears; this is straight out of Homer or late Shakespeare.* But he'd wept all his tears, very likely the tears of the rest of his life. What he felt was ease in the silent presence of a permanent feature of his usable landscape, the shadow of a broad hill he'd grown up beside. *Don't even* think *of the day he'll die.* After a minute with nothing from Grainger, Hutch said "They're waiting for me out there in the blistering sun. I better join them. I'll be up here again next week to see you with less on my mind. Tell Straw to call me if you need the least thing."

Grainger faced him then, the only judge Hutch had ever acknowledged.

It almost bowled Hutch over on his back—the total recognition in that broad skull, the record of all his life that survived in this lean face, the man that moved it, the ancient eyes that even here were still feeding constantly on what the day offered. *The only live thing, myself included, that's seen my whole life.* Hutch couldn't speak.

Grainger said "Son, let me see Wade please." The *please* was the shock; *please* had disappeared from Grainger's speech forty years ago.

The lid of the urn was taped neatly shut with silver duct tape. For an instant Hutch hesitated to obey; he sat upright on the edge of the bed still. But once the old man leaned far forward and waited for the sight, there was no more question of refusing consent. Hutch peeled back the tape, set the lid beside him on the taut bedspread and tilted the open urn toward Grainger.

Grainger leaned still farther till his eyes were less than a foot from the ashes. "You sure that's him?"

"As sure as anybody could be that didn't watch him burn. No sir, I trust the people that did it."

Grainger said "People didn't used to do this, you know—just cook people down like sand in the wind. You think Wade Mayfield can rise up at Judgment, all parched like this?" His right hand went to the lip of the urn.

Hutch knew that God or the likelihood of punishment had meant less to Grainger, in the past fifty years, than money or vengeance. *Is he changing here on the verge of the grave? No clean way to ask—he'd never tell me.* So Hutch said "I feel fairly sure Wade can rise, yes sir, if there's any such day. A lot of saints burned—you recall Joan of Arc, old Nero's martyrs, soldiers in firefights, your own friends in France, young children in buildings every night of the year."

Grainger was not fully satisfied, but he said "All right." He saw no reason to alarm Hutch further. Then again he moved to stand on his own.

Hutch reached for the lid.

"Leave it open, I told you." Again Grainger got to his feet, unaided. He went to the nearest kitchen drawer, reached toward the back and brought out a box maybe three inches long—an old cream-colored box tied with a ribbon that had once been red.

Hutch had never seen it.

Grainger came back with enormous care, stood before Hutch, untied the ribbon, reached under a yellowed scrap of cotton and drew out a gold ring—a wide plain band.

At first Hutch failed to recognize it.

But Grainger held the ring between thumb and finger and met Hutch's eyes again. "Make up your mind who this is for next." He didn't hand it over.

Hutch suddenly knew. It had to be his family's wedding ring—the one old Rob Mayfield gave his bride well over a century ago in Virginia. Nearly four decades had passed since Hutch had seen it. After his and Ann's sad interrupted Christmas in Italy, she'd abandoned the hope to use it as their wedding ring. Hutch had left it with Polly Drewry in Richmond; she'd warmed old Rob in his last sick years, then Rob's son Forrest (Hutch's own grandfather). Polly had conditionally accepted the ring but for safekeeping only. She'd written to say she'd hold it for Hutch, taped to the underside of her bed. Then while the years passed, Hutch forgot the ring. Polly had never mentioned it again; and when she died, in her peaceful confusion, Hutch sold her few sticks of furniture for minus nothing—no thought of a ring worth maybe no more than eighty dollars, with a burden of suffering locked in its round. Yet here, in its shining life, it was. Had Polly sent it to Grainger somehow before she died? She and Grainger had never been great friends; they loved the same men. Still seated on the bed, Hutch could only say "Is it what I think?"

Grainger said "Don't matter what you think."

"Polly sent it to you?"

Grainger only said "You do what you know is right with it next."

In real uncertainty, Hutch said "I'd appreciate some advice." With all its other history, he also knew that the ring had spent some years of its history on Grainger's wife's hand—hard beautiful burnt-out Gracie Walters, who'd abandoned Grainger and drunk herself deep into the ground, a young woman still.

So Grainger reached inside the urn and pressed the gold band into the absolute center of the ashes till it barely showed.

Hutch said "You want me to scatter it with him?"

Grainger said "I told you I got no plans. You the man here now."

It was hardly the first time Hutch had felt grown, though like most humans he secretly felt the same age always—some tentative year in mid-adolescence. Yet with this sudden license from Grainger, he did feel stronger. He stood in the short space between himself and the harsh old man and looked all round him.

The crowded wall of pictures beyond—poor scorched-out Gracie, Rob in his prime, Wade in his childhood (vivid as paint) and the whole constellation of kinfolk, statesmen, and murderous generals from Grainger's war—they all seemed spokes of a slow-turned wheel in which the old man was somehow, for lack of another, the hub and axle. As Hutch cradled the ashes and moved to leave, his left hand grazed the cloth of Grainger's shoulder.

Grainger said "Go on."

12

OUTSIDE, Straw stood with Ivory and Raven in the deep oak shade. The heat had stilled them, and they stood as separate as horses in a field; but when Hutch came down Grainger's few steps, he saw how the three of them looked like the harbor he'd longed for all his life and never found. *Ask for them, here and now—then they'll know I'm crazy.*

When Hutch reached them though, thinking of some right way to ask for such a gift, Straw spoke first. "Ivory and I want to give you privacy, if you want that, down there at the creek." He pointed to the woods.

It seemed unthinkable—coming from Straw who'd cared for Wade as much as anyone left alive (except maybe Ann; who could speak for Ann Gatlin?)—that Straw would surrender his place in Wade's last moments among them. Hutch was all but ready to say "God, no, I need you all."

But at that moment young Raven ran off toward the single-strand barbed wire fence that lay between here, the woods and the creek in its steep valley. The fence was thirty yards off in full sun; and when the boy reached the ugly strand of wire, he looked back toward the solemn adults and burst out in a low hilarious unbroken laugh.

It felt to Hutch like the first authentic joy the human race had earned.

Raven spun in place a few quick times, then stopped with arms out to calm his dizzy head. Finally he looked back and called out plainly. "Mother, I'm *gone* from here." Then he bent to pass through the wire to the strip of field that lay between him and the trees.

Ivory kept smiling but she said "You hold on right where you are, Mr. Smarty." She looked to Hutchins and, though her face was empty of anything like a threat or plea, she said "You think you could stand for him to walk down with you?"

Hutch thought *Wait—what are you telling me?* But in the presence of Ivory's commandingly peaceful eyes, he knew *She wants the child to go*; so he said at last "I'd be more than pleased."

She said "Then I'll wait back in the house." Her eyes had always seemed past weeping; they were still in her mind's full control, but what showed through them was a sorrow beyond what Hutch could have guessed.

Straw, in a sudden pool of green light, was his best old self—more vulnerable than any young runner at the end of his sprint, far more likely to last. He said to Hutch "You're really sure?"

"Of what?"

"Of me not walking down with you this time."

Hutch accepted that. "You'll be here the rest of your life though, right?"

Straw said "To the best of my knowledge, yes—it's my intention."

By then Ivory had walked halfway toward Raven. When he'd slowly obeyed her beckoning hand and stood before her, she told him to help

Mr. Mayfield politely, not to act silly and to show his respect for Wade and Wyatt.

Straw followed closely and gave his own warning. "Don't fall in a hole—there's an old well back there that eats careless boys."

Ivory looked concerned.

Straw shook his head and grinned.

Raven said nothing but ducked his chin. He'd been to funerals with his old grandmother, but this was the first time he'd known the dead man. He'd do what he could, as events unrolled.

By then Hutch had joined them, still waiting for fate to choose his companions.

Ivory turned and faced him a moment. The loss in her eyes was glaring and endless. She said "I'd go if I thought I could, but Raven will help you." Then though her composure had held, she passed Hutch and headed back toward the house. After a few steps, she looked round and said "Don't forget young Raven's a city boy; he wouldn't know a snake from a rolled-up sock."

Hutch silently mouthed two words—*He's safe*—and waved as if they were leaving for good.

But Straw told her "Put your mind at ease. No bad snakes around here." It was not strictly true—the odd copperhead turned up every few weeks.

Ivory took it though and went her way.

When she'd gone past earshot, Raven whispered "I'm hoping to see me a cobra."

Straw said "You're on the wrong continent, Son."

Hutch smiled. "That's a fact, more ways than one."

If anyone heard him, no one gave a sign.

Then the two men and the eager boy were silent for a moment, their eyes on the ground.

Straw stood long enough to reach out and touch the urn once more. Half facing Hutch, he said "So long"; then he touched his friend's shoulder and followed Ivory.

*   *   *

WHEN a safe distance had grown between them, Raven called to their backs—a notch louder than a whisper—"I'm big enough to take care of me *and* this man."

No one heard him but Hutch. He touched Raven's forehead and said "I hope you are."

But Raven tore off eight or ten giant steps toward the trees.

And Hutch saw that Maud, Straw's old black retriever—broad backed as a pony—had come up beside him and was fixed on Raven, running beyond her. She'd never harmed a live thing in her life, nearly thirteen years; and in her youth, Wade had been her favorite from humankind, an instinctive bonding that had pleased them both through hundreds of walks and hours on the porch. Hutch suspected she'd come to follow him down through shade to the creek, and he knew a single word would stop her. The day was hot for her age and her thick coat; Hutch also didn't trust his strength to be with her. So he scratched the loosening skin of her muzzle and said "Old lady, you guard the others."

Maud didn't look up—she was still calculating the distance before her, down through the woods. But finally she took Hutch's order and turned. No look, no trick, just a slow stiff-hipped surrender and exit.

Raven had stopped at the line of trees and was looking toward Hutch. So Hutch went on.

13

HUTCH set the urn down and crouched to thread himself through the rusty barbed wire.

Before he could stand upright again, Raven ran back to watch his progress; and as Hutch reclaimed the urn, the boy said "Who burned up the man?"

"Call him Wade. His name was Wade Mayfield. You remember Wade, your uncle's friend."

Raven's eyes were blank; he was making no commitment. In fact he hadn't seen Wade since Christmas, seven months ago.

Hutch reached his right hand out to Raven.

The boy looked it over, then surrendered his own. It was deeply lined already, a shrunk man's hand but fully fleshed.

When they were nearly into the pines, Hutch asked again "You remember my Wade?"

The boy watched the ground, unlike any ground he'd crossed till today. "Nobody told me he was yours."

"Well, you're right he wasn't, not mine to keep. But I was his father."

"When he was a child?"

Hutch said "That's pretty much how it was, yes—when Wade was a child very much like you." And for the first time, Hutch wondered if Ivory or Wade or Wyatt—or old Mrs. Bondurant on northshore Long Island—had given the boy any clue about Wade. *No way to ask, not for years anyhow.* Possible questions ran through Hutch's mind, but all seemed mildly obscene or cruel.

Then Raven forestalled him. "My mother and father have got a divorce."

"I heard that, yes. Do you see your father?"

"Too much. I hate him. One weekend a month way off in New Jersey. I hate that place."

Hutch said "Hate's probably not a good idea."

Raven looked up till he'd drawn Hutch's eyes to meet him. "You must not know my father then."

Hutch noted the courtliness with which the boy called his parents *mother* and *father* when the rest of America had accepted *mom* and *dad* from TV, but he dodged the boy's question. "I just meant hate hurts the person that hates more than anybody else."

Raven said "Man, you're wrong again."

"How's that?"

"Meanness is getting to be the big style. You never been to New York City, have you?"

Hutch laughed. "Not lately. I hear it's bad."

"*Bad!* They'll shoot you in kindergarten; don't wait till you're grown."

"But you're being extra careful, aren't you?"

"I can't stop bullets if that's what you mean." Raven held up both palms as if to show holes.

Till here it hadn't really struck Hutch that, if Wade was truly this boy's father, then his and Ann's one grandchild and their only heir was living up north in even more danger than he'd meet down here in the worst imaginable hands—the all but vanished white-trash Klansman or defeated punk. The apparently endless slaughter of innocence underway in American cities, a mindless raking down of bystanders, had overtaken hatred in its tracks and bludgeoned its way on at unchecked speeds. *Anything I can do about that? Not short of moving him down here with Ivory, no; and that can't happen—can't or won't.* Hutch said "You wish you lived somewhere else?"

"Not down here anyway if that's what you mean."

Hutch said "What's the problem with where we are?"

"*Hot*, red hot." The boy fanned his face.

"It's hot up north."

Raven said "Sometimes. But we got the ocean. Remember I live in *Sea* Cliff, New York."

Hutch laughed. "I'll do my best to remember." Yet even alone now he felt the need to cover his tracks. "I wasn't exactly inviting you down here. I just thought you said you liked all the trees."

They were well into the serious woods, the soft floor deep in dry leaves and pinestraw, the gradual downgrade toward the valley. In ten more yards the shade was dense as dusk.

Raven pressed Hutch's hand. "I didn't say that to hurt your feelings."

Hutch said "I understand—you're a city boy. You think you could come down and visit sometime though? We could go to the beach or the mountains maybe."

"Just you and me?"

"Ivory could come if she wanted to."

Raven's head all but agreed to the plan. "She does like it better than me down here." He went on thinking the option through. "Would that lady back at the house be with us?"

"Wade's mother? Ann?"

Raven signed a strong Yes again. "The dead man's mother—"

"Wade's mother—she might be; yes, she might. Her plans are still vague. But that wouldn't affect you."

"I like her." Then the boy looked around in half-comic carefulness and whispered "She gave me a five-dollar bill." He patted his hip pocket where a small wallet guarded the crisp new bill, plus the five and two ones he'd brought from New York (his grandmother gave him money to phone her in case he got lost).

Hutch said "Good. She's smart and well paid."

Raven seemed to consider that matter closed. He struck off on his own. "My mother is scared of airplanes, but I'm old enough to fly by myself. Children fly everywhere, tickets tied round their neck to show who they are."

"They do," Hutch said. "You name the day."

"You'd need to make those arrangements with my family." The boy's high-spoken gravity amused even him; when he'd heard his sentence, he beamed up at Hutch.

"I'll remember that, when the time comes, surely."

They'd gone a good way downhill before Raven said "When will that be?"

"Sir?"

"You said 'When the time comes.' What time is that—when you ask my mother?"

Hutch said "It could start anywhere from the minute we're back in Strawson's house till sunup tomorrow."

"And last for how long? How long would you need me?"

"Oh till you're a grown man and I'm out of sight."

Raven consulted himself in silence. "I don't think that's going to work, Mr. Mayfield. I'm missing day camp just walking with you in all this heat." He elaborately dried his neck with a hand, then fanned himself again.

"Call me *Hutch,* please sir—I heard about your camp. Sure, you need to finish that."

"And high school and college and the rest of my grandmother's life, I guess."

"How's that?"

"She'd die without me."

Hutch thought *That's very likely the truth.* "That doesn't leave us much hope then, do you think?"

Raven said "I wouldn't go far as that." His voice was plainly an echo of his elders but likewise in earnest.

"You got some spare time, somewhere in your life?"

"I'll see can I manage to work - you - in." Again the boy smiled his enormous delight at Hutch.

It found its mark. Hutch felt the slow rise in his chest and throat of that strange elation he'd felt in the early hours of rescuing Wade and bringing him home. When he could speak, he said "You phone me collect when you know."

"No way, Hutch," the boy said. "I'll pay for the call." He held up his pale small hand to offer a genuine high five, nobody's beggar.

As well as Hutch could, with the cradled ashes, he met the hand and confirmed the greeting.

By now they were near enough to the creek to hear its slender late-summer flow and the heartened birdcalls that signaled a cooler air and light than any available elsewhere for miles. Hutch recognized each sound as it came—the furious challenging cluck of a squirrel, a far-off dove in its lunar moan, the piercing *scree* of a red-tailed hawk nearby overhead. It all drew him down more surely toward his goal.

Raven had never been this near a wilderness, but the deepening peace above the strange sounds and the separate odors of natural water and ripened leaves were welcome findings.

Hutch said "This place where you and I are going was Wade's favorite place when he was your age. He used to come up here every summer and stay with the Stuarts and old Mr. Walters, and this was the place he made his own."

"For what?" Raven said.

"Oh being alone, thinking his own thoughts with nobody leaning or holding him back."

Raven said "I spend most of my time alone, when I'm home from school. My grandmother works till time to cook supper; then she watches TV past my bedtime."

"You mind that at all?"

"Shoot, no, I love it. I'm good company, Hutch."

"I'm beginning to notice. You'll almost certainly like Wade's creek then. With a little luck on the food and weather, a smart sane man could live a whole life here and never need more."

"How about a young boy? Could he make out?"

Hutch said "Maybe if he was, say, thirteen."

"That's five years from now."

Hutch said "You could probably manage it, with occasional visits from Strawson or me."

Raven let go of Hutch's hand and stepped ahead faster, but he still asked clearly "Why did Wade leave then?"

"Wait please," Hutch said. "Don't get there before me." He wanted to see the boy's eyes take in the heart of the place—first sight, first pleasure.

So Raven halted in his tracks, with his back turned, and waited till Hutch was precisely beside him. He asked again "Why you think Wade left?"

Hutch said "He had his grown life to find." For a moment he wanted to sit down here, beg the boy to sit and try not to leave. *Crazier still. Lead him on; do your job.* He said to Raven "You walk in my tracks," not explaining that his tracks would be safer on the slope, when they reached the downgrade.

So the boy looked to Hutch's feet and fell in behind him, stride for wide stride, till they came to the crest of the valley and stopped.

Full as the summer growth still was, this deep into shade, the stretch of creek that Grainger had channeled was plain below them. Its edges were softened by moss and vines since Hutch's visit in early spring, and summer rains had gnawed at the banks, but the big smooth boulders still broke the flow into tamer strands of water that now looked clear but dark brown like strong cold tea.

Raven's face was calm but his eyes had widened; and he said "Man, this is a Tarzan movie."

"Exactly. Hear him swinging our way—him and his monkeys?"

Raven gave Hutch the benefit of the doubt; he actually listened, then shook his head Yes and pulled ahead on Hutch's wrist. "Come *on*, man." The boy ran three steps down the steep embankment, then tumbled over, rolled a fast two yards, stopped himself and sprang to his feet.

Hutch had thought *God, don't let him be hurt with me. We've only started* and moved to help him.

But by then the boy was brushing leaves off his suit, picking at a narrow scratch in his right palm, then laughing to Hutch and giving a formal bow from the waist. "Son of Tarzan, at your service, sir."

Hutch said "Well, greetings" and returned the bow. For that long instant he felt all but fully rewarded for the spring and summer's pain.

Raven said "For a white dude, you doing all right."

"Thank you, friend—I try. I try when I can."

Raven was already thinking ahead. "Can I see the dead man now?"

Hutch was holding the urn in both arms, against his chest. "These are ashes, Son. They're all that's left of Wade Mayfield's body. Wade was my only son. You said you remembered Wade."

"A little bit. I think we had a picnic."

Hutch could see he was hedging. "When was that?"

"When I was a child, *way* back when." Raven's eyes were still fixed on the urn.

Hutch said "Let's do our duty then" and took the first careful step down the steep slope.

Reminded again of their serious errand, Raven came on several yards behind Hutch in long slow strides.

AT the edge of the creek, Hutch waited till the boy had caught up beside him. Then he crouched to the ground and again peeled the tape from the lid of the urn. He paused a moment to brace himself for what he might feel at this last sight. Then he looked to Raven who was in reach behind him, waiting too with eyes on the lid. So what Hutch felt was, again, the oldest feeling of his life—the literal medium in which he was born and had swum ever since: a bitter mix of pleasure and grief, thanks and irrecoverable loss. He took off the lid; the ashes were just as Grainger had left them. The gold ring barely showed, still pressed in the center. Hutch tilted the urn so Raven could see.

The boy crouched too and took a long look. Without facing Hutch he said "Is this all you got?"

"All of what?"

"The dead man—your Mr. Wade."

Hutch said "Not all, no."

"Who's got the rest?"

Hutch said "All of us, deep down in our minds. You'll know more about Wade once you get grown."

Raven said "I see him right this minute." When he looked across to Hutch, it was clear that the boy meant he was watching memories, however unsure and far in his past. Then his head bent closer to the urn. "Are they safe?"

"From what?"

"For me to touch—my uncle Wyatt wasn't safe when he died. They locked up the casket; said he was *catching*. I wouldn't even go in the room where they had him."

Hutch said "Wade's ashes are safe as sand. You do what you want."

Raven put out his right hand and set two fingers on the gritty surface. "That's his finger ring?"

"It should have been."

"You throwing it away too?"

Hutch said "Maybe. What do you think?"

Raven touched a single finger to the ring and pressed it deeper into the ash. "I think some child'll get a nice finger ring when he finds it down here."

"Or maybe it'll wash on down through the river and land on the ocean floor."

"A shark might eat it." The idea lit the boy's whole face.

Hutch said "He might."

Then they both were silent a long time, seeing only their private needs—Hutch searched for a small still cove by the bank; Raven scanned the tree limbs for pythons.

At last Hutch reached in, uncovered the ring and hooked it onto his right little finger. It hadn't touched him in so many years, but it felt normal here. He said to Raven "You still want to help me?"

"Yes, just say the word." The boy's face lit again with the solemn force it had in the chapel yesterday, not a ritual funeral look but the image of innocent awe at the final mystery left.

Hutch said "Reach in then, take a good handful and spread it on the water."

Careful as a good young priest, Raven performed the gesture like something he'd learned years back and brought to effortless ease today.

The tan ashes lay on top of the water for an instant, then sifted downward and on with the stream.

Raven kept his eyes on their course. "Let me do one more."

Hutch waited with the urn while the boy spread a second handful.

In a quick shaft of light, the ashes spread on the surface—rainbowed for a moment in their startling colors of tan, white, ochre, blues and purples. The bits of bone cast circles around them that rode out of sight.

But Raven stood where he'd stopped and watched them, his dusty right hand held out from his side.

Hutch had crouched through that. Now he stood, walking slowly upstream to scatter the rest. If he'd been thrown forward, dead of grief and regret in the dirt any instant here, he'd have felt no surprise. But his blood beat on, he stayed upright, and the ashes were gone even sooner than he'd guessed. He was left with the urn and a weight of loss—iron desolation—like none he'd ever borne till today. For half a minute again he thought he'd pitch to the ground. His heart contracted like a terrified fist and slammed at his ribs.

It was then Hutch knew that, against all reason, he still dreaded Wyatt—Wyatt Bondurant here in this real day. Whoever had fathered Ivory's Raven, there could be no doubt the child was Wyatt's nephew. *Wyatt may slam in here, any moment, to take this child. He'll never let me know him.* Wild as that tasted and felt in Hutch's mind, he half believed it; half expected it in this real daylight on land his family had owned for so long and worked with the usable entirely expendable lives of others, all of them buried in long-lost graves within reach of his voice, if he'd raise his voice here.

In Hutch's crowded head, he even saw an image—the child crushed down, with blood on his lip, by the unseen weight of a famished dead man. *We all end here—Wade, Ann and me; maybe even this child, whoever he is. And all my kin, back far as they go toward Eden and Gomorrah.* The entire story (the little Hutch knew of it and all the hidden mass with its thousand feeders)—all the likable, darkening, execrable routes each private life had dug toward its goal, its hunt for care and heat in the world, the self's desert triumph over others, over land and God; and the promise of some eventual rest: all the history of the world ended here, in no more than six or eight fistsful of ashes.

Oh to roll it back and scotch it at the start. Absurd as that sounded in his head, Hutch flushed it away but then felt his mind lunge forward at the boy here, with more real threat than he'd felt toward anyone since the awful moments of balked lust and abandonment in his early manhood. He was literally helpless not to think *End this child now, here, end him yourself. Spare him the slow and poisonous trek.* He turned to the boy.

Raven had followed three steps behind Hutch; he'd also watched the last of the ashes rest on the water and then sift inward. When they'd sunk and Hutch had swung round to face the boy—thinking any instant he must beg for help—Raven went on watching the creek as if the world harbored no threats stronger than pine trees and gangster jays. Then the boy said "Your Wade can enjoy himself from now on."

Hutch stood and took that, knowing not to ask for more by way of explanation. *All right; he ought to.* Hutch's heart opened slightly; he drew a short breath, ready at least to believe they were safe again. "Let's hope Wade enjoys the whole rest of things, as long as things last. God knows he paid for it." Then a second breath offered itself and went deeper into his lungs and mind. So Hutch walked forward, found the lid on a flat rock and closed the urn. He hadn't anticipated having a handsome empty pot to keep or destroy. *Smash it on the rocks. Leave it here with the dust.* That would break the enormous quiet around them. *Give it to Raven.* Hutch actually held it out before him to see if the boy would ask to have it.

By then though Raven had seen a red salamander on the moss and was watching it closely.

It eyed him back more urgently than any two eyes had watched him till now.

Hutch gave the boy another few seconds, then said "We need to climb back and head for home."

Raven said "There's four states between here and *my* home."

Hutch could smile. "Then we need to ball the jack." Again he offered the boy his hand, and they climbed carefully up the steep valley and on through gradually thinning trees—through Hutch's racing thoughts of a lifetime, long lifetimes behind him, the unseen future—till open ground was no more than fifty feet ahead, still flat under unblocked pounding sun. Hutch paused there, mainly to catch his breath.

Raven waited beside him, staring ahead.

Hutch finally said "You ready?"

"For what?" The great dark eyes went to Hutch again.

"Oh for life to start."

"Man, it's *started*," Raven said. "I'm near about grown."

There was more than a grain of truth in that, Hutch well understood. This boy might never come back here again; they actually might not meet again. However hard Hutch might want to see Raven through the years, that was Ivory's choice and must never be seized without her full assent and blessing. *Now, this instant, is all you know you'll get on Earth.* So Hutch bent and set the urn at the foot of a monumental beech, a giant elephant's leg. He slid old Rob's gold ring from his right hand, reached silently out, won Raven's consent and slid it onto the boy's left thumb.

Raven studied the wide band, still several sizes too large for his hand. He turned it slowly as if he already knew its power, the rune that perfectly worked its strength to bind whole lives and outride time. Not looking to Hutch, Raven almost whispered "You trying to say this is mine to keep?"

"Yours to keep or give away or fling in the sea."

"I live in Sea Cliff, you know that, right?"

"I do," Hutch said. "I'll know it forever."

Still not looking up, the boy said "Thank you."

"You may want to let your mother keep it safe till your hand grows to fit it."

Raven agreed to that. "It won't be long."

Hutch said "I bet it'll feel like forever, but really you're right. It'll come very quick."

The boy's smile broke out against his resistance, one of the last bursts of uncrossed joy he'd feel till his own middle age. He turned that actual beam on Hutch, said "Roll right on!" and pointed ahead.

For the first time since the line came to him last month at the crossroad mechanic's, Hutch suddenly knew he'd build a poem from the first given words. A second, a third, and part of a fourth line clicked into place here.

> This child knows the last riddle and answer.
> They wait far back in these mineshaft eyes
> Till he concedes your right to know them,
> Which may be never.

No other actual words arrived, neither riddle nor answer and no firm sense of a shapely life on a page of print or a possible length, just the strong assurance Hutch had barely known since his first mature poems— that a thoroughly sizable living creature was forming down in him, below his sight or natural vision. The creature would surface in its own time and cut its own path.

Not that a single poem, however deep, would count for much in whatever scale his life hung from or would hang from at the end. *An honorable piece of handiwork anyhow, a clean piece of carving to set in the long American gallery of cigar-store Indians and Abe Lincoln busts. That much, if no more.* The only other thing Hutch knew, here on the final edge of shade, was that somehow the poem would resurrect Wade in words more durable than any of his kin and join him finally with this likable child. The prospect felt like strength enough for days to come; and Raven's eyes were still fixed on him, still ready to guide.

So whoever they'd be for one another in the years between here and Raven's full manhood or Hutch's death, the two of them went on, hand in hand, through the last of the shade and broke into blinding clean sunlight. Though their stunned eyes saw only wavering heat and the withering grass, all that lay beyond Hutch and his new kin seemed to them both their only goal—Grainger's, the main house, the durable oaks, whatever people had waited them out, the car that would drive them south to the airport and part them again for months or for good. They could hardly see to walk toward shade and find the others to say they'd done one duty at least— one man's return to the bottomless ground; maybe even a family's end, its story told—but they looked on forward and took the first steps.

REYNOLDS PRICE

REYNOLDS PRICE was born in Macon, North Carolina in 1933. Educated in the public schools of his native state, he earned an A.B. *summa cum laude* from Duke University. In 1955 he traveled as a Rhodes Scholar to Merton College, Oxford University to study English literature. After three years and the B.Litt. degree, he returned to Duke where he continues in his fourth decade of teaching. He is James B. Duke Professor of English.

In 1962 his novel *A Long and Happy Life* appeared. It received the William Faulkner Award for a notable first novel and has never been out of print. Since, he has published more than two dozen books. Among them, his novel *Kate Vaiden* received the National Book Critics Circle Award in 1986. His *Collected Stories* appeared in 1993; he has also published volumes of poems, plays, essays, translations, and two volumes of memoir, *Clear Pictures* and *A Whole New Life*. The latter is his account of a ten-year survival of spinal cancer.

His television play *Private Contentment* was commissioned by "American Playhouse" and appeared in its premiere season on PBS. His trilogy of plays *New Music* premiered at the Cleveland Play House in 1989; and its three plays have been produced throughout the country, as has a newer play, *Full Moon*, his sixth.

He is a member of the American Academy of Arts and Letters, and his books have appeared in sixteen languages.